James H. Graff, Edmund Hodgson Yates

Land at Last

a novel

James H. Graff, Edmund Hodgson Yates

Land at Last
a novel

ISBN/EAN: 9783337349387

Printed in Europe, USA, Canada, Australia, Japan

Cover: Foto ©Andreas Hilbeck / pixelio.de

More available books at **www.hansebooks.com**

𝔄 𝔑𝔬𝔳𝔢𝔩.

BY

EDMUND YATES,

AUTHOR OF "FORLORN HOPE," "BLACK SHEEP," "RUNNING THE GAUNTLET,"

ETC., ETC.

"Post tenebras lux."

THIRD EDITION.

LONDON:

CHAPMAN AND HALL, 193, PICCADILLY.

1868.

CONTENTS.

BOOK I.

BOOK II.

Contents.

BOOK III.

LAND AT LAST.

Book the First.

CHAPTER I.

IN THE STREETS.

IT was between nine and ten o'clock on a January night, and the London streets were in a state of slush. During the previous night snow had fallen heavily, and the respectable portion of the community, which, according to regular custom, had retired to bed at eleven o'clock, had been astonished, on peering out from behind a corner of the window-curtain when they arose, to find the roads and the neighbouring housetops covered with a thick white incrustation. The pavements were already showing dank dabs of footmarks, which even the snow then falling failed to fill up; and the roadway speedily lost its winter-garment and became sticky with congealed mud. Then the snow ceased, and a sickly straggling bit of winter-sunlight, a mere parody on the real thing, half light and half warmth, came lurking out between the dun clouds; and under its influence the black-specked covering of the roofs melted, and the water-pipes ran with cold black liquid filth. The pavement had given it up long ago, and resumed its normal winter state of sticky slippery grease—grease which clung to the boots and roused the wildest rage of foot-passengers by causing them to slip backward when they wanted to make progress, and which accumulated in the direst manner on the landing-places and

B

street corners,—the first bits of refuge after the perils of the crossing,—where it heaped itself in aggravating lumps and shiny rings under the heels of foot passengers just arrived, having been shaken and stamped off the soles of passengers who had just preceded them. So it had continued all day; but towards the afternoon the air had grown colder, and a whisper had run round that it froze again. Cutlers who had been gazing with a melancholy air on the placards "Skates" in their window, and had determined on removing them, as a bad joke against themselves, decided on letting them remain. Boys who had been delighted in the morning at the sight of the snow, and proportionately chopfallen towards middle-day at the sight of the thaw, had plucked up again and seen visions of snowballing matches, slides on the gutters, and, most delicious of all, omnibus-horses both down at once on the slippery road. Homeward-bound City-clerks, their day's work over, shivered in the omnibuses, and told each other how they were afraid it had come at last, and reminded each other of what the newspapers had said about the flocks of wild-geese and other signs of a hard winter, and moaned lugubriously about the advanced price of coals and the difficulties of locomotion certain to be consequent on the frost.

But when the cruel black night had set regularly in, a dim sleek soft drizzle began to fall, and all hopes or fears of frost were at an end. Slowly and gently it came down, wrapping the streets as with a damp pall; stealing quietly in under umbrellas; eating its way through the thickest broadcloth, matting the hair and hanging in dank, unwholesome beads on the beards of all unlucky enough to be exposed to it. It meant mischief, this drizzle, and it carried out its intention. Omnibus-drivers and cabmen knew it at once from long experience, donned their heavy tarpaulin-capes, and made up their minds for the worst. The professional beggars knew it too. The pavement-chalking tramp, who had selected a tolerably dry spot under the lee of a wall, no sooner felt its first damp breath than he blew out his paper-lantern, put the candle into his pocket, stamped out as much of the mackerel and the ship at sea as he had already sten-cilled, and made off. The man in the exemplary shirt-collar and apron, who had planted himself before the chemist's window to procure an extra death-tinge from the light reflected from the blue bottle, packed up his linen and decamped, fearing lest his stock-in-trade—his virtue and his lucifers—might be injured by damp. The brass bands which had been playing outside the public-houses shouldered their instruments and went inside; the vendors of second-hand books covered their openly-displayed stock with strips of baize and dismissed their watchful boys, conscious that no petty thief would risk the weather for so small a prey. The hot-potato men blew fiercer jets of steam out of their tin kitchens, as though calling on the public to defy dull care and comfort themselves with an antidote to the general wretchedness; and the policemen stamped solemnly and slowly round their beats, as men impressed with the full knowledge that, as there was not the remotest chance of their being relieved from their miserable fate until the morning, they might as well bear themselves with as much dignity as possible under the circumstances.

It was bad everywhere; but in no place at the West-end of London was it so bad as at the Regent Circus. There the great tide of humanity had been ebbing and flowing all day; there hapless females in shoals had struggled across the roaring sea of Oxford Street, some conveyed by the crossing-sweeper, some drifting helplessly under the poles of omnibuses and the wheels of hansom cabs. There the umbrellas of the expectant omnibus-seekers jostled each other with extra virulence; and there the edges of the pavements were thick with dark alluvial deposits kicked hither and thither by the feet of thousands. All day there had been a bustle and a roar round this spot; and at ten o'clock at night it had but little diminished. Omnibus-conductors, like kites and vultures, clawed and wrangled over the bodies of their victims, who in a miserable little flock huddled together in a corner, and dashed out helplessly and without purpose as each lumbering vehicle drew up. Intermingled with these were several vagabond boys, whose animal spirits no amount of wet or misery could quell, and who constituted themselves a kind of vedette or outpost-guard, giving warning of the approach of the different omnibuses in much pleasantly familiar speech, "Now, guv'nor, for Bayswater! Hatlas comin' up! Ready now for Nottin' 'Ill!"

At the back of the little crowd, sheltering herself under the lee of the houses, stood a slight female figure, a mere slight slip of a girl, dressed only in a clinging gown and

B 2

a miserable tightly-drawn shawl. Her worn bonnet was pulled over her face, her arms were clasped before her, and she stood in a doorway almost motionless. The policeman tramping leisurely by had at first imagined her to be an omnibus-passenger waiting for a vehicle ; but some twenty minutes after he had first noticed her, finding her still in the same position, he took advantage of a pretended trial of the security of various street-doors to scrutinise her appearance. To the man versed in such matters the miserable garb told its own tale—its wearer was a pauper ; and a beggar the man in office surmised, although the girl had made no plaint, had uttered no word, had remained immovable and statue-like, gazing blankly before her. The policeman had been long enough in the force to know that the girl's presence in the doorway was an offence in the eyes of the law ; but he was a kindly-hearted Somersetshire man, and he performed his duty in as pleasant a way as he could, by gently pulling a corner of the drabbled shawl, and saying, " You musn't stand here, lass ; you must move on, please." The shawl-wearer never looked up or spoke, but shivering slightly, stepped out into the dank mist, and floated, phantom-like, across the road.

Gliding up the upper part of Regent Street, keeping close to the houses, and walking with her head bent down and her arms always folded tightly across her breast, she struck off into a bystreet to the right, and, crossing Oxford Market, seemed hesitating which way to turn. For an instant she stopped before the window of an eating-house, where thick columns of steam were yet playing round the attenuated remains of joints, or casting a greasy halo round slabs of pudding. As the girl gazed at these wretched remnants of a wretched feast, she raised her head, her eyes glistened, her pinched nostrils dilated, and for an instant her breath came thick and fast ; then, drawing her shawl more tightly round her, and bending her head to avoid as much as possible the rain, which came thickly scudding on the rising wind, she hurried on, and only stopped for shelter under the outstretched blind of a little chandler's shop—a wretched shelter, for the blind was soaked through, and the rain dripped from it in little pools, and the wind shook it in its frame, and eddied underneath it with a wet and gusty whirl ; but there was something of comfort to the girl in the warm look of the gaslit shop, in the smug rotund appearance of the chandler, in the distant glimmer of the fire on the glazed door of the parlour at the back. Staring vacantly before him while mechanically patting a conical lump of lard, not unlike the bald cranium of an elderly gentleman, the chandler became aware of the girl's face at the window; and seeing Want legibly inscribed by Nature's never-erring hand on every feature of that face, and being a humane man, he was groping in the till for some small coin to bestow in charity, when from the back room came a sharp shrill voice, "Jim, time to shut up!" and at the sound of the voice the chandler hastily retreated, and, a small boy suddenly appearing, pulled up the overhanging blind, and having lost its shelter, the girl set forth again.

But her course was nearly at an end. To avoid a troop of boys who, arm-in-arm, came breasting up the street singing the burden of a negro-song, she turned off again into the main thoroughfare, and had barely gained the broad shadow of the sharp-steepled church in Langham Place, when she felt her legs sinking under her, her brain reeling, her heart throbbing in her breast like a ball of fire. She tottered and clung to the church-railing for support. In the next instant she was surrounded by a little crowd, in which she had a vision of painted faces and glistening silks, a dream of faint words of commiseration overborne by mocking laughter and ribald oaths, oaths made more fearful still by being uttered in foreign accents, of bitter jests and broad hints of drunkenness and shame; finally, of the strident voice of the policeman telling her again to "move on!" The dead faintness, consequent on cold and wet and weariness and starvation, passed away for the time, and she obeyed the mandate. Passively she crept away a few steps up a deserted bystreet until her tormentors had left her quite alone; then she sunk down, shivering, on a door-step, and burying her face in her tattered shawl, felt that her end was come.

There she remained, the dead damp cold striking through her lower limbs and chilling them to stone, while her head was one blazing fire. Gradually her limbs became numbed and lost to all sensation, a sickening empty pain was round her heart, a dead apathy settling down over her mind and brain. The tramping of feet was close upon her, the noise of loud voices, the ringing shouts of loud laughter, were in her ears ; but she never raised her head from the tattered shawl, nor by speech or motion did she give the smallest sign of life. Men passed her constantly, all making for one goal, the portico next to that in which she had sunk down helpless—men with kindly hearts attuned to charity, who, had they known the state of the wretched wayfarer, would have exerted themselves bravely in her succour, but whom a London life had so inured to spectacles of casual misery and vice, that a few only cast a passing glance on the stricken woman and passed on. They came singly and in twos and threes ; but none spoke to her, none noticed her save by a glance and a shoulder shrug.

Then, as the icy hands of Cold and Want gradually stealing over her seemed to settle round the region of her heart, the girl gave one low faint cry, " God help me ! it's come at last—God help me ! " and fell back in a dead swoon.

CHAPTER II.

THE BRETHREN OF THE BRUSH.

THE house to which all the jovial fellows who passed the girl on the doorstep with such carelessness were wending their way was almost unique in the metropolis. The rumour ran that it had originally been designed for stables, and indeed there was a certain mews-ish appearance about its architectural elevation ; it had the squat, squabby, square look of those buildings from whose upper-floors clothes-lines stretch diagonally across stable-yards ; and you were at first surprised at finding an imposing portico with an imposing bell in a position where you looked for the folding-doors of a coach-house. Whether there had been any truth in the report or not, it is certain that the owner of the property speedily saw his way to more money than he could have gained by the ignoble pursuit of stabling horses, and made alterations in his building, which converted it into several sets of spacious, roomy, and comfortable, if not elegant chambers. The upper rooms were duly let, and speedily became famous—thus-wise. When Parmegiano Wilkins made his first great success with his picture of " Boadicea at Breakfast,"—connoisseurs and art-critics will recollect the marvellous manner in which the chip in the porridge of the Queen of the Iceni was rendered,—Mr. Caniche, the great picture-dealer, to whom Wilkins had mortgaged himself body and soul for three years, felt it necessary that his next works should be submitted to the private inspection of the newspaper-writers and the *cognoscenti* previous to their going into the Academy Exhibition. On receiving a letter to this effect from Caniche, Wilkins was at his wits' end. He was living, for privacy's sake, in a little cottage on the outskirts of Epping Forest, and having made a success, had naturally alienated all his friends whose rooms in town would otherwise have been available for the display of his pictures ; he thought—and there the astute picture-dealer agreed with him—that it would be unwise to send them to Caniche's shop (it was before such places were called "galleries"), as tending to make public the connection between them ; and Wilkins did not know what to do. Then Caniche came to his rescue. Little Jimmy Dabb, who had been Gold-Medallist and Travelling-Student at the Academy three years beforehand, and who, for sheer sake of bread-winning, had settled down as one of Caniche's Labourers, had a big studio in the stable-like edifice near Langham Church. In it he painted those bits of domestic life,—dying children on beds, weeping mothers, small table with cut-orange, Bible and physic by bedside, and pitying angel dimly hovering between mantelpiece and ceiling,—which, originally in oil, and subsequently in engravings, had such a vast sale, and brought so much ready money to Caniche's exchequer. The situation was central ; why not utilise it ? No sooner thought of than done : a red cotton-velvet coverlet was spread over Jimmy Dabb's bed in the corner ; a Dutch carpet, red with black flecks, was, at Caniche's expense, spread over the floor, paint-smeared and burnt with tobacco-ash ; two gorgeous easels, on which were displayed Wilkins's two pictures, "The Bird in the Hand"—every feather in the bird and the dirt in the nails of the ploughboy's hand marvellously delineated —and "Crumbs of Comfort," each crumb separate, and the loaf in the background so real, that the Dowager-Countess of Rundall, a celebrated household manager, declared it at once to be a "slack-baked quartern." Invitation-cards, wonderfully illuminated in Old-English characters, and utterly illegible, were sent forth to rank, fashion, and talent, who duly attended. Crowds of gay carriages choked up the little street : Dabb in his Sunday-clothes did the honours ; Caniche, bland, smiling, and polyglot, flitted here and there, his clerk took down orders for proof copies, and the fortune of the chambers was made. They were so original, so artistic, so convenient, they were just the place for a painter. Smudge, R.A., who painted portraits of the aristocracy, who wore a velvet-coat, and whose name was seen in the tail-end of the list of fashionables at evening-parties, took a vacant set at once ; and Clement Walkinshaw of the Foreign Office, who passed such spare time as his country could afford him in illuminating missals, in preparing designs for stained glass, and in hanging about art-circles generally, secured the remainder of the upper-floor, and converted it into a Wardour-Street Paradise, with hanging velvet *portières*, old oak cabinets, Venetian-glass, marqueterie tables, Sèvres china, escutcheons of armour, and Viennese porcelain pipes.

Meanwhile, utterly uncaring for and utterly independent of what went on upstairs, the denizens of the lower story kept quietly on. Who were the denizens of the lower story? who but the well-known Titian Sketching-Club ! How many men, who, after struggling through Suffolk Street and the Portland Gallery, have won their way to fame and fortune, have made their *coup d'essai* on the walls of the chambers rented by the Titian Sketching-Club ! Outsiders, who professed great love for art, but who only knew the two or three exhibitions of the season, and only recognised the score of names in each vouchsafed for by the newspaper-critics, would have been astonished to learn the amount of canvas covered, pains taken, and skill brought to bear upon the work of the Members of the Titian. There are guilds, and companies of Freemasons, and brotherhoods by the score in London ; but I know of none where the grand spirit of Camaraderie is so carried out as in this. It is the nearest thing to the *Vie de Bohème* of Paris of Henri Murger that we can show ; there is more liberty of speech and thought and action, less reticence, more friendship,—when friendship is understood by purse-sharing, by sick-bedside-watching, by absence of envy, jealousy, hatred, and all uncharitableness,—more singleness of purpose, more contempt for shams and im-postures and the dismal fetters of conventionality, than in any other circle of English Society with which I am acquainted.

It was a grand night with the Titians; no model was carefully posed on the "throne" that evening; no intelligent class was grouped round on the rising benches, copying from the "draped" or the "nude;" none of the wardrobe or properties of the club (and it is rich in both),—none of the coats of mail or suits of armour, hauberks and broadswords, buff boots, dinted breastplates, carved ebony crucifixes, ivory-hafted daggers, Louis-Onze caps, friars' gowns and rosaries, nor other portions of the stock-in-trade, were on view. The "sending-in" day for the approaching Exhibition of the British Institution was at hand; and the discoloured smoky old walls of the Titians, the rickety easels piled round the room, all available ledges and nooks, were covered with the works of the members of the club, which they fully intended to submit for exhibition. A very Babel, in a thick fog of tobacco-smoke, through which loomed the red face of Flexor the famous model, like the sun in November, greeted you on your entrance. Flexor pretended to take the hats, but the visitors seemed to know him too well, and contented themselves with nodding at him in a friendly manner, and retaining their property. Then you passed into the rooms, where you found yourself wedged up amongst a crowd of perhaps the most extraordinary-looking beings you ever encountered. Little men with big heads and long beards, big men with bald heads and shaved cheeks, and enormous moustaches and glowering spectacles; tall thin straggling men, who seemed all profile, and whose full face you could never catch; dirty shaggy little men, with heads of hair like red mops, and no apparent faces underneath, whose eyes flashed through their elf-locks, and who were explaining their pictures with singular pantomimic power of their sinewy hands, and notably of their ever-flashing thumbs; moon-faced solemn didactic men, prosing away on their views of art to dreary discontented listeners; and foppish, smart little fellows, standing a-tiptoe to get particular lights, shading their eyes with their hands, and backing against the company generally. Moving here and there among the guests was the Titians' president, honest old Tom Wrigley, who had been "at it," as he used to say, for thirty years, without making any great mark in his profession, but who was cordially beloved for his kind-heartedness and *bonhomie*, and who had a word and a joke for all. As he elbowed his way through the room he spoke right and left.

"Hallo, Tom Rogers!—hallo, Tom! That's an improvement, Tom, my boy! Got rid of the heavy browns, eh? weren't good, those heavy browns; specially for a Venetian atmosphere, eh, Tom? Much better, this.—How are you, Jukes? Old story, Jukes?—hen and chickens, ducks in the pond, horse looking over the gate? Quite right, Jukes; stick to that, if it pays. Much better than the death of J. Cæsar on a twenty-foot canvas, which nobody would be fool enough to buy. Stick to the ducks, Jukes, old fellow.— What's the matter, George? Why so savage, my son?"

"Here's Scumble!" said the young man addressed, in an undertone.

"And what of that, George? Mr. Scumble is a Royal Academician, it is true; and consequently a mark for your scorn and hatred, George. But it's not *his* fault; he never did anything to aspire to such a dignity. It's your British public, George, which is such an insensate jackass as to buy Scumble's pictures, and to tell him he's a genius."

"He was on the Hanging-Committee last year, and—"

"Ah, so he was; and your 'Aristides' was kicked out, and so was my 'Hope Deferred,' which was a deuced sight better than your big picture, Master George; but see how I shall treat him.—How do you do, Mr. Scumble? You're very welcome here, sir."

Mr. Scumble, R.A., who had a head like a tin-loaf, and a face without any earthly expression, bowed his acknowledgments, and threw as much warmth into his manner as he possibly could, apparently labouring under a notion that he was marked out for speedy assassination. "This is indeed a char-ming collection! Great talent among the ri-sing men, Mr.—pardon me—President! This now, for instance, a most charming landscape!"

"Yes, old boy; you may say that," said a square-built man smoking a clay-pipe, and leaning with his elbows on the easel on which the picture was placed. "I mean the real thing,—not this; which ain't bad though, is it? Not that I should say so; 'cause for why; which I did it!" and here the square-built man removed one of his elbows from the easel, and dug it into the sacred ribs of Scumble, R.A.

"Bad, sir!" said Scumble, recoiling from the thrust, and still with the notion of a secret dagger hidden behind the square-built man's waistcoat; "it's magnificent, superb, Mr.—!"

"Meaning me? Potts!" said the square-built man— "Charley Potts, artist, U.E., or unsuccessful exhibitor at every daub-show in London. That's the Via Mala, that is. I was there last autumn with Geoffrey Ludlow and Tom Bleistift. 'Show me a finer view than that,' I said to those fellows, when it burst upon us. 'If you'd a Scotchman with you,' said Tom, 'he'd say it wasn't so fine as the approach to Edinburgh.' 'Would he?' said I. 'If he said any-thing of that sort, I'd show him that view, and—and rub his nose in it!'"

Mr. Scumble, R.A., smiled in a sickly manner, bowed feebly, and passed on. Old Tom Wrigley laughed a great boisterous "Ha, ha!" and went on his way. Charley Potts remained before his picture, turning his back on it, and puffing out great volumes of smoke. He seemed to know everybody in the room, and to be known to and greeted by most of them. Some slapped him on the back, some poked him in the ribs, others laid their forefingers alongside their noses and winked; but all called him "Charley," and all had some pleasant word for him; and to all he had some-thing to say in return.

"Hallo, Fred Snitterfield!" he called out to a fat man in a suit of shepherd's-plaid dittoes. "Halloa, Fred! how's your brother Bill? What's he been doing? Not here to-night, of course?"

"No; he wasn't very well," said the man addressed. "He's got—"

"Yes, yes; I know, Fred!" said Charley Potts. "Wife won't let him! That's it, isn't it, old boy? He only dined out once in his life without leave, and then he sent home a telegram to say he was engaged; and when his wife received the telegram she would not believe it, because she said it wasn't his handwriting! Poor old Bill! Did he sell that 'Revenge' to what's-his-name—that Manchester man—Prebble?"

"Lord, no! Haven't you heard? Prebble's smashed up,—all his property gone to the devil!"

"Ah, then Prebble will find it again some day, no doubt. Look out! here's Bowie!"

Mr. Bowie was the art-critic of a great daily journal. In

early life he had courted art himself; but lacking executive
power, he had mixed up a few theories and quaint conceits
which he had learned with a great deal of acrid bile, with
which he had been gifted by nature, and wrote the most
pungent and malevolent art-notices of the day.   A tall, light-
haired, vacant-looking man, like a light-house without any
light in it, peering uncomfortably over his stiff white cravat,
and fumbling nervously at his watch-chain.   Clinging close
to him, and pointing out to him various pictures as they
passed them by, was quite another style of man,—Caniche,
the great picture dealer,—an under-sized lively Gascon,
black-bearded from his chin, round which it was closely cut,
to his beady black eyes, faultlessly dressed, sparkling in
speech, affable in manner, at home with all.

"Ah, ah!" said he, stopping before the easel, "the Via
Mala! Not bad—not at all bad!" he continued, with
scarcely a trace of a foreign accent.   "Yours, Charley Potts?
yours, *mon brave?*   De-caidedly an improvement, Charley!
You go on that way, mai boy, and some day—"

"Some day you'll give me twenty pound, and sell me for
a hundred! won't you, Caniche?—generous buffalo!" growled
Charley, over his pipe.

The men round laughed, but Caniche was not a bit
offended.   "Of course," he said, simply, "I will, indeed;
that is my trade!   And if you could find a man who would
give you thirty, you would throw me over in what you call
a brace of shakes!   *N'est-ce pas?*   Meanwhile, find the
man to give you thirty.   He is not here; I mean coming
now.—How do you do, Herr Stompff?"

Mr. Caniche (popularly known as Cannish among the
artists) winced as he said this, for Herr Stompff was his great
rival and bitterest enemy.

A short, bald-headed, gray-bearded man was Mr. Stompff,
—a Hamburger,—who, on his first arrival in England, had
been an importer of piping bullfinches at Hull; then a
tobacconist in St. Mary Axe; and who finally had taken up
picture-selling, and did an enormous business.   No one
could tell that he was not an Englishman from his talk, and
an Englishman with a marvellous fluency in the vernacular.
He had every slang saying as soon as it was out, and by
this used to triumph over his rival Caniche, who never could
follow his phraseology.

"Hallo, Caniche!" he said; "how are you? What's up?—running the rig on the boys here! telling Charley Potts his daubs are first-rate? Pickles!—We know all that game, don't we, Charley? What do you want for it, Charley? —How are you, Mr. Bowie? what's fresh with you, sir? Too proud to come and have a cut of mutton with me and Mrs. S. a-Sunday, I suppose? Some good fellows coming, too; Mugger from the Cracksideum, and Talboys and Sir Paul Potter—leastways I've asked him. Well, Charley, what's the figure for this lot, eh?"

"I'll trouble you not to 'Charley' me, Mr. Stump, or whatever your infernal name is!" said Potts, folding his arms and puffing out his smoke savagely. "I don't want any Havannah cigars, nor silk handkerchiefs, nor painted canaries, nor anything else in your line, sir; and I want your confounded patronage least of all!"

"Good boy, Charley! very good boy!" said Stompff, calmly pulling his whisker through his teeth—"shouldn't lose his temper, though. Come and dine a-Sunday, Charley. Mr. Potts said something, which the historian is not bound to repeat, turned on his heel, and walked away.

Mr. Stompff was not a bit disconcerted at this treatment. He merely stuck his tongue in his cheek, and looking at the men standing round, said, "He's on the high ropes, is Master Charley! Some of you fellows have been lending him half-a-crown, or that fool Caniche has bought one of his pictures for seven-and-six! Now, has anybody anything new to show, eh?" Of course everybody had something new to show to the great Stompff, the enterprising Stompff, the liberal Stompff, whose cheques were as good as notes of the Bank of England. How they watched his progress, and how their hearts beat as he loitered before their works! Jupp, who had a bed-ridden wife, a dear pretty little woman recovering from rheumatic fever at, Adalbert Villa, Elgiva Road, St. John's Wood; Smethurst, who had a 25*l.* bill coming due in a fortnight, and had three-and-sevenpence wherewith to meet it: Vogelstadt, who had been beguiled into leaving Düsseldorf for London on the rumours of English riches and English patronage, and whose capital studies of birds in the snow, and *treibe-jagds,* and boar-hunts, had called forth universal laudation, but had not as yet entrapped a single purchaser, so that Vogelstadt, who had come **down**

not discontentedly to living on bread-and-milk, had notions
of mortgaging his ancestral thumb-ring to procure even those
trifling necessaries,—how they all glared with expectation as
the ex-singing-bird-importer passed their pictures in review !
That worthy took matters very easily, strolling along with
his hands in his pockets, glancing at the easels and along
the walls, occasionally nodding his head in approval, or
shrugging his shoulders in depreciation, but never saying a
word until he stopped opposite a well-placed figure-subject
to which he devoted a two-minutes' close scrutiny, and then
uttered this frank though *argot*-tinged criticism, " That'll hit
'em up! that'll open their eyelids, by Jove !   Whose is it ?"

The picture represented a modern ballroom, in a corner
of which a man of middle age, his arms tightly folded across
his breast, was intently watching the movements of a young
girl, just starting off in a *valse* with a handsome dashing
young partner.   The expressions in the two faces were
admirably defined : in the man's was a deep earnest devotion
not unmingled with passion and with jealousy, his tightly-
clenched mouth, his deep-set earnest eyes, settled in rapt
adoration on the girl, showed the earnestness of his feeling,
so did the rigidly-fixed arms, and the *pose* of the figure,
which, originally careless, had become hardened and angular
through intensity of feeling.   The contrast was well marked;
in the girl's face, which was turned toward the man while
her eyes were fixed on him, was a bright saucy triumph,
brightening her eyes, inflating her little nostrils, curving the
corners of her mouth, while her figure was light and airy,
just obedient to the first notes of the *valse*, balancing itself
as it were on the arm of her partner before starting off down
the dance.   All the accessories were admirable : the dreary
wallflowers ranged round the room, the chaperons nid-
nodding together on the rout-seats, paterfamilias despondingly
consulting his watch, the wearied hostess, and the somno-
lently-inclined musicians,—all were there, portrayed not
merely by a facile hand but by a man conversant with
society.   The title of the picture; " Sic vos non vobis," was
written on a bit of paper stuck into the frame, on the other
corner of which was a card bearing the words " Mr. Geoffrey
Ludlow."

"Ah !" said Stompff, who, after carefully scanning the
picture close and then from a distance, had read the card

—"at last! Geoffrey Ludlow's going to fulfil the promise which he's been showing this ten years! A late birth, but a fine babby now it's born! That's the real thing and no flies! That's about as near a good thing as I've seen this long time—that; come, you'll say the same! That's a good picture, Mr. Wrigley!"

"Ah!" said old Tom, coming up at the moment, "you've made another lucky hit if you've bought that, Mr. Stompff! Geoff is so confoundedly undecided, so horribly weak in all things, that he's been all this time making up his mind whether he really would paint a good picture or not. But he's decided at last, and he has painted a clipper."

"Ye-es!" said Stompff, whose first enthusiasm had by no means died away—on the contrary, he thought so well of the picture that he had within himself determined to purchase it; but his business caution was coming over him strongly. "Yes! it's a clipper, as you say, Wrigley; but it's a picture which would take all a fellow knew to work it. Throw that into the market—where are you! Pouf! gone! no one thinking of it. Judicious advertisement, judicious squaring of those confounded fellows of the press; a little dinner at the Albion or the Star and Garter to two or three whom *we* know; and then the wonderful grasp of modern life, the singular manner in which the great natural feelings are rendered, the microscopic observation, and the power of detail—"

"Yes, yes," said Tom Wrigley; "for which, see *Catalogue of Stompff's Gallery of Modern Painters*, price 6*d*. Spare yourself, you unselfish encourager of talent, and spare Geoff's blushes; for here he is.—Did you hear what Stompff was saying on, Geoff?"

As he spoke, there came slouching up, shouldering his way through the crowd, a big, heavily-built man of about forty years of age, standing over six feet, and striking in appearance if not prepossessing. Striking in appearance from his height, which was even increased by his great shock head of dark-brown hair standing upright on his forehead, but curling in tight crisp waves round the back and poll of his head; from his great prominent brown eyes, which, firmly set in their large thickly-carved lids, flashed from under an overhanging pair of brows; from his large heavy nose, thick and fleshy, yet with lithe sensitive nostrils; from his short upper and protruding thick under lip; from the length of his

chin and the massive heaviness of his jaw, though the heavy
beard greatly concealed the formation of the lower portion of
his face. A face which at once evoked attention, which no
one passed by without noticing, which people at first called
"odd," and "singular," and "queer," according to their
vocabulary; then, following the same rule, pronounced
"ugly," or "hideous," or "grotesque,"—allowing all the
time that there "was something very curious in it." But a
face which, when seen in animation or excitement, in reflex
of the soul within, whose every thought was legibly portrayed
in its every expression, in light or shade, with earnest
watchful eyes, and knit brows and quivering nostrils and
working lips; or, on the other hand, with its mouth full of
sound big white teeth gleaming between its ruddy lips, and
its eyes sparkling with pure merriment or mischief;—then a
face to be preferred to all the dolly inanities of the Household Brigade, or even the matchless toga-draped dummies in
Mr. Truefitt's window. This was Geoffrey Ludlow, whom
everybody liked, but who was esteemed to be so weak and
vacillating, so infirm of purpose, so incapable of succeeding
in his art or in his life, as to have been always regarded as
an object of pity rather than envy; as a man who was his
own worst enemy, and of whom nothing could be said. He
had apparently caught some words of the conversation, for
when he arrived at the group a smile lit up his homely
features, and his teeth glistened again in the gaslight.

"What are you fellows joking about?" he asked, while he
roared with laughter, as if with an anticipatory relish of the
fun. "Some chaff at my expense, eh? Something about
my not having made up my mind to do something or not;
the usual nonsense, I suppose?"

"Not at all Geoff," said Tom Wrigley. "The question
asked by Mr. Stompff here was—whether you wished to sell
this picture, and what you asked for it."

"Ah!" said Geoffrey Ludlow, his lips closing and the fun
dying out of his eyes. "Well, you see it's of course a
compliment for you, Mr. Stompff, to ask the question; but
I've scarcely made up my mind—whether—and indeed as to
the price—"

"Stuff, Geoff! What rubbish you talk!" said Charley
Potts, who had rejoined the group. "You know well
enough that you painted the picture for sale. You know

equally well that the price is two hundred guineas. Are you answered, Mr. Stump?"

Ludlow started forward with a look of annoyance, but Stompff merely grinned, and said quietly, "I take it at the price, and as many more as Mr. Ludlow will paint of the same sort; stock, lock, and barrel, I'll have the whole bilin'. Must change the title though, Ludlow, my boy. None of your Sic wos non thingummy; none of your Hebrew classics for the British public. 'The Vow,' or 'The Last Farewell,' or something in that line.—Very neatly done of you, Charley, my boy; very neat bit of dealing, I call it. I ought to deduct four-and-nine from the next fifteen shillin' commission you get; but I'll make it up to you this way,—you've evidently all the qualities of a salesman; come and be my clerk, and I'll stand thirty shillings a-week and a commission on the catalogues."

Charley Potts was too delighted at his friend's success to feel annoyance at these remarks; he merely shook his fist laughingly, and was passing on, with his arm through Ludlow's; but the vivacious dealer, who had rapidly calculated where he could plant his newly-acquired purchase, and what percentage he could make on it, was not to be thus balked.

"Look here!" said he; "a bargain's a bargain, ain't it? People say your word's as good as your bond, and all that. Pickles! You drop down to my office to-morrow, Ludlow, and there'll be an agreement for you to sign—all straight and reg'lar, you know. And come and cut your mutton with me and Mrs. S. at Velasquez Villa, Nottin' 'Ill, on Sunday, at six. No sayin' no, because I won't hear it. We'll wet our connection in a glass of Sham. And bring Charley with you, if his dress-coat ain't up! You know, Charley! Tar, Tar!" And highly delighted with himself, and with the full conviction that he had rendered himself thoroughly delightful to his hearers, the great man waddled off to his brougham.

Meanwhile the news of the purchase had spread through the rooms, and men were hurrying up on all sides to congratulate Ludlow on his success. The fortunate man seemed, however, a little dazed with his triumph; he shook all the outstretched hands cordially, and said a few common-places of thanks, intermingled with doubts as to whether he

c

had not been too well treated; but on the first convenient opportunity he slipped away, and sliding a shilling into the palm of Flexor the model, who, being by this time very drunk, had arranged his hair in a curl on his forehead, and was sitting on the bench in the hall after his famous rendering of George the Fourth of blessed memory, Geoff seized his hat and coat and let himself out. The fresh night-air revived him wonderfully, and he was about starting off at his usual headstrong pace, when he heard a low dismal moan, and looking round, he saw a female figure cowering in a door-way. The next instant he was kneeling by her side.

CHAPTER III.

BLOTTED OUT.

THE strange caprices of Fashion were never more strangely illustrated than by her fixing upon St. Barnabas Square as one of her favourite localities. There are men yet living among us whose mothers had been robbed on their way from Ranelagh in crossing the spot, then a dreary swampy marsh, on which now stands the city of palaces known as Cubittopolis. For years on years it remained in its dismal condition, until an enterprising builder, seeing the army of civilisation advancing with grand strides south-westward, and perceiving at a glance the immediate realisation of an enormous profit on his outlay, bought up the entire estate, had it thoroughly cleansed and drained, and proceeded to erect thereon a series of terraces, places, and squares, each vying with the other in size, perfection of finish, and, let it be said, general ghastliness. The houses in St. Barnabas Square resemble those in Chasuble Crescent, and scarcely differ in any particular from the eligible residences in Reredos Road : they are all very tall, and rather thin ; they have all enormous porticoes, over which are little conservatories, railed in with ecclesiastical ironwork ; dismal little back-rooms no bigger than warm-baths, but described as "libraries" by the house-agents ; gaunt drawing-rooms connected by an arch ; vast landings, leading on to other little conservatories, where "blacks," old flower-pots, and a few geranium stumps, are principally conserved; and a series of gaunt towny bedrooms. In front they have Mr. Swiveller's prospect,—a delightful view of over-the-way; across the bit of square enclosure like a green pocket-handkerchief; while at the back they look immediately on to the back-premises of other eligible residences. The enterprising builder has done his best for his neighbourhood, but he has been unable to neutralise the effects of the neighbouring Thames; and the consequence is, that during the winter months a chronic fog drifts up from the pleasant Kentish marshes, and finding ample room and verge enough, settles permanently down in the St. Barnabas district; while in the summer, the new roads which intersect the locality, being mostly composed of a chalky foundation, peel off under every passing wheel, and emit enormous clouds of dust, which are generally drifting on the summer wind into the eyes and mouths of stray passengers, and in at the doors and windows of regular residents. Yet this is one of Fashion's chosen spots; here in this stronghold of stucco reside scores of those whose names and doings the courtly journalist delighteth to chronicle; hither do county magnates bring, to furnished houses, their wives and daughters, leaving them to entertain those of the proper set during the three summer months, while they, the county magnates themselves, are sleeping the sleep of the just on the benches of the House of Commons, or nobly discharging their duty to their country by smoking cigars on the terrace; here reside men high up in the great West-end public offices, commissioners and secretaries, anxious to imbue themselves with the scent of the rose, and *vivre près d'elle*, City magnates, judges of the land, and counsel learned in the law. The situation is near to Westminster for the lawyers and politicians; and the address has quite enough of the true ring about it to make it much sought after by all those who go-in for a fashionable neighbourhood.

A few hours before the events described in the preceding chapters took place, a brougham, perfectly appointed, and drawn by a splendid horse, came dashing through the fog and driving mist, and pulled up before one of the largest houses in St. Barnabas Square. The footman jumped from the box, and was running to the door, when, in obedience to a sharp voice, he stopped, and the occupant of the vehicle, who had descended, crossed the pavement with rapid strides,

C 2

and opened the door with a pass-key. He strode quickly through the hall, up the staircase, and into the drawing-room, round which he took a rapid glance. The room was empty; the gas was lit, and a fire burned brightly on the hearth; while an open piano, covered with music, on the one side of the fireplace, and a book turned down with open leaves, showed that the occupants had but recently left. The new-comer, finding himself alone, walked to the mantelpiece, and leaning his back against it, passed his hands rapidly across his forehead; then plunging both of them into his pockets, seemed lost in thought. The gaslight showed him to be a man of about sixty years of age, tall, wiry, well-proportioned; his head was bald, with a fringe of grayish hair, his forehead broad, his eyes deep-set, his mouth thin-lipped, and ascetic; he wore two little strips of whisker, but his chin was closely shaved. He was dressed in high stiff shirt-collars, a blue-silk neckerchief with white dots, in which gleamed a carbuncle pin; a gray overcoat, under which was a cutaway riding-coat, high waistcoat with onyx buttons, and tight-fitting cord-trousers. This was George Brakespere, third Earl Beauport, of whom and of whose family it behoves one to speak in detail.

They were *novi homines*, the Brakesperes, though they always claimed to be sprung from ancient Norman blood. Only seventy years ago old Martin Brakespere was a wool-stapler in Uttoxeter; and though highly respected for the wealth he was reported to have amassed, was very much jeered at privately, and with bated breath, for keeping an apocryphal genealogical tree hanging up in his back-shop, and for invariably boasting, after his second glass of grog at the Greyhound, about his lineage. But when, after old Martin had been some score years quietly resting in Uttoxeter churchyard, his son Sir Richard Brakespere, who had been successively solicitor and attorney general, was raised to the peerage, and took his seat on the woolsack as Baron Beauport, Lord High Chancellor of England, the Herald's College, and all the rest of the genealogical authorities, said that the line was thoroughly made out and received the revival of the ancient title with the greatest laudation. A wiry, fox-headed, thin chip of a lawyer, the first Baron Beauport, as knowing as a ferret, and not unlike one in the face. He administered the laws of his country very well, and he lent some of the money he had inherited from his father to the sovereign of his country and the first gentleman in Europe at a very high rate of interest, it is said. Rumour reports that he did not get all his money back again, taking instead thereof an increase in rank, and dying, at an advanced age, as Earl Beauport, succeeded in his title and estates by his only son, Theodore Brakespere, by courtesy Viscount Caterham.

When his father died, Lord Caterham, the second Earl Beauport, was nearly fifty years old, a prim little gentleman who loved music and wore a wig; a dried-up chip of a little man, who lived in a little house in Hans Place with an old servant, a big violoncello, and a special and peculiar breed of pug-dogs. To walk out with the pug-dogs in the morning, to be carefully dressed and tittivated and buckled and curled by the old servant in the afternoon, and either to play the violoncello in a Beethoven or Mozart selection with some other old amateur fogies, or to be present at a performance of chamber-music, or philharmonics, or oratorio-rehearsals in the evening, constituted the sole pleasure of the second Earl Beauport's life. He never married; and at his death some fifteen years after his father's, the title and, with the exception of a few legacies to musical charities, the estates passed to his cousin George Brakespere, Fellow of Lincoln College, Oxon, and then of Little Milman Street, Bedford Row, and the Northern Circuit, briefless barrister.

Just in the very nick of time came the peerage and the estates to George Brakespere, for he was surrounded by duns, and over head and ears in love. With all his hard work at Oxford, and he had worked hard, he had the reputation of being the best bowler at Bullingdon, and the hardest rider after hounds; of having the best old port and the finest cigars (it was before the days of claret and short pipes), and the best old oak furniture, library of books, and before-letter proofs in the University. All these could not be paid for out of an undergraduate's income; and the large remainder of unpaid bills hung round him and plagued him heavily long after he had left Oxford and been called to the bar. It was horribly up-hill work getting a connection among the attorneys; he tried writing for reviews, and succeeded, but earned very little money. And then, on circuit, at an assize-ball, he fell in love with Gertrude

Carrington, a haughty county beauty, only daughter of Sir Joshua Carrington, Chairman of Quarter Sessions; and that nearly finished him. Gertrude Carrington was very haughty and very wilful; she admired the clever face and the bold bearing of the young barrister; but in all probability she would have thought no more of him, had not the eminent Sir Joshua, who kept his eyes very sharply about him, marked the flirtation, and immediately expressed his total disapproval of it. That was enough for Gertrude, and she at once went in for George Brakespere, heart and soul. She made no objection to a clandestine correspondence, and responded regularly and warmly to George's passionate letters. She gave him two or three secret meetings under an old oak in a secluded part of her father's park,— Homershams was a five-hours' journey from town,—and these assignations always involved George's sleeping at an inn, and put him to large expense; and when she came up to stay with her cousins in town, she let him know all the parties to which they were going, and rendered him a mendicant for invitations. When the change of fortune came, and George succeeded to the title, Sir Joshua succumbed at once, and became anxious for the match. Had George inherited money only, it is probable that from sheer wilfulness Gertrude would have thrown him over; but the notion of being a countess, of taking precedence and *pas* of all the neighbouring gentry, had its influence, and they were married. Two sons were born to them,—Viscount Caterham and the Hon. Lionel Brakespere,—and a daughter, who only survived her birth a few weeks. As Earl Beauport, George Brakespere retained the energy and activity of mind and body, the love of exercise and field-sports, the clear brain and singleness of purpose, which had distinguished him as a commoner: but there was a skeleton in his house, whose bony fingers touched his heart in his gayest moments, numbed his energies, and warped his usefulness; whose dread presence he could not escape from, whose chilling influence nor wine, nor work, nor medicine, nor gaiety, could palliate. It was ever present in a tangible shape; he knew his weakness and wickedness in permitting it to conquer him,—he strove against it, but vainly; and in the dead watches of the night often he lay broad awake railing against the fate which had mingled so bitter an ingredient in his cup of happiness.

The door swung open and the Countess entered, a woman nearly fifty now, but not looking her age by at least eight years. A tall handsome woman, with the charms of her former beauty mellowed but not impaired; the face was more full, but the firm chiselling of the nose and lips, the brightness of the eyes, the luxurious dark gloss of the hair, were there still. As she entered, her husband advanced to meet her; and as he touched her forehead with his lips, she laid her hand on his, and asked " What news ?"

He shook his head sadly, and said, " The worst."

" The worst !" she repeated, faintly ; " he's not dead ? Beauport, you—you would not say it in that way—he's not dead ?"

" I wish to God he were !" said Lord Beauport through his teeth. " I wish it had pleased God to take him years and years ago ! No ! he's not dead." Then throwing himself into a chair, and staring vacantly at the fire, he repeated, " I wish to God he were !"

" Anything but that !" said the Countess, with a sense of immense relief; " anything but that ! whatever he has done may be atoned for, and repented, and—But what has he done ? where is he ? have you seen Mr. Farquhar ?"

" I have—and I know all. Gertrude, Lionel is a scoundrel and a criminal—no, don't interrupt me ! I myself have prosecuted and transported men for less crimes than he has committed ; years ago he would have been hanged. He is a forger !"

" A forger !"

" He has forged the names of two of his friends—old brother officers ; Lord Hinchenbrook is one, and young Latham the other—to bills for five thousand pounds. I've had the bills in my hands, and seen letters from the men denying their signatures to-night, and—"

" But Lionel—where is he ? in prison ?"

" No ; he saw the crash coming, and fled from it. Farquhar showed me a blotted letter from him, written from Liverpool, saying in a few lines that he had disgraced us all, that he was on the point of sailing under a feigned name for Australia, and that we should never see him again."

" Never see him again ! my boy, my own darling boy !" and Lady Beauport burst into an agony of tears.

" Gertrude," said her husband, when the first wild storm of grief had subsided, " calm yourself for one instant."

He rang the bell, and to the servant answering it, said :

"Tell Lord Caterham I wish to speak to him, and beg Miss Maurice to be good enough to step here."

Lady Beauport was about to speak, but the Earl said coldly :

"I wish it, if you please ;" and reiterated his commands to the servant, who left the room. "I have fully decided, Gertrude, on the step I am about to take. To-morrow those forged bills will be mine. I saw young Latham at Farquhar's, and he said—" Lord Beauport's voice shook here—"said everything that was kind and noble ; and Hinchenbrook has said the same to Farquhar. It—it cannot be kept quiet, of course. Every club is probably ringing with it now ; but they will let me have the bills. And from this moment, Gertrude, that boy's name must never be uttered, save in our prayers—in our prayers for his forgiveness and—and repentance—by you, his mother ; by me his father,—nor by any one in this house. He is dead to us for ever !"

"Beauport, for Heaven's sake—"

"I swear it, Gertrude, I swear it ! and most solemnly will keep the oath. I have sent for Caterham, who must know, of course ; his good sense will approve what I have done ; and for Annie, she is part of our household now, and must be told. Dead to us all henceforth ; dead to us all !"

He sank into a chair opposite the fire and buried his face in his hands, but roused himself at advancing footsteps. The door opened, and a servant entered, pushing before him a library-chair fitted on large wheels, in which sat a man of about thirty, of slight spare frame, with long arms and thin womanly hands—a delicately-handsome man, with a small head, soft grey eyes, and an almost feminine mouth ; a man whom Nature had intended for an Apollo, whom fortune had marked for her sport, blighting his childhood with some mysterious disease for which the doctors could find neither name nor cure, sapping his marrow and causing his legs to wither into the shrunken and useless members which now hung loosely before him utterly without strength, almost without shape, incapable of bearing his weight, and rendering him maimed, crippled, blasted for life. This was Viscount Caterham, Earl Beauport's eldest son, and heir to his title and estates. His father cast one short, rapid glance at him as he entered, and then turned to the person who immediately followed him.

This was a tall girl of two-and-twenty, of rounded form and winning expression. Her features were by no means regular; her eyes were brown and sleepy; she had a pert inquisitive nose; and when she smiled, in her decidedly large mouth gleamed two rows of strong white teeth. Her dark-brown hair was simply and precisely arranged; for she had but a humble opinion of her own charms, and objected to any appearance of coquetry. She was dressed in a tight-fitting black silk, with linen collar and cuffs, and her hands and feet were small and perfectly shaped. Darling Annie Maurice, orphan daughter of a second cousin of my lord's, transplanted from a suburban curacy to be companion and humble friend of my lady, the one bright bit of sunshine and reality in that palace of ghastly stucco and sham. Even now, as she came in, Lord Beauport seemed to feel the cheering influence of her presence, and his brow relaxed for an instant as he stepped forward and offered his hand; after taking which, she, with a bow to the Countess, glided round and stood by Lord Caterham's chair.

Lord Caterham was the first to speak.

"You sent for us—for Annie and me, sir," he said in a low tremulous voice; "I trust you have no bad news of Lionel."

Lady Beauport hid her face in her hands; but the Earl, who had resumed his position against the mantelpiece, spoke firmly.

"I sent for you, Caterham, and for you, Annie, as members of my family, to tell you that Lionel Brakespere's name must never more be mentioned in this house. He has disgraced himself, and us through him; and though we cannot wipe away that disgrace, we must strive as far as possible to blot him out from our memories and our lives. You know, both of you,—at least you, Caterham, know well enough,—what he has been to me—the love I had for him—the—yes, my God, the pride I had in him!"

His voice broke here, and he passed his hand across his eyes. In the momentary pause Annie Maurice glanced up at Lord Caterham, and marked his face distorted as with pain, and his head reclining on his chest. Then, gulping down the knot rising in his throat, the Earl continued:

"All that is over now ; he has left the country, and the chances are that we shall never see nor even hear from him again." A moan from the Countess shook his voice for a second, but he proceeded : "It was to tell you this that I sent for you. You and I, Caterham, will have to enter upon this subject once more to-morrow, when some business arrangements have to be made. On all other occasions, recollect, it is tabooed. Let his name be blotted out from our memories, and let him be as if he had never lived."

As Earl Beauport ceased speaking he gathered himself together and walked towards the door, never trusting himself to look for an instant towards where his wife sat cowering in grief, lest his firmness should desert him. Down the stairs he went, until entering his library he shut the door behind him, locked it, and throwing himself into his chair, leant his head on the desk, and covering it with his hands gave way to a passion of sobs which shook his strong frame as though he were convulsed. Then rising, he went to the book-case, and taking out a large volume, opened it, and turned to the page immediately succeeding the cover. It was a big old-fashioned Bible, bound in calf, with a hideous ancient woodcut as a frontispiece representing the Adoration of the Wise Men ; but the page to which Lord Beauport turned, yellow with age, was inscribed in various-coloured inks, many dim and faded, with the names of the old Brakespere family, and the dates of their births, marriages, and deaths. Old Martin Brakespere's headed the list ; then came his son's, with "created Baron Beauport" in the lawyer's own skimpy little hand, in which also was entered the name of the musical-amateur peer, his son ; then came George Brakespere's bold entry of his own name and his wife's, and of the names of their two sons. Over the last entry Lord Beauport paused for a few minutes, glaring at it with eyes which did not see it, but which had before them a chubby child, a bright handsome Eton boy, a dashing guardsman, a "swell" loved and petted by all, a fugitive skulking in an assumed name in the cabin of a sea-tossed ship ; then he took up a pen and ran it through the entry backwards and forwards until the name was completely blotted out ; and then he fell again into his train of thought. The family dinner-hour was long since passed ; the table was laid, all was ready, and the French cook and the grave butler were in despair : but Lord Beauport still sat alone in his library with old Martin Brakespere's Bible open before him.

---◦◦◦---

CHAPTER IV.

ON THE DOOR-STEP.

IT is cheap philosophy to moralise on the importance of events led up to by the merest trifles ; but the subject comes so frequently before us as to furnish innumerable pegs whereon the week-day preacher may hang up his little garland of reflections, his little wreath of homely truisms. If Ned Waldron had not been crossing into the Park at the exact moment when the shortsighted Godalming banker was knocked down by the hansom at the Corner, he would have still been enjoying eighty pounds a-year as a temporary extra-clerk at Whitehall, instead of groaning over the villanous extortion of the malt-tax, as a landed proprietor of some thousands of inherited acres. If Dr. Weston's red-lamp over the surgery-door had been blown out when the servant rushed off for medical advice for Master Percy Buckmaster's ear-ache, the eminent apothecary would never have had the chance of which he so skilfully availed himself —of paying dutiful attention to Mrs. Buckmaster, and finally stepping into the shoes of her late husband, the wealthy Indian indigo-planter.

If Geoffrey Ludlow, dashing impetuously onward in his career, had not heard that long low heart-breaking moan, he might have gone on leading his easy, shiftless, drifting life, with no break greater than the excitement consequent on the sale of a picture or the accomplishment of a resolution. But he *did* hear it, and, rare thing in him, acting at once on his first impulse, he dropped on his knees just in time to catch the fainting form in his outstretched arms. That same instant he would have shrunk back if he could ; but it was too late ; that same instant there came across him a horrible feeling of the ludicrousness of his position : there at midnight in a London thoroughfare holding in his arms—what ! a drunken tramp, perhaps ; a vagrant well known to the Mendicity Society ; a gin-sodden street-walker, who might requite his good Samaritanism with a leer and a laugh, or an oath and a blow. And yet the **groan** seemed to come from the lowest depths of a wrung and suffering heart; and the appearance—no, there could be no mistake about that. That thin, almost emaciated, figure; those pinched features; drawn, haggard, colourless cheeks; that brow, half hidden by the thick, damp, matted hair, yet in its deep lines and indentations revealing the bitter workings of the mind; the small thin bony hands now hanging flaccid and motionless—all these, if there were anything real in this life, were outward semblances such as mere imposters could not have brought forward in the way of trade.

Not one of them was lost on Geoffrey Ludlow, who, leaning over the prostrate figure, narrowly scanned its every feature, bent his face towards the mouth, placed his hands on the heart, and then, thoroughly alarmed, looked round and called for aid. Perhaps his excitement had something to do with it, but Geoff's voice fell flat and limp on the thick damp air, and there was no response, though he shouted again and again. But presently the door whence he had issued opened widely, and in the midst of a gush of tobacco smoke a man came out, humming a song, twirling a stick, and striding down the street. Again Geoffrey Ludlow shouted, and this time with success, for the new-comer stopped suddenly, took his pipe from his mouth, and turning his head towards the spot whence the voice proceeded, he called out, simply but earnestly, " Hallo there ! what's the row ? "

Ludlow recognised the speaker at once. It was Charley Potts, and Geoffrey hailed him by name.

" All right !" said Charley in return. " You've picked up my name fast enough, my pippin ; but that don't go far. Better known than trusted is your obedient servant, C. P. Hallo, Geoff, old man, is it you ? Why, what the deuce have you got there ? an 'omeless poor, that won't move on, or a —— By George, Geoff, this is a bad case !" He had leant over the girl's prostrate body, and had rapidly felt her pulse and listened at her heart. " This woman's dying of inanition and prostration. I know it, for I was in the red-bottle and Plaster-of-Paris-horse line before I went in for Art. She must be looked to at once, or she'll slip off the hooks while we're standing by her. You hold on here, old man, while I run back and fetch the brandy out of Dabb's room; I know where he keeps it. Chafe her hands, will you, Geoff? I shan't be a second."

Charley Potts rushed off, and left Geoffrey still kneeling by the girl's side. In obedience to his friend's instructions, he began mechanically to chafe her thin worn hands; but as he rubbed his own over them to and fro, to and fro, he peered into her face, and wondered dreamily what kind of eyes were hidden behind the drooped lids, and what was the colour of the hair hanging in dank thick masses over the pallid brow. Even now there began to spring in his mind a feeling of wonder not unmixed with alarm, as to what would be thought of him, were he discovered in his then position; whether his motives would be rightly construed; whether he were not acting somewhat indiscreetly in so far committing himself: for Geoffrey Ludlow had been brought up in the strict school of dire respectability, where a lively terror of rendering yourself liable to Mrs. Grundy's remarks is amongst the doctrines most religiously inculcated. But a glance at the form before him gave him fresh assurance; and when Charley Potts returned he found his friend rubbing away with all his energy.

"Here it is," said Charley; "Dabb's particular. I know it's first-rate, for Dabb only keeps it medicinally, taking Sir Felix Booth Bart. as his ordinary tipple. I know this water-of-life-of-cognac of old, sir, and always have internal qualms of conscience when I go to see Dabb, which will not be allayed until I have had what Caniche calls a suspicion. Hold her head for a second, Geoff, while I put the flask to her mouth. There! Once more, Geoff. Ah! I thought so. Her pulse is moving now, old fellow, and she'll rouse in a bit; but it was very nearly a case of Walker."

"Look at her eyes—they're unclosing."

"Not much wonder in that, is there, my boy? though it is odd, perhaps. A glass of brandy has made many people shut their eyes before now; but as to opening them—Hallo! steady there!"

He said this as the girl, her eyes glaring straight before her, attempted to raise herself into an erect position, but after a faint struggle dropped back, exclaiming feebly:

"I cannot, I cannot."

"Of course you can't, my dear," said Charley Potts, **not**

unkindly; "of course you can't. You musn't think of attempting it either. I say, Geoff,"—(this was said in a lower tone)
—"look out for the policeman when he comes round, and give
him a hail. Our young friend here must be looked after at
once, and he'd better take her in a cab to the workhouse."

As he said the last words, Geoffrey Ludlow felt the girl's
hand which he held thrill between his, and, bending down,
thought he saw her lips move.

"What's the matter?" said Charley Potts.

"It's very strange," replied Geoffrey; "I could swear I
heard her say 'Not there!' and yet—"

"Likely enough been there before, and knows the treatment. However, we must get her off at once, or she'll go
to grief; so let us—"

"Look here, Charley: I don't like the notion of this
woman's going to a workhouse, specially as she seems to—
object, eh? Couldn't we—isn't there any one where we
could—where she could lodge for a night or two, until—the
doctor, you know—one might see? Confound it all,
Charley, you know I never can explain exactly; can't you
help me, eh?"

"What a stammering old idiot it is!" said Charley Potts,
laughing. "Yes, I see what you mean—there's Flexor's
wife lives close by, in Little Flotsam Street—keeps a
lodging-house. If she's not full, this young party can go in
there. She's all right now so far as stepping it is concerned,
but she'll want a deal of looking after yet. O, by Jove! I
left Rollit in at the Titians, the army-doctor, you know, who
sketches so well. Let's get her into Flexor's, and I'll fetch
Rollit to look at her. Easy now! Up!"

They raised her to her feet, and half-supported, half-
carried her round the church and across the broad road,
and down a little bystreet on the other side. There Charley
Potts stopped at a door, and knocking at it, was soon confronted by a buxom middle-aged woman, who started with
surprise at seeing the group.

"Lor, Mr. Potts! what can have brought you 'ere, sir?
Flexor's not come in, sir, yet—at them nasty Titiums, he is,
and joy go with him. If you're wanting him, sir, you'd
better—"

"No, Mrs. Flexor, we don't want your husband just now.
Here's Mr. Ludlow, who—"

" Lord, and so it is ! but seeing nothing but the nape of your neck, sir, I did not recognise—"

" All right, Mrs. Flexor," said Geoffrey ; " we want to know if your house is full. If not, here is a poor woman for whom we—at least Mr. Potts—and I myself, for the matter of that—"

" Stuttering again, Geoff ! What stuff ! Here, Mrs. Flexor, we want a room for this young woman to sleep in ; and just help us in with her at once into your parlour, will you ? and let us put her down there while I run round for the doctor."

It is probable that Mrs. Flexor might have raised objections to this proposition ; but Charley Potts was a favourite with her, and Geoffrey Ludlow was a certain source of income to her husband ; so she stepped back while the men caught up their burden, who all this time had been resting, half-fainting, on Geoffrey's shoulder, and carried her into the parlour. Here they placed her in a big, frayed, ragged easy-chair, with all its cushion-stuffing gone, and palpable bits of shaggy wool peering through its arms and back ; and after dragging this in front of the expiring fire, and bidding Mrs. Flexor at once prepare some hot gruel, Charley Potts rushed away to catch Dr. Rollit.

And now Geoffrey Ludlow, left to himself once more (for the girl was lying back in the chair, still with unclosing eyes, and had apparently relapsed into a state of stupor), began to turn the events of the past hour in his mind, and to wonder very much at the position in which he found himself. Here he was in a room in a house which he had never before entered, shut up with a girl of whose name or condition he was as yet entirely ignorant, of whose very existence he had only just known ; he, who had always shirked anything which afforded the smallest chance of adventure, was actually taking part in a romance. And yet—nonsense ! here was a starving wanderer, whom he and his friend had rescued from the street ; an ordinary every-day case, familiar in a thousand phases to the relieving-officers and the poor-law guardians, who, after her certain allowance of warmth, and food, and physic, would start off to go—no matter where, and do—no matter what. And yet he certainly had not been deceived in thinking of her faint protest when Charley proposed to send her to the workhouse. She had

spoken then; and though the words were so few and the
tone so low, there was something in the latter which suggested education and refinement.   Her hands too, her poor
thin hands, were long and well-shaped, with tapering fingers
and filbert-nails, and bore no traces of hard work : and
her face—ah, he should be better able to see her face now.

He turned, and taking the flaring candle from the table,
held it above her head.   Her eyes were still closed; but as
he moved, they opened wide, and fixed themselves on him.
Such large, deep-violet eyes, with long sweeping lashes!
such a long, solemn, stedfast gaze, in which his own eyes
were caught fast, and remained motionless.   Then on to
his hand, leaning on the arm of the chair, came the cold
clammy pressure of feeble fingers ; and in his ear, bent and
listening, as he saw a fluttering motion of her lips, murmured
very feebly the words, "Bless you !—saved me !" twice repeated.   As her breath fanned his cheek, Geoffrey Ludlow's
heart beat fast and audibly, his hand shook beneath the
light touch of the lithe fingers ; but the next instant the
eyelids dropped, the touch relaxed, and a tremulousness
seized on the ashy lips.   Geoffrey glanced at her for an
instant, and was rushing in alarm to the door, when it
opened, and Charley Potts entered, followed by a tall grave
man, in a long black beard, whom Potts introduced as
Dr. Rollit.

"You're just in time," said Geoffrey ; "I was just going to
call for help.   She—"

"Pardon me, please," said the doctor, calmly pushing
him on one side.   "Permit me to—ah !" he continued, after a
glance—"I must trouble you to leave the room, Potts,
please, and take your friend with you.   And just send
the woman of the house to me, will you ?   There is a
woman, I suppose?"

"O yes, there is a woman, of course.—Here, Mrs. Flexor,
just step up, will you ?—Now, Geoff, what are you staring
at, man ?   Do you think the doctor's going to eat the girl?
Come on, old fellow ; we'll sit on the kitchen-stairs, and
catch blackbeetles to pass the time.   Come on !"

Geoff roused himself at his friend's touch, and went with
him, but in a dreamy sullen manner.   When they got into
the passage, he remained with outstretched ear, listening
eagerly ; and when Charley spoke, he savagely bade him

hold his tongue. Mr. Potts was so utterly astonished at this conduct, that he continued staring and motionless, and merely gave vent to his feelings in one short low whistle. When the door was opened, Geoffrey Ludlow strode down the passage at once, and confronting the doctor, asked him what news. Dr. Rollit looked his questioner steadily in the eyes for a moment; and when he spoke his tone was softer, his manner less abrupt than before. "There is no special danger, Mr. Ludlow," said he; "though the girl has had a narrow escape. She has been fighting with cold and want of proper nourishment for days, so far as I can tell."

"Did she say so?"

"She said nothing; she has not spoken a word." Dr. Rollit did not fail to notice that here Geoffrey Ludlow gave a sigh of relief. "I but judge from her appearance and symptoms. I have told this good person what to do; and I will look round early in the morning. I live close by. Now, good-night."

"You are sure as to the absence of danger?"

"Certain."

"Good-night; a thousand thanks!—Mrs. Flexor, mind that your patient has every thing wanted, and that I settle with you.—Now, Charley, come; what are you waiting for?"

"Eh?" said Charley. "Well, I thought that, after this little excitement, perhaps a glass out of that black bottle which I know Mrs. Flexor keeps on the second shelf in the right-hand cupboard—"

"Get along with you, Mr. Potts!" said Mrs. Flexor, grinning.

"You know you do, Mrs. F.—a glass of that might cheer and not inebriate.—What do you say, Geoff?"

"I say no! You've had quite enough; and all Mrs. Flexor's attention is required elsewhere.—Good-night, Mrs. Flexor; and"—by this time they were in the street—"good-night, Charley."

Mr. Potts, engaged in extracting a short-pipe from the breast-pocket of his pea-jacket, looked up with an abstracted air, and said, "I beg your pardon."

"Good-night, Charley."

"Oh, certainly, if you wish it. Good-night, Geoffrey Ludlow, Esquire; and permit me to add, Hey no nonny! Not a very lucid remark, perhaps, but one which exactly illustrates my state of mind." And Charley Potts filled his pipe, lit it, and remained leaning against the wall, and smoking with much deliberation until his friend was out of sight.

Geoffrey Ludlow strode down the street, the pavement ringing under his firm tread, his head erect, his step elastic, his whole bearing sensibly different even to himself. As he swung along he tried to examine himself as to what was the cause of his sudden light-heartedness; and at first he ascribed it to the sale of his picture, and to the warm promises of support he had received at the hands of Mr. Stompff. But these, though a few hours since they had really afforded him the greatest delight, now paled before the transient glance of two deep-violet eyes, and the scarcely-heard murmur of a feeble voice. "'Bless you !—saved me !' that's what she said !" exclaimed Geoff, halting for a second and reflecting. "And then the touch of her hand, and the —ah! Charley was right! Hey no nonny is the only language for such an ass as I'm making of myself." So home through the quiet streets, and into his studio, thinking he would smoke one quiet pipe before turning in. There, restlessness, inability to settle to any thing, mad desire to sketch a certain face with large eyes, a certain fragile helpless figure, now prostrate, now half-reclining on a bit of manly shoulder; a carrying-out of this desire with a bit of crayon on the studio-wall, several attempts, constant failure, and consequent disgust. A feeling that ought to have been pleasure, and yet had a strong tinge of pain at his heart, and a constant ringing of one phrase, "Bless you !—saved me !" in his ears. So to bed ; where he dreamt he saw his name, Geoffrey Ludlow, in big black letters at the bottom of a gold frame, the picture in which was Keat's "Lamia ;" and lo ! the Lamia had the deep-violet eyes of the wanderer in the streets.

CHAPTER V

THE LETTER.

THE houses in St. Barnabas Square have an advantage over most other London residences in the possession of a "third room" on the ground-floor. Most people who, purposing to change their domicile, have gone in for a study of the *Times* Supplement or the mendacious catalogues of house-agents, have read of the "noble dining-room, snug breakfast-room, and library," and have found the said breakfast-room to be about the size and depth of a warm-bath, and the "library" a soul-depressing hole just beyond the glazed top of the kitchen-stairs, to which are eventually relegated your old boots, the bust of the friend with whom since he presented it you have had a deadly quarrel, some odd numbers of magazines, and the framework of a shower-bath which, in a moment of madness, you bought at a sale and never have been able to fit together.

But the houses in St. Barnabas Square have each, built over what in other neighbourhoods is called "leads,"—a ghastly space where the cats creep stealthily about in the day-time, and whence at night they yowl with preternatural pertinacity,—a fine large room, devoted in most instances to the purposes of billiards, but at Lord Beauport's given up entirely to Lord Caterham. It had been selected originally from its situation on the ground-floor giving the poor crippled lad easy means of exit and entrance, and preventing any necessity for his being carried—for walking was utterly impossible to him—up and down stairs. It was *his* room; and there, and there alone, he was absolute master; there he was allowed to carry out what his mother spoke of as his "fads," what his father called "poor Caterham's odd ways." His brother, Lionel Brakespere, had been in the habit of dropping in there twice or three times a-week, smoking his cigar, turning over the "rum things" on the table, asking advice which he never took, and lounging round the room, reading the backs of the books which he did not understand, and criticising the pictures which he knew nothing about. It would have been impossible to tell to what manner of man the room belonged from a cursory survey of its contents. Three-fourths of the walls were covered with large bookcases filled with a heterogeneous assemblage of books. Here a row of poets, a big quarto *Shakespeare* in six volumes, followed by *Youatt on the Horse, Philip Van Artevelde,* and Stanhope's *Christian Martyr.* In the next shelf Voltaire, all the Tennysons, *Mr. Sponge's Sporting-Tour,* a work on Farriery, and *Blunt on the Pentateuch.* So the *mélange* ran throughout the bookshelves; and on the fourth wall, where hung the

D 2

pictures, it was not much better. For in the centre were Landseer's "Midsummer-Night's Dream," where that lovely Titania, unfairy-like if you please, but one of the most glorious specimens of pictured womanhood, pillows her fair face under the shadow of that magnificent ass's head; and Frith's "Coming of Age," and Delaroche's "Execution of Lady Jane Grey," and three or four splendid proof-engravings of untouchable Sir Joshua; and among them, dotted here and there, hunting-sketches by Alken, and coaching bits from Fores. Scattered about on tables were pieces of lava from Vesuvius, photographs from Pompeii, a collection of weeds and grasses from the Arctic regions (all duly labelled in the most precise handwriting), a horse's shoe specially adapted for ice-travelling, specimens of egg-shell china, a box of gleaming carpenter's tools, boxes of Tunbridge ware, furs of Indian manufacture, caricature statuettes by Danton, a case of shells, and another of geological specimens. Here stood an easel bearing a half-finished picture, in one corner was a sheaf of walking-sticks, against the wall a rack of whips. Before the fire was a carved-oak writing-desk, and on it, beside the ordinary blotting and writing materials, were an aneroid barometer, a small skeleton clock, and a silver handbell. And at it sat Viscount Caterham, his head drooping, his face pale, his hands idly clasped before him.

Not an unusual position this with him, not unusual by any means when he was alone. In such society as he forced himself to keep—for with him it was more than effort to determine occasionally to shake off his love of solitude, to be present amongst his father's guests, and to receive some few special favourites in his own rooms—he was more than pleasant, he was brilliant and amusing. Big, heavy, good-natured guardsmen, who had contributed nothing to the "go" of the evening, and had nearly tugged off their tawny beards in the vain endeavour to extract something to say, would go away, and growl in deep bas voices over their cigars about "that strordinary f'ler Caterham. Knows a lot, you know, that f'ler, 'bout all sorts things. Can't 'ceive where picks it all up; and as jolly as old boots, by Jove!"

Old friends of Lord Beauport's, now gradually dropping into fogiedom, and clutching year by year more tightly the conventional prejudices instilled into them in early life, listened with elevated eyebrows and dropping jaws to Lord

Caterham's outspoken opinions, now clothed in brilliant
tropes, now crackling with smart antithesis, but always fresh,
earnest, liberal, and vigorous; and when they talked him
over in club-windows, these old boys would say that "there
was something in that deformed fellow of Beauport's, but
that he was all wrong; his mind as warped as his body, by
George!" And women,—ah, that was the worst of all,—
women would sit and listen to him on such rare occasions
as he spoke before them, sit many of them steadfast-eyed
and ear-attentive, and would give him smiles and encouraging
glances, and then would float away and talk to their next
dancing-partner of the strange little man who had such odd
ideas, and spoke so—so unlike most people, you know.

He knew it all, this fragile, colourless, delicate cripple,
bound for life to his wheel-chair, dependent for mere motion
on the assistance of others; a something apart and almost
without parallel, helpless as a little child, and yet with the
brain, the heart, the passions of a man. No keener observer of outward show, no clearer reader of character than
he. From out his deep-set melancholy eyes he saw the
stare of astonishment, sometimes the look of disgust, which
usually marked a first introduction to him; his quick ear
caught the would-be compassionate inflection of the voice
addressing him on the simplest matters; he knew what the
old fogies were thinking of, as they shifted uneasily in their
chairs as he spoke; and he interpreted clearly enough the
straying glances and occasional interjections of the women.
He knew it all, and bore it—bore it as the cross is rarely
borne.

Only three times in his life had there gone up from his
lips a wail to the Father of mercies, a passionate outpouring
of his heart, a wild inquiry as to why such affliction had
been cast upon him. But three times, and the first of these
was when he was a lad of eighteen. Lord Beauport had
been educated at Charterhouse, where, as every one knows,
Founder's Day is kept with annual rejoicings. To one of
these celebrations Lord Beauport had gone, taking Lord
Caterham with him. The speeches and recitations were
over, and the crowd of spectators were filing out into the
quadrangle, when Lord Caterham, whose chair was being
wheeled by a servant close by his father's side, heard a
cheery voice say, " What, Brakespere ! Gad, Lord Beauport,

I mean! I forgot. Well, how are you, my dear fellow?
I haven't seen you since we sat on the same form in that
old place." Lord Caterham looked up and saw his father
shaking hands with a jolly-looking middle-aged man, who
rattled on—"Well, and you've been in luck and are a great
gun! I'm delighted to hear it. You're just the fellow to
bear your honours bravely. O yes, I'm wonderfully well,
thank God. And I've got my boy here at the old shop,
doing just as we used to do, Brakespere—Beauport, I mean.
I'll introduce you. Here, Charley!" calling to him a fine
handsome lad; "this is Lord Beauport, an old schoolfellow
of mine. And you, Beauport,—you've got children, eh?"

"O yes," said Lord Beauport—"two boys."

"Ah! that's right. I wish they'd been here; I should
have liked to have seen them." The man rattled on, but
Lord Caterham heard no more. He had heard enough.
He knew that his father was ashamed to acknowledge his
maimed and crippled child — ashamed of a comparison
between the stalwart son of his old schoolfellow and his own
blighted lad; and that night Lord Caterham's pillow was
wet with tears, and he prayed to God that his life might be
taken from him.

Twice since then the same feelings had been violently
excited; but the sense of his position, the knowledge that
he was a perpetual grief and affliction to his parents, was
ever present, and pervaded his very being. To tell truth,
neither his father nor his mother ever outwardly manifested
their disappointment or their sorrow at the hopeless physical
state of their firstborn son; but Lord Caterham read his
father's trouble in thousands of covert glances thrown
towards the occupant of the wheeled chair, which the elder
man thought were all unmarked, in short self-suppressed
sighs, in sudden shiftings of the conversation when any
subject involving a question of physical activity or muscular
force happened to be touched upon, in the persistent way in
which his father excluded him from those regular solemn
festivities of the season, held at certain special times, and at
which he by right should certainly have been present.

No man knew better than Lord Beauport the horrible
injustice he was committing; he felt that he was mutely
rebelling against the decrees of Providence, and adding to
the affliction already mysteriously dispensed to his unfortunate

son by his treatment. He fought against it, but without avail; he *could* not bow his head and kiss the rod by which he had been smitten. Had his heir been brainless, dissipated, even bad, he could have forgiven him. He did in his heart forgive his second son when he became all three; but that he, George Brakespere, handsome Brakespere, one of the best athletes of the day, should have to own that poor misshapen man as his son and heir !—it was too much. He tried to persuade himself that he loved his son; but he never looked at him without a shudder, never spoke of him with unflushed cheeks.

As for Lady Beauport, from the time that the child's malady first was proclaimed incurable, she never took the smallest interest in him, but devoted herself, as much as devotion was compatible with perpetual attendance at ball, concert, and theatre, to her second son. As a child, Lord Caterham had, by her express commands, been studiously kept out of her sight; and now that he was a man, she saw very much less of him than of many strangers. A dozen times in the year she would enter his room and remain a few minutes, asking for his taste in a matter of fancy-costume, or something of the kind; and then she would brush his forehead with her lips, and rustle away perfectly satisfied with her manner of discharging the duties of maternity.

And Lord Caterham knew all this; read it as in a book; and suffered, and was strong. Who know most of life, discern character most readily, and read it most deeply? We who what we call "mix in the world," hurry hither and thither, buffeting our way through friends and foes, taking the rough and the smooth, smiling here, frowning there, but ever pushing onward? Or the quiet ones, who lie by in the nooks and lanes, and look on at the strife, and mark the quality and effect of the blows struck; who see not merely how, but why the battle has been undertaken; who can trace the strong and weak points of the attack and defence, see the skirmishers thrown out here, the feigned retreat there, the mine ready prepared in the far distance? How many years had that crippled man looked on at life, standing as it were at the gates and peering in at the antics and dalliances, the bowings and scrapings, the mad moppings and idiotic mowings of the puppets performing? And had he not arrived during this period at a perfect knowledge of how the wires were pulled, and what was the result ?

Among them but not of them, in the midst of the whirl of London but as isolated as a hermit, with keen analytical powers, and leisure and opportunity to give them full swing, Lord Caterham passed his life in studying the lives of other people, in taking off the padding and the drapery, the paint and the tinsel, in looking behind the grins, and studying the motives for the sneers. Ah, what a life for a man to pass ! situated as Lord Caterham was, he must under such circumstances have become either a Quilp or an angel. The natural tendency is to the former : but Providence had been kind in one instance to Lord Caterham, and he, like Mr. Disraeli, went in for the angel.

His flow of spirits was generally, to say the least of it, equable. When the dark hour was on him he suffered dreadfully ; but this morning he was more than usually low, for he had been pondering over his brother's insane downfall, and it was with something like real pleasure that he heard his servant announce " Mr. Barford," and gave orders for that gentleman's admittance.

The Honourable Algernon Barford by prescriptive right, but " Algy Barford " to any one after two days' acquaintance with him, was one of those men whom it is impossible not to call by their Christian names ; whom it is impossible not to like as an acquaintance ; whom it is difficult to take into intimate friendship ; but with whom no one ever quarrelled. A big, broad-chested, broad-faced, light-whiskered man, perfectly dressed, with an easy rolling walk, a pleasant presence, a way of enarming and " old boy-ing " you, without the least appearance of undue familiarity ; on the contrary, with a sense of real delight in your society ; with a voice which, without being in the least affected, or in the remotest degree resembling the tone of the stage-nobleman, had the real swell ring and roll in it ; a kindly, sunny, chirpy, world-citizen, who, with what was supposed to be a very small income, lived in the best society, never borrowed or owed a sovereign, and was nearly always in good temper. Algy Barford was the very man to visit you when you were out of spirits. A glance at him was cheering ; it revived one at once to look at his shiny bald forehead fringed with thin golden hair, at his saucy blue eyes, his big grinning mouth furnished with sparkling teeth ; and when he spoke, his voice came ringing out with a cheery music of its own.

"Hallo, Caterham !" said he, coming up to the chair and placing one of his big hands on the occupant's small shoulder; "how goes it, my boy? Wanted to see you, and have a chat. How are you, old fellow, eh? Where does one put one's hat, by the way, dear old boy? Can't put it under my seat, you know, or I should think I was in church ; and there's no place in this den of yours; and—ah, that'll do, on that lady's head. Who is it? O, Pallas Athené ; ah, very well then, *non invitâ Minervâ*, she'll support my castor for me. Fancy my recollecting Latin, eh? but I think I must have seen it on somebody's crest. Well, and now, old boy, how are you?"

"Well, not very brilliant this morning, Algy. I—"

"Ah, like me, got rats, haven't you?"

"Rats?"

"Yes; whenever I'm out of spirits I think I've got rats— sometimes boiled rats. Oh, it's all very well for you to laugh, Caterham ; but you know, though I'm generally pretty jolly, sometimes I have a regular file-gnawing time of it. I think I'll take a peg, dear old boy—a sherry peg— just to keep me up."

"To be sure. Just ring for Stevens, will you ? he'll—"

"Not at all ; I recollect where the sherry is and where the glasses live. *Nourri dans le sérail, j'en connais les détours.* Here they are. Have a peg, Caterham?"

"No, thanks, Algy ; the doctor forbids me that sort of thing. I take no exercise to carry it off, you know ; but I thought some one told me you had turned teetotaller."

"Gad, how extraordinarily things get wind, don't you know ! So I did, honour !—kept to it all strictly, give you my word, for—ay, for a fortnight ; but then I thought I might as well die a natural death, so I took to it again. This is the second peg I've had to-day—took number one at the Foreign Office, with my cousin Jack Lambert. You know Jack?—little fellow, short and dirty, like a winter's day."

"I know him," said Caterham, smiling ; "a sharp fellow."

"O yes, deuced cute little dog—knows every thing. I wanted him to recommend me a new servant—obliged to send my man away—couldn't stand him any longer—always worrying me."

"I thought he was a capital servant?"

"Ye-es; knew too much though, and went to too many evening-parties—never would give me a chance of wearing my own black bags and dress-boots—kept 'em in constant requisition, by Jove! A greedy fellow too. I used to let him get just outside the door with the breakfast-things, and then suddenly call him back; and he never showed up without his mouth full of kidney, or whatever it was. And he always would read my letters — before I'd done with them, I mean. I'm short-sighted, you know, and obliged to get close to the light : he was in such a hurry to find out what they were about, that he used to peep in through the window, and read them over my shoulder. I found this out; and this morning I was ready for him with my fist neatly doubled-up in a thick towel. I saw his shadow come stealing across the paper, and then I turned round and let out at him slap through the glass. It was a gentle hint that I had spotted his game ; and so he came in when he had got his face right, and begged me to suit myself in a month, as he had heard of a place which he thought he should like better. Now, can you tell me of any handy fellow, Caterham?"

"Not I; I'm all unlikely to know of such people. Stay, there was a man that—"

"Yes ; and then you stop. Gad, you are like the rest of the world, old fellow: you have an *arrière pensée* which prevents your telling a fellow a good thing."

"No, not that, Algy. I was going to say that there was a man who was Lionel's servant. I don't know whether he has got another place ; but Lionel, you know—" and Lord Caterham stopped with a knot in his throat and burning cheeks.

"I know, dear old boy," said Algy Barford, rising from his seat and again placing his hand on Caterham's shoulder; "of course I know. You're too much a man of the world " —(Heaven help us! Caterham a man of the world! But this was Algy Barford's pleasant way of putting it)—"not to know that the clubs rang with the whole story last night. Don't shrink, old boy. It's a bad business ; but I never heard such tremendous sympathy expressed for a—for a

buffer—as for Lionel. Every body says he must have been
no end cornered before he—before he—well, there's no
use talking of it. But what I wanted to say to you is this,—
and I'm deuced glad you mentioned Lionel's name, old
fellow, for I've been thinking all the time I've been here
how I could bring it in. Look here! he and I were no end
chums, you know; I was much older than he; but we took
to each other like any thing, and—and I got a letter from
him from Liverpool with—with an enclosure for you, old
boy."

Algy Barford unbuttoned his coat as he said these last
words, took a long breath, and seemed immensely relieved,
though he still looked anxiously towards his friend.

"An enclosure for me?" said Lord Caterham, turning
deadly white; "no further trouble—no further misery for—"

"On my honour, Caterham, I dont' know what it is," said
Algy Barford; "he doesn't hint it in his letter to me. He
simply says, 'Let the enclosed be given to Caterham, and
given by your own hand.' He underlines that last sentence;
and so I brought it on. I'm a bungling jackass, or I should
have found means to explain it myself, by Jove! But as
you have helped me, so much the better."

"Have you it with you?"

"O yes; brought it on purpose," said Algy, rising and
taking his coat from a chair, and his hat from the head of
Pallas Athené; "here it is. I don't suppose anything from
poor Lionel can be very brilliant just now; but still, I know
nothing. Good-by, Caterham, old fellow; can't help me to
a servant-man, eh? See you next week; meantime,—and
this earnest, old boy,—if there's anything I can do to help
Lionel in any shape, you'll let me know, won't you, old
fellow?"

And Algy Barford handed Lord Caterham the letter,
kissed his hand, and departed in his usual airy, cheery
fashion.

That night Lord Caterham did not appear at the dinner-
table; and his servant, on being asked, said that his master
"had been more than usual queer-like," and had gone to
bed very early.

CHAPTER VI.

THE FIRST VISIT.

GEOFFREY LUDLOW was in his way a recognisant and a grateful man, grateful for such mercies as he knew he enjoyed; but from never having experienced its loss, he was not sufficiently appreciative of one of the greatest of life's blessings, the faculty of sleep at will. He could have slept, had he so willed it, under the tremendous cannonading, the *feu-d'enfer*, before Sebastopol, or while Mr. Gladstone was speaking his best speech, or Mr. Tennyson was reading aloud his own poetry; whenever and wherever he chose he could sleep the calm peaceful sleep of an infant. Some people tell you they are too tired to sleep —that was never the case with Geoffrey; others that their minds are too full, that they are too excited, that the weather is too hot or too cold, that there is too much noise, or that the very silence is too oppressive. But, excited or comatose, hot or cold, in the rumble of London streets or the dead silence of—well, he had never tried the Desert, but let us say Walton-on-the-Naze, Geoffrey Ludlow no sooner laid his head on the pillow than he went off into a sound, glorious, healthy sleep—steady, calm, and peaceful; not one of your stertorous, heavy, growling slumbers, nor your starting, fly-catching, open-mouthed, moaning states, but a placid, regular sleep, so quiet and undisturbed that he scarcely seemed to breathe; and often as a child had caused his mother to examine with anxiety whether the motionless figure stretched upon the little bed was only sleeping naturally, or whether the last long sleep had not fallen on it.

Dreams he had, no doubt; but they by no means disturbed the refreshing, invigorating character of his repose. On the night of his adventure in the streets, he dreamt the Lamia dream without its in the least affecting his slumber; and when he opened his eyes the next morning, with the recollection of where he was, and what day it was, and what he had to do—those post-waking thoughts which come to all of us—there came upon him an indefinable sensation of something pleasurable and happy, of something bright and sunshiny, of something which made his heart feel light within him, and caused him to open his eyes and grapple with the day at once.

Some one surely must long ere this have remarked how our manner of waking from slumber is affected by our state of mind. The instant that consciousness comes upon us, the dominant object of our thoughts, be it pleasant or horrible, is before us : the absurd quarrel with the man in the black beard last night, about—what *was* it about? the acceptance which Smith holds, which must be met, and can't be renewed ; the proposal in the conservatory to Emily Fairbairn, while she was flushed with the first *valse* after supper, and we with Mrs. Tresillian's champagne ;—or, *per contra*, as they say in the City, the thrilling pressure of Flora Maitland's hand, and the low whisper in which she gave us rendezvous at the Botanical Fête this afternoon ; the lawyer's letter informing us of our godfather's handsome legacy ;—all these, whether for good or ill, come before us with the first unclosing of our eyelids. If agreeable we rouse ourselves at once, and lie simultaneously chewing the cud of pleasant thoughts and enjoying the calm haven of our bed ; if objectionable, we try and shut them out yet for a little while, and turning round court sleep once more.

What was the first thought that flashed across Geoffrey Ludlow's brain immediately on his waking, and filled him with hope and joy? Not the remembrance of the purchase of his picture by Mr. Stompff, though that certainly occurred to him, with Stompff's promises of future employment, and the kind words of his old friends at the Titians, all floating simultaneously across his mind. But with these thoughts came the recollection of a fragile form, and a thin hand with long lithe fingers wound round his own, and a low feeble voice whispering the words "Bless you !—saved me !" in his listening ear.

Beneath the flickering gas-lamps, or in the dim half-light of Mrs. Flexor's room, he had been unable to make out the colour of the eyes, or of the thick hair which hung in heavy masses over her cheeks ; it was a spiritual recollection of her at the best ; but he would soon change that into a material inspection. So, after settling in his own mind—that mind which coincides so readily with our wishes—that it was benevolence which prompted his every action, and which roused in him the desire to know how the patient of the previous night was getting on, he sprang from his bed, and pulled the string of his shower-bath with an energy which not even the knowledge of the water's probable temperature could mitigate. But he had not proceeded half-way through his toilet, when the old spirit of irresolution began to exercise its dominion over him. Was it not somewhat of a Quixotic adventure in which he was engaging? To succour a starving frozen girl on a wet night was merely charitable and humane; there was no man of anything like decent feeling but would have acted as he had done, and—by George!— here the hair-brushes were suspended in mid-air, just threatening a descent one on either side of his bushy head—wouldn't it have been better to have accepted Charley Pott's suggestion, and let the policeman take her to the workhouse? There she would have had every attention and—bah! every attention! the truckle-bed in a gaunt bare room, surrounded by disease in every shape; the prefunctory visits of the parish-doctor; the—O no! and, moreover, had he not heard, or at all events imagined he heard, the pallid lips mutter "Not there!" No! there was something in her which—which—at all events—well, *ruat cœlum*, it was done, and he must take the consequences; and down came the two hair-brushes like two avalanches, and worried his unresisting scalp like two steam-harrows. The recollection of the fragile frame, and the thin hands, and the broken voice, supported by the benevolent theory, had it all their own way from that time out, until he had finished dressing, and sent him downstairs in a happy mood, pleased with what he had done, more pleased still with the notion of what he was about to do. He entered the room briskly, and striding up to an old lady sitting at the head of the breakfast-table, gave her a sounding kiss.

"Good-morning, dearest mother.—How do, Til, dear?" turning to a young woman who was engaged in pouring out the tea. "I'm late again, I see."

"Always on sausage mornings, I notice, Geoffrey," said Mrs. Ludlow, with a little asperity. It does not so much matter with haddock, though it becomes leathery; or eggs, for you like them hard; but sausages should be eaten hot, or not at all; and to-day, when I'd sent specially for these, knowing that nasty herb-stuffing is indigestible—let them deny it if they can—it does seem hard that—well, never mind—"

Mrs. Ludlow was a very good old lady, with one great failing : she was under the notion that she had to bear what she called "a cross," a most uncomfortable typical object, which caused all her friends the greatest annoyance, but in which, though outwardly mournful, she secretly rejoiced, as giving her a peculiar status in her circle. This cross intruded itself into all the social and domestic details of her life, and was lugged out metaphorically on all possible occasions.

"Don't mind me, mother," said Geoff; "the sausages will do splendidly. I overslept myself; I was a little late last night."

"O, at those everlasting Titians.—I declare I forgot," said the young woman who had been addressed as "Til," and who was Geoffrey's only sister. "Ah, poor fellow ! studying his art till two this morning, wasn't he ?" And Miss Til made a comic sympathetic *moue*, which made Geoff laugh.

"Two !" said Mrs. Ludlow; "nearer three, Matilda. I ought to know, for I had water running down my back all night, and my feet as cold as stone ; and I had a perfect recollection of having left the key of the linen closet in the door, owing to my having been hurried down to luncheon yesterday when I was giving Martha out the clean pillowcases. However, if burglars do break into that linen-closet, it won't be for my not having mentioned it, as I call you to witness, Matilda."

"All right, mother," said Geoffrey; "we'll run the risk of that. I'm very sorry I disturbed the house, but I *was* late, I confess ; but I did some good, though."

"O yes, Geoffrey, we know," said Matilda. "Got some new notions for a subject, or heard some æsthetic criticism ; or met some wonderful lion, who's going to astonish the world, and of whom no one ever hears again ! You always have done something extraordinary when you're out very late, I find."

"Well, I did something really extraordinary last night. I sold my picture the ' Ballroom,' you know; and for what do you think ?—two hundred pounds."

"O, Geoff, you dear, darling old Geoff! I am so glad! Two hundred pounds! O, Geoff, Geoff! You dear, lucky old fellow!" and Miss Till flung her arms round her brother's neck and hugged him with delight. Mrs. Ludlow said never a word; but her cross melted away momentarily, her eyes filled with tears, and her lips quivered. Geoffrey noticed this, and so soon as he had returned his sister's hearty embrace, he went up to his mother, and kneeling by her side, put up his face for her kiss.

"God bless you, my son!" said the old lady reverently, as she gave it; "God bless you! This is brave news, indeed. I knew it would come in time; but—"

"Yes; but tell us all about it, Geoff. How did it come about? and however did you pluck up courage, you dear, bashful, nervous old thing, to ask such a price?"

"I—why, Til, you know that I—and you, dear mother, you know too that—not that I am bashful, as Til says; but still there's something. O, I should never have sold the picture, I believe, if I'd been let alone. It was Charley Potts sold it for me."

"Charles Potts! That ridiculous young man! Well, I should never have thought it," said Mrs. Ludlow.

Miss Matilda said nothing, but a faint flush rose on her neck and cheeks, and died away again as quickly as it came.

"O, he's a capital man of business—for anybody else, that's to say. He don't do much good for himself. He sold the picture for me, and prevented my saying a word in the whole affair. And who do you think has bought it? Mr. Stompff, the great dealer, who tells me he'll take as many more of the same style as I like to paint."

"This is great news, indeed, my boy," said the old lady. "You've only to persevere, and your fortune's made. Only one thing, Geoffrey,—never paint on Sunday, or you'll never become a great man."

"Well but, mother," said Geoff, smiling, "Sir Joshua Reynolds painted always on Sundays until Johnson's death; and he was a great man."

"Ah, well, my dear," replied his mother forcibly, if not logically, "that's nothing to do with it."

Then Geoffrey, who had been hurrying through his sausage, and towards the last began to grow nervous and fidgety—

accounted for by his mother and sister from his anxiety to go and see Mr. Stompff, and at once fling himself on to fresh canvases—finished his breakfast, and went out to get his hat. Mrs. Ludlow, with her "cross" rapidly coming upon her, sat down to "do the books,"—an inspection of the household brigade of tradesmen's accounts which she carried on weekly with the sternest rigour; and Matilda, who was by no means either a romantic or a strong-minded woman, commenced to darn a basketful of Geoffrey's socks. Then the sock-destroyer put his head in at the door, his mouth ornamented with a large cigar, and calling out "Good-bye," departed on his way.

The fragile form, the thin hands, and the soft low voice had it all their own way with Geoffrey Ludlow now. He was going to see their owner; in less than an hour he should know the colour of the eyes and the hair; and figuratively Geoffrey walked upon air; literally, he strode along with bright eyes and flushed cheeks, swinging his stick, and, but for the necessity of clenching his cigar between his teeth, inclined to hum a tune aloud. He scarcely noticed any of the people he met; but such as he did casually glance at he pitied from the bottom of his soul : there were no thin hands or soft voices waiting for them. And it must be owned that the passers-by who noticed him returned his pity. The clerks on the omnibuses, sucking solemnly at their briar-root pipes, or immersed in their newspapers, solemn staid men going in "to business," on their regular daily routine, looked up with wonder on this buoyant figure, with its black wide-awake hat and long floating beard, its jerky walk, its swinging stick, and its general air of light-hearted happiness. The cynical clerks, men with large families, whom nothing but an increase of salary could rouse, interchanged shoulder-shrugs of contempt, and the omnibus-conductor, likewise a cynic, after taking a long stare at Geoffrey, called out to his driver, "'Appy cove that ! looks as if he'd found a fourpenny-piece, don't he ?"

Entirely ignorant of the attention he was attracting, Geoff blithely pursued his way. He lived at Brompton, and he was bound for the neighbourhood of Portland Place ; so he turned in at the Albert Gate, and crossing the enclosure and the Row, made for Grosvenor Gate. In the Park he was equally the object of remark : the nurse-girls called their charges to come

" to heel " out of the way of that " nasty ugly big man ;" the valetudinarians taking their constitutional in the Row loathed him for swinging his stick and making their horses shy as he passed ; the park-keepers watched him narrowly, as one probably with felonious intent to the plants or the ducks.

Still, utterly unconscious, Geoffrey went swinging along across Grosvenor Square, down Brook Street ; and not until he turned into Bond Street did he begin to realise entirely the step he was about to take.   Then he wavered, in mind and in gait ; he thought he would turn back : he did turn back, irresolute, doubtful.   Better have nothing more to do with it ; nip it in the bud ; send Charley Potts with a couple of sovereigns to Mrs. Flexor's, and tell her to set the girl on her way again, and wish her God-speed.   But what if she were still ill, unable to move ? people didn't gain sufficient strength in twelve hours ; and Charley, though kind-hearted, was rather *brusque;* and then the low voice, with the " Bless you !—saved me !" came murmuring in his ear ; and Geoffrey, like Whittington, turned again, and strode on towards Little Flotsam Street.

When he got near Flexor's door, he faltered again, and very nearly gave in : but looking up, saw Mrs. Flexor standing on the pavement ; and perceiving by her manner that his advent had been noticed, proceeded, and was soon alongside that matron.

"Good morning, Mrs. Flexor."

"Good mornin', sir ; thought you'd be over early, though not lookin' for you now, but for Reg'las, my youngest plague, so called after Mr. Scumble's Wictory of the Carthageniums, who has gone for milk for some posset for our dear ; who is much better this mornin', the Lord a mussy ! Dr. Rollix have been, and says we may sit up a little, if taking nourishment prescribed ; and pleased to see you we shall be.   A pretty creetur, Mr. Ludlow, though thin as thin and low as low : but what can we expect ?"

"She is better, then ?"

"A deal better, more herself like ; though not knowing what she was before, I can't exactly say.   Flexor was fine and buffy when he came home last night, after you was gone, sir.   Them nasty Titiums, he always gets upset there. And now he's gone to sit to Mr. Potts for—ah, well, some Roman party whose name I never can remember."

" Is your patient up, Mrs. Flexor ?"

"Gettin'   We shall be ready to see you in five minutes, sir.   I'll go and see to her at once."

Mrs. Flexor retired, and Geoffrey was left to himself for a quarter of an hour standing in the street, during which time he amused himself as most people would under similar circumstances.   That is to say, he stared at the houses opposite and at the people who passed ; and then he beat his stick against his leg, and then he whistled a tune, and then, having looked at his watch five times, he looked at it for the sixth.   Then he walked up the street, taking care to place his foot on the round iron of every coal-shoot ; and then he walked down the street, carrying out a determination to step in the exact centre of every flagstone ; and then, after he had pulled his beard a dozen times, and lifted his wideawake hat as many, that the air might blow upon his hot forehead, he saw Mrs. Flexor's head protrude from the doorway, and he felt very much inclined to run away.   But he checked himself in time, and entered the house, and, after a ghostly admonition from Mrs. Flexor "not to hagitate her," he opened the parlour-door, which Mrs. Flexor duly shut behind him, and entered the room.

Little light ever groped its way between the closely-packed rows of houses in Little Flotsam Street, even on the brightest summer day ; and on a dark and dreary winter's morning Mrs. Flexor's little front parlour was horribly dark.   The worthy landlady had some wild notion, whence derived no one knew, that an immense amount of gentility was derived from keeping the light out ; and consequently the bottom parts of her windows were fitted with dwarf wire-blinds, and the top parts with long linen-blinds, and across both were drawn curtains made of a kind of white fishing-net ; so that even so little daylight as Little Flotsam Street enjoyed was greatly diluted in the Flexorian establishment.

But Geoffrey Ludlow saw stretched out on a miserable black horsehair sofa before him there this fragile form which had been haunting his brain for the last twelve hours.   Ah, how thin and fragile it was ; how small it looked, even in its worn draggled black-merino dress !   As he advanced noiselessly, he saw that the patient slept ; her head was thrown back, her delicate white hands (and almost involuntarily Geoffrey remarked that she wore no wedding-

E 2

ring) were clasped across her breast, and her hair, put off her dead-white face, fell in thick clusters over her shoulders.

With a professional eye Geoffrey saw at once that whatever trouble she might have taken, she could not have been more artistically posed than in this natural attitude. The expression of her eyes was wanting; and, as he sunk into a chair at her feet, her eyes opened upon him. Then he saw her face in its entirety; saw large deep-violet eyes, with dark lashes and eyebrows; a thin, slightly aquiline nose; small thin close lips, and a little chin; a complexion of the deadest white, without the smallest colour; and hair, long thick rich luxuriant hair, of a deep, red-gold colour—not the poetic "auburn," not the vulgar "carrots;" a rich metallic red, unmistakable, admitting of no compromise, no darkening by grease or confining by fixature—a great mass of deep-red hair, strange, weird, and oddly beautiful. The deep-violet eyes, opening slowly, fixed their regard on his face without a tremor, and with a somewhat languid gaze; then brightening slowly, while the hands were unclasped, and the voice—how well Geoff remembered its tones, and how they thrilled him again!—murmured faintly, " It is you !"

What is that wonderful something in the human voice which at once proclaims the social status of the speaker? The proletary and the *roturier*, Nature willing, can have as good features, grow as flowing beards, be as good in stature, grace, and agility, as the noblest patrician, or the man in whose veins flows the purest *sangre azul;* but they fail generally in hands, always in voice. Geoffrey Ludlow, all his weakness and irresolution notwithstanding, was necessarily by his art a student of life and character; and no sooner did he hear those three little words spoken in that tone, than all his floating ideas of shamming tramp or hypocritical street-walker, as connected with the recipient of his last night's charity, died away, and he recognised at once the soft modulations of education, if not of birth.

But those three words, spoken in deep low quivering tones, while they set the blood dancing in Geoffrey Ludlow's veins, made him at the same time very uncomfortable. He had a dread of anything romantic; and there flashed through his mind an idea that he could only answer this remark by exclaiming, "'Tis I !" or " Ay, indeed !" or something else equally absurd and ridiculous. So he contented himself with bowing his head and putting out his hand—into which the long lithe fingers came fluttering instantly. Then with burning cheeks Geoffrey bent forward, and said, "You are better to-day?"

"Oh, so much—so much better! thanks to you, thanks to you!"

"Your doctor has been?" She bowed her head in reply.

"And you have everything you wish for?" She bowed again, this time glancing up—with, O, such a light in the deep-violet eyes—into Geoffrey's face!

"Then—then I will leave you now," said he, awkwardly enough. The glance fell as he said this; but flashed again full and earnest in an instant; the lithe fingers wound round his wrist, and the voice, even lower and more tremulously than before, whispered, "You'll come to-morrow?"

Geoff flushed again, stammered, "Yes, O, by all means!" made a clumsy bow, and went out.

Now this was a short, and not a particularly satisfactory, interview; but the smallest detail of it remained in Geoffrey Ludlow's mind, and was reproduced throughout the remainder of that day and the first portion of the succeeding night, for him to ponder over. He felt the clasp of her fingers yet on his wrist, and he heard the soft voice, "You'll come to-morrow?" It must be a long distance, he thought, that he would not go to gaze into those eyes, to touch that hand, to hear that voice again!

CHAPTER VII.

CHEZ POTTS.

MR. POTTS lived in Berners Street, on the second floor of a rambling big old-fashioned house, which in its palmy days had been inhabited by people of distinction; and in which it was rumoured in the art-world that the great Mr. Fuseli had once lived, and painted those horrors which sprung from the nightmare consequent on heavy suppers of pork-chops. But these were the days of its decadence, and each of its floors had now a separate and distinct tenant. The ground-floor was a kind of half show-room, half shop, held by Mr. Lectern, the great church-upholsterer. Specimens of stained-glass windows, croziers, and brass instruments like exaggerated beadles'-staves, gilt sets of communion-service, and splendidly-worked altar-cloths, occupied the walls; the visitor walked up to the desk at which Mr. Lectern presided between groves of elaborately-carved pulpits and reading-desks, and brazen eagles were extending their wings in every available corner. On the first-floor Mdlle. Stetti gave lessons to the nobility, gentry, and the public in general in the fashionable dances of the day, and in the Magyar sceptre-exercises for opening the chest and improving the figure. Mdlle. Stetti had a very large connection; and as many of her pupils were adults who had never learned to dance while they were supple and tender, and as, under the persevering tuition of their little instructress, they gambolled in a cumbrous and rather elephantine manner, they earned for themselves many hearty anathemas from Mr. Potts, who found it impossible to work with anything like a steady hand while the whole house was rocking under the influence of a stout stockbroker doing the "changes," or while the walls trembled at every bound of the fourteen-stone lady from Islington, who was being initiated into the mysteries of the gavotte. But Charley Potts' pipe was the only confidant of his growled anathemas, and on the whole he got on remarkably well with his neighbours; for Mr. Lectern had lent him bits of oak furniture to paint from; and once, when he was ill, Mdlle. Stetti, who was the dearest, cheeriest, hardest-working, best-tempered little creature in existence, had made him broths and "goodies" with her own hand, and when he was well, had always a kind word and a smile for him—and, indeed, revelled in the practical humour and buffoonery of "*ce farceur* Pott." For Mr. Potts was nothing if not funny; the staircase leading to his rooms began to be decorated immediately after you had passed Mdlle. Stetti's apartments; an enormous hand, sketched in crayon, with an outstretched finger, directed attention to an inscription—"To the halls of Potts!" Just above the little landing you were confronted by a big beef-eater's head, out of the mouth of which floated a balloon-like legend—"Walk up, walk up, and see the great Potts!" The aperture of the letter-box in the door formed the mouth in a capital caricatured head of Charley himself; and instead of a bell-handle there hung a hare's-foot, beneath

which was gummed a paper label with a written inscription—
" Tug the trotter."

Three days after the gathering at the Titian Sketching-
Club, Mr. Potts sat in his studio, smoking a pipe, and
glaring vacantly at a picture on an easel in front of him. It
was not a comfortable room; its owner's warmest friend
could not have asserted that. There was no carpet, and
the floor was begrimed with the dirt of ages, and with spilt
tobacco and trodden-in cigar-ash. The big window was
half stopped-up, and had no curtain. An old oak-cabinet
against the wall, surmounted by the inevitable plaster torso,
and studies of hands and arms, had lost one of its supporting
feet, and looked as though momentarily about to topple
forward. A table in the middle of the room was crowded
with litter, amongst which a pewter-pot reared itself con-
spicuously. Over an old sofa were thrown a big rough
Inverness-cape, a wideawake hat, and a thick stick; while
on a broken, ragged, but theatrically-tawdry arm-chair, by
the easel, were a big palette already " set," a colour-box,
and a sheaf of brushes. Mr. Potts was dressed in a shepherd's-plaid shooting coat, adorned here and there with
dabs of paint, and with semi-burnt brown patches, the result
of the incautious dropping of incandescent tobacco and
vesuvians. He had on a pair of loose rough trousers, red-
morocco slippers without heels, and he wore no neckcloth;
but his big turned-down shirt-collar was open at the throat.
He wore no beard, but had a large sweeping Austrian moustache, which curled fiercely at the ends; had thin brown
hair, light blue eyes, and the freshest and healthiest of com-
plexions. No amount of late hours, of drinking and smoking,
could apparently have any effect on this baby-skin; and
under the influence of cold water and yellow soap, both of
which he used in large quantities, he seemed destined to
remain—so far as his complexion was concerned—" beautiful
for ever,"—or at least until long after Madame Rachel's
clients had seen the worthlessness of pigments. Looking at
him as he sat there—his back bent nearly double, his eyes
fixed on his picture, his pipe fixed stiffly between his teeth,
and his big bony hands clasped in front of him—there was
no mistaking him for anything but a gentleman; ill-dressed,
slatternly, if you like; but a true gentleman, every inch of
him.

The " trotter " outside being tugged with tremendous violence, roused him from his reverie, and he got up and opened the door, saying, as he did so, " Why didn't you ring ? I would, if I'd been you. You're in the bell-hanging line, I should think, by the way you jerked my wire. Hollo, Bowker, my boy ! is it you ? What's the matter ? Are you chivied by a dun on the staircase, or fainting for a pull at the pewter, that you come with such a ring as that ? Bring your body in, old man ; there's a wind here enough to shave you."

Mr. Bowker preceded his friend into the room, looked into the pewter-pot, drained it, wiped his beard with a handkerchief, which he took out of his hat, and said, in a solemn deep voice : " Potts, my pipkin, how goes it ?"

" Pretty well, old man, pretty well — considering the weather. And you ?"

"Your William *se porte bien.* Hallo !" glancing at the casel, while he took a pipe from his pocket and filled it from a jar on the table ; "hallo ! something new ! What's the subject ? Who is the Spanish party in tights ? and what's the venerable buffer in the clerical get-up of the period putting out his hand about ?"

" Oh, it's a scene from *Gil Blas,* where the Archbishop of Grenada discharges him, you know."

" No, I don't, and I don't want to hear ; your William, dear boy, has discovered that life is too short to have anything explained to him : if he don't see it at first, he let's it pass. The young party's right leg is out of drawing, my chick ; just give your William a bit of chalk. There—not being a patient at the Orthopædic Hospital—that's where his foot would come to. The crimson of the reverend gent's gown is about as bad as anything I've seen for a long time, dear boy. Hand over the palette and brushes for two minutes. Your William is a rum old skittle ; but if there's one thing he knows about, it is colour." And Charley, who knew that, with all his eccentricity, Mr. Bowker, or " your William," as he always spoke of himself, was a thorough master of his art, handed him what he required, and sat by watching him.

A fat bald-headed man with a grizzled beard, a large paunch and flat splay feet, badly dressed and not too clean, Mr. Bowker did not give one the idea of ever having been an "object of interest" to any one save the waiter at the tavern where he dined, or the tobacconist where he bought his Cavendish. But yet there had been a day when bright eyes grew brighter at his approach, tiny ears latticed with chestnut-hair had eagerly drunk in the music of his voice, gentle hands had thrilled beneath his touch. He had bright blue eyes himself then, and long hair, and a slim figure. He was young Mr. Bowker, whose first pictures exhibited at Somerset House had made such a sensation, and who was so much noticed by Sir David Wilkie, and for whom Mr. Northcote prophesied such a future, and whom Mr. Fuseli called a "coot prave poy!" He was the young Mr. Bowker who was recommended by Sir Thomas Lawrence as drawing-master to the lovely young wife of old Mr. Van Den Bosch, the Dutch banker and financier long resident in London. He was "that scoundrel Bowker, sir," who, being wildly romantic, fell head-over-ears in love with his pupil; and finding that she was cruelly ill-treated by the old ruffian her husband, ran away with her to Spain, and by that rash act smashed-up his career and finally settled himself for ever. Old Van Den Bosch got a divorce, and died, leaving all his money to his nephews; and then William Bowker and the woman he had eloped with returned to England, to find himself universally shunned and condemned. His art was as good, nay a thousand times better than ever; but they would not hear of him at the Royal Academy now; would not receive his pictures; would not allow the mention of his name. Patrons turned their backs on him, debts accumulated, the woman for whom he had sacrificed everything died,—penitent so far as she herself was concerned, but adoring her lover to the last, and calling down blessings on him with her latest breath. And then William Bowker strove no more, but accepted his position and sunk into what he was, a kindly, jolly, graceless vagabond, doing no harm, but very little good. He had a little private money on which he lived; and as time progressed, some of his patrons, who found he painted splendidly and cheaply, came back to him and gave him commissions; but he never again attempted to regain his status; and so long as he had enough to supply his simple daily wants, seemed content. He was a great favourite with some half-dozen young men of Charley Potts's set, who had a real love and regard for him, and was never so happy as when helping them with advice and manual assistance.

Charley watched him at his work, and saw with delight the archbishop's robe gradually growing all a-glow beneath the master's touch ; and then, to keep him in good-humour and amused, began to talk, telling him a score of anecdotes, and finally asking him if he'd heard anything of Tommy Smalt.

"Tommy Smalt, sir ?" cried Bowker, in his cheery voice ; "Tommy Smalt, sir, is in clover ! Your William has been able to put Tommy on to a revenue of at least thirty shillings a-week. Tommy is now the right-hand man of Jacobs of Newman Street ; and the best judges say that there are no Ostades, Jan Steens, or Gerard Dows like Tommy's."

"What do you mean ?—copies ?"

"Copies ! no, sir : originals."

"Originals !"

"Certainly ! original Tenierses, of boors drinking ; Wouvermanns, not forgetting the white horse ; or Jan Steens, with the never-failing episode ;—all carefully painted by Tommy Smalt and his fellow-labourers ! Ah, Jacobs is a wonderful man ! There never was such a fellow ; he sticks at nothing ; and when he finds a man who can do his particular work, he keeps him in constant employment."

"Well, but is the imposition never detected ? Don't the pictures look new ?"

"Oh, most verdant of youths, of course not ! The painting is clobbered with liquorice-water ; and the varnish is so prepared that it cracks at once ; and the signature in the corner is always authentic ; and there's a genuine look of cloudy vacancy and hopeless bankruptcy about the whole that stamps it at once to the connoisseur as the real thing. Tommy's doing a 'Youth's Head' by Rembrandt now, which ought to get him higher pay ; it ought indeed. It's for a Manchester man. They're very hot about Rembrandts at Manchester."

"Well, you've put me up to a new wrinkle. And Jacobs lives by this ?"

"Lives by it ! ay, and lives like a prince too. Mrs. J. to fetch him every day in an open barouche, and coachman and footman in skyblue livery, and all the little J.'s hanging

over the carriage-doors, rendering Newman Street dark with
the shadow of their noses. Lives by it! ay, and why not?
There will always be fools in the world, thank Heaven!—or
how should you and I get on, Charley, my boy?—and so
long as people will spend money on what they know nothing
about, for the sake of cutting-out their friends, gaining a
spurious reputation for taste, or cutting a swell as 'patrons
of the fine-arts,'—patrons indeed! that word nearly chokes
me!—it's quite right that they should be pillaged and done.
No man can love art in the same manner that he can love
pancakes. He must know something about it, and have
some appreciation of it. Now no man with the smallest
knowledge would go to Jacobs; and so I say that the lords
and railway-men and cotton-men who go there simply as a
piece of duff—to buy pictures as they would carpets—are
deuced well served out. There! your William has not
talked so much as that in one breath for many a long day.
The pewter's empty. Send for some more beer, and let's
have a damp; my throat's as dry as a lime-burner's wig."

Charley Potts took up the pewter-measure, and going
on to the landing outside the door, threw open the
staircase-window, and gave a shrill whistle. This twice
repeated had some effect! for a very much-be-ribboned
young lady in the bar of the opposite public-house looked
up, and nodded with great complaisance; and then Charley,
having made a solemn bow, waved the empty quart-pot
three times round his head. Two minutes afterwards a
bare-headed youth, with his shirt-sleeves rolled up to his
shoulders, crossed the road, carefully bearing a pasteboard
hat-box, with which he entered the house, and which he
delivered into Mr. Potts' hands.

"Good boy, Richard! never forget the hat-box; come for
it this evening, and take back both the empty pewters in it.
—It would never do, Bowker, my boy, to have beer—vulgar
beer, sir—in its native pewter come into a respectable house
like this. The pious parties, who buy their rattletraps and
properties of old Lectern down below, would be scandalised;
and poor little Mossoo woman Stetti would lose her swell
connection. So Caroline and I—that's Caroline in the bar,
with the puce-coloured ribbons—arranged this little dodge;
and it answers first-rate."

"Ha—a!" said Mr. Bowker, putting down the tankard

half-empty, and drawing a long breath; "beer is to your William what what's-his-name is to thingummy; which, being interpreted, means that he can't get on without it. I never take a big pull at a pewter without thinking of our Geoff. How is our Geoff?"

"Our Geoff is—hush! some one coming up stairs. What's to-day? Friday. The day I told the tailor to call. Hush!"

The footsteps came creaking up the stairs until they stopped outside Charley Potts' door, on which three peculiar blows were struck,—one very loud, then two in rapid succession.

"A friend!" said Charley, going to the door and opening it. "Pass, friend, and give the countersign! Hallo, Flexor! is it you? I forgot our appointment for this morning. Come in."

It was, indeed, the great model, who, fresh-shaved, and with his hair neatly poodled under his curly-brimmed hat, entered the room with a swagger, which, when he perceived a stranger, he allowed to subside into an elaborate bow.

"Now then, Flexor, get to work! we won't mind my friend here; he knows all this sort of game of old," said Charley; while Flexor began to arrange himself into the position of the expelled secretary of the archbishop.

"Ay, and I know Mr. Flexor of old, that's another thing!" said Bowker, with a deep chuckle, expelling a huge puff of smoke.

"Do you, sir?" said Flexor, still rigid in the Gil-Blas position, and never turning his head; "maybe, sir; many gents knows Flexor."

"Yes; but many gents didn't know Flexor five-and-twenty years ago, when he stood for 'Mercutio discoursing of Queen Mab.'"

"Lor' a mussy!" cried Flexor, forgetting all about his duty, parting the smoke with his hand and bending down to look into William's face. "It's Mr. Bowker, and I ought to have knowed him by the voice. And how are you, sir? hearty you look, though you've got a paucity of nobthatch, and what 'air you 'ave is that gray, you might be your own grandfather. Why, I haven't seen you since you was gold-medallist at the 'cademy, 'cept once when you come with Mrs. ——"

"There, that'll do, Flexor! I'm alive still, you see; and so I see are you. And your wife, is she alive?"

"O yes, sir; but, Lord, how different from what you know'd her! None of your Wenuses, nor Dalilys, nor Nell Gwyns now! she's growed stout and cumbersome, and never sits 'cept some gent wants a Mrs. Primrose in that everlastin' Wicar, or a old woman a-scoldin' a gal because she wants to marry a poor cove, or somethin' in that line; and then I says, 'Well, Jane, you may as well earn a shillin' an hour as any one else,' I says."

"And you've been a model all these years, Flexor?"

"Well, no sir—off and on; but I've always come back to it. I was a actor for three years; did Grecian stators,—Ajax defyin' the lightnin'; Slave a-listenin' to conspirators; Boy a-sharpenin' his knife, and that game, you know, in a cirkiss. But I didn't like it; they're a low lot, them actors, with no feelin' for art. And then I was a gentleman's servant; but that wouldn't do; they do dam' and cuss their servants so, the gentlemen do, as I couldn't stand it; and I was a mute."

"A mute!—what, a funeral mute?"

"Yes, sir; black-job business; and wery good that is,—plenty of pleasant comp'ny and agreeable talk, and nice rides in the summer time on the 'earses to all the pleasant simmetries in the suburbs! But in the winter it's frightful! and my last job I was nearly killed. We had a job at 'Ampstead, in the debth of snow; and it was frightful cold on the top of the 'Eath. It was the party's good lady as was going to be interred, and the party himself were frightful near; in fact, a reg'lar screw. Well, me and my mate had been standin' outside the 'ouse-door with the banners in our 'ands for an hour, until we was so froze we could scarcely hold the banners. So I says, I won't stand no longer, I says; and I gev a soft rap, and told the servant we must have a drop of somethin' short, or we should be killed with cold. The servant goes and tells her master, and what do you think he says? 'Drink!' he says. 'Nonsense!' he says; '*if they're cold, let 'em jump about and warm 'emselves,*' he says. Fancy a couple of mutes with their banners in their 'ands a-jumpin' about outside the door just before the party was brought out. So that disgusted me, and I gev it up, and come back to the old game agen."

"Now, Flexor," said Charley, "if you've finished your biography, get back again."

"All right, sir !" and again Flexor became rigid, as the student of Santillane.

"What were we talking of when Flexor arrived? O, I remember; I was asking you about Geoff Ludlow. What of him ?"

"Well, sir, Geoff Ludlow has made a thundering *coup* at last. The other night at the Titians he sold a picture to Stompff for two hundred pounds; more than that, Stompff promised him no end of commissions."

"That's first-rate ! Your William pledges him !" and Mr. Bowker finished the stout.

"He'll want all he can make, gentlemen," said Flexor, who, seeing the pewter emptied, became cynical; "he'll want all he can make, if he goes on as he's doin' now."

"What do you mean ?" asked Bowker.

"He's in love, Mr. Ludlow is; that's wot I mean. That party—you know, Mr. Potts—as you brought to our place that night—he's been to see her every day, he has; and my missis says, from what she 'ave seen and 'eard—well, that's neither 'ere nor there," said Flexor, checking himself abruptly as he remembered that the keyhole was the place whence Mrs. Flexor's information had been derived.

Charley Potts gave a loud whistle, and said, " The devil !" then turning to Bowker, he was about to tell the story of the wet night's adventure, but William putting up his finger warningly, grunted out *"Nachher !"* and Charley, who understood German, ceased his chatter and went on with his painting.

When the sitting was over, and Flexor had departed, William Bowker returned to the subject, saying, "Now, Charley, tell your William all about this story of Geoff and his adventure."

Charley Potts narrated it circumstantially, Bowker sitting grimly by and puffing his pipe the while. When he had finished, Bowker never spoke for full five minutes; but his brow was knit, and his teeth clenched round his pipe. At length he said, " This is a bad business, so far as I see ; a devilish bad business ! If the girl were in Geoff's own station, or if he were younger, it wouldn't so much matter ; but Geoff must be forty now, and at that age a man's deuced hard to turn from any thing he gets into his head. Well, we must wait and see. I'd rather it were you, Charley, by a mile ; one might have some chance then. But you never think of any thing of that sort, eh ?"

What made Charley Potts colour as he said, "Well—not in Geoff's line, at all events ?"

William Bowker noticed the flush, and said ruefully, "Ah, I see ! Always the way ! Now let's go and get some beef or something to eat : I'm hungry."

CHAPTER VIII.

THROWING THE FLY.

MR. FLEXOR was by nature mendacious ; indeed his employers used pleasantly to remark, that when he did not lie, it was simply by accident ; but in what he had mentioned to Charley Potts about Geoffrey Ludlow's visits to the nameless female then resident in his, Flexor's, house, he had merely spoken the truth. To be sure there had been an *arrière pensée* in his remark ; the fact being that Flexor objected to matrimony as an institute amongst his patrons. He found that by an artist in a celibate state beer was oftener sent for, donations of cigars were more frequent, cupboards were more constantly unlocked, and irregularities of attendance on his part, consequent on the frivolities of the preceding night, were more easily overlooked, than when there was a lady to share confidence and keys, and to regard all models, both male and female, as "horrid creatures." But although Mr. Flexor had spoken somewhat disparagingly of Geoffrey's frequent visits, and had by his hints roused up a certain amount of suspicion in the breasts of Charley Potts and that grim old cynic William Bowker, he was himself far from knowing what real ground for apprehension existed, or how far matters had progressed, at least with one of the parties concerned.

For Geoffrey Ludlow was hard hit ! In vain he attempted to argue with himself that all he had done, was doing, and might do, was but prompted by benevolence. A secret voice within him told him that his attempts at self-deceit were of the feeblest, and that, did he but dare to confess it, he knew that there was in this woman whom he had rescued from starvation an attraction more potent than he had ever yet submitted to. It was, it may be said, his duty to call and see how she was getting on, to learn that she wanted for nothing, to hear from her own lips that his orders for her comfort had been obeyed; but it was not his duty to sit watching jealously every glance of her eye, every turn of her head, every motion of her lithe fingers. It was *not* his duty to bear away with him recollections of how she sat when she said this or answered that ; of the manner in which, following a habit of hers, she would push back the thick masses of her gleaming hair, and tuck them away behind her pretty ears ; or, following another habit, she would drum petulantly on the floor with her little foot, when talking of any thing that annoyed her—as, for instance, Mrs. Flexor's prying curiosity.

What was it that caused him to lie awake at night, tossing from side to side on his hot pillow, ever before him the deep-violet eyes, the pallid face set in masses of deep-red hair, the slight frail figure ? What was it that made his heart beat loudly, his breath come thickly, his whole being tingle with a strange sensation—now ecstatic delight, now dull blank misery ? Not philanthropy, I trow. The superintendents of boys' reformatories and refuges for the houseless poor may, in thinking over what good they have achieved, enjoy a comfortable amount of self-satisfaction and proper pride ; but I doubt if the feeling ever rises to this level of excitement. Not much wonder if Geoffrey himself, suffering acutely under the disease, knew not, or refused to avow to himself, any knowledge of the symptoms. Your darling child, peacefully sleeping in his little bed, shall show here and there an angry skin-spot, which you think heat or cold, or any thing else, until the experienced doctor arrives, and with a glance pronounces it scarlet-fever. Let us be thankful, in such a case, that the prostrate patient is young. Geoffrey's was as dire a malady, and one which, coming on at forty years of age, usually places the sufferer in a perilous state. It was called Love ; not the ordinary sober inclination of a middle-aged man, not that thin line of fire quivering amongst a heap of ashes which betokens the faded passion of the worn and sated voluptuary ; this was boy-love, calf-love, mad-spooniness—any thing by which you can express the silliest, wildest, pleasantest, most miserable phase of human existence. It never comes but once to any one. The *caprices* of the voluptuary are as like to each other as peas or grains of sand ; the platonic attachments or the sentimental *liaisons* indulged in by foolish persons of both sexes with nothing to do may have some slight shade of distinction, but are equally wanting in backbone and *vis*. Not to man or woman is it given to be ever twice "in love" —a simple phrase, which means every thing, but needs very little explanation. My readers will comprehend what I want to convey, and will not require my feeble efforts in depicting the state. Suffice it to say, that Geoffrey Ludlow, who had hitherto gone through life scot-free, not because he was case-hardened, not because he was infection-proof, or that he had run no risks, but simply from the merest chance, —now fell a victim to the disease, and dropped powerless before its attack.

He did not even strive to make head against it much. A little of his constitutional wavering and doubtfulness came into play for a short time, suggesting that this passion—for such he must allow it—was decidedly an unworthy one ; that at present he knew nothing of the girl's antecedents ; and that her actual state did not promise much for all she had to tell of what had gone before. At certain times too, when things present themselves in their least roseate garb, notably on waking in the morning, for instance, he allowed, to himself, that he was making a fool of himself ; but the confidence extended no farther. And then, as the day grew, and the sun came out, and he touched up his picture, and thought of the commissions Mr. Stompff had promised him, he became brighter and more hopeful, and he allowed his thoughts to feast on the figure then awaiting him in Little Flotsam Street, and he put by his sheaf of brushes and his palette, and went up and examined himself in the glass over the mantelpiece. He had caught himself doing this very frequently within the last few days, and, half-chuckling inwardly, had acknowledged that it was a bad sign. But though he laughed, he tweaked out the most prominent gray hairs in his beard, and gave his necktie a more knowing twist, and removed the dabs of stray paint from his shooting-coat. Straws thrown up show which way the wind blows,

F

and even such little sacrifices to vanity as these were in Geoffrey Ludlow very strong signs indeed.

He had paid three visits to Little Flotsam Street; and on the fourth morning, after a very poor pretence of work, he was at the looking-glass settling himself preparatory to again setting out. Ever since that midnight adventure after the Titians meeting, Geoffrey had felt it impossible to take his usual daily spell at the easel, had not done five-pounds' worth of real work in the whole time, had sketched-in and taken out, and pottered, and smoked over his canvas, perfectly conscious that he was doing no good, utterly unable to do any better. On this fourth morning he had been even more unsuccessful than usual; he was highly nervous; he could not even set his palette properly, and by no manner of means could he apply his thoughts to his work. He had had a bad night; that is, he had woke with a feeling that this kind of penny-journal romance, wherein a man finds a starving girl in the streets and falls desperately in love with her, could go on no longer in London and in the nineteenth century. She was better now, probably strong enough to get about; he would learn her history, so much of it at least as she liked to tell; and putting her in some way of earning an honest livelihood, take his leave of her, and dismiss her from his thoughts.

He arrived at this determination in his studio; he kept it as he walked through the streets; he wavered horribly when he came within sight of the door; and by the time he knocked he had resolved to let matters take their chance, and to act as occasion might suggest. It was not Mrs. Flexor who opened the door to him, but that worthy woman's youngest plague, Reg'las, who, with a brown eruption produced by liquorice round his lips, nodded his head, and calmly invited the visitor, as he would have done any one else, to "go up 'tairs." Geoffrey entered, patted the boy's head, and stopped at the parlour-door, at which he gave a low rap, and immediately turning the handle, walked in.

She was lying as usual on the sofa, immediately opposite the door; but, what he had never seen before, her hair was freed from the confining comb, and was hanging in full luxuriance over her shoulders. Great heavens, how beautiful she looked! There had been a certain piquancy and *chic* in her appearance when her hair had been taken saucily off her face and behind her ears; but they were nothing as compared to the profound expression of calm holy resignation in that dead-white face, set in that deep dead-gold frame of hair. Geoff started when he saw it; was it a Madonna of Raphael's, or a St. Teresa of Guido's, which flashed across his mind? And as he looked she raised her eyes, and a soft rosy flush spread over her face, and melted as quickly as it came. He seated himself on a chair by her side as usual, and took her hand as usual, the blood tingling in his fingers as he touched hers—as usual. She was the first to speak.

" You are very early this morning. I scarcely expected you so soon—as you may see ;" and with a renewed flush she took up the ends of her hair, and was about to twist them up, when Geoffrey stopped her.

" Leave it as it is," said he in a low tone ; "it could not be better; leave it as it is."

She looked at him as he spoke; not a full straight glance, but through half-closed lids; a prolonged gaze,—half-dreamy, half-intense ; then released her hair, and let it again fall over her shoulders in a rich red cloud.

" You are much better?"

" Thanks to you, very much ; thanks to you !" and her little hand came out frankly, and was speedily swallowed up in his big palm.

" No thanks at all; that is—well, you know. Let us change the subject. I came to say—that—that—"

" You hesitate because you are afraid of hurting my feelings. I think I can understand. I have learnt the world— God knows in no easy school ; you came to say that I had been long enough a pensioner on your charity, and now must make my own way. Isn't that it?"

" No, indeed; not, that is not entirely what I meant. You see—our meeting—so strange—"

" Strange enough for London and this present day. You found me starving, dying, and you took care of me; and you knew nothing of me—not even my name—not even my appearance."

There was a something harsh and bitter in her tone which Geoffrey had never remarked before. It jarred on his ear; but he did not further notice it. His eyes dropped a little as he said, "No, I didn't; I do not know your name."

She looked up at him from under her eyelids; and the harshness had all faded out of her voice as she said, "My name is Margaret Dacre." She stopped, and looked at him; but his face only wore its grave honest smile. Then she suddenly raised herself on the sofa, and looking straight into his face, said hurriedly, "You are a kind man, Mr. Ludlow; a kind, generous, honourable man; there are many men would have given me food and shelter—there are very few who would have done it unquestioning, as you have."

"You were my guest, Miss Dacre, and that was enough, though the temptation was strong. How one evidently born and bred a lady could have—"

"Ah, now," said she, smiling fainting, "you are throwing off your bonds, and all man's curiosity is at work."

"No, on my honour; but—I don't know whether you know, but any one acquainted with the world would see that —gad! I scarcely know how to put it—but—fact is, that— people would scarcely understand—you must excuse me, but —but the position, Miss Dacre!" and Geoff pushed his hands through his hair, and knew that his cheeks were flaming.

"I see what you mean," said she, "and you are only explaining what I have for the last day or two felt myself; that the—the position must be altered. But you have so far been my friend, Mr. Ludlow—for I suppose the preserver of one's life is to be looked upon as a friend, at all events as one actuated by friendly motives—that I must ask you to advise me how to support it."

"It would be impossible to advise unless—I mean, unless one knew, or had some idea—what, in fact, one had been accustomed to.

The girl sat up on the sofa, and this time looked him steadily in the face for a minute or so. Then she said, in a calm unbroken voice, "You are coming to what I knew must arise, to what is always asked, but what I hitherto have always refused to tell. You, however, have a claim to know —what I suppose people would call my history." Her thin lips were tightly pressed and her nostrils curved in scorn as she said these words. Geoffrey marked the change, and spoke out at once, all his usual hesitation succumbing before his earnestness of purpose.

"I have asked nothing," said he; "please to remember that; and further, I wish to hear nothing. You are my guest for so long as it pleases you to remain in that position. When you wish to go, you will do so, regretted but certainly unquestioned." If Geoffrey Ludlow ever looked handsome, it was at this moment. He was a little nettled at being suspected of patronage, and the annoyance flushed his cheek and fired his eyes.

"Then I am to be a kind of heroine of a German fairytale; to appear, to sojourn for a while—then to fade away and never to be heard of ever after, save by the good fortune which I leave behind me to him who had entertained an angel unawares. Not the last part of the story, I fear, Mr. Ludlow; nor indeed any part of it. I have accepted your kindness; I am grateful—God knows how grateful for it—and now, being strong again—you need not raise your eyebrows; I am strong, am I not, compared with the feeble creature you found in the streets?—I will fade away, leaving gratitude and blessings behind me."

"But what do you intend to do?"

"Ah! there you probe me beyond any possibility of reply. I shall—"

"I—I have a notion, Miss Dacre, just come upon me. It was seeing you with your hair down—at least, I think it was—suggested it; but I'm sure it's a good one. To sit, you know, as a model—of course I mean your face, you know, and hair, and all that sort of thing, so much in vogue just now; and so many fellows would be delighted to get studies of you—the pre-Raphaelite fellows, you know; and it isn't much—the pay, you know: but when one gets a connexion—and I'm sure that I could recommend—O, no end of fellows." It was not that this was rather a longer speech than usual that made Geoffrey terminate it abruptly; it was the expression in Margaret Dacre's gray eyes.

"Do you think I could become a model, Mr. Ludlow—at the beck and call of every man who chose to offer me so much per hour? Would you wish to see me thus?" and as she said the last words she knit her brows, leaning forward and looking straight at him under her drooping lids.

Geoffrey's eyes fell before that peculiar glance, and he

pushed his hands through his hair in sheer doubtful desperation.

"No!" he said, after a minute's pause; "it wouldn't do. I hadn't thought of that. You see, I—O, by Jove, another idea! You play? Yes, I knew you did by the look of your hands! and talk French and German, I daresay? Ah, I thought so! Well, you know, I give lessons in some capital families—drawing and water-colour sketching—and I'm constantly asked if I know of governesses. Now what's to prevent my recommending you?"

"What, indeed? You have known me so long! You are so thoroughly acquainted with my capabilities—so persuaded of my respectability!"

The curved lips, the petulant nostril, the harsh bitter voice again! Geoff winced under them. "I think you are a little prejudiced," he began. "A little—"

"A little nothing! Listen, Mr. Ludlow! You have saved me from death, and you are kind enough to wish me, under your auspices, to begin life again. Hear, first, what was my former life. Hear it, and then see the soundness of your well-intentioned plans. My father was an infantry captain, who was killed in the Crimea. After the news came of his death, my mother's friends, wealthy tradespeople, raised a subscription to pay her an annuity of 15*l*., on condition of her never troubling them again. She accepted this, and she and I went to live for cheapness at Tenby in Wales. There was no break in my life until two years since, when I was eighteen years old. Up to that time, school, constant practice at home (for I determined to be well educated), and attendance on my mother, an invalid, formed my life. Then came the usual character—without which the drama of woman's life is incomplete—a man!"

She hesitated for a moment, and looked up as Geoffrey Ludlow leaned forward, breathing thickly through his nostrils; then she continued—

"This one was a soldier, and claimed acquaintance with a dead comrade's widow; had his claim allowed, and came to us morning, noon, and night. A man of the world, they called him; could sit and talk with my mother of her husband's virtues and still-remembered name, and press my hand, and gaze into my eyes, and whisper in my ear whenever her head was turned."

" And you ? "

" And I ! What would a girl do, brought up at a sleepy watering-place, and seeing nobody but the curate or the doctor ? I listened to his every word, I believed his every look ; and when he said to me, 'On such a night fly with me,' I fled with him without remorse."

Geoffrey Ludlow must have anticipated something of this kind, and yet when he heard it, he dropped his head and shook it, as though under the effect of a staggering blow. The action was not unnoticed by Margaret.

" Ah," said she, in low tones and with a sad smile, " I saw how your schemes would melt away before my story."

This time it was his hand that came out and caught hers in its grip.

" Ah, wait until you have heard the end, now very close at hand. The old, old story : a coming marriage, which never came, protracted and deferred now for one excuse, now for another,—the fear of friends, the waiting for promotion, the—ah, every note in the whole gamut of lies ! And then—"

" Spare yourself and me—I know enough ! "

" No ; hear it out ! It is due to you, it is due to me. A sojourn in Italy, a sojourn in England—gradual coolness, final flight. But such flight ! One line to say that he was ruined, and would not drag me down in his degradation—no hope of a future meeting—no provision for present want. I lived for a time by the sale of what he had given me,—first jewels, then luxuries, then—clothes. And then, just as I dropped into death's jaws, you found me."

" Thank God ! " said Geoffrey earnestly, still retaining the little hand within his own ; " thank God ! I can hear no more to-day—yes ; one thing, his name ? "

" His name," said she, with fixed eyes, " I have never mentioned to mortal ; but to you I will tell it. His name was Leonard Brookfield."

" Leonard Brookfield," repeated Geoffrey. " I shall not forget it. Now adieu ! We shall meet to-morrow."

He bowed over her hand and pressed it to his lips, then was gone ; but as his figure passed the window, she raised herself upright, and ere he vanished from her sight, from between her compressed lips came the words, " At last ! at last ! "

CHAPTER IX.

SUNSHINE IN THE SHADE.

WHAT is a dull life? In what does the enjoyment of existence consist? It is a comparative matter, after all, I fancy. A Londoner, cantering homeward down the Row, will lift his hat as he passes three horsemen abreast, the middle one of whom, comely, stout, and pleasant-looking, bows in return; or, looking after an olive-coloured brougham with a white horse, out of the window of which looms a lined leery-looking face, will say, " How well Pam holds out!" and will go home to dinner without bestowing another thought on the subject; whereas the mere fact of having seen the Prince of Wales or Lord Palmerston would give a countryman matter for reflection and conversation for a couple of days. There are even Londoners who look upon a performance of chamber-music, or a visit to the Polytechnic Institute as an excitement; while in a provincial town to attend a lecture on " Mnemonics," or the dinner of the farmers' club, is the acme of dissipation. Some lives are passed in such a whirl that even the occasional advent among their kindred of the great date-marker, Death, is scarcely noticed; others dwindle away with such unvarying pulsations that the purchase of a new bonnet, the lameness of an old horse, the doctor's visit, the curate's cough, are all duly set down as notabilia worthy to be recorded. Who does not recollect the awe and reverence with which one regarded the Bishop of Bosphorus, when, a benevolent seraph in a wig (they wore wigs in those days) and lawn sleeves, he arrived at the parish church for the confirmation-service? It was exciting to see him; it was almost too much to hear his voice; but now, if you are a member of the Athenæum Club, you may see him, and two or three other prelates, reading the evening papers, or drinking their pint of sherry with the joint, and speaking to the waiters in voices akin to those of ordinary mortals; may even see him sitting next to Belmont the poet, whose *Twilight Musings* so delighted your youth, but whom you now find to be a fat man with a red face and a tendency to growl if there be not enough schalot sent up with his steak.

If there were ever a man who should have felt the influence of a dull life, it was Lord Caterham, who never repined.
And yet it would be difficult to imagine any thing more
terribly lonely than was that man's existence. Dressed by
his servant, his breakfast over, and he wheeled up to his
library-table, there was the long day before him; how was he
to get through it? Who would come to see him? His
father, perhaps, for five minutes, with a talk about the
leading topic treated of in the *Times*, a remark about the
change in the weather, a hope that his son would "get out
into the sunshine," and as speedy a departure as could be
decently managed. His mother, very rarely, and then only
for a frosty peck at his cheek, and a tittered hope that he
was better. His brother Lionel, when in town, when not else
engaged, when not too seedy after "a night of it,"—his
brother Lionel, who would throw himself into an easy-chair,
and, kicking out his slippered feet, tell Caterham what a " rum
fellow" he, Lionel, thought him; what a "close file;" what
a "reserved, oyster-like kind of a cove!" Other visitors
occasionally. Algy Barford, genial, jolly, and quaint; always
welcome for his bright sunshiny face, his equable temper, his
odd salted remarks on men and things. A bustling apothecary,
with telescopic shoulders and twinkling eyelids, who peered
down Lord Caterham's throat like a magpie looking into a
bone, and who listened to the wheezings of Lord Caterham's
chest with as much intentness as a foreigner in the Opera-pit
to the prayer in *Der Freischütz*. Two or three lounging
youths, fresh from school or college, who were pleased to go
away afterwards and talk of their having been with him,
partly because he was a lord, partly because he was a man
whose name was known in town, and one with whom it was
rather *kudos* to be thought intimate. There are people who,
under such circumstances, would have taken their servants into
their confidence; but Lord Caterham was not one of these.
Kindly and courteous to all, he yet kept his servant at the
greatest distance; and the man knew that to take the slightest
liberty was more than his place was worth. There were no
women to talk with this exile from his species; there were
none on sufficiently intimate footing to call on him and sit
with him, to talk frankly and unreservedly that pleasant
chatter which gives us the key-note to their characters; and
for this at least Lord and Lady Beauport were unfeignedly

thankful. Lord Beauport's knowledge of the world told him that there were women against whom his son's deformity and isolated state would be no defence, to whom his rank and position would be indefinable attractions, by whom he would probably be assailed, and with whom he had no chance of coping. Not bad women, not *intrigantes*,—such would have set forth their charms and wasted their dalliances in vain,—but clever heartless girls, brought up by match-making mothers, graduates in the great school of life, skilled in the deft and dexterous use of all aggressive weapons, unscrupulous as to the mode of warfare so long as victory was to be the result. In preventing Lord Caterham from making the acquaintance of any such persons, Lord Beauport took greater pains than he had ever bestowed on anything in connection with his eldest son ; and, aided by the astute generalship of his wife, he had succeeded wonderfully.

Only once did there seem a chance of an enemy's scaling the walls and entering the citadel, and then the case was really serious. It was at an Eton and Harrow match at Lord's that Lord Caterham first saw Carry Chesterton. She came up hanging on the arm of her brother, Con Chesterton, the gentleman farmer, who had the ground outside Homershams, Lady Beauport's family place, and who begged to present his sister to Lord Caterham, of whom she had heard so much. A sallow-faced girl, with deep black eyes, arched brows, and raven hair in broad bands, with a high forehead and a chiselled nose and tight thin lips, was Carry Chesterton ; and as she bent over Lord Caterham's chair and expressed her delight at the introduction, she shot a glance that went through Caterham's eyes, and into his very soul.

"She was a poetess, was Carry, and all that sort of thing," said honest Con ; "and had come up to town to try and get some of her writings printed, you know, and that sort of thing ; and your lordship's reputation as a man of taste, you know, and that sort of thing,—if you'd only look at the stuff and give your opinion, and that sort of thing."

"That sort of thing," *i.e.* the compulsory conversion into a Mecænas, Lord Caterham had had tried-on before ; but only in the case of moon-struck men, never from such a pair of eyes. Never had he had the request indorsed in such a deep-toned thrilling voice ; and so he acquiesced, and a meeting was arranged for the morrow, when Con was to

bring Carry to St. Barnabas Square; and that night Lord
Caterham lay in a pleasant state of fevered exitement,
thinking of his expected visitor. Carry came next day, but
not Con. Con had some arrangements to make about that
dreadful yeomanry which took up so much of his time, to see
Major Latchford or Lord Spurrier, the colonel, and arrange
about their horrid evolutions; but Carry came, and brought
her manuscript book of poems. Would she read them? she
could, and did, in a deep low *traînante* voice, with wonderful
art and pathos, illustrating them with elevations of her thick
brows and with fervid glances from her black eyes. They
were above the average of women's verse, had nothing
namby-pamby in them, and were not merely flowing and
musical, but strong and fervid; they were full of passion,
which was not merely a Byronic *refrain*, but had a warmth
and novelty of its own. Lord Caterham was charmed with
the verses, was charmed with the writer; he might suggest
certain improvements. in them, none in her. He pointed
out certain lines which might be altered; and as he pointed
them out, their hands met, touched but for an instant, and on
looking up, his eyes lost themselves in hers.

Ah, those hand-touches and eye-glances! The oldest
worldling has some pleasure in them yet, and can recall the
wild ecstatic thrill which ran through him when he first
experienced them in his salad-days. But we can conceive
nothing of their effect on a man who, under peculiar circumstances, had lived a reserved self-contained life until five-and-
twenty years of age,—a man with keen imagination and warm
passions, who had "never felt the kiss of love, nor maiden's
hand in his," until his whole being glowed and tingled under
the fluttering touch of Carry Chesterton's lithe fingers, and in
the fiery gaze of her black eyes. She came again and again;
and after every visit Lord Caterham's passion increased. She
was a clever woman with a purpose, to the fulfilment of
which her every word, her every action, tended. Softly,
delicately, and with the greatest *finesse*, she held up to him
the blank dreariness of his life, and showed him how it
might be cheered and consoled. In a pitying rather than
an accusing spirit, she pointed out the shortcomings of his
own relatives, and indicated how, to a person in his position,
there could be but one who should be all in all. This was
all done with the utmost tact and refinement; a sharp word,

an appearance of eagerness, the slightest showing of the
cards, and the game would have been spoilt; but Carry Chesterton knew her work, and did it well. She had been duly
presented by Lord Caterham to his father and mother, and
had duly evoked first their suspicion, then their rage. At
first it was thought that by short resolute measures the evil
might be got rid of. So Lord Beauport spoke seriously to
his son, and Lady Beauport spoke warningly; but all in vain.
For the first time in his life Lord Caterham rebelled, and in
his rebellion spoke his mind; and in speaking his mind he
poured forth all that bitterness of spirit which had been
collecting and fermenting so long. To the crippled man's
heartwrung wail of contempt and neglect, to his passionate
appeal for some one to love and to be loved by, the parents
had no reply. They knew that he had bitter cause for
complaint; but they also knew that he was now in pursuit
of a shadow; that he was about to assuage his thirst for love
with Dead-Sea apples; that the "set gray life and apathetic
end" were better than the wild fierce conflict and the warm-
ing of a viper in the fires of one's heart. Lady Beauport
read Carry Chesterton like a book, saw her ends and aims,
and told Lord Caterham plainly what they were. "This girl
is attracted by your title and position, Caterham,—nothing
else," she said, in her hard dry voice; "and the natural
result has ensued." But that voice had never been softened
by any infusion of maternal love. Her opinions had no
weight with her son. He made no answer, and the subject
dropped.

Lionel Brakespere, duly apprised by his mother of what
was going on, and urged to put a stop to it, took his turn at
his brother, and spoke with his usual mess-room frankness,
and in his usual engaging language. "Every body knew
Carry Chesterton," he said, "all the fellows at the Rag
knew her; at least all who'd been quartered in the neighbourhood of Flockborough, where she was a regular garrison
hack, and had been engaged to Spoonbill of the 18th
Hussars, and jilted by Slummer of the 160th Rifles, and was
as well known as the town-clock, by Jove; and Caterham
was a flat and a spoon, and he'd be dashed if he'd see the
fam'ly degraded; and I say, why the doose didn't Caterham
listen to reason!" So far Captain the Honourable Lionel
Brakespere; who, utterly failing in his purpose and intent,

and having any further access to Lord Caterham's rooms strictly denied him by Lord Caterham's orders, sought out Algy Barford and confided to him the whole story, and " put him on " to save the fam'ly credit, and stop Caterham's rediklous 'fatuation.

Now if the infatuation in question had been legitimate, and likely to lead to good results, Algy Barford would have been the very last man on earth to attempt to put a stop to it, or to interfere in any way save for its advancement. But this airy, laughing philosopher, with all his apparent carelessness, was a man of the world and a shrewd reader of human character ; and he had made certain inquiries, the result of which proved that Carry Chesterton was, if not all that Lionel Brakespere had made her out, at all events a heartless coquette and fortune-huntress, always rising at the largest fly. Quite recently jilted by that charming creature Captain Slummer of the Rifles, she had been heard to declare she would not merely retrieve the position hereby lost, but achieve a much greater one ; and she had been weak enough to boast of her influence over Lord Caterham, and her determination to marry him in spite of all his family's opposition. Then Algy Barford joined the ranks of the conspirators, and brought his thoroughly practical worldly knowledge to their camp. It was at a council held in Lady Beauport's boudoir that he first spoke on the subject, his face radiant with good humour, his teeth gleaming in the light, and his attention impartially divided between the matter under discussion and the vagaries of a big rough terrier which accompanied him every where.

"You must pardon me, dear Lady Beauport," said he ; " but you've all been harking forward on the wrong scent.— Down, Tinker ! Don't let him jump on your mother, Lionel ; his fleas, give you my honour, big as lobsters !—on the wrong scent ! Dear old Caterham, best fellow in the world ; but frets at the curb, don't you know ? Put him a couple of links higher up than usual, and he rides rusty and jibs—jibs, by Jove ! And that's what you've been doing now. Dear old Caterham ! not much to amuse him in life, don't you know ? goes on like a blessed old martyr ; but at last finds something which he likes, and you don't. Quite right, dear Lady Beauport ; *I* see it fast enough, because I'm an old lad, and have seen men and cities ; but dear

Caterham, who is all milk and rusks and green peas, and every thing that is innocent, don't you know, don't see it at all. And then you try to shake him by the shoulder and rouse him out of his dream, and tell him that he's not in fairyland, not in Aladdin's palace, not in a two-pair back in Craven Street, Strand. Great mistake that, Lionel, dear boy. Dear Lady Beauport, surely your experience teaches you that it is a great mistake to cross a person when they're in that state?"

"But, Mr. Barford, what is to be done?"

"Put the helm about, Lady Beauport, and—Tinker! you atrocious desperado, you shameless caitiff! will you get down?—put the helm about, and try the other tack. We've failed with dear old Caterham: now let's try the lady. Caterham is the biggest fish she's seen yet; but my notion is that if a perch came in her way, and seemed likely to bite, she'd forget she'd ever seen a gudgeon. Now my brother Windermere came to town last week, and he's an earl, you know, and just the sort of fellow who likes nothing so much as a flirtation, and is all the time thunderingly well able to take care of himself. I think if Miss Chesterton were introduced to Windermere, she'd soon drop poor dear Caterham."

Both Lionel and his mother agreed in this notion, and an early opportunity was taken for the presentation of Lord Windermere to Miss Chesterton. An acknowledged *parti;* a man of thews and sinews; frank, generous, and affable: apparently candid and unsuspecting in the highest degree, he seemed the very prize for which that accomplished fortune-huntress had long been waiting; and forgetting the old fable of the shadow and the substance, she at once turned a decided cold shoulder upon poor Lord Caterham, ceased visiting him, showed him no more poetry, and within a week of her making Lord Windermere's acquaintance, cut her old friend dead in Kensington Gardens, whither he had been wheeled in the hope of seeing her. Ah, in how few weeks, having discovered the sandy foundation on which she had been building, did she come back, crouching and fawning and trying all the old devices, to find the fire faded out of Caterham's eyes and the hope out of his breast, and the prospect of any love or companionship as distant from him as ever!

Yes, that was Lord Caterham's one experience of love; and after its lame and impotent conclusion he determined he would never have another. We have all of us determined that in our time; but few of us have kept to our resolution so rigidly as did Lord Caterham, possibly because opportunities have not been so wanting to us as to him. It is all that horrible opportunity which saps our strongest resolutions; it is the close proximity of the magnum of "something special" in claret which leads to the big drink; it is the shaded walk, and the setting sun behind the deep bank of purple clouds, and the solemn stillness, and the upturned eyes and the provoking mouth, which lead to all sorts of horrible mistakes. Opportunity after the Chesterton *escapade* was denied to Lord Caterham both by himself and his parents. He shut himself up in solitude: he would see no one save the apothecary and Algy Barford, who indeed came constantly, feeling all the while horribly treacherous and shamefaced. And then by degrees—by that blessed process of Time against which we rail so much, but which is so beneficial, of Time the anodyne and comforter, he fell back into his old ways of life; and all that little storm and commotion was as though it had never been. It left no marks of its fury on Caterham; he kept no relics of its bright burning days: all letters had been destroyed. There was not a glove nor a flower in his drawers—nothing for him to muse and shake his head over. So soon as his passion had spent itself—so soon as he could look calmly upon the doings of the few previous months, he saw how unworthy they had been, and blotted them from his memory for ever.

So until Annie Maurice had come to take up her position as his mother's companion, Lord Caterham had been entirely without female society, and since her advent he had first learned the advantages of associating with a pure, genuine healthy woman. Like Carry Chesterton, she seemed to take to the crippled man from her first introduction to him; but ah, how unlike that siren did sweet Annie Maurice show her regard! There was no more romance in her composition, so she would have told you herself, than in the statue at Charing Cross; no eyebrow elevations, no glances, no palpable demonstrations of interest. In quite a household

and domestic manner did this good fairy discharge her
duties. She was not the Elf, the Wili, the Giselle, in book-
muslin and starsprent hair; she was the ordinary "Brownie,"
the honest Troll, which shows its presence in help rather
than ornament. Ever since Miss Maurice had been an
inmate of the house in Barnabas Square, Caterham's books
had been dusted, his books and papers arranged, his diurnal
calendar set, his desk freshened with a glass of newly-
gathered flowers. Never before had his personal wants been
so readily understood, so deftly attended to. No one
smoothed his pillows so softly, wheeled his chair so easily,
his every look so quickly comprehended. To all that
dreary household Annie Maurice was a sunbeam; but on
no one did she shine so brightly as on that darkened spirit.
The Earl felt the beaming influence of her bright nature;
the Countess could not deny her meed of respect to one
who was always "in her place;" the servants, horribly
tenacious of interference, could find no fault with Miss
Maurice; but to none appeared she in so bright a light as
to Lord Caterham.

It was the morning after the receipt of the letter which
Algy Barford had left with him, and which had seemingly
so much upset him, that Caterham was sitting in his room,
his hands clasped idly before him, his looks bent, not on
the book lying open on the desk, but on the vacant space
beyond it. So delicately constituted was his frame, that
any mental jar was immediately succeeded by acute bodily
suffering; he was hurt, not merely in spirit but in body;
the machinery of his being was shaken and put out of gear,
and it took comparatively some length of time for all to get
into working order again. The strain on this occasion had
evidently been great, his head throbbed, his eyes were surrounded with bistre rings, and the nervous tension of his
clasped fingers showed the unrest of his mind. Then came
a gentle tap on the door, a sound apparently instantly
recognisable, for Lord Caterham raised his head, and bade
the visitor "Come in." It was Annie Maurice. No one
else opened the door so quickly and closed it so quietly
behind her, no one came with so light and yet so firm a
step, no one else would have seen that the sun was pouring
in through the window on to the desk, and would have

crossed the room and arranged the blind before coming up to the chair. Caterham knew her without raising his eyes, and had said, "Ah, Annie dear!" before she reached him.

"I feared you were ill, my lord," she commenced; but a deep growl from Caterham stopped her. "I feared you were ill, Arthur," she then said; "you did not show at dinner last night, nor in the evening; but I thought you might be disinclined for society—the Gervises were here, you know, and the Scrimgeours, and I know you don't care for our classical music, which is invariable on such occasions; but I met Stephens on the staircase, and he gave me such a desponding account, that I really feared you were ill."

"Only a passing dull fit, Annie; only a passing dull fit of extra heaviness, and consequently extra duration! Stephens is a croaker, you know; and having, I believe, an odd sort of Newfoundland-dog attachment to me, is frightened if I have a finger-ache. But I'm very glad you've come in, Annie, for I'm not really very bright even now, and you always help to set me straight. Well, and how goes it with you, young lady?"

"Oh, very well, Arthur, very well."

"You feel happier than you did on your first coming among us? You feel as though you were settling down into your home?"

"I should be worse than foolish if I did not, for every one tries to be kind to me."

"I did not ask you for moral sentiments, Annie, I asked you for facts. Do you feel settling down into your home?" And as Caterham said this, he shot a keen scrutinising glance at the girl.

She paused for a moment ere she answered, and when she spoke she looked at him straight out of her big brown eyes.

"Do I feel as if I were settling down into my home, Arthur? No; in all honesty, no. I have no home, as you know well enough; but I feel that—"

"Why no home?" he interrupted; "isn't—No, I understand."

"No, you do not understand; and it is for that reason I speak. You do not understand me, Lord—Arthur. You have notions which I want to combat, and set right at once, please. I know you have, for I've heard hints of them in

G

something you've said before. It all rises out of your gentlemanly and chivalrous feeling, I know; but, believe me, you're wrong. I fill the position of your mother's companion here, and you have fallen into the conventional notion that I'm not well treated, put upon, and all that kind of thing. On my honour, that is utterly wrong. No two people could be kinder, after their lights, than Lord and Lady Beauport are to me. Of your own conduct I need say no word. From the servants I have perfect respect; and yet—"

"And yet?"

"Well, simply you choose the wrong word; there's no homey feeling about it, and I should be false were I to pretend there were."

"But pardon me for thus pursuing the subject into detail, —my interest in you must be my excuse,—what 'homey feeling,' as you call it, had you at Ricksborough Vicarage, whence you came to us? The people there are no closer blood-relations than we are; nor did they, as far as I know—"

"Nor did they try more to make me happy. No, indeed, they could not have tried more in that way than you do. But I was much younger when I first went there, Arthur— quite a little child—and had all sorts of childish reminiscences of cow-milking, and haymaking, and harvest-homes, and all kinds of ruralities, with that great balloon-shaped shadow of St. Paul's ever present on the horizon keeping watch over the City, where dear old uncle Frank told me I should have to get my living after he was gone. Its home-influence gained on me even from the sorrow which I saw and partook of in it; from the sight of my aunt's death-bed and my uncle's meek resignation overcoming his desperate grief; from the holy comfort inspired in him by the discharge of his holy calling; by the respect and esteem in which he was held by all around, and which was never so much shown as when he wanted it most acutely. These things, among many others, made that place home to me."

"Yes," said Lord Caterham, in a harsh dry voice; "I understand easily enough. After such innocence and good-ness I can fully comprehend what it must be to you to read blue-books to my father, to listen to my mother's *fade* nonsense about balls, operas, and dresses, or to attend to the hypochondriacal fancies of a valetudinarian like myself—"

"Lord Caterham! I don't think that even you have a right to insult me in this way!"

"*Even* I! thank you for the compliment, which implies— Bah! what a brute I am! You'll forgive me, Annie, won't you? I'm horribly hipped and low. I've not been out for two days; and the mere fact of being a prisoner to the house always fills my veins with bile instead of blood. Ah, you won't keep that knit brow and those tightened lips any longer, will you? No one sees more plainly than I do that your life here wants certain—"

"Pray say no more, I—"

"Ah, Annie, for Heaven's sake don't pursue this miserable growl of mine. Have some pity for my ill-health. But I want to see you with as many surroundings natural to your age and taste as we can find in this—hospital. There's music: you play and sing very sweetly; but you can't—I know you can't—sit down with any ease or comfort to that great furniture-van of a grand-piano in that gaunt drawing-room; that's only fit for those long-haired foreigners who let off their fireworks on Lady Beauport's reception-nights. You must have a good piano of your own, in your own room or here, or somewhere where you can practise quietly. I'll see about that. And drawing—for you have a great natural talent for that; but you should have some lessons: you must keep it up; you must have a master. There's a man goes to Lady Lilford's, a capital fellow, whom I know; you must have him. What's his name? Ludlow—"

"What, Geoffrey Ludlow! dear old Geoff! He used to be papa's greatest friend when we were at Willesden, you know,—and before that dreadful bankruptcy, you know, Mr. Ludlow was always there. I've sat on his knee a thousand times; and he used to sketch me, and call me his little elf. Oh yes, dear Arthur, I should like that,—I should like to have lessons from Mr. Ludlow! I should so like to see him again!"

"Well, Annie, you shall. I'll get his address from the Lilfords and write to him, and settle about his coming. And now, Annie, leave me, dear; I'm a little tired, and want rest."

He was tired, and wanted rest; but he did not get it just then. Long after Annie left the room he sat pondering, pondering, with a strange feeling for which he himself could

not account, but which had its keynote in this: How
strongly she spoke of the man Ludlow; how he disliked
her earnestness on the subject; and what would he not
have given, could he have thought she would have spoken
so strongly of him.

CHAPTER X.

YOUR WILLIAM.

WHEN you feel yourself gradually becoming enthralled,
falling a victim to a fascination all-potent, but
scarcely all-satisfactory, be it melancholy, or gambling, or
drink, or love, there is nothing so counteracting to the
horrible influence as to brace your nerves together, and go
in for a grand spell of work. That remedy is always effi-
cacious, of course. It never fails, as Geoffrey Ludlow knew
very well; and that was the reason why, on the morning
after his last-described interview with Margaret Dacre, he
dragged out from behind a screen, where it had been turned
with its face to the wall, his half-finished picture intended
for the Academy, and commenced working on it with
wonderful earnestness. It was a large canvas with three
principal figures: a young man, a "swell" of modern days,
turning away from the bold and eager glances of a somewhat brazen coquette, and suddenly struck by the modest
bashful beauty of a girl of the governess-order seated at a
piano. "Scylla and Charybdis" Geoff had intended calling
it, with the usual *Incidit in &c.* motto; and when the idea
first struck him he had taken pains with his composition,
had sketched his figures carefully, and had painted-in the
flirt and the man very successfully. The governess had as
yet been a failure; he had had no ideal to work from; the
model who had sat to him was a little coarse and clumsy,
and irritated at not being able to carry out his notion, he
had put the picture by. But he now felt that work was
required of him, not merely as a distraction from thought,
but as an absolute duty which he owed to himself; and as
this was a subject likely to be appreciated by Mr. Stompff,
he determined to work at it again, and to have it ready for
submission to the Hanging Committee of the Academy.
He boggled over it a little at first; he smoked two pipes,

staring at the canvas, occasionally shading his eyes with one hand, and waving the other in a dreamy possessed manner in front of him. Then he took up a brush and began to lay on a bit of colour, stepping back from time to time to note the effect; and then the spirit came upon him, and he went to work with all his soul.

What a gift is that of the painter, whose whole story can be read at one glance, who puts what we require three thick volumes to narrate into a few feet of canvas, who with one touch of his brush gives an expression which we pen-and-ink workers should take pages to convey, and even then could never hope to do it half so happily!—who sees his work grow beneath his hand, and can himself judge of its effect on others;—who can sit with his pipe in his mouth, and chirp away merrily to his friend, the while his right hand is gaining him wealth and honour and fame!

The spirit was on Geoffrey Ludlow, and the result came out splendidly. He hoped to gain a good place on the Academy walls, he hoped to do justice to the commissions which Mr. Stompff had given him; but there was something beyond these two incentives which spurred his industry and nerved his touch. After all his previous failures, it seemed as though Scylla the governess would have the best of it at last. Charybdis was a splendid creature, a bold, black-eyed, raven-haired charmer, with her hair falling in thick masses over her shoulders, and with a gorgeous passion-flower hanging voluptuously among her tresses; a goddess amongst big Guardsmen, who would sit and suck their yellow moustaches and express their admiration in fragmentary ejaculations, or amongst youths from the Universities, with fluff instead of hair, and blushes in place of *aplomb*. But in his later work the artist's heart seemed to have gone with Scylla, who was to her rival as is a proof after Sir Joshua to a French print, as a glass of Amontillado to a *petit verre* of Chartreuse,—a slight delicate creature, with violet eyes and pallid complexion, and deep-red hair brought down in thick braids, and tucked away behind such dainty little ears; her modest gray dress contrasting, in its quaker-like simplicity, with the brilliant-hued robe and rich laces of her rival. His morning's work must have been successful, for—rare thing with him—Geoff himself was pleased with it; no doubt of the inspiration now, he tried to deny it to himself, but could not—the likeness came out so wonderfully. So he gave way to the charm, and as he sat before the canvas, thoughtfully gazing at it, he let his imagination run riot, and gave his pleasant memories full play.

He had worked well and manfully, and had tolerably satisfied himself, and was sitting resting, looking at what he had done, and thinking over what had prompted his work, when there came a tap at the door, and his sister Til crept noiselessly in. She entered softly, as was her wont when her brother was engaged, and took up her position behind him. But Miss Til was demonstrative by nature, and after a minute's glance could not contain herself.

"Oh, you dear old Geoff, that is charming! oh, Geoff, how you have got on! But I say, Geoff, the governess— what do you call her? I never can recollect those Latin names, or Greek is it?—you know, and it does not matter; but she is—you know, Geoff, I know you don't like me to say so, but I can't find any other word—she is stunning! Not that I think—I don't know, you know, of course, because we don't mix in that sort of society—not that—that I think that people who—well, I declare, I don't know any other word for them!—I mean swells—would allow their governess to have her hair done in that style; but she is de-licious! You've got a new model, Geoff; at least you've never attempted any thing in that style before, and I declare you've made a regular hit. You don't speak, Geoff; don't you like what I'm saying?"

"My dear child, you don't give me the chance of saying any thing. You rattle on with 'I know' and 'you know' and 'don't you know,' till I can scarcely tell where I am. One thing I do manage to glean, however, and that is that you are pleased with the picture, which is the very best news that I could have. For though you're a most horrible little rattletrap, and talk nineteen to the dozen, there is some sense in what you say and always a great deal of truth."

"Specially when what I say is complimentary, eh, Geoff? Not that I think I have ever said much in any other strain to you. But you haven't told me about your new model, Geoff. Where did she come from?"

"My new model?"

"Yes, yes, for the governess, you know. That's new—

I mean that hair and eyes, and all that. You've never painted any thing like· that before. Where did she come from?"

There were few things that Geoffrey Ludlow would have kept from his sister, but this was one of them ; so he merely said :

"O, a model, Til dear—one of the usual shilling-an-hour victims."

"Sent you by Mr. Charles Potts, I suppose," said Miss Til, with unusual asperity ; "sent you for—" But here a knock at the door cut short the young lady's remarks. "O, but if that is Mr. Potts," she resumed, "don't say a word about what I said just now ; don't, Geoff, there's a dear."

It was not Mr. Potts who responded to Geoffrey Ludlow's "Come in." It was Mr. Bowker's head which was thrust through the small space made by the opening of the door ; and it was Mr. Bowker's deep voice which exclaimed :

"Engaged, eh? Your William will look in again."

But 'Til, with whom Mr. Bowker was a special favourite, from his strange unconventional manners and rough *bonhomie*, called out at once : "Mr. Bowker, it's only I—Geoff's sister Til;" and Geoff himself roaring out that "Bowker was growing modest in his old age," that gentleman was persuaded to come in ; and closing the door lightly behind him, he went up to the young lady, and bending over her hand, made her a bow such as any *preux chevalier* might have envied. A meeting with a lady was a rare oasis in the desert of William Bowker's wasted life ; but whenever he had the chance he showed that he had been something more than the mere pot-walloping boon-companion which most men thought him.

"Geoff's sister Til !" he repeated, looking at the tall handsome girl before him,—"Geoff's sister Til ! Ah, then it's perfectly right that I should have lost all my hair, and that my beard should be grizzled, and that I have a general notion of the omnipresence of old age. I was inclined to grumble ; but if 'Geoff's sister Til,' who I thought was still a little child, is to come up and greet me in this guise, I recant : Time is right; and your William is the only old fool in the matter."

"It is your own fault, Mr. Bowker, that you don't know the changes that take place in us. You know we are always glad to see you, and that mamma is always sending you messages by Geoff."

"You are all very good, and—well, I suppose it is my fault; let's say it is, at all events. What! going? There, you see the effect my presence has when I come up on a chance visit."

"Not at all," said Til; "I should have gone five minutes ago if you had not come in. I'll make a confidant of you, Mr. Bowker, and let you into a secret. Those perpetual irritable pulls at the bell are the tradespeople waiting for orders; and I must go and settle about dinner and all sorts of things. Now good-bye." She shook hands with him, nodded brightly at her brother, and was gone.

"That's a nice girl," said William Bowker, as the door closed after her; "a regular nice girl—modest, ladylike, and true; none of your infernal fal-lal affectations—honest as the day; you can see that in her eyes and in every word she says. Where do you keep your tobacco? All right. Your pipes want looking after, Geoff. I've tried three, and each is as foul as a chimney. Ah, this will do at last; now I'm all right, and can look at your work. H—m! that seems good stuff. You must tone-down that background a little, and put a touch of light here and there on the dress, which is infernally heavy and Hamlet-like. Hallo, Geoff, are you going in for the P.-R.-B. business?"

"Not I. What do you mean?"

"What do *you* mean by this red-haired party, my boy? This is a new style for you, Geoff, and one which no one would have thought of your taking up. You weren't brought up to consider this the right style of thing in old Sassoon's academy, Geoff. If the old boy could rise from his grave, and see his favourite pupil painting a frizzy, red-haired, sallow-faced woman as the realisation of beauty, I think he'd be glad he'd been called away before such awful times."

There was a hesitation in Geoff's voice, and a hollowness in his smile, as he answered:

"P.-R.-B. nonsense! Old Sassoon couldn't teach everything; and as for his ideas of beauty, look how often he made us paint Mrs. S. and the Miss S.'s, who, Heaven knows, were anything but reproductions of the Venus Calipyge. The simple question, as I take it, is this—is the thing a good thing or a bad one? Tell me that."

" **As** a work of art ?"

"Of course ; as you see it. What else could I mean?"

" As a work of art, it's good—undeniably good, in tone, and treatment, and conception ; as a work of prudence, it's infernally bad."

Geoff looked at him sharply for a minute, and William Bowker, calmly puffing at his pipe, did not shrink from his friend's glance. Then, with a flush, Geoff said :

"It strikes me that it is as a work of art you have to regard it. As to what you say about a work of prudence, you have the advantage of me. I don't understand you."

" Don't you ?" said William. " I'm sorry for you. What model did you paint that head from ?"

" From no model."

" From life ?"

" N-no ; from memory—from— Upon my soul, Bowker, I don't see what right you have to cross-question me in this way."

" Don't you ?" said Bowker. " Give your William some-thing to drink, please ; he can't talk when he's dry. What is that? B. and soda. Yes, that'll do. Look here, Geoffrey Ludlow, when you were little more than a boy, grinding away in the Life-School, and only too pleased if the Visitor gave you an encouraging word, your William, who is ten years your senior, had done work which made him be looked upon as the coming man. He had the ball at his foot, and he had merely to kick it to send it where he chose. He does not say this out of brag--you know it ?"

Geoffrey Ludlow inclined his head in acquiescence.

" Your William didn't kick the ball ; something interfered just as his foot was lifted to send it flying to the goal— a woman."

Again Geoffrey Ludlow nodded in acquiescence.

"You have heard the story. Every body in town knew it, and each had his peculiar version ; but I will tell you the whole truth myself. You don't know how I struggled on against that infatuation ;—no, you may think you do, but I am a much stronger man than you—am, or was—and I saw what I was losing by giving way. I gave way. I knocked down the whole fabric which, from the time I had had a man's thoughts, a man's mind, a man's energy and **power,**

I had striven to raise. I kicked it all down, as Alnaschar did his basket of eggs, and almost as soon found how vain had been my castle-building. I need scarcely go into detail with you about that story: it was published in the Sunday news-papers of the time ; it echoed in every club-room ; it has remained lingering about art-circles, and in them is doubtless told with great gusto at the present day, should ever my name be mentioned. I fell in love with a woman who was married to a man of more than double her age,—a woman of education, taste, and refinement; of singular beauty too —and that to a young artist was not her least charm—tied for life to an old heartless scoundrel. My passion for her sprung from the day of my first seeing her ; but I choked it down. I saw as plainly as I see this glass before me now what would be the consequence of any absurd escapade on my part; how it would crush me, how, infinitely more, it would drag *her* down. I knew what was working in each of us; and, so help me Heaven ! I tried to spare us both. I tried—and failed, dismally enough. It was for no want of arguing with myself—from no want of forethought of all the consequences that might ensue. I looked at all point-blank; for though I was young and mad with passion, I loved that woman so that I could even have crushed my own selfishness lest it should be harm to her. I could have done this : I did it until—until one night I saw a blue livid mark on her shoulder. God knows how many years that is ago, but I have the whole scene before me at this moment. It was at some fine ball (I went into what is called 'society' then), and we were standing in a conservatory, when I noticed this mark. I asked her about it, and she hesitated; I taxed her with the truth, which she first feebly denied, then admitted. He had struck her, the hound ! in a fit of jealous rage,—had struck her with his clenched fist ! Even as she told me this, I could see him within a few yards of us, pretending to be rapt in conversation, but obviously noting our conduct. I suppose he guessed that she had told me of what had occurred. I suppose he guessed it from my manner and the expression of my face, for a deadly pallor came over his grinning cheeks; and as we passed out of the conservatory, he whispered to her—not so low but that I caught the words—'You shall pay for this, madam—you shall pay for this !' That determined

me, and that night we fled.—Give me some more brandy and
soda, Geoff. Merely to tell this story drags the heart out
of my breast."

Geoff pushed the bottle over to his friend, and after a gulp
Bowker proceeded :

"We went to Spain, and remained there many months ;
and there it was all very well. That slumbering country is
even now but little haunted by your infernal British tourist ;
but then scarcely any Englishman came there. Such as we
came across were all bachelors, your fine lady can't stand
the mule-travelling and the roughing it in the posadas ; and
they either had not heard the story, or didn't see the propriety
of standing on any squeamishness, more especially when the
acquaintance was all to their advantage, and we got on
capitally. Nelly had seen nothing, poor child, having left
school to be married; and all the travel, and the picturesque
old towns, and the peasantry, and the Alhambra, and all the
rest of it, made a sort of romantic dream for her. But then
old Van den Bosch got his divorce ; and so soon as I had
heard of that, like a madman as I was, I determined to come
back to England. The money was running short, to be sure ;
but I had made no end of sketches, and I might have sent
them over and sold them ; but I wanted to get back. A
man can't live on love alone ; and I wanted to be amongst
my old set again, for the old gossip and the old *camaraderie;*
and so back we came. I took a little place out at Ealing,
and then I went into the old haunts, and saw the old fellows,
and—for the first time—so help me Heaven ! for the first
time I saw what I had done. They cut me, sir, right and
left ! There were some of them—blackguards who would
have hobnobbed with Greenacre, if he'd stood the drink—
who accepted my invitations, and came Sunday after Sunday,
and would have eaten and drunk me out of house and home.
if I'd have stood it ; but the best—the fellows I really cared
about—pretty generally gave me the cold shoulder. Some of
them had married during my absence, and of course they
couldn't come; others were making their way in their art,
working under the patronage of big swells in the Academy,
and hoping for election there, and they daren't be mixed up
with such a notoriously black sheep as your William. I felt
this, Geoff, old boy. By George, it cut me to the heart ; it
took all the change out of me ; it made me low and hipped,

and, I fear, sometimes savage. And I suppose I showed it at home ; for poor Nell seemed to change and wither from the day of our return. She had her own troubles, poor darling, though she thought she kept them to herself. In a case like that, Geoff, the women get it much hotter than we do. There were no friends for her, no one to whom she could tell her troubles. And then the story got known, and people used to stare and nudge each other, and whisper as she passed. The parson called when we first came, and was a good pleasant fellow; but a fortnight afterwards he'd heard all about it, and grew purple in the face as he looked straight over our heads when we met him. And once a butcher, who had to be spoken to for cheating, cheeked her and alluded to her story ; but I think what I did to him prevented any repetition of that kind of conduct. But I couldn't silence the whole world by thrashing it, old fellow; and Nell drooped and withered under all the misery—drooped and—died ! And I—well, I became the graceless, purposeless, spiritless brute you see me now !"

Mr. Bowker stopped and rubbed the back of his hand across his eyes, and gave a great cough before finishing his drink; and then Geoffrey patted him on the shoulder and said, " But you know how we all love you, old friend ; how that Charley Potts, and I, and Markham, and Wallis, and all the fellows, would do anything for you."

Mr. Bowker gave his friend's hand a tight grip as he said, "I know, Geoff; I know you boys are fond of your William; but it wasn't to parade my grief, or to cadge for sympathy from them, that I told you that story. I had another motive."

" And that was—"

" To set myself up as an example and a warning to—any one who might be going to take a similar step. You named yourself just now, Geoff, amongst those who cared for me. Your William is a bit of a fogy, he knows ; but some of you do care for him, and you amongst them."

"Of course. You know that well enough."

"Then why not show your regard for your William, dear boy ? "

" Show my regard—how shall I show it ? "

" By confiding in him, Geoff; by talking to him about yourself; telling him your hopes and plans ; asking him for

some of that advice which seeing a great many men and
cities, and being a remarkably downy old skittle, qualifies
him to give. Why not confide in him, Geoff?"

"Confide in you? About what? Why on earth not speak
out plainly at once?"

"Well, well, I won't beat about the bush any longer. I
daresay there's nothing in it; but people talk and cackle
so confoundedly, and, by George, men—some men, at least
—are quite as bad as women in that line; and they say
you're in love, Geoff; regularly hard hit—no chance of
recovery!"

"Do they?" said Geoff, flushing very red—"do they?
Who are 'they,' by the way?—not that it matters, a pack of
gabbling fools! But suppose I am, what then?"

"What then! Why, nothing then—only it's rather odd
that you've never told your William, whom you've known so
long and so intimately, any thing about it. Is that" (pointing
to the picture) "a portrait of the lady?"

"There—there is a reminiscence of her—her head and
general style."

"Then your William would think that her head and general
style must be doosid good. Any sisters?"

"I—I think not."

"Are her people pleasant—do you get on with them?"

"I don't know them."

"Ah, Geoff, Geoff, why make me go on in this way?
Don't you know me well enough to be certain that I'm not
asking all these questions for impertinence and idle curiosity?
Don't you see that I'm dragging bit by bit out of you because
I'm coming to the only point any of your friends can care
about? Is this girl a good girl; is she respectable; is she
in your own sphere of life; can you bring her home and tell
the old lady to throw her arms round her neck, and welcome
her as a daughter? Can you introduce her to that sweet
sister of yours who was here when I came in?"

There came over Geoffrey Ludlow's face a dark shadow
such as William Bowker had never seen there before. He
did not speak nor turn his eyes, but sat fixed and rigid as a
statue.

"For God's sake think of all this, Geoff! I've told you a
thousand times that you ought to be married; that there
was no man more calculated to make a woman happy, or to

have his own happiness increased by a woman's love. But then she must be of your own degree in life, and one of whom you could be every where proud. I would not have you married to an ugly woman or a drabby woman, or any thing that wasn't very nice; how much less, then, to any one whom you would feel ashamed of, or who could not be received by your dear ones at home! Geoff, dear old Geoff, for heaven's sake think of all this before it is too late! Take warning by my fatal error, and see what misery you would prepare for both of you."

Geoffrey Ludlow still sat in the same attitude. He made no reply for some minutes; then he said, dreamily, "Yes—yes, you're quite right, of course,—quite right. But I don't think we'll continue the conversation now. Another time, Bowker, please—another time." Then he ceased, and Mr. Bowker rose and pressed his hand, and took his departure. As he closed the door behind him, that worthy said to himself: "Well, I've done my duty, and I know I've done right; but it's very little of Geoff's mutton that your William will cut, and very little of Geoff's wine that your William will drink, if that marriage comes off. For of course he'll tell her all I've said, and *won't* she love your William!"

And for hours Geoffrey Ludlow sat before his easel, gazing at the Scylla head, and revolving all the detail of Mr. Bowker's story in his mind.

CHAPTER XI.

PLAYING THE FISH.

WHEN did the giver of good, sound, unpalatable, wholesome advice ever receive his due? Who does not possess, amongst the multitude of acquaintances, a friend who says, "Such and such are my difficulties: I come to you because I want advice;" and who, after having heard all that, after a long struggle with yourself, you bring yourself to say, wrings your hand, goes away thinking what an impertinent idiot you are, and does exactly the opposite of all you have suggested? All men, even the most self-opinionated and practical, are eager for advice. None,

even the most hesitating and diffident, take it, unless it
agrees with their own preconceived ideas. There are, of
course, exceptions by which this rule is proved; but there
are two subjects on which no man was ever yet known to
take advice, and they are horses and women. Depreciate
your friend's purchase as delicately as Agag came unto Saul;
give every possible encomium to make and shape and
breeding; but hint, *per contra*, that the animal is scarcely up
to his weight, or that that cramped action looks like a
possible blunder; suggest that a little more slope in the
shoulder, a little less cowiness in the general build, might be
desirable for riding purposes, and your friend will smile, and
shake his head, and canter away, convinced of the utter
shallowness of your equine knowledge. In the other matter
it is much worse. You must be very much indeed a man's
friend if you can venture to hint to him, even after his
iterated requests for your honest candid opinion, that the
lady of his love is any thing but what he thinks her. And
though you iterate and reiterate, moralise as shrewdly as
Ecclesiasticus, bring chapter and verse to support your text,
he must be more or less than a man, and cast in very
different clay from that of which we poor ordinary mortals
are composed, if he accepts one of your arguments or gives
way one atom before your elucidations.

Did William Bowker's forlorn story, commingled with his
earnest passionate appeal, weigh one scruple with Geoffrey
Ludlow? Not one. Geoff was taken aback by the story.
There was a grand human interest in that laying bare before
him of a man's heart, and of two persons' wasted lives,
which aroused his interest and his sympathy, made him
ponder over what might have been, had the principal actors
in the drama been kept asunder, and sent him into a fine
drowsy state of metaphysical dubiety. But while Bowker
was pointing his moral, Geoff was merely turning over the
various salient points which had adorned his tale.

He certainly heard Bowker drawing a parallel between his
own unhappy passion and Geoff's regard for the original
owner of that "Scylla head;" but as the eminent speaker
was arguing on hypothetical facts, and drawing deductions
from things of which he knew absolutely nothing, too much
reliance was not to be placed on his arguments. In
Bowker's case there had been a public scandal, a certain

betrayal of trust, which was the worst feature in the whole affair, a trial and an *exposé*, and a denunciation of the—well, the world used hard words—the seducer; which—though Bowker was the best fellow in the world, and had obviously a dreadful time of it — was only according to English custom. Now, in his own case, Margaret (he had already accustomed himself to think of her as Margaret) had been victimised by a scoundrel, and the blame—for he supposed blame would, at least in the minds of very strait-laced people, attach to her—was mitigated by the facts. Besides —and here was his great thought—nothing would be known of her former history. Her life, so far as any one in his set could possibly know any thing about it, began on the night when he and Charley Potts found her in the street. She was destitute and starving, granted; but there was nothing criminal in destitution and starvation, which indeed would, in the eyes of a great many weak and goodnatured (the terms are synonymous) persons, bind a kind of romance to the story. And as to all that had gone before, what of that? How was any thing of that love ever to become known? This Leonard Brookfield, an army swell, a man who, under any circumstances, was never likely to come across them, or to be mixed up in Geoff's artist-circle, had vanished, and with him vanished the whole dark part of the story. Vanished for ever and aye! Margaret's life would begin to date from the time when she became his wife, when he brought her home to——Ah, by the way, what was that Bowker said about her worthiness to associate with his mother and sister? Why not? He would tell them all about it. They were good women, who fully appreciated the grand doctrine of forgiveness; and yet—He hesitated; he knew his mother to be a most excellent church-going woman, bearing her "cross" womanfully, not to say rather flaunting it than otherwise; but he doubted whether she would appreciate an introduction to a Magdalen, however penitent. To subscribe to a charity for "those poor creatures;" to talk pleasantly and condescendingly to them, and to leave them a tract on visiting a "Home" or a "Refuge," is one thing; to take them to your heart as daughters-in-law is another. And his sister! Well, young girls didn't understand this kind of thing, and would put a false construction on it, and were always chattering, and a great deal of harm might be done by Til's want of reticence; and so, perhaps, the best thing to be done was to hold his tongue, decline to answer any questions about former life, and leave matters to take their course. He had already arrived at that state of mind that he felt, if any disagreements arose, he was perfectly ready to leave mother and sister, and cleave to his wife—that was to be.

So Geoffrey Ludlow, tossing like a reed upon the waters, but ever, like the same reed, drifting with the resistless current of his will, made up his mind; and all the sage experience of William Bowker, illustrated by the story of his life, failed in altering his determination. It is questionable whether a younger man might not have been swayed by, or frightened at, the council given to him. Youth is impressible in all ways; and however people may talk of the headstrong passion of youth, it is clear that—nowadays at least—there is a certain amount of selfish forethought mingled with the heat and fervour; that love—like the measles—though innocuous in youth, is very dangerous when taken in middle life; and Geoffrey Ludlow was as weak, and withal as stubborn, an im-patient, as ever caught the disease.

And yet?—and yet?—was the chain so strong, were the links already so well riveted, as to defy every effort to break them? Or, in truth, was it that the effort was wanting? An infatuation for a woman had been painted in very black shadows by William Bowker; but it was a great question to Geoff whether there was not infinite pleasure in the mere fact of being infatuated. Since he had seen Margaret Dacre —at all events, since he had been fascinated by her—not merely was he a different man, so far as she was concerned, but all life was to him a different and infinitely more pleasurable thing. That strange doubting and hesitation which had been his bane through life seemed, if not to have entirely vanished, at all events to be greatly modified; and he had recently, in one or two matters, shown a decision which had astonished the members of his little household. He felt that he had at last—what he had wanted all through his life—a purpose; he felt that there was something for him to live for; that by his love he had learned something that he had never known before; that his soul was opened, and the whole aspect of nature intensified and beautified;

H

that he might have said with Maud's lover in that exquisite poem of the Laureate's, which so few really appreciate—

> " It seems that I am happy, that to me
> A livelier emerald twinkles in the grass,
> A purer sapphire melts into the sea."

Then he sat down at his easel again, and worked away at the Scylla head, which came out grandly, and soon grew all a-glow with Margaret Dacre's peculiar expression; and then, after contemplating it long and lovingly, the desire to see the original came madly upon him, and he threw down his palette and brushes, and went out.

He walked straight to Mrs. Flexor's, and, on his knocking, the door was opened to him by that worthy dame, who announced to him, with awful solemnity, that he'd "find a change upstairs."

"A change !" cried Geoffrey, his heart thumping audibly, and his cheek blanched ; "a change !"

"O, nothin' serious, Mr. Ludlows ; but she have been a worritin' herself, poor lamb, and a cryin' her very eyes out. But what it is I can't make out, though statin' put your trust in one where trust is doo, continual."

"I don't follow you yet, Mrs. Flexor. Your lodger has been in low spirits—is that it?"

"Sperrits isn't the name for it, Mr. Ludlows, when downer than dumps is what one would express. As queer as Dick's hatband have she been ever since you went away yesterday; and I says to her at tea last evening—"

"I can see her, I suppose ?"

"Of course you can, sir; which all I was doing was to prepare you for the—" but here Mrs. Flexor, who had apparently taken something stronger than usual with her dinner, broke down and became inarticulate.

Geoffrey pushed past her, and, knocking at the parlour-door, entered at once. He found Margaret standing, with her arms on the mantelshelf, surveying herself in the wretched little scrap of looking-glass which adorned the wall. Her hair was arranged in two large full bands, her eyes were swollen, and her face was blurred and marked by tears. She did not turn round at the opening of the door, nor, indeed, until she had raised her head and seen in the glass Geoff's reflection; even then she moved languidly, as though in pain, and her hand, when she placed it in his, was dry with burning heat.

"That chattering idiot down stairs was right after all," said Geoff, looking alarmedly at her; "you are ill?"

"No," she said, with a faint smile; "not ill, at all events not now. I have been rather weak and silly; but I did not expect you yet. I intended to remove all traces of such folly by the time you came. It was fit I should, as I want to talk to you most seriously and soberly."

"Do we not always talk so? did we not the last time I was here—yesterday?"

"Well, generally, perhaps; but not the last time—not yesterday. If I could have thought so, I should have spared myself a night of agony and a morning of remorse."

Geoff's face grew clouded.

"I am sorry for your agony, but much more sorry for your remorse, Miss Dacre," said he.

"Ah, Mr. Ludlow," cried Margaret, passionately, "don't *you* be angry with me; don't *you* speak to me harshly, or I shall give way all together! O, I watched every change of your face; and I saw what you thought at once; but indeed, indeed it is not so. My remorse is not for having told you all that I did yesterday; for what else could I do to you who had been to me what you had? My remorse was for what I had done—not for what I had said—for the wretched folly which prompted me to yield to a wheedling tongue, and so ruin myself for ever."

Her tears burst forth again as she said this, and she stamped her foot upon the ground.

"Ruin you for ever, Margaret!" said Geoffrey, stealing his arm round her waist as she still stood by the mantel-shelf; "O no, not ruin you, dearest Margaret—"

"Ah, Mr. Ludlow," she interrupted, neither withdrawing from nor yielding to his arm, "have I not reason to say ruin? Can I fail to see that you have taken an interest in me which—which—"

"Which nothing you have told me can alter—which I shall preserve, please God," said Geoff, in all simplicity and sincerity, "to the end of my life."

She looked at him as he said these words with a fixed regard, half of wonder, half of real unfeigned earnest admiration.

H 2

"I—I'm a very bad hand at talking, Margaret, and know I ought to say a great deal for which I can't find words. You see," he continued, with a grave smile, "I'm not a young man now, and I suppose one finds it more difficult to express oneself about—about such matters. But I'm going to ask you—to—to share my lot—to be my wife!"

Her heart gave one great bound within her breast, and her face was paler than ever, as she said:

"Your wife! your wife! Do you know what you are saying, Mr. Ludlow? or is it I who, as the worldling, must point out to you—"

"I know all," said Geoffrey, raising his hand deprecatingly; but she would not be silenced.

"I must point out to you what you would bring upon yourself—what you would have to endure. The story of my life is known to you and to you alone; not another living soul has ever heard it. My mother died while I was in Italy; and of—the other person—nothing has ever been heard since his flight. So far, then, I do not fear that my—my shame—we will use the accepted term—would be flung in your teeth, or that you would be made to wince under any thing that might be said about me. But you would know the facts yourself; you could not hide them from your own heart; they would be ever present to you; and in introducing me to your friends, your relatives, if you have any, you would feel that—"

"I don't think we need go into that, Margaret. I see how right and how honourable are your motives for saying all this; but I have thought it over, and do not attach one grain of importance to it. If you say 'yes' to me, we shall live for ourselves, and with a very few friends who will appreciate us for ourselves. Ah, I was going to say that to you. I'm not rich, Margaret, and your life would, I'm afraid, be dull. A small income and a small house, and—"

"It would be my home, and I should have you;" and for the first time during the interview she gave him one of her long dreamy looks out of her half-shut eyes.

"Then you will say 'yes,' dearest?" asked Geoff passionately.

"Ah, how can I refuse! how can I deny myself such happiness as you hold out to me after the misery I have gone through!"

"Ah, darling, you shall forget that—"

"But you must not act rashly—must not do in a moment what you would repent your life long. Take a week for consideration. Go over every thing in your mind, and then come back to me and tell me the result."

"I know it now. O, don't hesitate, Margaret; don't let me wait the horrid week!"

"It is right, and so we will do it. It will be more tedious to me than to you, my—my Geoffrey."

Ah, how caressingly she spoke, and what a look of love and passion glowed in her deep-violet eyes!

"And I am not to see you during this week?"

"No; you shall be free from whatever little influence my presence may possess. You shall go now. Good-bye."

"God bless you, my darling!" He bent down and kissed her upturned mouth, then was gone. She looked after him wistfully; then after some time said softly to herself: "I did not believe there lived so good a man."

CHAPTER XII.

UNDER THE HARROW.

MR. BOWKER was not the only one of Geoffrey Ludlow's friends to whom that gentleman's intentions towards the lodger at Flexor's occasioned much troubled thought. Charley Potts regarded his friend's intimacy in that quarter with any thing but satisfaction; and an enormous amount of bird's-eye tobacco was consumed by that rising young artist in solemn cogitation over what was best to be done in the matter. For though Geoffrey had reposed no confidence in his friend, and, indeed, had never called upon him, and abstained as much as possible from meeting him since the night of the adventure outside the Titian Sketching-Club, yet Mr. Potts was pretty accurately informed of the state of affairs, through the medium of Mr. Flexor, then perpetually sitting for the final touches to Gil Blas; and having a tolerable acquaintance with human nature,—or being, as he metaphorically expressed it, "able to reckon how many blue beans made five,"—Mr. Potts was enabled to arrive at a pretty accurate idea of how affairs

stood in Little Flotsam Street.   And affairs, as they existed
in Little Flotsam Street, were by no means satisfactory to
Mr. Charles Potts.   Had it been a year ago, he would have
cared but little about it.   A man of the world, accustomed
to take things as they were, without the remotest idea of
ever setting himself up to correct abuses, or protest against
a habitude of being not strictly in accordance with the views
of the most strait-laced, Charley Potts had floated down the
stream of life, objecting to nothing, objected to by none.
There were fifty ladies of his acquaintance, passing as the
wives of fifty men of his acquaintance, pleasant genial
creatures, capital punch-mixers,—women in whose presence
you might wear your hat, smoke, talk slang, chaff, and sing ;
women who knew all the art-gossip, and entered into it ;
whom one could take to the Derby, or who would be
delighted with a cheap-veal-and-ham-pie, beer-in-a-stone-jar,
and bottle-of-hot-sherry picnic in Bushey Park,—the copy
of whose marriage-licenses Charley never expected to see.
It was nothing to him, he used to say.   It might or it might
not be ; but he didn't think that Joe's punch would be any
the stronger, or Tom's weeds any the better, or Bill's bary-
tone voice one atom more tuneful and chirpy, if the Archbishop of Canterbury had given out the bans and performed
the ceremony for the lot.   There was in it, he thought, a
glorious phase of the *vie de Bohême*, a scorn of the respectable
conventionalities of society, a freedom of thought and action
possessing a peculiar charm of their own ; and he looked
upon the persons who married and settled, and paid taxes
and tradesmen's bills, and had children, and went to bed
before morning, and didn't smoke clay pipes and sit in their
shirt-sleeves, with that softened pity with which the man
bound for Epsom Downs regards the City clerk going to
business on the Clapham omnibus.

But within the last few months Mr. Potts's ideas had
very considerably changed.   It was not because he had
attained the venerable age of thirty, though he was at first
inclined to ascribe the alteration to that ; it was not that his
appetite for fun and pleasure had lost any of its keenness,
nor that he had become "awakened," or "enlightened," or
subjected to any of the preposterous revival influences of
the day.   It was simply that he had, in the course of his
intimacy with Geoffrey Ludlow, seen a great deal of Geoffrey

Ludlow's sister, Til; and that the result of his acquaintance
with that young lady was the entire change of his ideas on
various most important points.   It was astonishing, its effect
on him : how, after an evening at Mrs. Ludlow's tea-table—
presided over, of course, by Miss Til—Charley Potts, going
somewhere out to supper among his old set, suddenly had
his eyes opened to Louie's blackened eyelids and Bella's
painted cheeks; how Georgie's *h*-slips smote with tenfold
horror on his ear, and Carry's cigarette-smoking made him
wince with disgust.   He had seen all these things before,
and rather liked them ; it was the contrast that induced the
new feeling.   Ah, those preachers and pedants,— well-
meaning, right-thinking men,—how utterly futile are the
means which they use for compassing their ends !   In these
sceptical times, their pulpit denunciations, their frightful
stories of wrath to come, are received with polite shoulder-
shrugs and grins of incredulity ; their twopence coloured
pictures of the Scarlet Woman, their time-worn renderings
of the street-wanderer, are sneered at as utterly fictitious
and untrue ; and meanwhile detached villas in St. John's
Wood, and first-floors in quiet Pimlico streets, command
the most preposterous rents.   Young men will of course be
young men ; but the period of young-man-ism in that sense
narrows and contracts every year.   The ranks of her
Scarlet Ladyship's army are now filled with very young
boys who do not know any better, or elderly men who
cannot get into the new groove, and who still think that to
be gentlemanly it is necessary to be immoral.   Those
writers who complain of the "levelling" tone of society,
and the "fast" manners of our young ladies, scarcely reflect
upon the improved morality of the age.   Our girls—all the
outcry about fastness and selling themselves for money
notwithstanding—are as good and as domestic as when
formed under the literary auspices of Mrs. Chapone ; and—
granting the existence of Casinos and Anonymas—our young
men are infinitely more wholesome than the class for whose
instruction Philip Dormer Stanhope, Earl of Chesterfield,
penned his delicious letters.
   So Mr. Charles Potts, glowing with newly-awakened ideas
of respectability, began to think that, after all, the *vie de
Bohême* was perhaps a mistake, and not equal, in the average
amount of happiness derived from it, to the *vie de* Camden

Town. He began to think that to pay rent and taxes and
tradesmen's bills was very likely no dearer, and certainly
more satisfactory, than to invest in pensions for cast-off
mistresses and provisions for illegitimate children. He
began to think, in fact, that a snug little house in the
suburbs, with his own Lares and Penates about him, and
Miss Matilda Ludlow, now looking over his shoulder and
encouraging him at his work, now confronting him at the
domestic dinner-table, was about the pleasantest thing which
his fancy could conjure up in his then frame of mind.

Thinking all this, devoutly hoping it might so fall out,
and being, like most converts, infinitely more rabid in the
cause of Virtue than those who had served her with tolerable
fidelity for a series of years, Mr. Charley Potts heard with
a dreadful amount of alarm and amazement of Geoffrey
Ludlow's close connection with a person whose antecedents
were not comeatable and siftable by a local committee of
Grundys. A year ago, and Charley would have laughed the
whole business to scorn; insisted that every man had a
right to do as he liked; slashed at the doubters; mocked
their shaking heads and raised shoulders; and taken no
heed of any thing that might have been said. But matters
were different now. Not merely was Charley a recruit in
the Grundy ranks, having pinned the Grundy colours in his
coat, and subscribed to the Grundy oath; but the person
about to be brought before the Grundy *Fehmgericht*, or
court-marshal, was one in whom, should his hopes be realised, he would have the greatest interest. Though he had
never dared to express his hopes, though he had not the
smallest actual foundation for his little air-castle, Charles
Potts naturally and honestly regarded Matilda Ludlow as
the purest and most honourable of her sex—as does every
young fellow regard the girl he loves; and the idea that she
should be associated, or intimately connected, with any one
under a moral taint, was to him terrible and loathsome.

The moral taint, mind, was all hypothetical. Charles
Potts had not heard one syllable of Margaret Dacre's history,
had been told nothing about it, knew nothing of her except
that he and Geoffrey had saved her from starvation in the
streets. But when people go in for the public profession of
virtue, it is astonishing to find how quickly they listen to
reports of the shortcomings and backslidings of those who

are not professedly in the same category. It seemed a bit
of fatalism too, that this acquaintance should have occurred
immediately on Geoffrey's selling his picture for a large sum
to Mr. Stompff. Had he not done this, there is no doubt
that the other thing would have been heard of by few,
noticed by none; but in art, as in literature, and indeed
in most other professions, no crime is so heavily visited as
that of being successful. It is the sale of your picture, or
the success of your novel, that first makes people find out
how you steal from other people, how your characters are
mere reproductions of your own personal friends,—for which
you ought to be shunned,—how laboured is your pathos,
and how poor your jokes. It is the repetition of your
success that induces the criticism; not merely that you are
a singular instance of the badness of the public taste, but
that you have a red nose, a decided cast in one eye, and
that undoubtedly your grandmother had hard labour for
stealing a clock. Geoff Ludlow the struggling might have
done as he liked without comment; on Geoff Ludlow the
possessor of unlimited commissions from the great Stompff
it was meet that every vial of virtuous wrath should be
poured.

Although Charles Potts knew the loquacity of Mr. Flexor,
—the story of Geoff's adventure and fascination had gone
the round of the studios,—he did not think how much of
what had occurred, or what was likely to occur, was actually
known, inasmuch as that most men, knowing the close intimacy existing between him and Ludlow, had the decency
to hold their tongues in his presence. But one day he
heard a good deal more than every thing. He was painting
on a fancy head which he called "Diana Vernon," but
which, in truth, was merely a portrait of Miss Matilda Ludlow very slightly idealised (the "Gil Blas" had been sent
for acceptance or rejection by the Academy Committee),
and Bowker was sitting by smoking a sympathetic pipe,
when there came a sharp tug at the bell, and Bowker,
getting up to open the door, returned with a very rueful
countenance, closely followed by little Tidd. Now little
Tidd, though small in stature, was a great ruffian. A
soured, disappointed little wretch himself, he made it the
business of his life to go about maligning every one who
was successful, and endeavouring, when he came across

them personally, to put them out of conceit by hints and innuendoes. He was a nasty-looking little man, with an always grimy face and hands, a bald head, and a frizzled beard. He had a great savage mouth with yellow tusks at either end of it; and he gave you, generally, the sort of notion of a man that you would rather not drink after. He had been contemporary with Geoffrey Ludlow at the Academy, and had been used to say very frankly to him and others, "When I become a great man, as I'm sure to do, I shall cut all you chaps;" and he meant it. But years had passed, and Tidd had not become a great man yet; on the contrary, he had subsided from yards of high-art canvas into portrait-painting, and at that he seemed likely to remain.

"Well, how do *you* do, Potts?" said Mr. Tidd. "I said 'How do you do?' to our friend Mr. Bowker at the door. Looks well, don't he? His troubles seem to sit lightly on him." Here Mr. Bowker growled a bad word, and seemed as if about to spring upon the speaker.

"And what's this you're doing, Potts? A charming head! a charming—n-no! not quite so charming when you get close to it; nose a little out of drawing, and—rather spotty, eh? What do you say, Mr. Bowker?"

"I say, Mr. Tidd, that if you could paint like that, you'd give one of your ears."

"Ah, yes—well, that's not complimentary, but—soured, poor man; sad affair! Yes, well! You've sent your Gil Blas to the Academy, I suppose, Potts?"

"O yes; he's there, sir; very likely at this moment being held up by a carpenter before the Fatal Three."

"Ah! don't be surprised at its being kicked out."

"I don't intend to be."

"That's right; they're sending them back in shoals this year, I'm told—in shoals. Have you heard any thing about the pictures?"

"Nothing, except that Landseer's got something stunning."

"Landseer, ah!" said Mr. Tidd. "When I think of that man, and the prices he gets, my blood boils, sir—boils! That the British public should care about and pay for a lot of stupid horses and cattle-pieces, and be indifferent to real art, is—well, never mind!" and Mr. Tidd gave himself a great blow in the chest, and asked, "What else?"

"Nothing else—O yes! I heard from Rushworth, who's

on the Council, you know, that they had been tremendously struck by Geoff Ludlow's pictures, and that one or two more of the same sort are safe to make him an Associate."

" What !" said Mr. Tidd, eagerly biting his nails. "What! —an Associate ! Geoffrey Ludlow an Associate !"

" Ah, that seems strange to you, don't it, Tidd ?" said Bowker, speaking for the first time. " I recollect you and Geoff together drawing from the life. You were going to do every thing in those days, Tidd ; and old Geoff was as quiet and as modest as—as he is now. It's the old case of the hare and the tortoise ; and you're the hare, Tidd ;—though, to look at you," added Mr. Bowker under his breath, "you're a d—d sight more like the tortoise, by Jove !"

" Geoffrey Ludlow an Associate !" repeated Mr. Tidd, ignoring Mr. Bowker's remark, and still greedily biting his nails. "Well, I should hardly have thought that ; though you can't tell what they won't do down in that infernal place in Trafalgar Square. They've treated me badly enough ; and it's quite like them to make a pet of him."

" How have they treated you badly, Tidd ?" asked Potts, in the hope of turning the conversation away from Ludlow and his doings.

" How !" screamed Tidd ; " in a thousand ways ! They've a personal hatred of me, sir—that's what they have ! I've tried every dodge and painted in every school, and they won't have me. The year after Smith made a hit with that miserable picture 'Measuring Heights,' from the *Vicar of Wakefield*, I sent in ' Mr. Burchell cries Fudge !'—kicked out ! The year after, Mr. Ford got great praise for his wretched daub of ' Dr. Johnson reading Goldsmith's Manu- script.' I sent in ' Goldsmith, Johnson, and Bozzy at the Mitre Tavern '—kicked out !—a glorious bit of humour, in which I'd represented all three in different stages of drunken- ness—kicked out !"

" I suppose you've not been used worse than most of us, Tidd," growled Mr. Bowker. " She's an unjust stepmother, is the R.A. of A. But she snubs pretty nearly every body alike."

" Not at all !" said Tidd. " Here's this Ludlow—"

" What of him ?" interposed Potts quickly.

" Can any one say that his painting is—ah, well ! poor devil ! it's no good saying any thing more about him ; he'll have quite enough to bear on his own shoulders soon."

"What, when he's an Associate!" said Bowker, who inwardly was highly delighted at Tidd's evident rage.

"Associate!—stuff! I mean when he's married."

"Married? Is Ludlow going to be married?"

"Of course he is. Haven't you heard it? it's all over town." And indeed it would have been strange if the story had not permeated all those parts of the town which Mr. Tidd visited, as he himself had laboured energetically for its circulation. "It's all over town—O, a horrible thing! horrible thing!"

Bowker looked across at Charley Potts, who said, "What do you mean by a horrible thing, Tidd? Speak out and tell us; don't be hinting in that way."

"Well, then, Ludlow's going to marry some dreadful bad woman. O, it's a fact; I know all about it. Ludlow was coming home from a dinner-party one night, and he saw this woman, who was drunk, nearly run over by an omnibus at the Regent Circus. He rushed into the road, and pulled her out; and finding she was so drunk she couldn't speak, he got a room for her at Flexor's and took her there, and has been to see her every day since; and at last he's so madly in love with her that he's going to marry her."

"Ah!" said Mr. Bowker; "who is she? Where did she come from?"

"Nobody knows where she came from; but she's a reg'lar bad 'un,—as common as dirt. Pity too, ain't it? for I've heard Ludlow's mother is a nice old lady, and I've seen his sister, who's stunnin'!" and Mr. Tidd winked his eye.

This last proceeding finished Charley Potts, and caused his wrath, which had been long simmering, to boil over. "Look here, Mr. Tidd!" he burst forth; "that story about Geoff Ludlow is all lies—all lies, do you hear! And if I find that you're going about spreading it, or if you ever mention Miss Ludlow as you did just now, I'll break your infernal neck for you!"

"Mr. Potts!" said Tidd,—"Mr. Potts, such language! Mr. Bowker, did you hear what he said?"

"I did," growled old Bowker over his pipe; "and from what I know of him, I should think he was deuced likely to do it."

Mr. Tidd seemed to be of the same opinion, for he moved towards the door, and slunk out, muttering ominously.

"There's a scoundrel for you!" said Charley, when the door shut behind the retreating Tidd; "there's a ruffian for you! I've not the least doubt that vagabond got a sort of foundation smattering from that blabbing Flexor, and invented all that about the omnibus and the drunken state and the rest of it himself. If that story gets noised about, it will do Geoff harm."

"Of course it will," said Bowker; "and that's just what Tidd wants. However, I think your threat of breaking his neck has stopped that little brute's tongue. There are some fellows, by Jove! who'll go on lying and libelling you, and who are only checked by the idea of getting a licking, when they shut up like telescopes. I don't know what's to be done about Geoff. He seems thoroughly determined and infatuated."

"I can't understand it."

"*I* can," said old Bowker, sadly; "if she's any thing like the head he's painted in his second picture—and I think from his manner it must be deuced like her—I can understand a man's doing any thing for such a woman. Did she strike you as being very lovely?"

"I couldn't see much of her that night, and she was deadly white and ill; but I didn't think her as good-looking as—some that I know."

"Geoff ought to know about this story that's afloat."

"I think he ought," said Charley. "I'll walk up to his place in a day or two, and see him about it."

"See *him?*" said Bowker. "Ah, all right! Yesterday was not your William's natal day."

CHAPTER XIII.

AT THE PRIVATE VIEW.

THE grand epoch of the artistic year had arrived; the tremendous Fehmgericht—appointed to decide on the merits of some hundreds of struggling men, to stamp their efforts with approval or to blight them with rejection—had issued their sentence. The Hanging-Committee had gone through their labours and eaten their dinners; every inch of space on the walls in Trafalgar Square was duly covered; the successful men had received intimation of the "varnishing day," and to the rejected had been despatched a comforting missive, stating that the amount of space at the command of the Academy was so small, that, sooner than place their works in an objectionable position, the Council had determined to ask for their withdrawal. Out of this ordeal Geoffrey Ludlow had come splendidly. There had always been a notion that he would "do something;" but he had delayed so long—near the mark, but never reaching it—that the original belief in his talents had nearly faded out. Now, when realisation came, it came with tenfold force. The old boys—men of accepted name and fame—rejoiced with extra delight in his success because it was one in their own line, and without any giving in to the doctrines of the new school, which they hated with all their hearts. They liked the "Sic vos non vobis" best (for Geoffrey had sternly held to his title, and refused all Mr. Stompff's entreaties to give it a more popular character); they looked upon it as a more thoroughly legitimate piece of work. They allowed the excellences of the "Scylla and Charybdis," and, indeed, some of them were honest enough to prefer it, as a bit of real excellence in painting; but others objected to the pre-Raphaelite tendency to exalt the white face and the dead-gold hair into a realisation of beauty. But all were agreed that Geoffrey Ludlow had taken the grand step which was always anticipated from him, and that he was, out and away, the most promising man of the day. So Geoff was hung on the line, and received letters from half-a-dozen great names congratulating him on his success, and was in the seventh heaven of happiness, principally from the fact that in all this he saw a prospect of excellent revenue, of the acquisition of money and honour to be shared with a person then resident in Mr. Flexor's lodgings, soon to be mistress of his own home.

The kind Fates had also been propitious to Mr. Charles Potts, whose picture of "Gil Blas and the Archbishop" had been well placed in the North Room. Mr. Tidd's "Boadicea in her Chariot," ten feet by six, had been rejected; but his portrait of W. Bagglehole, Esq., vestry-clerk of St. Wabash, Little Britain, looked down from the ceiling of the large room and terrified the beholders.

So at length arrived that grand day of the year to the

Academicians, when they bid certain privileged persons to the private view of the pictures previous to their public exhibition. The *profanum vulgus*, who are odi'd and arceo'd, pine in vain hope of obtaining a ticket for this great occasion. The public press, the members of the Legislature carefully sifted, a set of old dowagers who never bought a sketch, and who scarcely know a picture from a pipkin, and a few distinguished artists,—these are the happy persons who are invited to enter the sacred precincts on this eventful day. Geoffrey Ludlow never had been inside the walls on such an occasion—never expected to be : but on the evening before, as he was sitting in his studio smoking a pipe, and thinking that within twenty-four hours he would have Margaret's final decision, looking back over his short acquaintance with her in wonder, looking forward to his future life with her in hope, when a mail-phaeton dashed up to the door, and in the strident tones, " Catch hold, young 'un," shouted to the groom, Geoff recognised the voice of Mr. Stompff, and looking out saw that great capitalist descending from the vehicle.

" Hallo, Ludlow !" said Mr. Stompff, entering the studio ; " how are you ? Quiet pipe after the day's grind ? That's your sort ! What will I take, you were going to say ? Well, I think a little drop of sherry, if you've got it pale and dry, —as, being a man of taste, of course you have. Well, those duffers at the Academy have hung you well, you see ! Of course they have. You know how that's done, of course ?"

" I had hoped that the—" Geoff began to stutter directly it became a personal question with him—" that the—I was going to say that the pictures were good enough to—"

" Pictures good enough ! — all stuff ! pickles ! The pictures are good—no use in denying that, and it would be deuced stupid in me, who've bought 'em ! But that's not why they're so well hung. My men all on the Hanging-Committee—*twiggez-vous ?* Last year there were two of Caniche's men, and a horrible fellow who paints religious dodges, which no one buys : not one of my men on the line, and half of them turned out ! I determined to set that right this year, and I've done it. Just you look where Caniche's men are to-morrow, that's all !"

" To-morrow ?"

" O, ah ! that's what brought me here ; I forgot to tell

you. Here's a ticket for the private view. I think you
ought to be there,—show yourself, you know, and that kind
of thing. And look here: if you see me pointing you out
to people, don't you be offended. I've lived longer in the
world than you, and I know what's what. Besides, you're
part of my establishment just now, and I know the way to
work the oracle. So don't mind it, that's all. Very decent
glass of sherry, Ludlow! I say—excuse me, but if you
could wear a white waistcoat to-morrow, I think I should
like it. English gentleman, you know, and all that! Some
of Caniche's fellows are very seedy-looking duffers."

Geoff smiled, took the ticket, and promised to come,
terribly uncomfortable at the prospect of notoriety which
Mr. Stompff had opened for him. But that worthy had not
done with him yet.

"After it's all over," said he, "you must come and dine
with me at Blackwall. Regular business of mine, sir. I
take down my men and two or three of the newspaper chaps,
after the private view, and give 'em as good a dinner as
money can buy. No stint! I say to Lovegrove, 'You
know me! The best, and damn the expense!' and Lovegrove does it, and it's all right! It would be difficult for a
fellow to pitch into any of my men with a recollection of my
Moselle about him, and a hope that it'll come again next
year, eh? Well—won't detain you now; see you to-
morrow; and don't forget the dinner."

Do you not know this kind of man, and does he not
permeate English society? — this coarse ruffian, whose
apparent good-nature disarms your nascent wrath, and yet
whose good-nature you know to be merely vulgar ostentatious
self-assertion under the guise of *bonhomie*. I take the character I have drawn, but I declare he belongs to all classes.
I have seen him as publisher to author, as attorney to young
barrister, as patron to struggler generally. Geoffrey Ludlow
shrank before him, but shrank in his old feeble hesitating
way; he had not the pluck to shake off the yoke, and bid
his employer go to the devil. It was a new phase of life
for him—a phase which promised competence at a time
when competence was required; which, moreover, rid him
of any doubt or anxiety about the destination of his labour,
which to a man of Ludlow's temperament was all in all.
How many of us are there who will sell such wares as

Providence has given us the power of producing at a much less rate than we could otherwise obtain for them, and to most objectionable people, so long as we are enabled to look for and to get a certain price, and are absorbed from the ignominy of haggling, even though by that haggling we should be tenfold enriched! So Geoffrey Ludlow took Mr. Stompff's ticket, and gave him his pale sherry, and promised to dine with him, and bowed him out ; and then went back into his studio and lit a fresh pipe, and sat down to think calmly over all that was about to befall him.

What came into his mind first? His love, of course. There is no man, as yet unanchored in the calm haven of marriage, who amidst contending perplexities does not first think of what storms and shoals beset his progress in that course. And who, so long as there he can see a bit of blue sky, a tolerably clear passage, does not, to a great extent, ignore the black clouds which he sees banking up to windward, the heavy swell crested with a thin, dangerous, white line of wave, which threatens his fortunes in another direction. Here Geoffrey Ludlow thought himself tolerably secure. Margaret had told him all her story, had made the worst of it, and had left him to act on her confession. Did she love him ? That was a difficult question for a man of Geoff's diffidence to judge. But he thought he might unhesitatingly answer it in the affirmative. It was her own proposition that nothing should be done hurriedly ; that he should take the week to calmly reflect over the position, and see whether he held by his first avowal. And to-morrow the week would be at an end, and he would have the right to ask for her decision.

That decision, if favourable, would at once settle his plans, and necessitate an immediate communication to his mother. This was a phase of the subject which Geoffrey characteristically had ignored, put by, and refrained from thinking of as long as possible. But now there was no help for it. Under any circumstances he would have endeavoured, on marrying, to set up a separate establishment for himself ; but situated as he was, with Margaret Dacre as his intended wife, he saw that such a step was inevitable. For though he loved his mother with all his heart, he was not blind to her weaknesses, and he knew that the " cross " would never be more triumphantly brought forward, or more loudly com-

I

plained of, than when it took the form of a daughter-in-law, —a daughter-in-law, moreover, whose antecedents were not held up for the old lady's scrutinising inspection. And here, perhaps, was the greatest tribute to the weird influence of the dead-gold hair, the pallid face, and the deep-violet eyes. A year ago, and Geoff Ludlow would have told you that nothing could ever have made him alter his then style of life. It had continued too long, he would have told you ; he had settled down into a certain state of routine, living with the old lady and Til : they understood his ways and wishes, and he thought he should never change. And Mrs. Ludlow used to say that Geoffrey would never marry now ; he did not care for young chits of girls, who were all giggle and nonsense, my dear ; a man at his time of life looked for something more than that, and where it was to come from she, for one, did not know. Miss Matilda had indeed different views on the subject ; she thought that dear old Geoff would marry, but that it would probably come about in this way. Some lovely female member of the aristocracy, to whom Geoff had given drawing-lessons, or who had seen his pictures, and become imbued with the spirit of poetry in them, would say to her father, the haughty earl, "I pine for him ; I cannot live without him ;" and to save his darling child's health, the earl would give his consent, and bestow upon the happy couple estates of the annual value of twenty thousand pounds. But then you see Miss Matilda Ludlow was given to novel-reading, and though perfectly practical and unromantic as regards herself and her career, was apt to look upon all appertaining to her brother, whom she adored, through a surrounding halo of circulating-library.

How this great intelligence would, then, be received by his home-tenants set Geoff thinking after Stompff's departure, and between the puffs of his pipe he turned the subject hither and thither in his mind, and proposed to himself all kinds of ways for meeting the difficulty ; none of which, on reconsideration, appearing practicable or judicious, he reverted to an old and favourite plan of his, that of postponing any further deliberation until the next day, when, as he argued with himself, he would have "slept upon it"—a most valuable result when the subject is systematically ignored up to the time of going to sleep, and after the hour of waking—he would have been to the private view at the

Academy—which had, of course, an immense deal to do with it—and he would have received the final decision from Margaret Dacre. O yes, it was useless to think any more of it that night. And fully persuaded of this, Geoff turned in and fell fast asleep.

"And there won't be a more gentlemanly-looking man in the rooms than our dear old Geoff !"

" Stuff, Til ! don't be absurd !"

" No, I mean it ; and you know it too, you vain old thing ; else why are you perpetually looking in the glass ?"

" No, but—Til, nonsense !—I suppose I'm all right, eh ?"

"All right !—you're charming, Geoff ! I never saw you such a—I can't help it you know—swell before ! Don't frown, Geoff; there's no other word that expresses it. One would think you were going to meet a lady there. Does the Queen go, or any of the young princesses ?"

" How can you be so ridiculous, Til ! Now, good-bye ;" and Geoff gave his sister a hearty kiss, and started off. Miss Matilda was right; he did look perfectly gentlemanly in his dark-blue coat, white waistcoat, and small-check trousers. Nature, which certainly had denied him personal beauty or regularity of feature, had given him two or three marks of distinction : his height, his bright earnest eyes, and a certain indefinable odd expression, different from the ordinary ruck of people—an expression which attracted attention, and invariably made people ask who he was.

It was three o'clock before Geoff arrived at the Academy, and the rooms were crowded. The scene was new to him, and he stared round in astonishment at the brilliancy of the *toilettes*, and what Charley Potts would have called the "air of swelldom" which pervaded the place. It is scarcely necessary to say that his first act was to glance at the Catalogue to see where his pictures were placed; his second, to proceed to them to see how they looked on the walls. Round each was a little host of eager inspectors, and from what Geoff caught of their conversation, the verdict was entirely favourable. But he was not long left in doubt. As he was looking on, his arm was seized by Mr. Stompff, who, scarcely waiting to carry him out of earshot, began, " Well ! you've done it up brown this time, my man, and no flies ! Your pictures have woke 'em up. They're

I 2

talking of nothing else. I've sold 'em both. Lord Everton —that's him over there : little man with a double eyeglass, brown coat and high velvet collar—he's bought the 'Sic wos ;' and Mr. Shirtings of Manchester's got the other. The price has been good, sir ; I'm not above denyin' it. There's six dozen of Sham ready to go into your cellar whenever you say the word : I ain't mean with my men like some people. Power of nobs here to-day. There's the Prime Minister, and the Chancellor of the Exchequer—that's him in the dirty white hat and rumpled coat—and no end of bishops and old ladies of title. That's Shirtings, that fat man in the black satin waistcoat. Wonderful man, sir,— factory-boy in Manchester ! Saved his shillin' a-week, and is now worth two hundred thousand. Fine modern collection he's got ! That little man in the turn-down collar, with the gold pencil-case in his hand, is Scrunch, the art-critic of the *Scourge.* A bitter little beast ; but I've squared him. I gave him five-and-twenty pounds to write a short account of the Punic War, which was given away with Bliff's picture of 'Regulus,' and he's never pitched into any of my people since. He's comin' to dinner to-day. O, by the bye, don't be late ! I'll drive you down."

"Thank you," said Geoff ; "I—I've got somewhere to go to. I'll find my own way to Blackwall."

"Ha !" said Stompff, "then it is true, is it? Never mind ; mum's the word ! I'm tiled ! Look here : don't you mind me if you see me doing any thing particular. It's all good for business."

It may have been so, but it was undoubtedly trying. During the next two hours Geoff was conscious of Mr. Stompff's perpetually hovering round him, always acting as cicerone to some different man, to whom he would point out Geoff with his forefinger, then whisper in his companion's ear, indicate one of Geoff's pictures with his elbow, and finish by promenading his friend just under Geoff's nose ; the stranger making a feeble pretence of looking at some highly-hung portrait, but obviously swallowing Geoff with his eyes, from his hair to his boots.

But he had also far more pleasurable experiences of his success. Three or four of the leading members of the Academy, men of world-wide fame, whom he had known by sight, and envied—so far as envy lay in his gentle disposition

—for years, came up to him, and introducing themselves, spoke warmly of his picture, and complimented him in most flattering terms. By one of these, the greatest of them all, Lord Everton was subsequently brought up; and the kind old man, with that courtesy which belongs only to the highest breeding, shook hands with him, and expressed his delight at being the fortunate possessor of Mr. Ludlow's admirable picture, and hoped to have the pleasure of receiving him at Everton house, and showing him the gallery of old masters, in whose footsteps he, Mr. Ludlow, was so swiftly following.

And then, as Geoffrey was bowing his acknowledgments, he heard his name pronounced, and turning round found himself close by Lord Caterham's wheel-chair, and had a hearty greeting from its occupant.

"How do you do, Mr. Ludlow? You will recollect meeting me at Lady Lilford's, I daresay. I have just been looking at your pictures, and I congratulate you most earnestly upon them. No, I never flatter. They appear to me very remarkable things, especially the evening-party scene, where you seem to have given an actual spirit of motion to the dancers in the background, so different from the ordinary stiff and angular representation.—You can leave the chair here for a minute, Stephens.—In such a crowd as this, Mr. Ludlow, it's refreshing—is it not?—to get a long look at that sheltered pool surrounded by waving trees, which Creswick has painted so charmingly. The young lady who came with me has gone roving away to search for some favourite, whose name she saw in the Catalogue; but if you don't mind waiting with me a minute, she will be back, and I know she will be glad to see you, as —ah! here she is!"

As Geoffrey looked round, a tall young lady with brown eyes, a pert inquisitive nose, an undulating figure, and a bright laughing mouth, came hurriedly up, and without noticing Geoffrey, bent over Lord Caterham's chair, and said, "I was quite right, Arthur; it is—" then, in obedience to a glance from her companion, she looked up and exclaimed, "What, Geoffrey!—Mr. Ludlow, I mean—O, how *do* you do? Why, you don't mean to say you don't recollect me?"

Geoff was a bad courtier at any time, and now the

expression of his face at the warmth of this salutation showed how utterly he was puzzled.

"You *have* forgotten, then? And you don't recollect those days when—"

"Stop!" he exclaimed, a sudden light breaking upon him; "little Annie Maurice that used to live at Willesden Priory! My little fairy, that I have sketched a thousand times. Well, I ought not to have forgotten you, Miss Maurice, for I have studied your features often enough to have impressed them on my memory. But how could I recognise my little elf in such a dashing young lady?"

Lord Caterham looked up at them out of the corners of his eyes as they stood warmly shaking hands, and for a moment his face wore a pained expression; but it passed away directly, and his voice was as cheery as usual as he said, "*Et nos mutamur in illis*, eh, Mr. Ludlow? Little fays grow into dashing young ladies, and indolent young sketchers become the favourites of the Academy."

"Ay," said Annie; "and the dear old Priory let to other people, and many of those who made those times so pleasant are dead and gone. O, Geoffrey—Mr. Ludlow, I mean—"

"Yes," said Geoff, interrupting her; "and Geoffrey turned into Mr. Ludlow, and Annie into Miss Maurice: there's another result of the flight of time, and one which I, for my part, heartily object to."

"Ah, but, Mr. Ludlow, I must bespeak a proper amount of veneration for you on the part of this young lady," said Lord Caterham; "for I am about to ask you to do me a personal favour in which she is involved."

Geoff bowed absently; he was already thinking it was time for him to go to Margaret.

"Miss Maurice is good enough to stay with my family for the present, Mr. Ludlow; and I am very anxious that she should avail herself of the opportunity of cultivating a talent for drawing which she undoubtedly possesses."

"She used to sketch very nicely years ago," said Geoff, turning to her with a smile; and her face was radiant with good humour as she said:

"O, Geoffrey, do you recollect my attempts at cows?"

"So, in order to give her this chance, and in the hope of making her attempt at cows more creditable than it seems they used to be, I am going to ask you, Mr. Ludlow, to undertake Miss Maurice's artistic education, to give her as much of your time as you can spare, and, in fact, to give what I think I may call her genius the right inclination."

Geoffrey hesitated of course—it was his normal state—and he said doubtingly : " You're very good ; but I—I'm almost afraid—"

" You are not bashful, I trust, Mr. Ludlow," said Lord Caterham ; " I have seen plenty of your work at Lady Lilford's, and I know you to be perfectly competent."

" It was scarcely that, my lord ; I rather think that—" but when he got thus far he looked up and saw Annie Maurice's brown eyes lifted to his in such an appealing glance that he finished his sentence by saying : " Well, I shall be very happy indeed to do all that I can—for old acquaintance-sake, Annie ;" and he held out his hand frankly to her.

" You are both very good," she said ; " and it will be a real pleasure to me to re-commence my lessons, and to try to prove to you, Geoffrey, that I'm not so impatient or so stupid as I was. When shall we begin?"

" The sooner the better, don't you think, Mr. Ludlow ?" said Lord Caterham.

Geoff felt his face flush as he said : " I—I expect to be going out of town for a week or two ; but when I return I shall be delighted to commence."

" When you return we shall be delighted to see you. I can fully understand how you long for a little rest and change after your hard work, Mr. Ludlow. Now good-bye to you ; I hope this is but the beginning of an intimate acquaintance." And Lord Caterham, nodding to Geoffrey, called Stephens and was wheeled away.

" I like that man, Annie," said he, when they were out of earshot ; " he has a thoroughly good face, and the truth and honesty of his eyes overbalance the weakness of the mouth, which is undecided, but not shifty. His manner is honest, too ; don't you think so?"

He waited an instant for an answer, but Annie did not speak.

" Didn't you hear me, Annie ? or am I not worth a reply ?"

"I—I beg your pardon, Arthur. I heard you perfectly; but I was thinking. O yes, I should think Mr. Ludlow was as honest as the day."

"But what made you *distraite?* What were you thinking of?"

"I was thinking what a wonderful difference a few years made. I was thinking of my old ideas of Mr. Ludlow when he used to come out to dine with papa, and sleep at our house; how he had long dark hair, which he used to toss off his face, and poor papa used to laugh at him and call him an enthusiast. I saw hundreds of silver threads in his hair just now, and he seemed—well, I don't know—so much more constrained and conventional than I recollect him."

"You seem to forget that you had frocks and trousers and trundled a hoop in those days, Annie. You were a little fay then; you are a Venus now: in a few years you will be married, and then you must sit to Mr. Ludlow for a Juno. It is only your pretty flowers that change so much; your hollies and yews keep pretty much the same throughout the year."

From the tone of voice in which Lord Caterham made this last remark, Annie knew very well that he was in one of those bitter humours which, when his malady was considered, came surprisingly seldom upon him, and she knew that a reply would only have aggravated his temper, so she forbore and walked silently by his side.

No sooner did he find himself free than Geoffrey Ludlow hurried from the Academy, and jumping into a cab, drove off at once to Little Flotsam Street. Never since Margaret Dacre had been denizened at Flexor's had Geoff approached the neighbourhood without a fluttering at his heart, a sinking of his spirits, a general notion of fright and something about to happen. But now, whether it was that his success at the Academy and the kind words he had had from all his friends had given him courage, it is impossible to say, but he certainly jumped out of the hansom without the faintest feeling of disquietude, and walked hurriedly perhaps, but by no means nervously, up to Flexor's door.

Margaret was in, of course. He found her, the very perfection of neatness, watering some flowers in her window which he had sent her. She had on a tight-fitting cotton dress of a very small pattern, and her hair was neatly braided over her ears. He had seen her look more voluptuous, never more *piquante* and irresistible. She came across the room to him with outstretched hand and raised eyebrows.

"You have come!" she said; "that's good of you, for I scarcely expected you."

Geoff stopped suddenly. "Scarcely expected me! Yet you must know that to-day the week is ended."

"I knew that well enough; but I heard from the woman of the house here that to-day is the private view of the Academy, and I knew how much you would be engaged."

"And did you think that I should suffer any thing to keep me from coming to you to-day?"

She paused a minute, then looked him full in the face. "No; frankly and honestly I did not. I was using conventionalisms and talking society to you. I never will do so again. I knew you would come, and—and I longed for your coming, to tell you my delight at what I hear is your glorious success."

"My greatest triumph is in your appreciation of it," said Geoff. "Having said to you what I did a week ago, you must know perfectly that the end and aim of all I think, of all I undertake, is connected with you. And you must not keep me in suspense, Margaret, please. You must tell me your decision."

"My decision! Now did we not part, at my suggestion, for a week's adjournment, during which you should turn over in your mind certain positions which I had placed before you? And now, the week ended, you ask for my decision! Surely rather I ought to put the question."

"A week ago I said to you, 'Margaret, be my wife.' It was not very romantically put, I confess; but I'm not a very romantic person. You told me to wait a week, to think over all the circumstances of our acquaintance, and to see whether my determination held good. The week is over; I've done all you said; and I've come again to say, Margaret, be my wife."

It was rather a long speech this for Geoff; and as he uttered it his dear old face glowed with honest fervour.

"You have thoroughly made up your mind, considered every thing, and decided?"

"I have."

"Mind, in telling you the story of my past life, I spoke out freely, regardless of my own feelings and of yours. You owe me an equal candour. You have thought of all?"

"Of all."

"And you still—"

"I still repeat that one demand."

"Then I say 'Yes,' frankly and freely. Geoffrey Ludlow, I will be your wife; and by Heaven's help I will make your life happy, and atone for my past. I—"

And she did not say any more just then, for Geoff stopped her lips with a kiss.

"What *can* have become of Ludlow?" said Mr. Stompff for about the twentieth time, as he came back into the dining-room, after craning over the balcony and looking all round.

"Giving himself airs on account of his success," said genial Mr. Bowie, the art-critic. "I wouldn't wait any longer for him, Stompff."

"I won't," said Stompff. "Dinner!"

The dinner was excellent, the wine good and plentiful, the guests well assorted, and the conversation as racy and salted as it usually is when a hecatomb of absent friends is duly slaughtered by the company. Each man said the direst things he could about his own personal enemies; and there were but very few cases in which the rest of the *convives* did not join in chorus. It was during a pause in this kind of conversation—much later in the evening, when the windows had been thrown open, and most of the men were smoking in the balcony—that little Tommy Smalt, who had done full justice to the claret, took his cigar from his mouth, leaned lazily back, and looking up at the moonlit sky, felt in such a happy state of repletion and tobacco as to be momentarily charitable—the which feeling induced him to say:

"I wish Ludlow had been with us!"

"His own fault that he's not," said Mr. Stompff; "his own fault entirely. However, he's missed a pleasant evening. I rather think we've had the pull of him."

Had Geoff missed a pleasant evening? He thought otherwise. He thought he had never had such an evening in his life; for the same cold steel-blue rays of the early

spring moon which fell upon the topers in the Blackwall
balcony came gleaming in through Mr. Flexor's first-floor
window, lighting up a pallid face set in a frame of dead-gold
hair and pillowed on Geoffrey Ludlow's breast.

CHAPTER XIV.

THOSE TWAIN ONE FLESH.

SO it was a settled thing between Margaret Dacre and
Geoffrey Ludlow. She had acceded to his earnest
demand—demand thrice repeated—after due consideration
and delay, and she was to become his wife forthwith.
Indeed, their colloquy on that delicious moonlight evening
would have been brought to a conclusion much sooner than
it was, had not Geoff stalwartly declared and manfully held
to his determination, spite of every protest, not to go until
they had settled upon a day on which to be married. He
did not see the use of waiting, he said; it would get buzzed
about by the Flexors; and all sorts of impertinent remarks
and congratulations would be made, which they could very
well do without. Of course, as regarded herself, Margaret
would want a—what do you call it?—outfit, *trousseau*, that
was the word. But it appeared to him that all he had to do
was to give her the money, and all she had to do was to go
out and get the things she wanted, and that need not take
any time, or hinder them from naming a day—well, let us
say in next week. He himself had certain little arrangements
to make; but he could very well get through them all in
that time. And what did Margaret say?

Margaret did not say very much. She had been lying
perfectly tranquil in Geoffrey's arms; a position which, she
said, first gave her assurance that her new life had indeed
begun. She should be able to realise it more fully, she
thought, when she commenced in a home of her own, and
in a fresh atmosphere; and as the prying curiosity of the
Flexors daily increased, and as Little Flotsam Street, with
its normal pavement of refuse and its high grim house-rows
scarcely admitting any light, was an objectionable residence,
she could urge no reason for delay. So a day at the end of
the ensuing week was fixed upon; and no sooner had it

been finally determined than Geoff, looking round at preparations which were absolutely necessary, was amazed at
their number and magnitude.

He should be away a fortnight, he calculated, perhaps
longer; and it was necessary to apprise the families and the
one or two "ladies' colleges" in which he taught drawing of
his absence. He would also let Stompff know that he would
not find him in his studio during the next few days (for it
was the habit of this great *entrepreneur* to pay frequent visits
to his *protégés*, just to "give 'em a look-up," as he said; but
in reality to see that they were not doing work for any
opposition dealer); but he should simply tell Stompff that
he was going out of town for a little change, leaving that
worthy to imagine that he wanted rest after his hard work.
And then came a point at which he hitched up at once, and
was metaphorically thrown on his beam-ends. What was
he to say to his mother and sister and to his intimate friends?

To the last, of course, there was no actual necessity to say
any thing, save that he knew he must have some one to
"give away" the bride, and he would have preferred one of
his old friends, even at the risk of an explanation, to Flexor,
hired for five shillings, and duly got up in the costume of
the old English gentleman. But to his mother and sister it
was absolutely necessary that some kind of notice should be
given. It was necessary they should know that the little
household, which, despite various small interruptions, had
been carried on so long in amity and affection, would be
broken up, so far as he was concerned; also necessary that
they should know that his contribution to the household
income would remain exactly the same as though he still
partook of its benefits. He had to say all this; and he was
as frightened as a child. He thought of writing at first, and
of leaving a letter to be given to his mother after the ceremony was over; of giving a bare history in a letter, and an
amount of affection in the postscript which would melt the
stoniest maternal heart. But a little reflection caused him
to think better of this notion, and determined him to seek an
interview with his mother. It was due to her, and he would
go through with it.

So one morning, when he had watched his sister Til safe
off into a prolonged diplomatic controversy with the cook, involving the reception of divers ambassadors from the butcher

and other tradespeople, Geoff made his way into his mother's room, and found her knitting something which might have been either an antimacassar for a giant or a counterpane for a child, and at once intimated his pleasure at finding her alone, as he had " something to say to her."

This was an ominous beginning in Mrs. Ludlow's ears, and her " cross " at once stood out visibly before her ; Constantine himself had never seen it plainer.   The mere pronunciation of the phrase made her nervous ; she ought to have " dropped one and taken up two ;" but her hands got complicated, and she stopped with a knitting-needle in mid-air.

" If you're alluding to the butcher's book, Geoffrey," she said, " I hold myself blameless.   It was understood, thoroughly understood, that it should be eightpence a pound all round ; and if Smithers chooses to charge ninepence-half-penny for lamb, and you allow it, I don't hold myself responsible.   I said to your sister at the time—I said, ' Matilda, I'm sure Geoffrey—' "

" It's not that, mother, I want to talk to you about," said Geoff, with a half-smile ; " it's a bigger subject than the price of butcher's meat.   I want to talk to you about myself —about my future life."

" Very well, Geoffrey ; that does not come upon me unawares.   I am a woman of the world.   I ought to be, considering the time I had with your poor father ; and I suppose that now you're making a name, you'll find it necessary to entertain.   He did, poor fellow, though it's little enough name or money he ever made !   But if you want to see your friends round you, there must be help in the kitchen.   There are certain things—jellies, and that like—that must come from the pastry-cook's ; but all the rest we can do very well at home with a little help in the kitchen."

" You don't comprehend me yet, mother.   I—I'm going to leave you."

" To leave us !—O, to live away !   Very well, Geoffrey," said the old lady, bridling up ; " if you've grown too grand to live with your mother, I can only say I'm sorry for you. Though I never saw my name in print in the *Times* newspaper, except among the marriages ; and if that's to be the effect it has upon me, I hope I never shall."

" My dear mother, how *can* you imagine any thing so absurd !   The truth is—"

"O yes, Geoffrey, I understand. I've not lived for sixty years in the world for nothing. Not that there's been ever the least word said about your friends coming pipe-smoking at all times of the night, or hot water required for spirits when Emma was that dead with sleep she could scarcely move ; nor about young persons—female models you call them—trolloping misses I say."

It is worthy of remark that in all business matters Mrs. Ludlow was accustomed to treat her son as a cipher, forgetting that two-thirds of the income by which the house was supported were contributed by him. There was no thought of this, however, in honest old Geoff's mind as he said,

" Mother, you won't hear me out ! The fact is, I'm going to be married."

" To be married, Geoffrey !" said the old lady, in a voice that was much softer and rather tremulous ; " to be married, my dear boy ! Well, that is news !" Her hands trembled as she laid them on his big shoulders and put up her face to kiss him. "Well, well, to be sure ! I never thought you'd marry now, Geoffrey. I looked upon you as a confirmed old bachelor. And who is it that has caught you at last? Not Miss Sanders, is it ?"

Geoffrey shook his head.

" I thought not. No, that would never do. Nice kind of girl too ; but if we're to hold our heads so high when all our money comes out of sugar-hogsheads in Thames Street, why where will be the end of it, I should like to know ? It isn't Miss Hall ?"

Geoffrey repeated his shake.

" Well, I'm glad of it ; not but what I'm very fond of Emily Hall ; but that half-pay father of hers ! I shouldn't like some of the people about here to know that we were related to a half-pay captain with a wooden leg ; and he'd be always clumping about the house, and be horrible for the carpets ! Well, if it isn't Minnie Beverley, I'll give it up ; for you'd never go marrying that tall Dickenson, who's more like a dromedary than a woman !"

" It is not Minnie Beverley, nor the young lady who's like a dromedary," said Geoff, laughing. "The young lady I am going to marry is a stranger to you ; you have never even seen her."

" Never seen her ! O Geoff !" cried the old lady, with

horror in her face, " you're never going to marry one of those trolloping models, and bring her home to live with us ?"

" No, no, mother; you need be under no alarm. This young lady, who is from the country, is thoroughly ladylike and well educated. But I shall not bring her home to you ; we shall have a house of our own."

" And what shall we do, Til and I ? O, Geoffrey, I shall never have to go into lodgings at my time of life, shall I, and after having kept house and had my own plate and linen for so many years?"

" Mother, do you imagine I should increase my own happiness at the expense of yours? Of course you'll keep this house, and all arrangements will go on just the same as usual, except that I sha'n't be here to worry you."

" You never worried me, my dear," said the old lady, as all his generosity and noble unselfishness rose before her mind; " you never worried me, but have been always the best of sons ; and pray God that you may be happy, for you deserve it." She put her arms round his neck and kissed him fondly, while the tears trickled down her cheeks. " Ah, here's Til," she continued, drying her eyes ; " it would never do to let her see me being so silly."

" O, here you are at last !" said Miss Til, who, as they both noticed, had a very high colour and was generally suffused about the face and neck; " what have you been conspiring about ? The Mater looks as guilty as possible, doesn't she, Geoff? and you're not much better, sir. What is the matter?"

" I suspect you're simply attempting the authoritative to cover your own confusion, Til. There's something—"

" No, no ! I won't be put off in that manner ! What *is* the matter?"

" There's nothing the matter, my dear," said Mrs. Ludlow, who by this time had recovered her composure; " though there is some great news. Geoffrey's going to be married !"

" What !" exclaimed Miss Til, and then made one spring into his arms. " O, you darling old Geoff, you don't say so ? O, how quiet you have kept it, you horrible hypocrite, seeing us day after day and never breathing a word about it ! Now, who is it, at once ? Stop, shall I guess ? Is it any one I know ?"

" No one that you know."

"O, I am so glad! Do you know, I think I hate most people I know—girls, I mean; and I'm sure none of them are nice enough for my Geoff. Now, what's she like, Geoff?"

"O, I don't know."

"That's what men always say—so tiresome! Is she dark or fair?"

"Well, fair, I suppose."

"And what coloured hair and eyes?"

"Eh? well, her hair is red, I think."

"Red! Lor, Geoff! what they call carrots?"

"No; deep-red, like red gold—"

"O, Geoff, I know, I know! Like the Scylla in the picture. O, you worse than fox, to deceive me in that way, telling me it was a model, and all the rest of it. Well, if she's like that, she must be wonderful to look at, and I'm dying to see her. What's her name?"

"Margaret."

"Margaret! That's very nice; I like Margaret very much. Of course you'll never let yourself be sufficiently childishly spoony to let it drop into Peggy, which is atrocious. I'm very glad she's got a nice name; for, do all I could, I'm certain I never could like a sister-in-law who was called Belinda or Keziah, or any thing dreadful."

"Have you fixed your wedding-day, Geoffrey?"

"Yes, mother; for Thursday next."

"Thursday!" exclaimed Miss Til. "Thursday next? why there'll be no time for me to get anything ready; for I suppose, as your sister, Geoff, I'm to be one of the bridesmaids?"

"There will be no bridesmaids, dear Til," said Geoffrey; "no company, no breakfast. I have always thought that, if ever I married, I should like to walk into the church with my bride, have the service gone through, and walk out again, without the least attempt at show; and I'm glad to find that Margaret thoroughly coincides with me."

"But surely, Geoffrey," said Mrs. Ludlow, "your friends will—"

"O my! Talking of friends," interrupted Miss Til, "I quite forgot in all this flurry to tell you that Mr. Charles Potts is in the drawing-room, waiting to see you, Geoffrey."

"Dear me! is he indeed? ah, that accounts for a flushed face—"

" Don't be absurd, Geoff ! Shall I tell him to come here?"

" You may if you like ; but don't come back with him, as I want five minutes' quiet talk with him."

So Mrs. Ludlow and her daughter left the studio, and in a few minutes Charley Potts arrived. As he walked up to Geoffrey and wrung his hand, both men seemed under some little constraint. Geoff spoke first.

" I'm glad you're here, Charley. I should have gone up to your place if you hadn't looked in to-day. I have something to tell you, and something to ask of you."

" Tell away, old boy ; and as for the asking, look upon it as done,—unless it's tin, by the way ; and there I'm no good just now."

" Charley, I'm going to be married next Thursday to Margaret Dacre—the girl we found fainting in the streets that night of the Titians."

Geoff expected some exclamation, but his friend only nodded his head.

" She has told me her whole life : insisted upon my hearing it before I said a word to her ; made me wait a week after I had asked her to be my wife, on the chance that I should repent ; behaved in the noblest way."

Geoffrey again paused, and Mr. Potts again nodded.

" We shall be married very quietly at the parish-church here ; and there will be nobody present but you. I want you to come ; will you ?"

" Will I ? Why, old man, we've been like brothers for years ; and to think that I'd desert you at a time like this ! I—I didn't quite mean that, you know ; but if not, why not ? You know what I do mean."

" Thanks, Charley. One thing more : don't talk about it until after it's over. I'm an awkward subject for chaff, particularly such chaff as this would give rise to. You may tell old Bowker, if you like ; but no one else."

And Mr. Potts went away without delivering that tremendous philippic with which he had come charged. Perhaps it was his conversation with Miss Til in the drawing-room which had softened his manners and prevented him from being brutal.

They were married on the following Thursday ; Margaret looking perfectly lovely in her brown-silk dress and white bonnet. Charley Potts could not believe her to be the

K

haggard creature in whose rescue he had assisted; and simple old William Bowker, peering out from between the curtains of a high pew, was amazed at her strange weird beauty. The ceremony was over; and Geoff, happy and proud, was leading his wife down the steps of the church to the fly waiting for them, when a procession of carriages, coachmen and footmen with white favours, and gaily-clad company, all betokening another wedding, drove up to the door. The bride and her bridesmaids had alighted, and the bridegroom's best-man, who with his friend had just jumped out of his cabriolet, was bowing to the bridesmaids as Geoff and Margaret passed. He was a pleasant airy fellow, and seeing a pretty woman coming down the steps, he looked hard at her. Their eyes met, and there was something in Margaret's glance which stopped him in the act of raising his hand to his hat. Geoffrey saw nothing of this; he was waving his hand to Bowker, who was standing by; and they passed on to the fly.

"Come on, Algy!" called out the impatient intended bridegroom; "they'll be waiting for us in the church. What on earth are you staring at?"

"Nothing, dear old boy!" said Algy Barford, who was the best man just named,—"nothing but a resurrection!—only a resurrection; by Jove, that's all!"

𝔅ook the 𝔖econd.

CHAPTER I.

NEW RELATIONS.

THE fact of her having a daughter-in-law whom she had never seen, of whose connections and antecedents she knew positively nothing, weighed a good deal on Mrs. Ludlow's mind. "If she had been an Indian, my dear," she said to her daughter Matilda, "at least, I don't mean an Indian, not black you know; of course not—ridiculous; but one of those young women who are sent out to India by their friends to pick up husbands,—it would be a different matter. Of course, then I could not have seen her until she came over to England; and as Geoff has never been in India, I don't quite see how it could have happened; but you know what I mean. But to think that she should have been living in London, within the bills of thingummy— mortality, and Geoff never to bring her to see me, is most extraordinary—most extraordinary! However, it only goes to prove what I've said—that I have a cross to bear; and now my son's marrying himself in a most mysterious and Arabian-nights-like manner is added to the short-weight which we always get from the baker, and to the exceeding forwardness shown by that young man with the pomatumed hair and the steel heart stuck into his apron, whenever you go into the grocer's shop."

And although Miss Matilda combated this idea with great resolution, albeit by no means comfortable in her own mind as to Geoffrey's proceedings, the old lady continued in a state of mind in which indignation at a sense of what she imagined the slight put upon her was only exceeded by her curiosity to catch a glimpse of her son's intended: under the influence of which latter feeling she even proposed to Til that they should attend the church on the occasion of the marriage-ceremony. "I can put on my Maltese-lace veil, you know, my dear: and if we gave the pew-opener

K 2

sixpence, she'd put us into a place in the gallery where we could hide behind a pillar, and be unseen spectators of the proceedings." But this suggestion was received with so much disfavour by her daughter that the old lady was compelled to abandon it, together with an idea, which she subsequently broached, of having Mr. Potts to supper,— giving him sprats, or tripe, or some of those odd things that men like; and then, when he was having a glass of spirits-and-water and smoking a pipe, getting him to tell us all about it, and how it went off. So Mrs. Ludlow was obliged to content herself with a line from Geoffrey,—received two or three days after his marriage, saying that he was well and happy, and that his Margaret sent her love ("She might have written that herself, I think!" said the old lady; "it would have been only respectful; but perhaps she can't write. Lord, Lord! to think we should have come to this!"),—and with a short report from Mr. Potts, whom Til had met, accidentally of course, walking one morning near the house, and who said that all had gone off capitally, and that the bride had looked perfectly lovely.

But there was balm in Gilead; and consolation came to old Mrs. Ludlow in the shape of a letter from Geoffrey at the end of the first week of his absence, requesting his mother and sister to see to the arrangement of his new house, the furniture of which was all ordered, and would be sent in on a certain day, when he wished Til and his mother to be present. Now the taking of this new house, and all in connection with it, had been a source of great disquietude and much conversation to the old lady, who had speculated upon its situation, its size, shape, conveniences, &c., with every one of her little circle of acquaintance. "Might be in the moon, my dear, for all we know about it," she used to say; "one would think that one's own son would mention where he was going to live—to his mother, at least: but Geoff is that tenacious, that—well, I suppose it's part of the cross of my life." But the information had come at last, and the old lady was to have a hand, however subordinate, in the arrangements; and she was proportionately pleased. "And now, Til, where is it, once more! Just read the letter again, will you?—for we're to be there the first thing to-morrow morning, Geoff says. What?—O, the vans will be there the first thing to-morrow morning! Yes, I know what the vans' first thing is—eleven o'clock or thereabouts; and then the men to go out for dinner at twelve, and not come back till half-past two, if somebody isn't there to hunt them up! The Elm Lodge, Lowbar! Lowbar! Why, that's Holloway and Whittington, and all that turn-again nonsense about the bells! Well, I'm sure! Talk about the poles being asunder, my dear; they're not more asunder than Brompton and Lowbar. O, of course that's done that he needn't see more of us than he chooses, though there was no occasion for that, I'm sure, at least so far as I'm concerned; I know when I'm wanted fast enough, and act accordingly."

"I don't think there was any such idea in Geoff's mind, mamma," said Til; "he always had a wish to go to the other side of town, as he found this too relaxing."

"Other side of town, indeed, my dear?—other side of England, you mean! This side has always been good enough for me; but then, you see, I never was a public character. However, if we are to go, we'd better have Brown's fly; it's no good our trapesing about in omnibuses that distance, and perhaps taking the wrong one, and I don't know what."

But the old lady's wrath (which, indeed, did not deserve the name of wrath, but would be better described as a kind of perpetual grumble, in which she delighted) melted away when, on the following morning, Brown's fly, striking off to the left soon after it commenced ascending the rise of Lowbar Hill, turned into a pretty country road, and stopped before a charming little house, bearing the name "Elm Lodge" on its gate-pillars. The house, which stood on a small eminence, was approached by a little carriage-sweep; had a little lawn in front, on which it opened from French windows, covered by a veranda, nestling under climbing clematis and jasmine; had the prettiest little rustic portico, floored with porcelain tiles; a cosy dining-room, a pretty little drawing-room with the French windows before named, and a capital painting-room. From the windows you had a splendid view over broad fields leading to Hampstead, with Harrow church fringing the distant horizon. Nobody could deny that it was a charming little place; and Mrs. Ludlow admitted the fact at once.

"Very nice, very nice indeed, my dear Til!" said she;

"Geoffrey has inherited my taste—that I will say for him. Rather earwiggy, I should think, all that green stuff over the balcony; too much so for me; however, I'm not going to live here, so it don't matter. Oh! the vans have arrived! Well, my stars! all in suites! Walnut and green silk for the drawing room, black oak and dark-brown velvet for the dining-room, did you say, man? It's never—no, my dear, I thought not; it's *not* real velvet,—Utrecht, my dear; I just felt it. I thought Geoff would never be so insane as to have real; though, as it is, it must have cost a pretty penny. Well, he never gave us any thing of this sort at Brompton; of course not."

"O, mother, how can you talk so!" said Til; "Geoff has always been nobly generous; but recollect he's only just beginning to make money."

"Quite true, my dear, quite true; and he's been the best of sons. Only I should have liked for once to have had the chance of showing my taste in such matters. In your poor father's time every thing was so heavy and clumsy compared to what it is nowadays, and—there! I would have had none of your rubbishing Cupids like that, holding up those stupid baskets."

So the old lady chattered on, by no means allowing her energy to relax by reason of her talk, but bustling about with determined vigour. When she had tucked up her dress, and got a duster into her hand, she was happy, flying at looking-glasses and picture-frames, and rubbing off infinitesimal atoms of dirt; planting herself resolutely in every body's way, and hunting up, or, as she termed it "hinching," the upholsterer's men in the most determined manner.

"I know 'em, my dear; a pack of lazy carpet-caps; do nothing unless you hinch 'em;" and so she worried and nagged and hustled and drove the men, until the pointed inquiry of one of them as to "who *was* that *h*old cat?" suggested to Miss Til the propriety of withdrawing her mother from the scene of action. But she had done an immense deal of good, and caused such progress to be made, that before they left, the rooms had begun to assume something like a habitable appearance. They went to take one more look round the house before getting into Brown's fly; and it was while they were upstairs that Mrs. Ludlow opened a door which she had not seen before—a door leading into a charming little room, with light chintz paper and chintz hangings, with a maple writing-table in the window, and a cosy lounge-chair and a *prie-dieu;* and niches on either side the fire-place occupied by little book-cases, into which the foreman of the upholsterers was placing a number of handsomely-bound books, which he took from a box on the floor.

"Why, good Lord! what's this?" said the old lady, as soon as she recovered her breath.

"This is the budwaw, mum," said the foreman, thinking he had been addressed.

"The what, man? What does he say, Matilda?"

"The budwaw, mum; Mrs. Ludlow's own room as is to be. Mr. Ludlow was most partickler about this room, mum; saw all the furniture for it before he went away, mum; and give special directions as to where it was to be put."

"Ah, well, it's all right, I daresay. Come along, my dear."

But Brown's horse had scarcely been persuaded by his driver to comprehend that he was required to start off homewards with Brown's fly, when the old lady turned round to her daughter, and said solemnly:

"You mark my words, Matilda, and after I'm dead and gone don't you forget 'em—your brother's going to make a fool of himself with this wife of his. I don't care if she were an angel, he'd spoil her. Boudoir, indeed!—room all to herself, with such a light chintz as that, and maple too; there's not one woman in ten thousand could stand it; and Geoffrey's building up a pretty nest for himself, you mark my words."

Two days later a letter was received from Geoffrey to say that they had arrived home, and that by the end of the week the house would be sufficiently in order, and Margaret sufficiently rested from her fatigue, to receive them, if they would come over to Elm Lodge to lunch. As the note was read aloud by Til, this last word struck upon old Mrs. Ludlow's ear, and roused her in an instant.

"To what, my dear?" she asked. "I beg your pardon, I didn't catch the word."

"To lunch, mamma."

"O, indeed; then I did catch the word, and it wasn't

your mumbling tone that deceived me. To lunch, eh? Well, upon my word! I know I'm a stupid old woman, and I begin to think I live in heathenish times; but I know in my day that a son would no more have thought of asking his mother to lunch than—well, it's good enough for us, I suppose."

"Mamma, how *can* you say such things! They're scarcely settled yet, and don't know any thing about their cook; and no doubt Margaret's a little frightened at first—I'm sure I should be, going into such a house as that."

"Well, my dear, different people are differently constituted. I shouldn't feel frightened to walk into Buckingham Palace as mistress to-morrow. However, I daresay you're right;" and then Mrs. Ludlow went into the momentous question of "what she was to go in." It was lucky that in this matter she had Til at her elbow; for whatever the old lady's taste may have been in houses and furniture, it was very curious in dress, leaning towards wild stripes and checks and large green leaves, with veins like caterpillars, spread over brown grounds; towards portentous bonnets, bearing cockades and bows of ribbon where such things were never seen before; to puce-coloured gloves, and parasols rescued at an alarming sacrifice from a cheap draper's sale. But under Til's supervision Mrs. Ludlow was relegated to a black-silk dress, and the bonnet which Geoffrey had presented to her on her birthday, and which Til had chosen; and to a pair of lavender gloves which fitted her exactly, and had not those caverns at the tips of the fingers and that wrinkled bagginess in the thumbs which were usually to be found in the old lady's handcoverings; and as she took her seat in Brown's fly, the neighbours on either side, with their noses firmly pressed against their parlour-windows, were envious of her personal appearance, though both of them declared afterwards that she wanted a "little more lighting-up."

When the fly was nearing its destination, Mrs. Ludlow began to grow very nervous, a state which was exhibited by her continually tugging at her bonnet-strings and shaking out the skirt of her dress, requesting to be informed whether she was "quite straight," and endeavouring to catch the reflection of herself in the front glasses of the fly. These performances were scarcely over before the fly stopped at the gate, and Mrs. Ludlow descending was received into her son's strong arms. The old lady's maternal feelings were strongly excited at that moment, for she never uttered a word of complaint or remonstrance, though Geoff squeezed up all the silk skirt which she had taken such pains to shake out, and hugged her until her bonnet was all displaced. Then, after giving Til a hearty embrace, Geoff took his mother's hand and led her across the little lawn to the French window, at which Margaret was waiting to receive her.

Naturally enough, old Mrs. Ludlow had thought very much over this interview, and had pictured it to herself in anticipation a score of times. She had never taken any notice of the allusions to the likeness between her daughter-in-law that was to be and the Scylla-head which Geoff had painted; but had drawn entirely upon her own imagination for the sort of person who was to be presented to her. This ideal personage had at various times undergone a good deal of change. At one time she would appear as a slight girl with long fair hair and blue eyes ("what I call a wax-doll beauty," the old lady would think); then she would have large black eyes, long black hair, and languishing manners; then she would be rather plain, but with a finely-developed figure, Mrs. Ludlow having a theory that most artists thought of figure more than face; but in any case she would be some little chit of a girl, just the one to catch such a man as our Geoff, who stuck to his paintings, and had seen so little of the world.

So much for Mrs. Ludlow's ideal; the realisation was this. On the step immediately outside the window stood Margaret, a slight rose-flush tinting her usually pale cheeks just under her eyes; her deep-violet eyes wider open than usual, but still soft and dreamy; her red-gold hair in bands round her face, but twisted up at the back into one large knot at the top of her head. She was dressed in a bright-blue cambric dress, which fell naturally and gracefully round her, neither bulging out with excess of crinoline, nor sticking limply to her like a bathing-gown; across her shoulders was a large white muslin-cape, such as that which Marie Antoinette is represented as wearing in Delaroche's splendid picture; muslin-cuffs and a muslin-apron. A gleam of sun shone upon her, bathing her in light; and as the old lady stood staring at her in amazement, a recollection came across her of something which she had not seen for more than forty years, nor ever thought of since,—a reminiscence of a stained-glass figure of the Virgin in some old Belgian cathedral, pointed out to her by her husband in her honeymoon.

As this idea passed through her mind, the tears rose into Mrs. Ludlow's eyes. She was an excitable old lady and easily touched; and simultaneously with the painted figure she thought of the husband pointing it out,—the young husband then so brave and handsome, now for so many years at rest,—and she only dimly saw Margaret coming forward to meet her. But remembering that tears would be a bad omen for such an introduction, she brushed them hastily away, and looked up in undisguised admiration at the handsome creature moving gracefully towards her. Geoffrey, in a whirl of stuttering doubt, said, " My mother, Margaret ; mother, this is—Margaret—my wife ;" and each woman moved forward a little, and neither knew what to do. Should they shake hands or kiss? and from whom should the suggestion come ? It came eventually from the old lady, who said simply, " I'm glad to see you, my dear ;" and putting one hand on Margaret's shoulder, kissed her affectionately. There was no need of introduction between the others. Til's bright eyes were sparkling with admiration and delight ; and Margaret, seeing the expression in them, reciprocated it at once, saying, " And this is Til !" and then they embraced, as warmly as girls under such circumstances always do. Then they went into the house, Mrs. Ludlow leaning on her son's arm, and Til and Margaret following.

" Now, mother," said Geoff, as they passed through the little hall, " Margaret will take you upstairs. You'll find things much more settled than when you were here last." And upstairs the women went accordingly.

When they were in the bedroom, Mrs. Ludlow seated herself comfortably in a chair, with her back to the light, and said to Margaret :

" Now, my dear, come here and let me have a quiet look at you. I've thought of you a thousand times, and wondered what you were like; but I never thought of any thing like this."

" You—you are not disappointed, I hope," said Margaret. She knew it was a dull remark, and she made it in a constrained manner. But what else was she to say?

"Disappointed! no, indeed, my dear. But I won't flatter you; you'll have quite enough of that from Geoffrey. I shall always think of you in future as a saint; you're so like the pictures of the saints in the churches abroad."

"You see you flatter me at once."

"No, my dear, I don't. For you are like them, I'm sure; not that you're to wear horsehair next your skin, or be chopped up into little pieces, or made to walk on hot iron, or any thing of that sort, you know; but I can see by your face that you're a good girl, and will make my Geoff a good wife."

"I will try to do so, Mrs. Ludlow," said Margaret, earnestly.

"And you'll succeed, my dear. I knew I could always trust Geoff for that; he might marry a silly girl, one that hadn't any proper notions of keeping house or managing those nuisances of servants; but I knew he would choose a good one. And don't call me 'Mrs. Ludlow,' please, my dear. I'm your mother now; and with such a daughter-in-law I'm proud of the title!" This little speech was sealed with a kiss, which drove away the cloud that was gathering on Margaret's brow, and they all went down to lunch together. The meal passed off without any particular incident to be recorded. Margaret was self-possessed, and did the honours of her table gracefully, paying particular attention to her guests, and generally conducting herself infinitely better than Geoff, who was in a flurry of nervous excitement, and was called to order by his mother several times for jumping up to fetch things when he ought to have rung the bell. "A habit that I trust you'll soon break him of, Margaret, my dear; for nothing goes to spoil a servant so quickly; and calling over the bannisters for what he wants is another trick, as though servants' legs weren't given them to answer bells." But Mrs. Ludlow did not talk much, being engaged, during the intervals of eating, in mentally appraising the articles on the table, in quietly trying the weight of the spoons, and in administering interrogative taps to the cow on the top of the butter-dish to find if she were silver or plated, in private speculations as to which quality of Romford ale Geoffrey had ordered and what he paid for it, and various other little domestic details whereto her experience as a household manager prompted her. Geoffrey too was silent; but the conversation, though not loud, was very brisk between Margaret and Til, who seemed, to Geoff's intense delight, to have taken a great fancy for each other.

It was not until late in the afternoon, when the hour at which Brown's fly had been ordered was rapidly approaching, and they were all seated in the veranda enjoying the distant view, the calm stillness, and the fresh air, that the old lady, who had been looking with a full heart at Geoffrey—who, seated close behind Margaret, was playing with the ends of her hair as she still kept up her conversation with Til—said:

"Well, Geoffrey, I don't think I ought to leave you to-night without saying how much I am pleased with my new daughter. O, I don't mind her hearing me; she's too good a girl to be upset by a little truthful praise—ain't you, my dear? Come and sit by me for a minute and give me your hand, Margaret; and you, Geoff, on the other side. God bless you both, my children, and make you happy in one another! You're strange to one another, and you'll have some little worries at first; but you'll soon settle down into happiness. And that's the blessing of your both being young and fresh. I'm very glad you didn't marry poor Joe Telford's widow, Geoff, as we thought you would, ten years ago. I don't think, if I had been a man, I should have liked marrying a widow. Of course every one has their little love-affairs before they marry, but that's nothing; but with a widow it's different, you know; and she'd be always comparing you with the other one, and perhaps the comparison might not be flattering. No; it's much better to begin life both together, with no past memories to—why, Geoffrey, how your hand shakes, my dear! What's the matter? it can't be the cold, for Margaret is as steady as a rock."

Geoffrey muttered something about "a sudden shiver," and just at that moment the fly appeared at the gate. So they parted with renewed embraces and promises of meeting again very shortly; Geoffrey was to bring Margaret over to Brompton, and the next time they came to Elm Lodge they must spend a long day, and perhaps sleep there; and it was not until Brown's fly turned the corner which shut the house out of sight that Mrs. Ludlow ceased stretching her head out of the window and nodding violently. Then she burst out at once with her long-pent-up questioning.

" Well, Matilda, and what do you think of your new relation? I'm sure you've been as quiet as quiet; there's been no getting a word out of you. But I suppose you don't mind telling your mother. What *do* you think of her?"

" She is very handsome, mamma, and seems very kind, and very fond of Geoff."

" Handsome, my dear! She's really splendid! There's a kind of *je ne sais quoi* about her that—and tall too, like a duchess! Well, I don't think the Wilkinsons in the Crescent will crow any longer. Why, that girl that Alfred Wilkinson married the other day, and that they all went on so about, isn't a patch upon Margaret. Did you notice her cape and cuffs, Matilda? Rather Frenchified, I thought; rather like that nurse that the Dixons brought from Boulogne last year, but very pretty. I hope she'll wear them when she comes to spend the day with us, and that some of those odious people in the Crescent will come to call. Their cook seems to have a light hand at pie-crust; and *did* you taste the jelly, my dear? I wonder if it was made at home; if so, the cook's a treasure, and dirt-cheap at seventeen and every thing found except beer, which Margaret tells me is all she gives! I see they didn't like my arrangement of the furniture; they've pulled the grand-piano away from the wall, and put the ottoman in its place : nice for the people who sit on it to rub the new paper with their greasy heads !"

And so the old lady chattered on until she felt sleepy, and stumbled out at her own door in an exhausted state, from which the delicious refreshment of a little cold brandy-and-water and a particularly hard and raspy biscuit did not rouse her. But just as Til was stepping into bed her mother came into the room, perfectly bright and preternaturally sharp, to say, " Do you know, my dear, I think, after all, Geoffrey was very fond of Joe Telford's widow? You were too young then to recollect her; for when I was speaking about her to-night, and saying how much better it was that both husband and wife should come fresh to each other, Geoff's hand shook like an aspen-leaf, and his face was as pale as death."

CHAPTER II.

MARGARET.

MARGARET had carried out what she knew would be the first part of the new programme of her life. During their short honeymoon, Geoffrey had talked so much of his mother and sister, and of his anxiety that they should be favourably impressed with her, that she had determined to put forth all the strength and tact she had to make that first meeting an agreeable one to them. That she had done so, that she had succeeded in her self-imposed task, was evident. Mrs. Ludlow, in her parting words, had expressed herself delighted with her new daughter-in-law; but by her manner, much more than by any thing she had said, Geoff knew that his mother's strong sympathies had been enlisted, if her heart had not been entirely won. For though the old lady so far gave in to the prejudices of the world as to observe a decent reticence towards objects of her displeasure—though she never compromised herself by outraging social decency in verbal attacks or disparaging remarks—a long experience had given her son a thorough appreciation of, and power of translating, certain bits of facial pantomime of a depreciatory nature, which never varied; notably among them, the uplifted eyebrow of astonishment, the prolonged stare of "wonder at her insolence," the shoulder-shrug of "I don't understand such things," and the sniff of unmitigated disgust. All these Geoff had seen brought to bear on various subjects quite often enough to rate them at their exact value; and it was, therefore, with genuine pleasure that he found them conspicuous by their absence on the occasion of his mother's first visit to Elm Lodge.

For although Geoff was not particularly apt as a student of human nature,—his want of self-confidence, and the quiet life he had pursued, being great obstacles to any such study,—he must, nevertheless, have had something of the faculty originally implanted in him, inasmuch as he had contrived completely, and almost without knowing it himself, to make himself master of the key to the characters of the two people with whom his life had been passed. It was this knowledge of his mother that made him originally propose that the first meeting between her and Margaret should take place at Brompton, where he could take his wife over as a visitor. He thought that very likely any little latent jealousy which the old lady might feel by reason of her deposition, not merely from the foremost place in her son's affections, but from the head of his table and the rulership of his house,—and it is undeniable that with the very best women these latter items jar quite as unpleasantly as the former,—whatever little jealousy Mrs. Ludlow may have felt on these accounts would be heightened by the sight of the new house and furniture in which it had pleased Geoff to have his new divinity enshrined. There is a point at which the female nature rebels ; and though Geoff neither knew, nor professed to know, much about female nature, he was perfectly certain that as a young woman is naturally more likely to "take up with" another who is her inferior in personal attractions, so Mrs. Ludlow would undoubtedly be more likely to look favourably on a daughter-in-law whose *status*, artificially or otherwise, should not appear greater than her own. It was Margaret who dissuaded Geoff from his original intention, pitting against her husband's special acquaintance with his mother's foibles her ordinary woman's cleverness, which told her that, properly managed, the new house and furniture, and all their little luxury, could be utilised for, instead of against, them with the old lady, making her part and parcel of themselves, and speaking of all the surroundings as component parts of a common stock, in which with them she had a common interest. This scheme, talked over in a long desultory lovers' ramble over the green cliffs at Niton in the ever-lovely Isle of Wight, resulted in the letter requesting Mrs. Ludlow to superintend the furniture-people, of which mention has already been made, and in the meeting taking place at Elm Lodge, as just described.

This first successful stroke, which Geoff perhaps unduly appreciated (but any thing in which his mother was involved had great weight with him), originated by Margaret and carried out by her aid, had great effect on Geoffrey Ludlow, and brought the woman whom he had married before him in quite a new light. The phrase "the woman he had married" is purposely chosen, because the fact of having a wife, in its largest and most legitimate sense, had not yet dawned upon him. We read in works of fiction of how men weigh and balance before committing matrimony, —carefully calculate this recommendation, calmly dissect that defect ; we have essay-writers, political economists, and others, who are good enough to explain these calculations, and to show us why it ought to be, and how it is to be done ; but, spite of certain of my brother-fictionists and these last-named social teachers, I maintain that, in ninety-nine cases out of a hundred, a man who is a man, " with blood, bones, passion, marrow, feeling," as Byron says, marries a girl because he is smitten with the charms either of her person or her manner—because there is something *simpatico*, as the Italians call it, between them—because he is "in love with her," as the good old English phrase runs ; but without having paid any thing but the most cursory attention to her disposition and idiosyncrasy. Is it so, or is it not ? Such a state of things leads, I am perfectly aware, to the acceptance of stone for bread and scorpions for fish ; but it exists, hath existed, and will continue to exist. Brown now helplessly acknowledges Mrs. B.'s "devil of a temper ;" but even if he had had proof positive of it, he would have laughed it away merrily enough that summer at Margate, when Mrs. B. was Emily Clark, and he was under the thrall of her black eyes. Jones suffers under his wife's "low fits," and Robinson under Mrs. Robinson's religion, which she takes very hot and strong, with a great deal of groaning and anathematising ; but though these peculiarities of both ladies might have been learned " on application " to any of the various swains who had been rejected by them, no inquiry was ever made by the more fortunate men who took them honestly on trust, and on account of their visible personal attractions. And though these instances seem drawn from a lower class of life, I contend that the axiom holds good in all states of society, save, of course, in the case of purely mercenary marriages, which, however, are by no means so common in occurrence, or at all events so fatal in their results, as many of our novel-writers wish us to believe.

It was undoubtedly the case with Geoffrey Ludlow. He was a man as free from gross passions, as unlikely to take a sudden caprice, or to give the reins to his will, as any of his kind. His intimates would as soon have thought of the bronze statue of Achilles "committing" itself as Geoff Ludlow ; and yet it was for the dead-gold hair, the deep-violet eyes, and the pallid face, that he had married Margaret Dacre ; and on her mental attributes he had not bestowed one single thought. He had not had much time, certainly ; but however long his courtship might have been, I doubt whether he would have penetrated very far into the mysteries of her idiosyncrasy. He had a certain theory that she was "artistic;" a word which, with him, took the place of "romantic" with other people, as opposed to "practical." Geoff hated "practical" people ; perhaps because he had suffered from an over-dose of practicality in his own home. He would far sooner that his wife should *not* have been able to make pies and puddings, and cut-out baby-linen, than that she should have excelled in those notable domestic virtues. But none of these things had entered his head when he asked Margaret Dacre to join her lot with his,— save, perhaps, an undefined notion that no woman with such hair and such eyes could be so constituted. You would have looked in vain in Guinevere for the characteristics of Mrs. Rundell, or Miss Acton.

He had thought of her as his peerless beauty, as his realisation of a thousand waking dreams ; and that for the time was enough. But when he found her entering into and giving shape and colour to his schemes, he regarded her with worship increased a hundredfold. Constitutionally inert and adverse to thinking and deciding for himself,— with a wholesome doubt, moreover, of the efficacy of his own powers of judgment,—it was only the wide diversity of opinion which on nearly every subject existed between his mother and himself that had prevented him from long ago giving himself up entirely to the old lady's direction. But he now saw, readily enough, that he had found one whose guiding hand he could accept, who satisfied both his inclin-ations and his judgment ; and he surrendered himself with more than resignation—with delight, to Margaret's control.

And she ? It is paying her no great compliment to say that she was equal to the task ; it is making no strong accusation against her to say that she had expected and accepted the position from the first. I am at a loss how

L

exactly to set forth this woman's character as I feel it, fearful of enlarging on defects without showing something in their palliation—more fearful of omitting some mental ingredient which might serve to explain the twofold workings of her mind. When she left her home it was under the influence of love and pride ; wild girlish adoration of the " swell :" the man with the thick moustache, the white hands, the soft voice, the well-made boots ; the man so different in every respect from any thing she had previously known ; and girlish pride in enslaving one in social rank far beyond the railway-clerks, merchants' book-keepers, and Custom-House agents, who were marked down as game by her friends and compeers. The step once taken, she was a girl no more ; her own natural hardihood came to her aid, and enabled her to hold her own wherever she went. The man her companion,—a man of society simply from mixing with society, but naturally sheepish and stupid,—was amazed at her wondrous calmness and self-possession under all sorts of circumstances. It was an odd sort of *camaraderie* in which they mixed, both at home and abroad; one where the *laissez-aller* spirit was always predominant, and where those who said and did as they liked were generally most appreciated ; but there was a something in Margaret Dacre which compelled a kind of respect even from the wildest. Where she was, the drink never degenerated into an orgie ; and though the *cancans* and *doubles entendres* might ring round the room, all outward signs of decency were preserved. In the wild crew with which she was mixed she stood apart, sometimes riding the whirlwind with them, but always directing the storm; and while invariably showing herself the superior, so tempering her superiority as to gain the obedience and respect, if not the regard, of all those among whom she was thrown. How did this come about ? Hear it in one sentence—that she was as cold as ice, and as heartless as a stone. She loved the man who had betrayed her with all the passion which had been vouchsafed to her. She loved him, as I have said, at first, from his difference to all her hitherto surroundings ; then she loved him for having made her love him and yield to him. She had not sufficient mental power to analyse her own feelings; but she recognised that she had not much heart, was not easily moved; and

therefore she gave extraordinary credit, which he did not deserve, to him who had had the power to turn her as he listed.

But still, on him, her whole powers of loving stopped—
spent, used-up. Her devotion to him—inexplicable to
herself—was spaniel-like in its nature. She took his re-
proaches, his threats, at the last his desertion, and loved him
still. During the time they were together she had temptation on every side ; but not merely did she continue faithful,
but her fidelity was never shaken even in thought. Although
in that shady *demi-monde* there is a queer kind of honour-
code extant among the Lovelaces and the Juans, far stricter
than they think themselves called upon to exercise when out
of their own territory, there are of course exceptions, who
hold the temptation of their friend's mistress but little less
piquante than the seduction of their friend's wife ; but none
of these had the smallest chance with Margaret. What in
such circles is systematically known by the name of a *caprice*
never entered her mind. Even at the last, when she found
herself deserted, penniless, she knew that a word would
restore her to a position equivalent, apparently, to that she
had occupied ; but she would not have spoken that word
to have saved her from the death which she was so nearly
meeting.

In those very jaws of death, from which she had just been
rescued, a new feeling dawned upon her. As she lay back
in the arm-chair in Flexor's parlour, dimly sounding in her
ears, at first like the monotonous surging of the waves, afterwards shaping itself into words, but always calm and grave
and kind, came Geoff's voice. She could scarcely make out
what was said, but she knew what was meant from the mo-
dulation and the tone. Then, when Mr. Potts had gone to
fetch Dr. Rollit, she knew that she was left alone with the
owner of the voice, and she brought all her strength together
to raise her eyelids and look at him. She saw the quiet
earnest face, she marked the intense gaze, and she let her
light fingers fall on the outstretched hand, and muttered her
" Bless you !—saved me !" with a gratitude which was not
merely an expression of grateful feeling for his rescuing her
from death, but partook more of the cynic's definition of the
word—a recognition of benefits to come.

It sprung up in her mind like a flame. It did more
towards effecting her cure, even in the outset, than all the

stimulants and nourishment which Dr. Rollit administered. It was with her while consciousness remained, and flashed across her the instant consciousness returned. A home, the chances of a home—nothing but that—somewhere, with walls, and a fire, and a roof to keep off the pelting of the bitter rain. Walls with pictures and a floor with carpets; not a workhouse, not such places as she had spent the night in on her weary desolate tramp; but such as she had been accustomed to. And some one to care for her—no low whisperings, and pressed hands, and averted glances, and flight; but a shoulder to rest her head against, a strong arm round her to save her from—O God!—those awful black pitiless streets. Rest, only rest,—that was her craving. Let her once more be restored to ordinary strength, and then let her rest until she died. Ah, had she not had more than the ordinary share of trouble and disquietude, and could not a haven be found for her at last? She recollected how, in the first flush of her wildness, she had pitied all her old companions soberly settling down in life; and now how gladly would she change lots with them! Was it come? was the chance at hand? Had she drifted through the storm long enough, and was the sun now breaking through the clouds? She thought so, even as she lay nearer death than life, and through the shimmering of her eyelids caught a fleeting glimpse of Geoff Ludlow's face, and heard his voice as in a dream; she knew so after the second time of his calling on her in her convalescence; knew she might tell him the story of her life, which would only bind a man of his disposition more strongly to her; knew that such a feeling engendered in such a man at his time of life was deep and true and lasting, and that once taken to his heart, her position was secure for ever.

And what was her feeling for him who thus rose up out of the darkness, and was to give her all for which her soul had been pining? Love? Not one particle. She had no love left. She had not been by any means bounteously provided with that article at the outset, and all that she had she had expended on one person. Of love, of what we know by love, of love as he himself understood it, she had not one particle for Geoffrey. But there was a feeling which she could hardly explain to herself. It would have been respect, respect for his noble heart, his thorough uprightness, and strict sense of honour; but this respect was diluted by an appreciation of his dubiety, his vacillation, his utter impotency of saying a harsh word or doing a harsh thing; and diluted in a way which invested the cold feeling of respect with a warmer hue, and rendered him, if less perfect, certainly more interesting in her eyes. Never, even for an instant, had she thought of him with love-passion; not when she gazed dreamily at him out of the voluptuous depths of her deep-violet eyes; not when, on that night when all had been arranged between them, she had lain on his breast in the steel-blue rays of the spring moon. She had—well, feigned it, if you like,—though she would scarcely avow that, deeming rather that she had accepted the devotion which he had offered her without repelling it. *Il y a toujours l'un qui baise, l'autre qui tend la joue.* That axiom, unromantic, but true in most cases, was strictly fulfilled in the present instance. Margaret proffered no love, but accepted, if not willingly, at least with a thorough show of graciousness, all that was proffered to her. And in the heartfelt worship of Geoffrey Ludlow there was something inexplicably attractive to her. Attractive, probably, because of its entire novelty and utter unselfishness. She could compare it with nothing she had ever seen or known. To her first lover there had been the attraction of enchaining the first love of a very young girl, the romance of stolen meetings and secret interviews, the enchantment of an elopement, which was looked upon as a great sin by those whom he scorned, and a great triumph by those whose applause he envied; the gratification of creating the jealousy of his compeers, and of being talked about as an example to be shunned by those whom he despised. He had the satisfaction of flaunting her beauty through the world, and of gaining that world's applause for his success in having made it succumb to him. But how was it with Geoffrey? The very opposite, in every way. At the very best her early history must be shrouded in doubt and obscurity. If known it might act prejudicially against her husband with his patrons, and those on whom he was dependent for his livelihood. Even her beauty could not afford him much source of gratification, save to himself; he could seldom or never enjoy that reflected pleasure which a sensible man feels at the world's admiration of his wife; for had he not himself told her that their life would be of the quietest, and that they would mix with very few people?

No! if ever earnest, true, and unselfish love existed in the world, it was now, she felt, bestowed upon her. What in the depths of her despair she had faintly hoped for, had come to her with treble measure. Her course lay plain and straight before her. It was not a very brilliant course, but it was quiet and peaceful and safe. So away all thoughts of the past! drop the curtain on the feverish excitement, the wild dream of hectic pleasure! Shut it out; and with it the dead dull heartache, the keen sense of wrong, the desperate struggle for bare life.

So Margaret dropped that curtain on her wedding-day, with the full intention of never raising it again.

CHAPTER III.

ANNIE.

LORD CATERHAM'S suggestion that Annie Maurice should cultivate her drawing-talent was made after due reflection. He saw, with his usual quickness of perception, that the girl's life was fretting away within her; that the conventional round of duties which fell to her lot as his mother's companion was discharged honestly enough, but without interest or concern. He never knew why Lady Beauport wanted a companion. So long as he had powers of judging character, he had never known her have an intimate friend; and when, at the death of the old clergyman with whom Annie had so long been domesticated, it was proposed to receive her into the mansion at St. Barnabas Square, Lord Caterham had been struck with astonishment, and could not possibly imagine what duties she would be called upon to fulfil. He heard that the lady henceforth to form a part of their establishment was young, and that mere fact was in itself a cause for wonder. There was no youth there, and it was a quality which was generally openly tabooed. Lady Beauport's woman was about fifty, a thorough mistress of her art, an artist in complexion before whom Madame Rachel might have bowed; a cunning and skilled labourer in all matters appertaining to the hair; a person

whose anatomical knowledge exceeded that of many medical
students, and who produced effects undreamt of by the
most daring sculptors. There were no nephews or nieces to
come on visits, to break up the usual solemnity reigning
throughout the house, with young voices and such laughter
as is only heard in youth, to tempt the old people into
a temporary forgetfulness of self, and into a remembrance
of days when they had hopes and fears and human interest in matters passing around them. There were sons
—yes! Caterham himself, who had never had one youthful thought or one youthful aspiration, whose playmate
had been the physician, whose toys the wheel-chair in which
he sat and the irons by which his wrecked frame was supported, who had been precocious at six and a man at twelve ;
and Lionel—but though of the family, Lionel was not of the
house ; he never used to enter it when he could make any
possible excuse ; and long before his final disappearance his
visits had been restricted to those occasions when he thought
his father could be bled or his mother cajoled. What was a
girl of two-and-twenty to do in such a household, Caterham
asked ; but got no answer. It had been Lady Beauport's
plan, who knew that Lord Beauport had been in the habit of
contributing a yearly something towards Miss Maurice's
support ; and she thought that it would be at least no extra
expense to have the young woman in the house, where she
might make herself useful with her needle, and could
generally sit with Mrs. Parkins the housekeeper.

But Lord Beauport would not have this. Treated as a
lady, as a member of his own family in his house, or properly
provided for out of it, should Annie Maurice be : my lady's
companion, but my cousin always. No companionship with
Mrs. Parkins, no set task or suggested assistance. Her
own room, her invariable presence when the rest of the
family meet together, if you please. Lady Beauport did
not please at first ; but Lord Beauport was firm, firm as
George Brakespere used to be in the old days ; and Lady
Beauport succumbed with a good grace, and was glad of it
ever after. For Annie Maurice not merely had the sweetest
temper and the most winning ways,—not merely read in the
softest voice, and had the taste to choose the most charming
"bits," over which Lady Beauport would hum first with
approval and then with sleep,—not merely played and sung

delightfully, without ever being hoarse or disinclined,—not merely could ride with her back to the horses, and dress for the Park exactly as Lady Beauport wished—neither dowdy nor swell,—but she brought old-fashioned receipts for quaint country dishes with which she won Mrs. Parkins's heart, and she taught Hodgson, Lady Beauport's maid, a new way of *gauffreing* which broke down all that Abigail's icy spleen. Her bright eyes, her white teeth, her sunny smile, did all the rest for her throughout the household : the big footmen moved more quickly for her than for their mistress; the coachman, with whom she must have interchanged confidential communications, told the groom she "knowed the p'ints of an 'oss as well as he did—spotted them wind-galls in Jack's off 'ind leg, and says, 'a cold-water bandage for them,' she says;" the women-servants, more likely than any of the others to take offence, were won by the silence of her bell and her independence of toilette assistance.

Lord Caterham saw all this, and understood her popularity; but he saw too that with it all Annie Maurice was any thing but happy. Reiteration of conventionality,—the reception of the callers and the paying of the calls, the morning concerts and afternoon botanical promenades, the occasional Opera-goings, and the set dinner-parties at home,—these weighed heavily on her. She felt that her life was artificial, that she had nothing in common with the people with whom it was passed, save when she escaped to Lord Caterham's room. He was at least natural ; she need talk or act no conventionality with him ; might read, or work, or chat with him as she liked. But she wanted some purpose in life—that Caterham saw, and saw almost with horror ; for that purpose might tend to take her away ; and if she left him, he felt as though the only bright portion of his life would leave him too.

Yes ; he had begun to acknowledge this to himself. He had fought against the idea, tried to laugh it off, but it had always recurred to him. For the first time in his life, he had moments of happy expectancy of an interview that was to come, hours of happy reflection over an interview that was past. Of course the Carry-Chesterton times came up in his mind ; but these were very different. Then he was in a wild state of excitement and tremor, of flushed cheeks and beating heart and trembling lips ; he thrilled at the sound of her voice; his blood, usually so calm, coursed through his veins at the touch of her hand; his passion was a delirium as alarming as it was intoxicating. The love of to-day had nothing in common with that bygone time. There was no similarity between Carry Chesterton's dash and *aplomb* and Annie Maurice's quiet domestic ways. The one scorched him with a glance; the other soothed him with a word. How sweet it was to lie back in his chair with half-shut eyes, as in a dream, and watch her moving quietly about, setting every thing in order, putting fresh flowers in his vases, dusting his writing-table, laughingly upbraiding the absent Algy Barford, and taxing him with the delinquency of a half-smoked cigar on the mantel-piece, and a pile of cigar-ash on the carpet. Then he would bid her finish her house-work, and she would wheel his chair to the table and read the newspapers to him, and listen to his quaint, shrewd, generally sarcastic comments on all she read. And he would sit, listening to the music of her voice, looking at the quiet charms of her simply-banded glossy dark-brown hair, at the play of feature illustrating every thing she read. It was a brother's love he told himself at first, and fully believed it; a brother's love for a favourite sister. He thought so until he pictured to himself her departure to some friend's or other, until he imagined the house without her, himself without her, and—and she with some one else. And then Lord Caterham confessed to himself that he loved Annie Maurice with all his soul, and simultaneously swore that by no act or word of his should she or any one else ever know it.

The Carry-Chesterton love-fever had been so sharp in its symptoms, and so prostrating in its results, that this second attack fell with comparative mildness on the sufferer. He had no night-watches now, no long feverish tossings to and fro waiting for the daylight, no wild remembrance of parting words and farewell hand-clasps. She was there; her "good-night" had rung out sweetly and steadily without a break in the situation; her sweet smile had lit up her face; her last words had been of some projected reading or work for the morrow. It was all friend and friend or brother and sister to every one but him. The very first night after Miss Chesterton had been presented to Lady Beauport, the latter, seeing with a woman's quickness the position of affairs, had spoken of the young lady from Homersham as "that dreadful person," "that terribly-forward young woman," and thereby goaded Lord Caterham into worse love-madness. Now both father and mother were perpetually congratulating themselves and him on having found some one who seemed to be able to enter into and appreciate their eldest son's "odd ways." This immunity from parental worry and supervision was pleasant, doubtless; but did it not prove that to eyes that were not blinded by love-passion there was nothing in Miss Maurice's regard for her cousin more than was compatible with cousinly affection, and with pity for one so circumstanced? So Lord Caterham had it; and who shall say that his extreme sensitiveness had deceived him?

It was the height of the London season, and Lady Beauport was fairly in the whirl. So was Annie Maurice, whose position was already as clearly defined amongst the set as if she had been duly ticketed with birth, parentage, education, and present employment. Hitherto her experience had decidedly been pleasant, and she had found that all the companion-life, as set forth in fashionable novels, had been ridiculously exaggerated. From no one had she received any thing approaching a slight, any thing approaching an insult. The great ladies mostly ignored her, though some made a point of special politeness; the men received her as a gentlewoman, with whom flirtation might be possible on an emergency, though unremunerative as a rule. Her perpetual attendance on Lady Beauport had prevented her seeing as much as usual of Lord Caterham; and it was with a sense of relief that she found a morning at her disposal, and sent Stephens to intimate her coming to his master.

She found him as usual, sitting listlessly in his wheel-chair, the newspaper folded ready to his hand, but unfolded and unread. He looked up, and smiled as she entered the room, and said: "At last, Annie, at last! Ah, I knew such a nice little girl who came here from Ricksborough, and lightened my solitary hours; but we've had a fashionable lady here lately, who is always at concerts or operas, or eating ices at Gunter's, or crushing into horticultural marquees, or—"

"Arthur, you ought to be ashamed of yourself! You know, however, I won't stoop to argue with you, sir. I'll only say that the little girl from Ricksborough has come back again, and that the fashionable lady has got a holiday and gone away."

"That's good; but I say, just stand in the light, Annie."

"Well, what's the matter now?"

"What has the little girl from Ricksborough done with all her colour? Where's the brightness of her eyes?"

"Ah, you don't expect every thing at once, do you, sir? Her natural colour has gone; but she has ordered a box from Bond Street; and as for the brightness of her eyes—"

"O, there's enough left; there is indeed, especially when she fires up in that way. But you're not looking well, Annie. I'm afraid my lady's doing too much with you."

"She's very kind, and wishes me to be always with her."

"Yes; but she forgets that the vicarage of Ricksborough was scarcely good training-ground for the races in which she has entered you, however kindly you take to the running." He paused a minute as he caught Annie's upturned gaze, and said: "I don't mean that, dear Annie. I know well enough you hate it all; and I was only trying to put the best face on the matter. What else can I do?"

"I know that, Arthur; nor is it Lady Beauport's fault that she does not exactly comprehend how a series of gaieties can be any thing but agreeable to a country-bred young woman. There are hundreds of girls who would give any thing to be 'brought out' under such chaperonage and in such a manner."

"You are very sweet and good to say so, Annie, and to look at it in that light, but I would give any thing to get you more time to yourself."

"That proves more plainly than any thing, Arthur, that you don't consider me one of the aristocracy; for their greatest object in life appears to me to prevent their having any time to themselves."

"Miss Maurice," said Lord Caterham with an assumption of gravity, "these sentiments are really horrible. I thought I missed my *Mill on Liberty* from the bookshelves. I am afraid, madame, you have been studying the doctrines of a man who has had the frightful audacity to think for himself."

"No, indeed, Arthur; nothing of the sort. I did take down the book—though of course you had never missed it; but it seemed a dreary old thing, and so I put it back again. No, I haven't a radical thought or feeling in me—except sometimes."

"And when is the malignant influence at work, pray?"

" When I see those footmen dressed up in that ridiculous costume, with powder in their heads, I confess then to being struck with wonder at a society which permits such monstrosity, and degrades its fellow-creatures to such a level."

" O, for a stump !" cried Caterham, shaking in his chair and with the tears running down his cheeks ; " this display of virtuous indignation is quite a new and hitherto undiscovered feature in the little girl from Ricksborough ; though of course you are quite wrong in your logic. Your fault should be found with the creatures who permit themselves to be so reduced. That 'dreary old thing,' Mr. Mill, would tell you that if the supply ceased, the demand would cease likewise. But don't let us talk about politics, for heaven's sake, even in fun. Let us revert to our original topic."

" What was that ?"

" What was that ! Why you, of course ! Don't you recollect that we decided that you should have some drawing-lessons ?"

" I recollect you were good enough to—"

" Annie ! Annie ! I thought it was fully understood that my goodness was a tabooed subject. No ; you remember we arranged, on the private-view day of the Exhibition, with that man who had those two capital pictures—what's his name ?—Ludlow, to give you some lessons."

" Yes ; but Mr. Ludlow himself told us that he could not come for some little time ; he was going out of town."

" I've had a letter from him this morning, explaining the continuance of his absence. What do you think is the reason ?"

" He was knocked up, and wanted rest ?"

" N-no ; apparently not."

" He's not ill ? O, Arthur, he's not ill ?"

" Not in the least, Annie,—there's not the least occasion for you to manifest any uneasiness." Lord Caterham's voice was becoming very hard and his face very rigid. " Mr. Ludlow's return to town was delayed in order that he might enjoy the pleasures of his honeymoon in the Isle of Wight."

" His what ?"

" His honeymoon ; he informs me that he is just married."

" Married ? Geoff married ? Who to ? What a very extraordinary thing ! Who is he married to ?"

" He has not reposed sufficient confidence in me to ac-

quaint me with the lady's name, probably guessing rightly
that I was not in the least curious upon the point, and that
to know it would not have afforded me the slightest satisfaction."

"No, of course not; how very odd!" That was all
Annie Maurice said, her chin resting on her hand, her eyes
looking straight before her.

"What is very odd?" said Caterham, in a harsh voice.
"That Mr. Ludlow should get married? Upon my honour
I can't see the eccentricity. It is not, surely, his extreme youth that should provoke astonishment, nor his
advanced age, for the matter of that. He's not endowed
with more wisdom than most of us to prevent his making a
fool of himself. What there is odd about the fact of his
marriage I cannot understand."

"No, Arthur," said Annie, very quietly, utterly ignoring
the querulous tone of Caterham's remarks; "very likely you
can't understand it, because Mr. Ludlow is a stranger to you,
and you judge him as you would any other stranger. But if
you'd known him in the old days when he used to come up
to us at Willesden, and papa was always teasing him about
being in love with the French teacher at Minerva House, a
tall old lady with a moustache; or with the vicar's daughter,
a sandy-haired girl in spectacles; and then poor papa would
laugh,—O, how he would laugh!—and declare that Mr.
Ludlow would be a bachelor to the end of his days. And
now he's married, you say? How very, very strange!"

If Lord Caterham had been going to make any further
unpleasant remark, he checked himself abruptly, and looking
into Annie's upturned pondering face, said, in his usual
tone,

"Well, married or not married, he won't throw us over;
he will hold to his engagement with us. His letter tells me
he will be back in town at the end of the week, and will then
settle times with us; so that we shall have our drawing-
lessons after all."

But Annie, evidently thoroughly preoccupied, only answered
methodically, "Yes—of course—thank you—yes." So Lord
Caterham was left to chew the cud of his own reflections,
which, from the manner in which he frowned to himself, and
sat blankly drumming with his fingers on the desk before
him, was evidently no pleasant mental pabulum. So that

he was not displeased when there came a sonorous tap at the door, to which, recognising it at once, he called out, " Come in !"

CHAPTER IV.

ALGY BARFORD'S NEWS.

IT was the Honourable Algy Barford who opened the door, and came in with his usual light and airy swing, stopping the minute he saw a lady present, to remove his hat and to give an easy bow. He recognised Annie at once, and, as she and he were great allies, he went up to her and shook hands.

"Charmed to see you, Miss Maurice. This is delightful— give you my word! Come to see this dear old boy here— how are you, Caterham, my dear fellow?—and find you in his den, lighting it up like—like—like—I'm regularly basketed, by Jove! You know what you light it up like, Miss Maurice."

Annie laughed as she said, " O, of course I know, Mr. Barford ; but I'm sorry to say the illumination is about immediately to be extinguished, as I must run away. So good-bye ; good-bye, Arthur. I shall see you to-morrow." And she waved her hand, and tripped lightly away.

" Gad, what a good-natured charming girl that is !" said Algy Barford, looking after her. " I always fancy that if ever I could have settled down—but I never could—impossible ! I'm without exception the most horrible scoundrel that—what's the matter, Caterham, dear old boy? you seem very down this morning, floundered, by Jove, so far as flatness is concerned. What is it ?"

" I—oh, I don't know, Algy ; a little bored, perhaps, this morning—hipped, you know."

" Know! I should think I did. I'm up to my watch-guard myself—think I'll take a sherry peg, just to keep myself up. This is a dull world, sir ; a very wearying orb. Gad, sometimes I think my cousin, poor Jack Hamilton, was right, after all."

" What did he say?" asked Caterham, not caring a bit, but for the sake of keeping up the conversation.

"Say! well, not much; he wasn't a talker, poor Jack; but what he did say was to the purpose. He was a very lazy kind of bird, and frightfully easily bored; so one day he got up, and then he wrote a letter saying that he'd lived for thirty years, and that the trouble of dressing himself every morning and undressing himself every night was so infernal that he couldn't stand it any longer; and then he blew his brains out."

"Ah," said Lord Caterham; "he got tired of himself, you see; and when you once do that, there's nobody you get so tired of."

"I daresay, dear old boy, though it's a terrific notion. Can't say I'm tired of myself quite yet, though there are times when I have a very low opinion of myself, and think seriously of cutting myself the next time we meet. What's the news with you, my dear Caterham?"

"News! what should be the news with me, Algy? Shut up in this place, like a rat in a cage, scarcely seeing any one but the doctor."

"Couldn't see a better fellow for news, my dear old boy. Doctors were always the fellows for news,—and barbers!— Figaro hé and Figaro la, and all that infernal rubbish that people laugh at when Ronconi sings it, always makes me deuced melancholy, by Jove. Well, since you've no news for me, let me think what I heard at the Club. Deuced nice club we've got now; best we've ever had since that dear old Velvet Cushion was done up."

"What's it called?"

"The Pelham; nothing to do with the Newcastle people or any thing of that sort; called after some fellow who wrote a book about swells; or was the hero of a book about swells, or something. Deuced nice place, snug and cosy; a little overdone with Aldershot, perhaps, and, to a critical mind, there might be a thought too much Plunger; but I can stand the animal tolerably well."

"I know it; at least I've heard of it," said Caterham. "They play very high, don't they?"

"O, of course you've heard it, I forgot; dear old Lionel belonged to it. Play! n-no, I don't think so. You can if you like, you know, of course. For instance, Lampeter— Lamb Lampeter they call him; he's such a mild-looking party—won two thousand of Westonhanger the night before

last at *écarté*—two thousand pounds, sir, in crisp bank-notes!
All fair and above board too. They had a corner table
at first; but when Westonhanger was dropping his money
and began doubling the stakes, Lampeter said, 'All right,
my lord; I'm with you as far as you like to go; but when
so much money's in question, it perhaps might be advisable
to take one of the tables in the middle of the room, where
any one can stand round and see the play.' They did, and
Westonhanger's estate is worse by two thou'"

"As you say, that does not look at all as if they played
there."

"What I meant was that I didn't think dear old Lionel
ever dropped much there. I don't know, though; I rather
think Gamson had him one night. Wonderful little fellow,
Gamson!—tremendously good-looking boy!—temporary
extra-clerk at two guineas a-week in the Check and Counter-
check Office; hasn't got another regular rap in the world
besides his pay, and plays any stakes you like to name.
Seems to keep luck in a tube, like you do scent, and
squeezes it out whenever he wants it. I am not a playing
man myself; but I don't fancy it's very hard to win at the
Pelham. These Plungers and fellows up from the Camp,
they always will play; and as they've had a very heavy
dinner and a big drink afterwards, it stands to reason that
any fellow with a clear head and a knowledge of the game
can pick them up at once, without any sharp practice."

"Yes," said Lord Caterham, "it seems a very charming
place. I suppose wheel-chairs are not admitted? How
sorry I am! I should have so enjoyed mixing with the
delightful society which you describe, Algy. And what news
had Mr. Gamson and the other gentlemen?"

"Tell you what it is, Caterham, old boy, you've got a
regular wire-drawing fit on to-day. Let's see; what news
had I to tell you?—not from Gamson, of course, or any
of those hairy Yahoos from Aldershot, who are always
tumbling about the place. O, I know! Dick Ffrench has
just come up from Denne,—the next place, you know,
to Eversfield, your old uncle Ampthill's house; and he
says the old boy's frightfully ill—clear case of hooks, you
know; and I thought it might be advisable that your people
should know, in case any thing might be done towards
working the testamentary oracle. The old gentleman used

to be very spoony on Lionel, years ago, I think I've heard him say."

" Well, what then ?"

"Gad, you catch a fellow up like the Snapping-Turtle, Caterham. I don't know what then; but I thought if the thing were properly put to him—if there was any body to go down to Eversfield and square it with old Ampthill, he might leave his money—and there's no end of it, I hear —or some of it at least, to poor old Lionel."

"And suppose he did. Do you think, Algy Barford, after what has happened, that Lionel Brakespere could show his face in town? Do you think that a man of Lionel's spirit could face-out the cutting which he'd receive from every one ?—and rightly too; I'm not denying that. I only ask you if you think he could do it ?"

"My dear old Caterham, you are a perfect child !—coral and bells and blue sash, and all that sort of thing, by Jove ! If Lionel came back at this instant, there are very few men who'd remember his escapade, unless he stood in their way ; then, I grant you, they would bring it up as unpleasantly as they could. But if he were to appear in society as old Ampthill's heir, there's not a man in his old set that wouldn't welcome him; no, by George, not a woman of his acquaintance that wouldn't try and hook him for self or daughter, as the case might be."

"I'm sorry to hear it," was all Caterham said in reply.

What did Lord Caterham think of when his friend was gone? What effect had the communication about Mr. Ampthill's probable legacy had on him? But one thing crossed his mind. If Lionel returned free, prosperous, and happy, would he not fall in love with Annie Maurice? His experience in such matters had been but limited; but judging by his own feelings, Lord Caterham could imagine nothing more likely.

CHAPTER V.

SETTLING DOWN.

IT was not likely that a man of Geoffrey Ludlow's temperament would for long keep himself from falling into
what was to be the ordinary tenor of his life, even had his
newly-espoused wife been the most exacting of brides, and
delighted in showing her power by keeping him in perpetual
attendance upon her. It is almost needless to say that
Margaret was guilty of no weakness of this kind. If the
dread truth must be told, she took far too little interest in
the life to which she had devoted herself to busy herself
about it in detail. She had a general notion that her whole
future was to be intensely respectable ; and in the minds of
all those persons with whom she had hitherto been associated,
respectability meant dulness of the most appalling kind ;
meant two-o'clock-shoulder-of-mutton-and-weak-Romford-ale
dinner, five o'clock tea, knitting, prayers, and a glass of
cold water before going to bed ; meant district-visiting and
tract-distributing, poke bonnets and limp skirts, a class on
Sunday afternoons, and a visit to the Crystal Palace with
the school-children on a summer's day. She did not think
it would be quite as bad as this in her case ; indeed, she
had several times been amused—so far as it lay in her now
to be amused—by hearing Geoffrey speak of himself, with
a kind of elephantine liveliness, as a roisterer and a Bohemian. But she was perfectly prepared to accept whatever
happened ; and when Geoff told her, the day after his
mother's visit, that he must begin work again and go on as
usual, she took it as a matter of course.

So Geoff arranged his new studio, and found out his best
light, and got his easel into position ; and Flexor arrived
with the lay-figure which had been passing its vacation in
Little Flotsam Street; and the great model recognised Mrs.
Geoffrey Ludlow, who happened to look in, with a deferen-
tial bow, and, with what seemed best under the circumstances,
a look of extreme astonishment, as though he had never
seen her before, and expected to find quite a different
person.

Gradually and one by one all the old accessories of Geoff's

daily life seemed closing round him. A feeble ring, heard while he and his wife were at breakfast, would be followed by the servant's announcement of "the young person, sir, a-waitin' in the stujo;" and the young person—a model— would be found objurgating the distance from town, and yet appreciative of the beauty of the spot when arrived at.

And Mr. Stompff had come; of course he had. No sooner did he get Geoff's letter announcing his return than he put himself into a hansom cab, and went up to Elm Lodge. For Mr. Stompff was a man of business. His weak point was, that he judged other men by his own standard; and knowing perfectly well that if any other man had had the success which Geoffrey Ludlow had achieved that year, he (Stompff) would have worked heaven and earth to get him into his clutches, he fancied that Caniche, and all the other dealers, would be equally voracious, and that the best thing he could do would be to strike the iron while it was hot, and secure Ludlow for himself. He thought too that this was rather a good opportunity for such a proceeding, as Ludlow's exchequer was likely to be low, and he could the more easily be won over. So the hansom made its way to Elm Lodge; and its fare, under the title of "a strange gentleman, sir!" was ushered into Geoff's studio.

"Well, and how are you, Ludlow! What did she say, 'a strange gentleman'? Yes, Mary, my love! I am a strange gentleman, as you'll find out before I've done with you." Mr. Stompff laid his finger to his nose, and winked with exquisite facetiousness. "Well, and how are you? safe and sound, and all the rest of it! And how's Mrs. L.? Must introduce me before I go. And what are you about now, eh? What's this?"

He stopped before the canvas on the easel, and began examining it attentively.

"That's nothing!" said Geoffrey; "merely an outline of a notion I had of the Esplanade at Brighton. I don't think it would make a bad subject. You see, here I get the invalids in Bath-chairs, the regular London swells pro- menading it, the boatmen; the Indian-Mutiny man, with his bandaged foot and his arm in a sling and his big beard; some excursionists with their baskets and bottles; some Jews, and—"

M 2

"Capital! nothing could be better! Hits the taste of the day, my boy; shoots folly, and no flies, as the man said. That's your ticket! Any body else seen that!"

"Well, literally not a soul. It's only just begun, and no one has been here since I returned."

"That's all right! Now what's the figure? You're going to open your mouth, I know; you fellows always do when you've made a little success."

"Well, you see," began old Geoff, in his usual hesitating diffident manner, "it's a larger canvas than I've worked on hitherto, and there are a good many more figures, and—"

"Will five hundred suit you?"

"Ye-es! Five hundred would be a good price, for—"

"All right! shake hands on it! I'll give you five hundred for the copyright—right and away, mind!—sketch, picture, and right of engraving. We'll get it to some winter-gallery, and you'll have another ready for the Academy. Nothing like that, my boy! I know the world, and you don't. What the public likes, you give them as much of as you can. Don't you believe in over-stocking the market with Ludlows; that's all stuff! Let 'em have the Ludlows while they want 'em. In a year or two they'll fight like devils to get a Jones or a Robinson, and wonder how the deuce any body could have spent their money on such a dauber as Ludlow. Don't you be offended, my boy; I'm only speakin' the truth. I buy you because the public wants you; and I turn an honest penny in sellin' you again; not that I'm any peculiar nuts on you myself, either one way or t'other. Come, let's wet this bargain, Ludlow, my boy; some of that dry sherry you pulled out when I saw you last at Brompton, eh?"

Geoffrey rang the bell; the sherry was produced, and Mr. Stompff enjoyed it with great gusto.

"Very neat glass of sherry as ever I drank. Well, Ludlow, success to our bargain! Give it a good name, mind; that's half the battle; and, I say, I wouldn't do too much about the Jews, eh? You know what I mean; none of that d—d nose-trick, you know. There's first-rate customers among the Jews, though they know more about pictures than most people, and won't be palmed off like your Manchester coves; but when they do like a thing, they will have it; and though they always insist upon discount, yet even then,

with the price one asks for a picture, it pays. Well, you'll
be able to finish that and two others—O, how do you do,
mam?"

This last to Margaret, who, not knowing that her husband
had any one with him, was entering the studio. She bowed,
and was about to withdraw; but Geoff called her back, and
presented Mr. Stompff to her.

" Very glad to make your acquaintance, mam," said that
worthy, seizing her hand; "heard of you often, and recognise
the picture of Scyllum and Something in an instant. Enjoyed yourself in the country, I 'ope. That's all right.
But nothing like London; that's the place to pick up the
dibs. I've been telling our friend here he must stick to
it, now he's a wife to provide for; for we know what's what,
don't we, Mrs. Ludlow? Three pictures a year, my boy,
and good-sized 'uns too; no small canvases: that's what we
must have out of you."

Geoffrey laughed as he said, " Well, no; not quite so
much as that. Recollect, I intend to take my wife out occasionally; and besides, I've promised to give some drawing
lessons."

" What!" shrieked Mr. Stompff; "drawing-lessons! a man
in your position give drawing-lessons! I never heard such
madness! You musn't do that, Ludlow."

The words were spoken so decidedly that Margaret bit
her lips, and turned to look at her husband, whose face
flushed a deep red, and whose voice stuttered tremendously
as he gasped out, " B-but I shall! D-don't you say 'must,'
please, to me, Mr. Stompff; because I don't like it; and
I don't know what the d-deuce you mean by using such a
word!"

" Mr. Stompff glanced at Margaret, whose face expressed
the deepest disgust; so, clearly perceiving the mistake he
had made, he said, " Well, of course I only spoke as a
friend; and when one does that he needn't be in much
doubt as to his reward. When I said 'must,' which seems
to have riled you so, Ludlow, I said it for your own sake.
However, you and I sha'n't fall out about that. Don't you
give your pictures to any one else, and we shall keep square
enough. Where are you going to give drawing-lessons, if
one may be bold enough to ask?"

" In St. Barnabas Square, to a young lady, a very old

friend of mine, and a *protégée* of Lord Caterham's," said Geoffrey, whose momentary ire had died out.

"O, Lord Caterham's! that queer little deformed chap. Good little fellow, too, they say he is ; sharp, and all that kind of thing. Well, there's no harm in that. I thought you were going on the philanthropic dodge—to schools and working-men, and that lay. There's one rule in life,—you never lose any thing by being civil to a bigwig; and this little chap, I daresay, has influence in his way. By the way, you might ask him to give a look in at my gallery, if he's passing by. Never does any harm, that kind of thing. Well, I can't stay here all day. Men of business must always be pushing on, Mrs. Ludlow. Good day to you; and, I say, when—hem ! there's any thing to renounce the world, the flesh, and the—hey, you understand? any body wanted to promise and vow, you know,—I'm ready; send for me. I've got my eye on a silver mug already. Good-bye, Ludlow ; see you next week. Three before next May, recollect, and all for me. Ta-ta !" and Mr. Stompff stepped into his cab, and drove off, kissing his fat pudgy little hands, with a great belief in Geoffrey Ludlow and a holy horror of his wife.

In the course of the next few days Geoffrey wrote to Lord Caterham, telling him that he was quite ready to commence Miss Maurice's instruction ; and shortly after-wards received an answer naming a day for the lessons to commence. On arriving at the house Geoff was shown into Lord Caterham's room, and there found Annie waiting to receive him. Geoff advanced, and shook hands warmly ; but he thought Miss Maurice's manner was a little more reserved than on the last occasion of their meeting.

" Lord Caterham bade me make his excuses to you, Mr. Ludlow," said she. "He hopes to see you before you go; but he is not very well just now, and does not leave his room till later in the day."

Geoff was a little hurt at the "Mr. Ludlow." Like all shy men, he was absurdly sensitive ; and at once thought that he saw in this mode of address a desire on Annie's part to show him his position as drawing-master. So he merely said he was "sorry for the cause of Lord Caterham's absence ;" and they proceeded at once to work.

But the ice on either side very soon melted away. Geoff had brought with him an old sketch-book, filled with scraps of landscape and figures, quaint *bizarre* caricatures, and little bits of every-day life, all drawn at Willesden Priory or in its neighbourhood, all having some little history of their own appealing to Annie's love of those old days and that happy home. And as she looked over them, she began to talk about the old times; and very speedily it was, "O, Geoff, don't you remember?" and "O, Geoff, will you ever forget?" and so on; and they went on sketching and talking until, to Annie at least, the present and the intervening time faded away, and she was again the petted little romp, and he was dear old Geoff, her best playmate, her earliest friend, whom she used to drive round the gravel-paths in her skipping-rope harness, and whose great shock head of hair used to cause her such infinite wonder and amusement.

As she sat watching him bending over the drawing, she remembered with what anxiety she used to await his coming at the Priory, and with what perfect good-humour he bore all her childish whims and vagaries. She remembered how he had always been her champion when her papa had been *brusque* or angry with her, saying, "Fairy was too small to be scolded;" how when just before that horrible bankruptcy took place and all the household were busy with their own cares, she, suffering under some little childish illness, was nursed by Geoff, then staying in the house with a vague idea of being able to help Mr. Maurice in his trouble; how he carried her in his arms to and fro, to and fro, during the whole of one long night, and hushed her to sleep with the soft tenderness of a woman. She had thought of him often and often during her life at Ricksborough Vicarage, always with the same feelings of clinging regard and perfect trust; and now she had found him. Well, no, not him exactly; she doubted very much whether Mr. Ludlow the rising artist was the same as the "dear old Geoff" of the Willesden-Priory days. There was—and then, as she was thinking all this, Geoff raised his eyes from the drawing, and smiled his dear old happy smile, and put his pencil between his teeth, and slowly rubbed his hands while he looked over his sketch, so exactly as he used to do fifteen years before, that she felt more than ever annoyed at that news which Arthur had told her a few days ago about Mr. Ludlow being married.

Yes, it was annoyance she felt! there was no other word
for it.   In the old days he had belonged entirely to her, and
why should he not now?   Her papa had always said that it
was impossible Geoff could ever be any thing but an old
bachelor, and an old bachelor he should have remained.
What a ridiculous thing for a man at his time of life to
import a new element into it by marriage!   It would have
been so pleasant to have had him then, just in the old way;
to have talked to him and teased him, and looked up to him
just as she used to do, and now—O, no! it could not be the
same! no married man is ever the same with the friends of
his bachelorhood, especially female friends, as he was before.
And Mrs. Ludlow, what was she like? what could have
induced Geoff to marry her?   While Geoff's head was bent
over the drawing, Annie revolved all this rapidly in her mind,
and came to the conclusion that it must have been for
money that Geoff plunged into matrimony, and that Mrs.
Ludlow was either a widow with a comfortable jointure,
in which case Annie pictured her to herself as short, stout,
and red-faced, with black hair in bands and a perpetual
black-silk dress; or a small heiress of uncertain age, thin,
with hollow cheeks and a pointed nose, ringlets of dust-
coloured hair, a pinched waist, and a soured temper.   And
to think of Geoff's going and throwing away the rest of his
life on a person of this sort, when he might have been so
happy in his old bachelor way!

The more she thought of this the more she hated it.   Why
had he not announced to them that he was going to be
married, when she first met him after that long lapse of years?
To be sure, the rooms at the Royal Academy were scarcely
the place in which to enter on such a matter; but then—
who could she be? what was she like?   It was so long
since Geoff had been intimate with any one; she knew that
of course his range of acquaintance might have been changed
a hundred times and she not know one of them.   How very
strange that he did not say any thing about it now!   He
had been here an hour sketching and pottering about, and
yet had not breathed a word about it.   O, she would soon
settle that!

So the next time Geoff looked up from his sketch, she
said to him: "Are you longing to be gone, Geoffrey?
Getting fearfully bored?   Is a horrible *heimweh* settling

down upon your soul? I suppose under the circumstances it ought to be, if it isn't."

"Under what circumstances, Annie? I'm not bored a bit, nor longing to be gone. What makes you think so?"

"Only my knowledge of a fact which I've learned, though not from you—your marriage, Geoffrey."

"Not from me! Pardon me, Annie; I begged Lord Caterham, to whom I announced it, specially to name it to you. And, if you must know, little child, I wondered you had said nothing to me about it."

He looked at her earnestly as he said this; and there was a dash of disappointment in his honest eyes.

"I'm so sorry, Geoff—so sorry! But I didn't understand it so; really I didn't," said Annie, already half-penitent. "Lord Caterham told me of the fact, but as from himself, not from you; and—and I thought it odd that, considering all our old intimacy, you hadn't—"

"Odd! why, God bless my soul! Annie, you don't think that I shouldn't; but, you see, it was all so—At all events, I'm certain I told Lord Caterham to tell you."

Geoff was in a fix here. His best chance of repudiating the idea that he had willfully neglected informing Annie of his intended marriage was the true reason, that the marriage itself was, up to within the shortest time of its fulfilment, so unlooked for; but this would throw a kind of slur on his wife; at all events, would prompt inquiries; so he got through it as best he could with the stuttering excuses above recorded.

They seemed to avail with Annie Maurice; for she only said, "O, yes; I daresay it was some bungle of yours. You always used to make the most horrible mistakes, Geoff, I've heard poor papa say a thousand times, and get out of it in the lamest manner." Then, after a moment, she said, "You must introduce me to your wife, Geoffrey;" and, almost against her inclination, added, "What is she like?"

"Introduce you, little child? Why, of course I will, and tell her how long I have known you, and how you used to sit on my knee, and be my little pet," said old Geoff, in a transport of delight. "O, I think you'll like her, Annie. She is—yes, I may say so—she is very beautiful, and—and very quiet and good."

Geoff's ignorance of the world is painfully manifested in

this speech. No woman could possibly be pleased to hear of her husband having been in the habit of having any little pet on his knee ; and in advancing her being " very beautiful" as a reason for liking his wife, Geoff showed innocence which was absolutely refreshing.

Very beautiful ! Was that mere conjugal blindness or real fact ? Taken in conjunction with " very quiet and good," it looked like the former ; but then where beauty was concerned Geoff had always been a stern judge ; and it was scarcely likely that he would suffer his judgment, founded on the strictest abstract principles, to be warped by any whim or fancy. Very beautiful !—the quietude and goodness came into account,—very beautiful !

" O, yes ; I must come and see Mrs. Ludlow, please. You will name a day before you go ?"

" Name a day ! What for, Annie ?"

Lord Caterham was the speaker, sitting in his chair, and being wheeled in from his bedroom by Stephens. His tone was a little harsh ; his temper a little sharp. He had all along determined that Annie and Geoff should not be left alone together on the occasion of her first lesson. But *l'homme propose et Dieu dispose;* and Caterham had been unable to raise his head from his pillow, with one of those fearful neuralgic headaches which occasionally affected him.

" What for ! Why, to be introduced to Mrs. Ludlow ! By the way, you seem to have left your eyes in the other room, Arthur. You have not seen Mr. Ludlow before, have you ?"

" I beg Mr. Ludlow a thousand pardons !" said Caterham, who had forgotten the announcement of Geoffrey's marriage, and who hailed the recalling of the past with intense gratification. " I'm delighted to see you, Mr. Ludlow ; and very grateful to you for coming to fill up so agreeably some of our young lady's blank time. If I thought you were a conventional man, I should make you a pretty conventional speech of gratulation on your marriage ; but as I'm sure you're something much better, I leave that to be inferred."

" You are very good," said Geoff. " Annie was just saying that I should introduce my wife to her, and—"

" Of course, of course !" said Caterham, a little dashed by the familiarity of the " Annie." " I hope to see Mrs. Ludlow here ; not merely as a visitor to a wretched bachelor like myself; but I'm sure my mother would be very pleased to welcome her, and will, if you please, do herself the honour of calling on Mrs. Ludlow."

"Thank you, Arthur; you are very kind, and I appreciate it," said Annie, in a low voice, crossing to his chair; "but my going will be a different thing; I mean, as an old friend of Geoff's, *I* may go and see his wife."

An old friend of Geoff's! Still the same bond between them, in which he had no part—an intimacy with which he had nothing to do.

"Of course," said he; "nothing could be more natural."

"Little Annie coming to be introduced to Margaret!" thought Geoff, as he walked homeward, the lesson over. This, then, was to be Margaret's first introduction to his old friend. Not much fear of their not getting on together. And yet, on reflection, Geoff was not so sure of that, after all.

CHAPTER VI.

AT HOME.

THE people of Lowbar, lusty citizens with suburban residences — lawyers, proctors, and merchants, all warm people in money matters—did not think much of the advent into their midst of a man following an unrecognised profession, which had no ledger-and-day-book responsibility, employed no clerks, and ministered to no absolute want. It was not the first time indeed that they had heard of an artist being encamped among them; for in the summer several brethren of the brush were tempted to make a temporary sojourn in the immediate vicinity of the broad meadows and suburban prettinesses. But these were mere birds of passage, who took lodgings over some shop in the High Street, and who were never seen save by marauding schoolboys or wandering lovers, who would come suddenly upon a bearded man smoking a pipe, and sketching away under the shade of a big white umbrella. To wear a beard and, in addition to that enormity, to smoke a pipe, were in themselves sufficient, in the eyes of the worthy inhabitants of Lowbar, to prove that a man was on the high-road to destruction; but they consoled themselves with the reflection that the evil-doer was but a sojourner amongst them. Now, however, had arrived a man in the person of Geoffrey Ludlow, who not merely wore a beard and smoked a pipe, but further flew in the face of all decently-constituted society by having a beautiful wife. And this man had not come into lodgings, but had regularly established himself in poor Mrs. Pierce's house, which he had had all done up and painted and papered and furnished in a manner—so at least Mr. Brandram the doctor said—that might be described as gorgeous.

Now, as the pretty suburb of Lowbar is still a good score of years behind the world, its inhabitants could not understand this at all, and the majority of them were rather scandalised than otherwise, when they found that the vicar and his wife had called on the new-comers. Mr. Brandram the doctor had called too ; but that was natural. He was a pushing man was Brandram, and a worldly man, so unlike Priestley, the other doctor, who was a retiring gentleman. So at least said Priestley's friends and Brandram's enemies. Brandram was a little man of between fifty and sixty, neat, and a little horsy in his dress, cheerful in his manner, fond of recommending good living, and fond of taking his own prescription. He was a little " fast " for Lowbar, going to the theatre once or twice in the year, and insisting upon having novels for the Book-Society ; whereas Priestley's greatest dissipation was attending a " humorous lecture " at the Mechanics' Institute, and his lightest reading a book of Antipodean travel. Brandram called at Elm Lodge, of course, and saw both Geoff and Margaret, and talked of the Academy pictures,—which he had carefully got up from the catalogue and the newspaper-notices,—and on going away, left Mrs. Brandram's card. For three weeks afterwards, that visit supplied the doctor with interesting discourse for his patients : he described all the alterations which had been made in the house since Mrs. Pierce's death; he knew the patterns of the carpets, the colours of the curtains, the style of the furniture. Finally, he pronounced upon the new-comers ; described Geoff as a healthy man of a sanguineous temperament, not much cut out for the Lowbar folk ; and his wife as a beautiful woman, but lymphatic.

These last were scarcely the details which the Lowbar folk wanted to know. They wanted to know all about the

ménage ; in what style the new-comers lived ; whether they
kept much or any company ; whether they agreed well
together.   This last was a point of special curiosity ; for,
in common with numberless other worthy, commonplace,
stupid people, the Lowbar folk imagined that the private
lives of "odd persons"—under which heading they included all professors of literature and art of any kind—were
passed in dissipation and wrangling.   How the information
was to be obtained was the great point, for they knew that
nothing would be extracted from the vicar, even if he had
been brimful of remarks upon his new parishioners, which,
indeed, he was not, as they neither of them happened to
be at home when he called.   It would be something to be
well assured about their personal appearance, especially
her personal appearance ; to see whether there were really
any grounds for this boast of beauty which Dr. Brandram
went talking about in such a ridiculous way.   The church
was the first happy hunting-ground pitched upon ; and
during the first Sunday after Geoff's and Margaret's arrival
the excitement during divine service was intense ; the wor-
shippers in the middle and side aisles, whose pews all faced
the pulpit, and whose backs were consequently turned to
the entrance-door, regarding with intense envy their friends
whose pews confronted each other between the pulpit and
the altar, and who, consequently, while chanting the responses
or listening to the lesson, could steal furtive glances on every
occasion of the door's opening, without outraging propriety.
But when it was found that the new-comers did not attend
either morning or evening service,—and unquestionably a
great many members of the congregation had their dinner
of cold meat and salad (it was considered sinful in Lowbar
to have hot dinners on Sunday) at an abnormally early
hour for the purpose of attending evening service on the
chance of seeing the new arrivals,—it was considered necessary to take more urgent measures ; and so the little Misses
Coverdale—two dried-up little chips of spinsters with cork-
screw ringlets and black-lace mittens, who kept house for
their brother, old Coverdale, the red-faced, white-headed
proctor, Geoffrey's next-door neighbour—had quite a little
gathering the next day, the supposed object of which was to
take tea and walk in the garden, but the real object to
peep furtively over the wall and try and catch a glimpse

of her who was already sarcastically known as " Dr. Brand-ram's beauty." Some of the visitors, acquainted with the peculiarities of the garden, knowing what mound to stand on and what position to take up, were successful in catching a glimpse of the top of Margaret's hair—"all taken off her face like a schoolgirl's, and leaving her cheeks as bare as bare," as they afterwards reported—as she wandered list-lessly round the garden, stooping now and then to smell or gather a flower. One or two others were also rewarded by the sight of Geoffrey in his velvet painting-coat; among them, Letty Coverdale, who pronounced him a splended man, and, O, so romantic-looking! for all ideas of matrimony had not yet left Miss Letty Coverdale, and the noun-sub-stantive Man yet caused her heart to beat with an extra throb in her flat little chest; whereas Miss Matty Coverdale, who had a face like a horse, and who loudly boasted that she had never had an offer of marriage in her life, snorted out her wonder that Geoff did not wear a surtout like a Christian, and her belief that he'd be all the cleaner after a visit to Mr. Ball, who was the Lowbar barber.

But bit by bit the personal appearance of both of them grew sufficiently familiar to many of the inhabitants, some of the most courageous of whom had actually screwed themselves up to that pitch of boldness necessary for the accomplishment of calling and leaving cards on strangers pursuing a profession unnamed in the *Directory,* and certainly not one of the three described in *Mangnall's Questions.* The calls were returned, and in some cases were succeeded by invitations to dinner. But Geoffrey cared little for these, and Margaret earnestly begged they might be declined. If she found her life insupportably dull and slow, this was not the kind of relief for which she prayed. A suburban dinner-party would be but a dull parody on what she had known; would give her trouble to dress for, without the smallest compensating amusement; would leave her at the mercy of stupid people, among whom she would probably be the only stranger, the only resource for staring eyes and questioning tongues. That they would have stared and questioned, there is little doubt; but they certainly intended hospitality. The "odd" feeling about the Ludlows prevalent on their first coming had worn off, and now the tide seemed setting the other way. Whether it was that

the tradesmen's books were regularly paid, that the lights
at Elm Lodge were seldom or never burning after eleven
o'clock, that Geoffrey's name had been seen in the *Times*,
as having been present at a dinner given by Lord Everton,
a very grand dinner, where he was the only untitled man
among the company, or for whatever other reason, there
was a decided disposition to be civil to them. No doubt
Margaret's beauty had a great deal to do with it, so far
as the men were concerned. Old Mr. Coverdale, who had
been portentously respectable for half a century, but concerning whom there was a floating legend of " jolly dog-ism "
in his youth, declared he had seen nothing like her since
the Princess Charlotte ; and Abbott, known as Captain
Abbott, from having once been in the Commissariat, who
always wore a chin-tip and a tightly-buttoned blue frock-
coat and pipe-clayed buckskin gloves, made an especial
point of walking past Elm Lodge every afternoon, and
bestowing on Margaret, whenever he saw her, a peculiar
leer which had done frightful execution amongst the nurse-
maids of Islington. Mrs. Abbott, a mild meek little woman,
who practised potichomanie, delcomanie, the art of making
wax-flowers, any thing whereby to make money to pay
the tradespeople and supply varnish for her husband's boots
and pocket-money for his *menus plaisirs*, was not, it is
needless to say, informed of these vagaries on the captain's
part.

They were discussed every where : at the Ladies' Clothing-
Club, where one need scarcely say that the opinions concerning Margaret's beauty were a little less fervid in expression ;
and at the Gentlemen's Book-Society, where a proposition
to invite Geoff to be of their number, started by the vicar
and seconded by old Mr. Coverdale, was opposed by Mr.
Bryant (of Bryant and Martin, coach-builders, Long Acre),
on the ground that the first of the rules stated that this
should be an association of gentlemen ; and who could
say what would be done next if artists was to be received ?
The discussion on this point waxed very warm, and during
it Mr. Cremer the curate incurred Mr. Bryant's deepest
hatred for calling out to him, on his again attempting to
address the meeting, " Spoke, spoke !" which Mr. Bryant
looked upon as a sneer at his trade, and remembered
bitterly when the subscription was got up in the parish

for presenting Mr. Cremer with the silver teapot and two hundred sovereigns, with which (the teapot at least) he proceeded to the rectory of Steeple Bumstead, in a distant part of the country.   They were discussed by the regulars in the nine-o'clock omnibus, most of whom, as they passèd by Elm Lodge and saw Geoff through the big window just commencing to set his palette, pitied him for having to work at home, and rejoiced in their own freedom from the possibility of conjugal inroad ; or, catching a glimpse of Margaret, poked each other in the ribs and told each other what a fine woman she was.   They were discussed by the schoolboys going to school, who had a low opinion of art, and for the most part confined the remarks about Geoffrey to his having a "stunnin' beard," and about Margaret to her being a "regular carrots," the youthful taste being strongly anti-pre-Raffaellitic, and worshipping the raven tresses and straight noses so dear to the old romancers.

And while all these discussions and speculations were rife, the persons speculated on and discussed were leading their lives without a thought of what people were saying of them.   Geoff knew that he was doing good work ; he felt that intuitively as every man does feel it, quite as intuitively as when he is producing rubbish ; and he knew it further from the not-too-laudatorily-inclined Mr. Stompff, who came up from time to time, and could not refuse his commendation to the progress of the pictures.   And then Geoff was happy—at least, well, Margaret might have been a little more lively perhaps ; but then—O, no ; he was thoroughly happy ! and Margaret—existed !   The curtain had dropped on her wedding-day, and she had been groping in darkness ever since.

Time went on, as he does to all of us, whatever our appreciation of him may be, according to the mood we may happen to be in : swiftly to the happy and the old, slowly to the young and the wearied.   There is that blessed compensation which pervades all human things, even in the flight of time.   No matter how pleasant, how varied, how completely filled is the time of the young, it hangs on them somehow ; they do not feel it rush past them nor melt away, the hours swallowed up in days, the days in years, as do the elder people, who have no special excitement, no particular delight. The fact still remains that the young want time to fly, the old want him to crawl; and that, fulfilling the wishes of neither, he speeds on *æquo pede*, grumbled at by both.

The time went on. So Margaret knew by the rising and setting of the sun, by the usual meals, her own getting up and going to bed, and all the usual domestic routine. But by what else? Nothing. She had been married now nearly six months, and from that experience she thought she might deduce something like an epitome of her life. What was it? She had a husband who doated on her; who lavished on her comforts, superfluities, luxuries; who seemed never so happy as when toiling at his easel, and who brought the products of his work to her to dispose of as she pleased. A husband who up to that hour of her thought had never in the smallest degree failed to fulfil her earliest expectations of him,—generous to a degree, kind-hearted, weak, and easily led. Weak! weak as water. —Yes, and O yes! What you like, my dear! What you think best, my child! That is for your decision, Margaret. I—I don't know; I scarcely like to give an opinion. Don't you think you had better settle it? I'll leave it all to you, please, dearest.—Good God! if he would only say *something*—as opposed to her ideas as possible, the more opposed the better—some assertion of self, some trumpet-note of argument, some sign of his having a will of his own, or at least an idea from which a will might spring. Here was the man who in his own art was working out the most admirable genius, showing that he had within him more of the divine afflatus than is given to nine hundred and ninety-nine in every thousand amongst us—a man who was rapidly lifting his name for the wonder and the envy of the best portion of the civilised world, incapable of saying "no" even to a proposition of hashed mutton for dinner, shirking the responsibility of a decision on the question of the proper place for a chair.

Indeed, I fear that, so far as I have stated, the sympathies of women will go against old Geoff, who must, I fancy, have been what they are in the habit of calling "very trying." You see he brought with him to the altar a big generous old heart, full of love and adoration of his intended wife, full of

N

resolution, in his old blunt way, to stand by her through evil and good report, and to do his duty by her in all honour and affection. He was any thing but a self-reliant man; but he knew that his love was sterling coin, truly unalloyed; and he thought that it might be taken as compensation for numerous deficiencies, the existence of which he readily allowed. You see he discovered his power of loving simultaneously almost with his power of painting; and I think that this may perhaps account for a kind of feeling that, as the latter was accepted by the world, so would the former be by the person to whom it was addressed. When he sent out the picture which first attracted Mr. Stompff's attention, he had no idea that it was better than a score others which he had painted during the course of his life; when he first saw Margaret Dacre, he could not tell that the instinctive admiration would lead to any thing more than the admiration which he had already silently paid to half-a-hundred pretty faces. But both had come to a successful issue; and he was only to paint his pictures with all the talent of his head and hand, and to love his wife with all the affection of his heart, to discharge his duty in life.

He did this; he worshipped her with all his heart. Whatever she did was right, whatever ought to have been discussed she was called upon to settle. They were very small affairs, as I have said,—of hashed mutton and jams, of the colour of a ribbon, or the fashion of a bonnet. Was there never to be any thing further than this? Was life to consist in her getting up and struggling through the day and going to bed at Elm Lodge? The short breakfast, when Geoff was evidently dying to be off into the painting-room; the long, long day,—composed of servants' instruction, newspaper, lunch, sleep, little walk, toilette, dinner, utterly feeble conversation, yawns and head-droppings, and finally bed. She had pictured to herself something quiet, tranquil, without excitement, without much change; but nothing like this.

Friends?—relations? O yes! old Mrs. Ludlow came to see her now and then; and she had been several times to Brompton. The old lady was very kind in her pottering stupid way, and her daughter Matilda was kind also, but as once gushing and prudish; so Margaret thought. And they both treated her as if she were a girl; the old lady perpetually haranguing her with good advice and feeble suggestion, and Matilda—who, of course, like all girls, had, it was perfectly evident, some silly love-affair on with some youth who had not as yet declared himself—wanting to make her half-confidences, and half-asking for advice, which she never intended to take. A girl? O yes, of course, she must play out that farce, and support that terribly vague story which old Geoff, pushed into a corner on a sudden, and without any one to help him at the instant, had fabricated concerning her parentage and belongings. And she must listen to the old lady's praises of Geoff, and how she thought it not improbable, if things went on as they were going, that the happiest dream of her life would be fulfilled—that she should ride in her son's carriage. " It would be yours, of course, my dear; I know that well enough; but you'd let me ride in it sometimes, just for the honour and glory of the thing." And they talked like this to her: the old lady of the glory of a carriage; Matilda of some hawbuck wretch for whom she had a liking;—to her! who had sat on the box-seat of a drag a score of times, with half-a-score of the best men in England sitting behind her, all eager for a word or a smile.

She saw them now, frequently, whenever she came over to Brompton,—all the actors in that bygone drama of her life, save the hero himself. It was the play of *Hamlet* with Hamlet left out, indeed. But what vast proportions did she then assume compared to what she had been lately! There were Rosencrantz and Guildenstern,—the one in his mail-phaeton, the other on his matchless hack; there was old Polonius in the high-collared bottle-green coat of thirty years back, guiding his clever cob in and out among the courtiers; there was the Honourable Osric, simpering and fooling among the fops. She hurried across the Drive or the Row on her way to or from Brompton, and stood up, a little distance off, gazing at these comrades of old times. She would press her hands to her head, and wonder whether it was all true or a dream; whether she was going back to the dull solemnity of Elm Lodge, when a dozen words would put her into that mail-phaeton—on to that horse! How often had Rosencrantz ogled! and was it not Guildenstern's billet that, after reading, she tore up and threw in his face? It was an awful temptation; and she was obliged, as an antidote, to picture to herself the tortures she had suffered from cold and want and starvation, to bring her round at all to a sensible line of thought.

Some one else had called upon her two or three times. O yes, a Miss Maurice, who came in a coroneted carriage, and to whom she had taken a peculiar detestation; not from any airs she had given herself—O no; there was nothing of that kind about her. She was one of those persons, don't you know, who have known your husband before his marriage, and take an interest in him, and must like you for his sake; one of those persons who are so open and honest and above-board, that you take an immediate distrust of them at first sight, which you never get over. O no, Margaret was perfectly certain she should never like Annie Maurice.

Music she had, and books; but she was not very fond of the first, and only played desultorily. Geoff was most passionately fond of music; and sometimes after dinner he would ask for "a tune," and then Margaret would sit down at the piano and let her fingers wander over the keys, gradually finding them straying into some of the brilliant dance-music of Auber and Musard, of Jullien and Kœnig, with which she had been familiarised during her Continental experience. And as she played, the forms familiarly associated with the music came trooping out of the mist—Henri, so grand in the *Cavalier seul*, Jules and Eulalie, so unapproachable in the *En avant deux*. There they whirled in the hot summer evenings; the *parterre*, illuminated with a thousand lamps glittering like fireflies, the sensuous strains of the orchestra soaring up to the great yellow-faced moon looking down upon it; and then the cosy little supper, the sparkling iced drink, the—"Time for bed, eh, dear?" from old Geoff, already nodding with premature sleep; and away flew the bright vision at the rattle of the chamber-candlestick.

Books! yes, no lack of them. Geoff subscribed for her to the library, and every week came the due supply of novels. These Margaret read, some in wonder, some in scorn. There was a great run upon the Magdalen just then in that style of literature; writers were beginning to be what is called "out-spoken;" and young ladies familiarised with the outward life of the species, as exhibited in the Park and at the Opera, read with avidity of their diamonds and their ponies, of the interior of the *ménage*, and of their spirited conversations with the cream of the male aristocracy. A deference to British virtue, and a desire to stand well with the librarian's subscribers, compelled an amount of repentance in the third volume which Margaret scarcely believed to be in accordance with truth. The remembrance of childhood's days, which made the ponies pall, and rendered the diamonds disgusting,—the inherent natural goodness, which took to eschewing of crinoline and the adoption of serge, which swamped the colonel in a storm of virtuous indignation, and brought the curate safely riding over the billows,—were agreeable incidents, but scarcely, she thought, founded on fact. Her own experience at least had taught her otherwise ; but it might be so after all.

So her life wore drearily on. Would there never be any change in it? Yes, one change at least Time brought in his flight. Dr. Brandram's visits were now regular ; and one morning a shrill cry resounded through the house, and the doctor placed in its father's arms a strong healthy boy.

CHAPTER VII.

WHAT THEIR FRIENDS THOUGHT.

GEOFFREY LUDLOW had married and settled himself in a not-too-accessible suburb, but he had not given up such of his old companions as were on a footing of undeniable intimacy with him. These were few in number; for although Geoff was a general favourite from his urbanity and the absence of any thing like pretentiousness in his disposition, he was considered slow by most of the bolder spirits among the artist-band. He was older than many of them certainly, but that was scarcely the reason ; for there were jolly old dogs whose presence never caused the smallest reticence of song or story—gray and bald-headed old boys, who held their own in scurrility and slang, and were among the latest sitters and the deepest drinkers of the set. It is needless to say that in all their popularity—and they were popular after a fashion—there was not mingled one single grain of respect; while Geoffrey was respected as much as he was liked. But his shyness, his quiet domestic habits, and his perpetual hard work gave him little time for the cultivation of acquaintance, and he had only two really intimate friends, who were Charley Potts and William Bowker.

Charley Potts had been "best man" at the marriage, and Geoffrey had caught a glimpse of old Bowker in hiding behind a pillar of the church. It was meet, then, that they—old companions of his former life—should see him under his altered circumstances, should know and be received by his wife, and should have the opportunity, if they wished for it, of keeping up at least a portion of the *camaraderie* of old days. Therefore after his return to London, and when he and his wife were settled down in Elm Lodge, Geoffrey wrote to each of his old friends, and said how glad he would be to see them in his new house.

This note found Mr. Charles Potts intent upon a representation of Mr. Tennyson's "Dora," sitting with the child in the cornfield, a commission which he had received from Mr. Caniche, and which was to be paid for by no less a sum than a hundred and fifty pounds. The "Gil Blas" had proved a great success in the Academy, and had been purchased by a country rector, who had won a hundred-pound prize in the Art-Union; so that Charley was altogether in very high feather and pecuniary triumph. He had not made much alteration in the style of his living or in the furniture of his apartment; but he had cleared off a long score for beer and grog standing against him in the books kept by Caroline of signal fame; he had presented Caroline herself with a cheap black-lace shawl, which had produced something like an effect at Rosherville Gardens! and he had sent a ten-pound note to the old aunt who had taken care of him, after his mother's death, and who wept tears of gratified joy on its receipt, and told all Sevenoaks of the talent and the goodness of her nephew. He had paid off some other debts also, and lent a pound or two here and there among his friends, and was even after that a capitalist to the extent of having some twenty pounds in the stomach of a china sailor, originally intended as a receptacle for tobacco. His success had taken effect on Charley. He had begun to think that there was really something in him,

…ter all; that life was, as the working-man observed, "not all beer and skittles;" and that if he worked honestly on, he might yet be able to realise a vision which had occasionally loomed through clouds of tobacco-smoke curling round his head; a vision of a pleasant cottage out at Kilburn, or better still at Cricklewood; with a bit of green lawn and a little conservatory, and two or three healthy children tumbling about; while their mother, uncommonly like Matilda Ludlow, looked on from the ivy-covered porch; and their father, uncommonly like himself, was finishing in the studio that great work which was to necessitate his election into the Academy. This vision had a peculiar charm for him; he worked away like a horse; the telegraphic signals to Caroline and the consequent supply of beer became far less frequent; he began to eschew late nights, which he found led to late mornings; and the "Dora" was growing under his hand day by day.

He was hard at work and had apparently worked himself into a knot, for he was standing a little distance from his easel, gazing vacantly at the picture and twirling his moustache with great vigour,—a sure sign of worry with him,—when the "tugging of the trotter" was heard, and on his opening the door, Mr. Bowker presented himself and walked in.

"'Tis I! Bowker the undaunted! Ha, Ha!" and Mr. Bowker gave two short stamps, and lunged with his walking-stick at his friend. "Give your William drink; he is athirst. What! nothing of a damp nature about? Potts, virtue and industry are good things; and your William has been glad to observe that of late you have been endeavouring to practise both; but industry is not incompatible with pale ale, and nimble fingers are oft allied to a dry palate. That sounds like one of the headings of the pages from Maunders' *Treasury of Knowledge.*—Send for some beer!"

The usual pantomime was gone through by Mr. Potts, and while it was in process, Bowker filled a pipe and walked towards the easel. "Very good, Charley; very good indeed. Nice fresh look in that girl—not the usual burnt-umber rusticity; but something—not quite—like the real ruddy peasant bronze. Child not bad either; looks as if it had got its feet in boxing-gloves, though; you must alter that;

and don't make its eyes quite so much like willow-pattern saucers. What's that on the child's head?"

"Hair, of course."

"And what stuff's that the girl's sitting in?"

"Corn! cornfield—wheat, you know, and that kind of stuff. What do you mean? why do you ask?"

"Only because it seems to your William that both substances are exactly alike. If it's hair, then the girl is sitting in a hair-field; if it's corn, then the child has got corn growing on its head."

"It'll have it growing on its feet some day, I suppose," growled Mr. Potts, with a grin. "You're quite right, though, old man; we'll alter that at once.—Well, what's new with you?"

"New? Nothing! I hear nothing, see nothing, and know nobody. I might be a hermit-crab, only I shall never creep into any body else's shell; my own—five feet ten by two feet six—will be ready quite soon enough for me. Stop! what stuff I'm talking! I very nearly forgot the object of my coming round to you this morning. Your William is asked into society! Look; here's a letter I received last night from our Geoff, asking me to come up to see his new house and be introduced to his wife."

"I had a similar one this morning."

"I thought that was on the cards, so I came round to see what you were going to do."

"Do? I shall go, of course. So will you, won't you?"

"Well, Charley, I don't know. I'm a queer old skittle, that has been knocked about in all manner of ways, and that has had no women's society for many years. So much the better, perhaps. I'm not pretty to look at; and I couldn't talk the stuff women like to have talked to them, and I should be horribly bored if I had to listen to it. So —and yet—God forgive me for growling so!—there are times when I'd give any thing for a word of counsel and comfort in a woman's voice, for the knowledge that there was any woman—good woman, mind!—no matter what— mother, sister, wife—who had an interest in what I did. There! never mind that."

Mr. Bowker stopped abruptly. Charley Potts waited for a minute; then putting his hand affectionately on his friend's shoulder, said: "But our William will make an exception for our Geoff. You've known him so long, and you're so fond of him."

"Fond of him! God bless him! No one could know Geoff without loving him, at least no one whose love was worth having. But you see there's the wife to be taken into account now."

"You surely wouldn't doubt your reception by her? The mere fact of your being an old friend of her husband's would be sufficient to make you welcome."

"O, Mr. Potts, Mr. Potts! you are as innocent as a sucking-dove, dear Mr. Potts, though you have painted a decent picture! To have known a man before his marriage is to be the natural enemy of his wife. However, I'll chance that, and go and see our Geoff."

"So shall I," said Potts, "though I'm rather doubtful about *my* reception. You see I was with Geoff that night, —you know, when we met the —his wife, you know."

"So you were. Haven't you seen her since?"

"Only at the wedding, and that all in a hurry—just an introduction; that was all."

"Did she seem at all confused when she recognised you?"

"She couldn't have recognised me, because when we found her she was senseless, and hadn't come-to when we left. But of course Geoff had told her who I was, and she didn't seem in the least confused."

"Not she, if there's any truth in physiognomy," muttered old Bowker; "well, if she showed no annoyance at first meeting you, she's not likely to do so now, and you'll be received sweetly enough, no doubt. We may as well go together, eh?"

To this proposition Mr. Potts consented with great alacrity, for though a leader of men in his own set, he was marvellously timid, silent, and ill at ease in the society of ladies. The mere notion of having to spend a portion of time, however short, in company with members of the other sex above the rank of Caroline, and with whom he could not exchange that free and pleasant *badinage* of which he was so great a master, inflicted torture on him sufficient to render him an object of compassion. So on a day agreed upon, the artistic pair set out to pay their visit to Mrs. Geoffrey Ludlow.

Their visit took place at about the time when public opinion in Lowbar was unsettled as to the propriety of knowing the Ludlows; and the dilatoriness of some of the inhabitants in accepting the position of the new-comers may probably be ascribed to the fact of the visitors having been encountered in the village. It is undeniable that the appearance of Mr. Potts and of Mr. Bowker was not calculated to impress the beholder with a feeling of respect, or a sense of their position in society. Holding this to be a gala-day, Mr. Potts had extracted a bank-note from the stomach of the china sailor, and expended it at the "emporium" of an outfitter in Oxford Street, in the purchase of a striking, but particularly ill-fitting, suit of checked clothes—coat, waistcoat, and trousers to match. His boots, of an unyielding leather, had very thick clump soles, which emitted curious wheezings and groanings as he walked; and his puce-coloured gloves were baggy at all the fingers' ends, and utterly impenetrable as regarded the thumbs. His white hat was a little on one side, and his moustaches were twisted with a ferocity which, however fascinating to the maid-servants at the kitchen-windows, failed to please the ruralising cits and citizenesses, who were accustomed to regard a white hat as the distinctive badge of card-sharpers, and a moustache as the outward and visible sign of swindling. Mr. Bowker had made little difference in his ordinary attire. He wore a loose shapeless brown garment which was more like a cloth dressing-gown than a paletot; a black waistcoat frayed at the pockets from constant contact with his pipe-stem, and so much too short that the ends of his white-cotton braces were in full view; also a pair of gray trousers of the cut which had been in fashion when their owner was in fashion—made very full over the boot, and having broad leather straps. Mr. Bowker also wore a soft black wideawake hat, and perfumed the fragrant air with strong cavendish tobacco, fragments of which decorated his beard. The two created a sensation as they strode up the quiet High Street; and when they rang at Elm Lodge Geoffrey's pretty servant-maid was ready to drop between admiration at Mr. Potts's appearance and a sudden apprehension that Mr. Bowker had come after the plate.

She had, however, little time for the indulgence of either

feeling; for Geoffrey, who had been expecting the arrival of his friends, with a degree of nervousness unintelligible to himself, no sooner heard the bell than he rushed out from his studio and received his old comrades with great cordiality. He shook hands heartily with Charley Potts; but a certain hesitation mingled with the warmth of his greeting of Bowker; and his talk rattled on from broken sentence to broken sentence, as though he were desirous of preventing his friend from speaking until he himself had had his say.

"How d'ye do, Charley? so glad to see you; and you, Bowker, my good old friend: it is thoroughly kind of you to come out here; and—long way, you know, and out of your usual beat, I know. Well, so you see I've joined the noble army of martyrs,—not that I mean that of course; but—eh, you didn't expect I would do it, did you? I couldn't say, like the girl in the Scotch song, 'I'm owre young to marry yet,' could I? However, thank God, I think you'll say my wife is—what a fellow I am! keeping you fellows out here in this broiling sun; and you haven't— at least you, Bowker, haven't been introduced to her. Come along—come in!"

He preceded them to the drawing-room, where Margaret was waiting to receive them. It was a hot staring day in the middle of a hot staring summer. The turf was burnt brown; the fields spreading between Elm Lodge and Hampstead, usually so cool and verdant, were now arid wastes; the outside blinds of the house were closed to exclude the scorching light, and there was no sound save the loud chirping of grasshoppers. A great weariness was on Margaret that day; she had tried to rouse herself, but found it impossible, so had sat all through the morning staring vacantly before her, busy with old memories. Between her past and her present life there was so little in common, that these memories were seldom roused by associations. The dull never-changing domestic day, and the pretty respectability of Elm Lodge, did not recal the wild Parisian revels, the rough pleasant Bohemianism of garrison-lodgings, the sumptuous luxury of the Florentine villa. But there was something in the weather to-day—in the bright fierce glare of the sun, in the solemn utterly-unbroken stillness—which brought back to her mind one when she and Leonard and some others were cruising off the Devonshire coast in Tom

Marshall's yacht; a day on which, with scarcely a breath of air to be felt, they lay becalmed in Babbicombe Bay; under an awning, of course, over which the men from time to time worked the fire-hose; and how absurdly funny Tom Marshall was when the ice ran short. Leonard said——The gate-bell rang, and her husband's voice was heard in hearty welcome of his friends.

In welcome of his friends! Yes, there at least she could do her duty; there she could give pleasure to her husband. She could not give him her love; she had tried, and found it utterly impossible; but equally impossible was it to withhold from him her respect. Day by day she honoured him more and more; as she watched his patient honesty, his indomitable energy, his thorough helplessness; as she learned —in spite of herself as it were—more of himself; for Geoff had always thought one of the chiefest pleasures of matrimony must be to have some one capable of receiving all one's confidences. As she, with a certain love of psychological analysis possessed by some women, went through his character, and discovered loyalty and truth in every thought and every deed, she felt half angry with herself for her inability to regard him with that love which his qualities ought to have inspired. She had been accustomed to tell herself, and half-believed, that she had no conscience; but this theory, which she had maintained during nearly all the earlier portion of her life, vanished as she learned to know and to appreciate her husband. She had a conscience, and she felt it; under its influence she made some struggles, ineffectual indeed, but greater than she at one time would have attempted. What was it that prevented her from giving this man his due, her heart's love? His appearance? No; he was not a "girl's man" certainly, not the delicious military vision which sets throbbing the hearts of sweet seventeen: by no means romantic-looking, but a thoroughly manly gentleman—big, strong, and well-mannered. Had he been dwarfed or deformed, vulgar, dirty—and even in the present days of tubbing and Turkish baths, there are men who possess genius and are afraid it may come off in hot water,—had he been "common," an expressive word meaning something almost as bad as dirt and vulgarity,— Margaret could have satisfied her newly-found conscience, or at least accounted for her feelings. But he was none of these, and she admitted it; and so at the conclusion of her self-examination fell back, not without a feeling of semi-complacency, to the conviction that it was not he, but she herself who was in fault; that she did not give him her heart simply because she had no heart to give; that she had lived and loved, but that, however long she might yet live, she could never love again.

These thoughts passed rapidly through her mind, not for the first, nor even for the hundredth time, as she sat down upon the sofa and took up the first book which came to hand, not even making a pretence of reading it, but allowing it to lie listlessly on her lap. Geoffrey came first, closely followed by Charley Potts, who advanced in a sheepish way, holding out his hand. Margaret smiled slightly and gave him her hand with no particular expression, a little dignified perhaps, but even that scarcely noticeable. Then Bowker, who had kept his keen eyes upon her from the moment he entered the room, and whom she had seen and examined while exchanging civilities with Potts, was brought forward by Geoffrey, and introduced as "one of my oldest and dearest friends." Margaret advanced as Bowker approached, her face flushed a little, and her eyes wore their most earnest expression, as she said, "I am very glad to see you, Mr. Bowker. I have heard of you from Geoffrey. I am sure we shall be very good friends." She gripped his hand and looked him straight in the face as she said this, and in that instant William Bowker divined that Margaret had heard of, and knew and sympathised with, the story of his life.

She seemed tacitly to acknowledge that there was a bond of union between them. She was as polite as could be expected of her to Charley Potts; but she addressed herself especially to Bowker when any point for discussion arose. These were not very frequent, for the conversation carried on was of a very ordinary kind. How they liked their new house, and whether they had seen much of the people of the neighbourhood; how they had enjoyed their honeymoon in the Isle of Wight; and trivialities of a similar character. Charley Potts, prevented by force of circumstances from indulging in his peculiar humour, and incapable from sheer ignorance of bearing his share of general conversation when a lady was present, had several times attempted to introduce the one subject, which, in any society, he could discuss at his ease, art—" shop ;" but on each occasion had found his proposition rigorously ignored both by Margaret and Bowker, who seemed to consider it out of place, and who were sufficiently interested in their own talk.   So Charley fell back upon Geoff, who, although delighted at seeing how well his wife was getting on with his friend, yet had sufficient kindness of heart to step in to Charley's rescue, and to discuss with him the impossibility of accounting for the high price obtained by Smudge ; the certainty that Scumble's popularity would be merely evanescent ; the disgraceful favouritism displayed by certain men "on the council ;" in short, all that kind of talk which is so popular and so unfailing in the simple kindly members of the art-world.   So on throughout lunch ; and, indeed, until the mention of Geoffrey's pictures then in progress necessitated the generalising of the conversation, and they went away (Margaret with them) to the studio. Arrived within those walls, Mr. Potts, temporarily oblivious of the presence of a lady, became himself again.   The mingled smell of turpentine and tobacco, the sight of the pictures on the easels, and of Geoff's pipe-rack on the wall, a general air of carelessness and discomfort, all came gratefully to Mr. Potts, who opened his chest, spread out his arms, shook himself as does a dog just emerged from the water—probably in his case to get rid of any clinging vestige of respectability—and said in a very hungry tone :

"Now, Geoff, let's have a smoke, old boy."

"You might as well wait until you knew whether Mrs. Ludlow made any objection, Charley," said Bowker, in a low tone.

"I beg Mrs. Ludlow's pardon," said Potts, scarlet all over ; "I had no notion that she—"

"Pray don't apologise, Mr. Potts ; I am thoroughly accustomed to smoke ; have been for—"

"Yes, of course ; ever since you married Geoff you have been thoroughly smoke-dried," interrupted Bowker, at whom Margaret shot a short quick glance, half of interrogation, half of gratitude.

They said no more on the smoke subject just then, but proceeded to a thorough examination of the picture, which Charley Potts pronounced "regularly stunning," and which Mr. Bowker criticised in a much less explosive manner.   He praised the drawing, the painting, the general arrangement ;

he allowed that Geoffrey was doing every thing requisite to obtain for himself name, fame, and wealth in the present day ; but he very much doubted whether that was all that was needed. With the French judge he would very much have doubted the necessity of living, if to live implied the abnegation of the first grand principles of art, its humanising and elevated influence. Bowker saw no trace of these in the undeniable cleverness of the Brighton Esplanade ; and though he was by no means sparing of his praise, his lack of enthusiasm, as compared with the full-flavoured ecstasy of Charley Potts, struck upon Margaret's ear. Shortly afterwards, while Geoffrey and Potts were deep in a discussion on colour, she turned to Mr. Bowker, and said abruptly :

" You are not satisfied with Geoffrey's picture ?"

He smiled somewhat grimly as he said, "Satisfied is a very strong word, Mrs. Ludlow. There are some of us in the world who have sufficient good sense not to be satisfied with what we do ourselves—"

" That's true, Heaven knows," she interrupted involuntarily.

" And are consequently not particularly likely to be content with what's done by other people. I think Geoff's picture good, very good of its sort ; but I don't—I candidly confess—like its sort. He is a man full of appreciation of nature, character, and sentiment ; a man who, in the expression of his own art, is as capable of rendering poetic feeling as—By Jove, now why didn't he think of that subject that Charley Potts has got under weigh just now? That would have suited Geoff exactly."

" What is it ?"

" Dora—Tennyson's Dora, you know." Margaret bowed in acquiescence. " There's a fine subject, if you like. Charley's painting it very well, so far as it goes; but he doesn't feel it. Now Geoff would. A man must have something more than facile manipulation ; he must have the soul of a poet before he could depict the expression which must necessarily be on such a face. There are few who could understand, fewer still who could interpret to others, such heart-feelings of that most beautiful of Tennyson's creations as would undoubtedly show themselves in her face; the patient endurance of unrequited love, which ' loves on through

all ills, and loves on till she dies;' which neither the contem
nor the death of its object can extinguish, but which the
flows, in as pure, if not as strong, a current towards h
widow and his child."

Margaret had spoken at first, partly for the sake of sayii
something, partly because her feeling for her husband a
mitted of great pride in his talent, which she thought Bowk
had somewhat slighted. But now she was thoroughly rouse
her eyes bright, her hair pushed back off her face, listenir
intently to him. When he ceased, she looked up strangel
and said:

" Do you believe in the existence of such love ?"

"O yes," he replied; "it's rare, of course. Especial
rare is the faculty of loving hopelessly without the lea
chance of return—loving stedfastly and honestly as Do:
did, I mean. With most people unrequited love turns in
particularly bitter hatred, or into that sentimental maudl
state of 'broken heart,' which is so comforting to its po
sessor and so wearying to his friends. But there *are* exce
tional cases where such love exists, and in these, no matt
how fought against, it can never be extinguished."

" I suppose you are right," said Margaret; "there mu
be such instances."

Bowker looked hard at her, but she had risen from he
seat and was rejoining the others.

" What's your opinion of Mrs. Ludlow, William ?" aske
Charley Potts, as they walked away puffing their pipes in th
calm summer night air. " Handsome woman, isn't she ?"

" Very handsome !" replied Bowker; "wondrously hanc
some !" Then reflectively—" It's a long time since you
William has seen any thing like that. All in all—face, figuri
manner—wondrously perfect! She walks like a Spaniard
and—"

" Yes, Geoff's in luck; at least I suppose he is. There
something about her which is not quite to my taste. I thin
I like a British element, which is not to be found in her.
don't know what it is—only something—well, something les
of the duchess about her. I don't think she's quite in ou
line—is she, Bowker, old boy?"

" That's because you're very young in the world's ways

Charley, and also because Geoff's wife is not very like Geoff's sister, I'm thinking." Whereat Mr. Potts grew very red, told his friend to "shut up!" and changed the subject.

"That night Mr. Bowker sat on the edge of his truckle-bed in his garret in Hart Street, Bloomsbury, holding in his left hand a faded portrait in a worn morocco case. He looked at it long and earnestly, while his right hand wafted aside the thick clouds of tobacco-smoke pouring over it from his pipe. He knew every line of it, every touch of colour in it ; but he sat gazing at it this night as though it were an entire novelty, studying it with a new interest.

"Yes," said he at length, "she's very like you, my darling, very like you,—hair, eyes, shape, all alike ; and she seems to have that same clinging, undying love which you had, my darling—that same resistless, unquenchable, undying love. But that love is not for Geoff ; God help him, dear fellow ! that love is not for Geoff !"

CHAPTER VIII.

MARGARET AND ANNIE.

THE meeting between Margaret and Annie Maurice, which Geoffrey had so anxiously desired, had taken place, but could scarcely be said to have been successful in its result. With the best intention possible, and indeed with a very earnest wish that these two women should like each other very much, Geoff had said so much about the other to each, as to beget a mutual distrust and dislike before they became acquainted. Margaret could not be jealous of Geoffrey ; her regard for him was not sufficiently acute to admit any such feeling. But she rebelled secretly against the constant encomiastic mention of Annie, and grew wearied at and annoyed with the perpetually-iterated stories of Miss Maurice's goodness with which Geoffrey regaled her. A good daughter ! Well, what of that ? She herself had been a good daughter until temptation assailed her, and probably Miss Maurice had never been tempted.—So simple, honest, and straightforward ! Yes, she detested women of that kind ; behind the mask of innocence and virtue they frequently

o

carried on the most daring schemes. Annie in her turn thought she had heard quite enough about Mrs. Ludlow's hair and eyes, and wondered Geoff had never said any thing about his wife's character or disposition. It was quite right, of course, that he, an artist, should marry a pretty person; but he was essentially a man who would require something more than mere beauty in his life's companion, and as yet he had not hinted at any accomplishments which his wife possessed. There was a something in Lord Caterham's tone, when speaking to and of Geoffrey Ludlow, which had often jarred upon Annie's ear, and which she now called to mind in connection with these thoughts—a certain tinge of pity more akin to contempt than to love. Annie had noticed that Caterham never assumed this tone when he was talking to Geoffrey about his art; then he listened deferentially or argued with spirit; but when matters of ordinary life formed the topics of conversation her cousin seemed to regard Geoffrey as a kind of large-hearted boy, very generous, very impulsive, but thoroughly inexperienced. Could Arthur Caterham's reading of Geoffrey Ludlow's character be the correct one? Was he, out of his art, so weak, vacillating, and easily led? and had he been caught by mere beauty of face? and had he settled himself down to pass his life with a woman of whose disposition he knew nothing? Annie Maurice put this question to herself with a full conviction that she would be able to answer it after her introduction to Mrs. Ludlow.

About a week after Geoffrey had given his first drawing-lesson in St. Barnabas Square, Annie drove off one afternoon to Elm Lodge in Lady Beauport's barouche. She had begged hard to be allowed to go in a cab, but Lord Caterham would not hear of it; and as Lady Beauport had had a touch of neuralgia (there were very few illnesses she permitted to attack her, and those only of an aristocratic nature), and had been confined to the house, no objection was made. So the barouche, with the curly-wigged coachman and silver-headed footmen on the box, went spinning through Camden and Kentish Towns, where the coachman pointed with his whip to rows of small houses bordering the roadside, and wondered what sort of people could live "in such little 'oles;" and the footman expressed his belief that the denizens were "clerks and poor coves of that kind." The children of the neighbourhood ran out in admiration of the whole turn-out, and especially of the footman's hair, which afforded them subject-matter for discussion during the evening, some contending that his head had been snowed upon; some insisting that it "grew so;" and others propounding a belief that he was a very old man, and that his white hair was merely natural. When the carriage dashed up to the gates of Elm Lodge, the Misses Coverdale next door were, as they afterwards described themselves, "in a perfect twitter of excitement;" because, though good carriages and handsome horses were by no means rare in the pretty suburb, no one had as yet ventured to ask his servant to wear hair-powder; and the coronet, immediately spied on the panels, had a wonderful effect.

The visit was not unexpected by either Margaret or Geoffrey; but the latter was at the moment closely engaged with Mr. Stompff, who had come up to make an apparently advantageous proposition; so that when Annie Maurice was shown into the drawing-room, she found Margaret there alone. At sight of her, Annie paused in sheer admiration. Margaret was dressed in a light striped muslin; her hair taken off her face and twisted into a large roll behind; her only ornaments a pair of long gold earrings. At the announcement of Miss Maurice's name, a slight flush came across her face, heightening its beauty. She rose without the smallest sign of hurry, grandly and calmly, and advanced a few paces. She saw the effect she had produced and did not intend that it should be lessened. It was Annie who spoke first, and Annie's hand was the first outstretched.

"I must introduce myself, Mrs. Ludlow," said she, "though I suppose you have heard of me from your husband. He and I are very old friends."

"O, Miss Maurice?" said Margaret, as though half doubtful to whom she was talking. "O yes; Geoffrey has mentioned your name several times. Pray sit down."

All this in the coldest tone and with the stiffest manner. Prejudiced originally, Margaret, in rising, had caught a glimpse through the blinds of the carriage, and regarded it as an assertion of dignity and superiority on her visitor's part, which must be at once counteracted.

"I should have come to see you long before, Mrs.

Ludlow, but my time is not my own, as you probably know ; and—"

"Yes, Mr. Ludlow told me you were Lady Beauport's companion." A hit at the carriage there.

"Yes," continued Annie with perfect composure, though she felt the blow, "I am Lady Beauport's companion, and consequently not a free agent, or, as I said, I should have called on you long ago."

Margaret had expected a hit in exchange for her own, which she saw had taken effect. A little mollified by her adversary's tolerance, she said :

"I should have been very glad to see you, Miss Maurice ; and in saying so I pay no compliment; for I should have been very glad to see any body to break this fearful monotony."

"You find it dull here ?"

"I find it dreary in the extreme."

"And I was only thinking how perfectly charming it is. This sense of thorough quiet is of all things the most pleasant to me. It reminds me of the place where the happiest days in my life have been passed; and now, after the fever and excitement of London, it seems doubly grateful. But perhaps you have been accustomed to gaiety."

"Yes ; at least, if not to gaiety, to excitement ; to having every hour of the day filled up with something to do ; to finding the time flown before I scarcely knew it had arrived, instead of watching the clock and wondering that it was not later in the day."

"Ah, then of course you feel the change very greatly at first; but I think you will find it wear off. One's views of life alter so after we have tried the new phase for a little time. It seems strange my speaking to you in this way, Mrs. Ludlow; but I have had a certain amount of experience. There was my own dear home ; and then I lived with my uncle at a little country parsonage, and kept house for him ; and then I became—Lady Beauport's companion."

A bright red patch burned on Margaret's cheek as Annie said these words. Was it shame ? Was the quiet earnestness, the simple courtesy and candour of this frank, bright-eyed girl getting over her ?

" That was very difficult at first, I confess," Annie continued; "every thing was so strange to me, just as it may be to you here, but I had come from the quietude to the gaiety; and I thought at one time it would be impossible for me to continue there. But I held on, and I manage to get on quite comfortably now. They are all very kind to me; and the sight of Mr. Ludlow occasionally insures my never forgetting the old days."

" It would be strange if they were not kind to you," said Margaret, looking fixedly at her. " I understand now what Geoffrey has told me about you. We shall be friends, shall we not?" suddenly extending her hand.

" The very best of friends!" said Annie, returning the pressure; "and, dear Mrs. Ludlow, you will soon get over this feeling of dulness. These horrible household duties, which are so annoying at first, become a regular part of the day's business, and, unconsciously to ourselves, we owe a great deal to them for helping us through the day. And then you must come out with me whenever I can get the carriage,—O, I've brought Lady Beauport's card, and she is coming herself as soon as she gets out again,—and we'll go for a drive in the Park. I can quite picture to myself the sensation you would make."

Margaret smiled—a strange hard smile—but said nothing.

" And then you must be fond of reading; and I don't know whether Mr. Ludlow has changed, but there was nothing he used to like so much as being read to while he was at work. Whenever he came to the Priory, papa and I used to sit in the little room where he painted and take it in turns to read to him. I daresay he hasn't liked to ask you, fearing it might bore you; and you haven't liked to suggest it, from an idea that you might interrupt his work."

" O yes, I've no doubt it will come right," said Margaret, indisposed to enter into detail; "and I know I can rely on your help; only one thing—don't mention what I have said to Geoffrey, please; it might annoy him; and he is so good, that I would not do that for the world."

" He will not hear a word of it from me. It would annoy him dreadfully, I know. He is so thoroughly wrapped up in you, that to think you were not completely happy would cause him great pain. Yes, he is good. Papa used to say he did not know so good a man, and—"

The door opened as she spoke, and Geoff entered the room. His eyes brightened as he saw the two women together in close conversation; and he said with a gay laugh:

"Well, little Annie, you've managed to find us out, have you?—come away from the marble halls, and brought 'vassals and serfs by your side,' and all the king's horses and all the king's men, up to our little hut. And you introduced yourself to Margaret, and you're beginning to understand one another, eh?"

"I think we understand each other perfectly; and what nonsense you talk about the vassals and king's horses, and all that! They would make me have the carriage; and no one but a horrible democrat like you would see any harm in using it."

"Democrat?—I?—the stanchest supporter of our aristocracy and our old institutions. I intend to have a card printed, with 'Instruction in drawing to the youthful nobility and gentry. References kindly permitted to the Earl of B., Lord C., &c.'—Well, my child," turning to Margaret, "you'll think your husband more venerable than ever after seeing this young lady; and remembering that he used to nurse her in his arms."

"I have been telling Miss Maurice that now I have seen her, I can fully understand all you have said about her; and she has promised to come and see me often, and to take me out with her."

"That's all right," said Geoffrey; "nothing will please me better.—It's dull for her here, Annie, all alone; and I'm tied to my easel all day."

"O, that will be all right, and we shall get on capitally together, shall we not, Annie?"

And the women kissed one another, and followed Geoffrey into the garden.

That was the brightest afternoon Margaret had spent for many a day. The carriage was dismissed to the inn, there to be the admiration of the ostlers and idlers; while the coachman and footman, after beer, condescended to play skittles and to receive the undisguised compliments of the village boys. Geoffrey went back to his work; and Margaret and Annie had a long talk, in which, though it was not very serious, Annie's good sense perpetually made itself felt, and at the end of which Margaret felt calmer, happier, and more hopeful than she had felt since her marriage. After the carriage had driven away, she sat pondering over all that had been said. This, then, was the Miss Maurice against whom she had conceived such a prejudice, and whom "she was sure she could never like?" And now, here, at their very first meeting, she had given her her confidence, and listened to her as though she had been her sister! What a calm quiet winning way she had! with what thorough good sense she talked! Margaret had expected to find her a prim old-maidish kind of person, younger, of course, but very much of the same type as the Miss Coverdales next door, utterly different from the fresh pretty-looking girl full of spirits and cheerfulness. How admirably she would have suited Geoff as a wife! and yet what was there in her that she (Margaret) could not acquire? It all rested with herself; her husband's heart was hers, firmly and undoubtedly, and she only needed to look her lot resolutely in the face, to conform to the ordinary domestic routine, as Annie had suggested, and all·would be well. O, if she could but lay the ghosts of that past which haunted her so incessantly, if she could but forget *him,* and all the associations connected with him, her life might yet be thoroughly happy!

And Annie, what did she think of her new acquaintance? Whatever her sentiments were, she kept them to herself, merely saying in answer to questions that Mrs. Geoffrey Ludlow was the most beautiful woman she had ever seen; that she could say with perfect truth and in all sincerity; but as to the rest, she did not know—she could scarcely make up her mind. During the first five minutes of their interview she hated her, at least regarded her with that feeling which Annie imagined was hate, but which was really only a mild dislike. There were few women, Annie supposed, who could in cold blood, and without the slightest provocation, have committed such an outrage as that taunt about her position in Lady Beauport's household; but then again there were few who would have so promptly though silently acknowledged the fault and endeavoured to make reparation for it. How openly she spoke! how bitterly she bemoaned the dulness of her life! That did not argue well for Geoffrey's happiness; but doubtless Mrs. Ludlow had reason to feel dull, as have most brides taken from their home and friends, and left to spend the day by themselves; but if she had really loved her husband, she would have hesitated before thus complaining to a stranger—would for his sake have either endeavoured to throw some explanatory gloss over the subject, or remained silent about it. She did not seem, so far as Annie saw, to have made any attempt to please her husband, or indeed to care to do so. How different she was from what Annie had expected! how different from all her previous experience of young married women, who indeed generally "gushed" dreadfully, and were painfully extravagant in their laudations of their husbands when they were absent, and in their connubialities when they were present. Geoffrey's large eloquent eyes had melted into tenderness as he looked at her; but she had not returned the glance, had not interchanged with him one term of endearment, one chance pressure of the hand. What did it all mean? What was that past gaiety and excitement to which she said she had been accustomed? What were her antecedents? In the whole of her long talk with Annie, Margaret had spoken always of the future, never of the past. It was of what she should do that she asked counsel; never mentioning what she had done; never alluding to any person, place, or circumstance connected with her existence previously to her having become Geoffrey Ludlow's wife. What were her antecedents? Once or twice during their talk she had used an odd word, a strange phrase, which grated on Annie's ear; but her manner was that of a well-bred gentlewoman; and in all the outward and visible signs of race, she might have been the purest aristocrat.

Meantime her beauty was undeniable, was overwhelming. Such hair and eyes Annie had dreamed of, but had never seen. She raved about them until Caterham declared she must puzzle her brain to find some excuse for his going to Elm Lodge to see this wonderful woman. She described Margaret to Lady Beauport, who was good enough to express a desire to see "the young person." She mentioned her to Algy Barford, who listened and then said, "Nice! nice! Caterham, dear old boy! you and I will take our slates and go up to—what's the name of the place?—to learn drawing. Must learn on slates, dear boy. Don't you recollect the house of our childhood with the singular perspective and an enormous amount of smoke, like wool, coming out of the chimneys? Must have been a brewery by the amount of smoke, by Jove! And the man in the cocked-hat, with no stomach to speak of, and both his arms very thin, with round blobs at the end growing out of one side. Delicious reminiscences of one's childhood, by Jove!"

And then Annie took to sketching after-memory portraits of Margaret, first mere pencil outlines, then more elaborate shaded attempts, and finally a water-colour reminiscence, which was any thing but bad. This she showed to Lord Caterham, who was immensely pleased with it, and who insisted that Barford should see it. So one morning when that pleasantest of laughing philosophers was smoking his after-breakfast cigar (at about noon) in Caterham's room, mooning about amongst the nick-nacks, and trotting out his little scraps of news in his own odd quaint fashion, Annie, who had heard from Stephens of his arrival, came in, bringing the portrait with her.

"Enter, Miss Maurice!" said Algy; "always welcome, but more especially welcome when she brings some delicious little novelty, such as I see she now holds under her arm. What would the world be without novelty?—Shakespeare. At least, if that delightful person did not make that remark, it was simply because he forgot it; for it's just one of those sort of things which he put so nicely. And what is Miss Maurice's novelty?"

"O! it's no novelty at all, Mr. Barford. Only a sketch of Mrs. Geoffrey Ludlow, of whom I spoke to you the other day. You recollect?"

"Recollect! the Muse of painting! Terps—Clio—no matter! a charming person from whom we were to have instruction in drawing, and who lives at some utterly unsearchable place! Of course I recollect! And you have a sketch of her there? Now, my dear Miss Maurice, don't keep me in suspense any longer, but let me look at it at once." But when the sketch was unrolled and placed before him, it had the very singular effect of reducing Algy Barford to a state of quietude. Beyond giving one long whistle he never uttered a sound, but sat with parted lips and uplifted eyebrows gazing at the picture for full five minutes. Then he said, "This is like, of course, Miss Maurice?"

"Well, I really think I may say it is. It is far inferior to the original in beauty, of course; but I think I have preserved her most delicate features."

"Just so. Her hair is of that peculiar colour, and her eyes a curious violet, eh?"

"Yes."

"This sketch gives one the notion of a tall woman with a full figure."

"Yes; she is taller than I, and her figure is thoroughly rounded and graceful."

"Ye-es; a very charming sketch, Miss Maurice; and your friend must be very lovely if she at all resembles it."

Shortly after, when Mr. Algy Barford had taken his leave, he stopped on the flags in St. Barnabas Square, thus soliloquising: "All right, my dear old boy, my dear old Algy! it's coming on fast—a little sooner than you thought; but that's no matter. Colney Hatch, my dear boy, and a padded room looking out over the railway. That's it; that's your hotel, dear boy! If you ever drank, it might be *del. trem.*, and would pass off; but you don't. No, no; to see twice within six months, first the woman herself, and then the portrait of the woman—just married and known to credible witnesses—whom you have firmly believed to be lying in Kensal Green! Colney Hatch, dear old boy; that is the apartment, and nothing else!"

CHAPTER IX.

MR. AMPTHILL'S WILL.

THE acquaintance between Margaret and Annie, which commenced so auspiciously, scarcely ripened into intimacy. When Lady Beauport's neuralgia passed away,—and her convalescence was much hurried by the near approach of a specially-grand entertainment given in honour of certain Serene Transparencies then visiting London,—she found that she could not spare Miss Maurice to go so long a distance, to be absent from her and her work for such a length of time. As to calling at Elm Lodge in person, Lady Beauport never gave the project another thought. With the neuralgia had passed away her desire to see that "pretty young person," Mrs. Geoffrey Ludlow; and in sending her card by Annie, Lady Beauport thought she had more than fulfilled any promises and vows of politeness which might have been made by her son in her name.

Lord Caterham had driven out once to Elm Lodge with Annie, and had been introduced to Margaret, whom he admired very much, but about whom he shook his head alarmingly when he and Annie were driving towards home. "That's an unhappy woman!" he said; "an unhappy woman, with something on her mind—something which she does not give way to and groan about, but against which she frets and fights and struggles with as with a chain. When she's not spoken to, when she's not supposed to be *en évidence*, there's a strange, half-weary, half-savage gleam in those wondrous eyes, such as I have noticed only once before, and then among the patients of a lunatic asylum. There's evidently something strange in the history of that marriage. Did you notice Ludlow's devotion to her, how he watched her every movement? Did you see what hard work it was for her to keep up with the conversation, not from want of power,—for, from one or two things she said, I should imagine her to be a naturally clever as well as an educated woman,—but from want of will? How utterly worn and wearied and *distraite* she looked, standing by us in Ludlow's studio, while we talked about his pictures, and how she only seemed to rouse into life when I compared that Brighton Esplanade with the Drive in the Park, and talked about some of the frequenters of each. She listened to all the fashionable nonsense as eagerly as any country miss, and yet—— She's a strange study, that woman, Annie. I shall take an early opportunity of driving out to see her again; but I'm glad that the distance will prevent her being very intimate with you."

The opportunity of repeating his visit did not, however, speedily occur. The fierce neuralgic headaches from which Lord Caterham suffered had become much more frequent of late, and worse in their effect. After hours of actual torture, unable to raise his head or scarcely to lift his eyes, he would fall into a state of prostration, which lasted two or three days. In this state he would be dressed by his servant and carried to his sofa, where he would lie with half-closed eyes dreaming the time away, comparatively happy in being free from pain, quite happy if, as frequently happened, on looking up he saw Annie Maurice moving noiselessly about the room dusting his books, arranging his desk, bringing fresh flowers for his glasses. Looking round at him from time to time, and finding he had noticed her presence, she would lay her finger on her lip enjoining silence, and then refresh his burning forehead and hands with eau-de-cologne, turn and smooth his pillows, and wheel his sofa to a cooler position. On the second day after an attack she would read to him for hours in her clear musical voice from his favourite authors ; or, if she found him able to bear it, would sit down at the cabinet-piano, which he had bought expressly for her, and sing to him the songs he loved so well—quiet English ballads, sparkling little French *chansons*, and some of the most pathetic music of the Italian operas ; but every thing for his taste must be soft and low : all roulades and execution, all the fireworks of music, he held in utter detestation.

Then Annie would be called away to write notes for Lady Beauport, or to go out with her or for her, and Caterham would be left alone again. Pleasanter his thoughts now : there were the flowers she had gathered and placed close by him, the books she had read from, the ivory keys which her dear fingers had so recently touched ! Her cheerful voice still rung in his ear, the touch of her hand seemed yet to linger on his forehead. O angel of light and almost of hope to this wretched frame, O sole realisation of womanly love and tenderness and sweet sympathy to this crushed spirit, wilt thou ever know it all? Yes, he felt that there would come a time, and that without long delay, when he should be able to tell her all the secret longings of his soul, to tell her in a few short words, and then—ay, then !

Meanwhile it was pleasant to lie in a half-dreamy state, thinking of her, picturing her to his fancy. He would lie on that sofa, his poor warped useless limbs stretched out before him, but hidden from his sight by a light silk *couvrette* of Annie's embroidering, his eyes closed, his whole frame n a state of repose. Through the double windows came deadened sounds of the world outside—the roll of carriages, the clanging of knockers, the busy hum of life. From the Square-garden came the glad voices of children, and now and then—solitary fragment of rusticity—the sound of the Square-gardener whetting his scythe. And Caterham lay day by day dreaming through it all, unroused even by the repetition of Czerny's pianoforte-exercises by the children in the next house; dreaming of his past, his present, and his future. Dreaming of the old farmhouse where they had sent him when a child to try and get strength—the quaint red-faced old house with its gable ends and mullioned windows, and its eternal and omnipresent smell of apples; of the sluggish black pool where the cattle stood knee-deep; the names of the fields—the home-croft, and the lea pasture, and the forty acres; the harvest-home, and the songs that they sung then, and to which he had listened in wonder sitting on the farmer's knee. He had not thought of all this from that day forth; but he remembered it vividly now, and could almost hear the loud ticking of the farmer's silver watch which fitted so tightly into his fob. The lodgings at Brighton, where he went with some old lady, never recollected but in connection with that one occasion, and called Miss Macraw,—the little lodgings with the bow-windowed room looking sideways over the sea; the happiness of that time, when the old lady perpetually talked to and amused him, when he was not left alone as he was at home, and when he had such delicious tea-cakes which he toasted for himself. The doctors who came to see him there; one a tall white-haired old man in a long black coat reaching to his heels, and another a jolly bald-headed man, who, they said, was surgeon to the King. The King—ay, he had seen him too, a red-faced man in a blue coat, walking in the Pavilion Gardens. Dreaming of the private tutor, a master at Charter House, who came on Wednesday and Saturday afternoons, and who struggled so hard and with such little success to conceal his hatred to Homer, Virgil, and the other classic poets, and his longing to be in the cricket-field, on the river, any where, to shake off that horrible conventional toil of tutorship, and to be a man and not a teaching-machine. Other recollections he had, of Lionel's pony and Lionel's Eton school-fellows, who came to see him in the holidays, and who stared in mute wonder at his wheel-chair and his poor crippled limbs. Recollections of his father and mother passing down the staircase in full dress on their way to some court-ball, and of his hearing the servants say what a noble-looking man his father was, and what a pity that Master Lionel had not been the eldest son. Recollections of the utter blankness of his life until she came—ah, until she came! The past faded away, and the present dawned. She was there, his star, his hope, his love! He was still a cripple, maimed and blighted; still worse than an invalid, the prey of acute and torturing disease; but he would be content— content to remain even as he was, so that he could have her near him, could see her, hear her voice, touch her hand. But that could not be. She would marry, would leave him, and then—ah then!—Let that future which he believed to be close upon him come at once. Until he had known hope, his life, though blank enough, had been supportable; now hope had fled; "the sooner it's over the sooner to sleep." Let there be an end of it!

There were but few days that Algy Barford did not come; bright, airy, and cheerful, bringing sunshine into the sick-room; never noisy or obtrusive, always taking a cheery view of affairs, and never failing to tell the invalid that he looked infinitely better than the last time he had seen him, and that this illness was "evidently a kind of clearing-up shower before the storm, dear old boy," and was the precursor of such excellent health as he had never had before. Lord Caterham, of course, never believed any of this; he had an internal monitor which told him very different truths; but he knew the feelings which prompted Algy Barford's hopeful predictions, and no man's visits were so agreeable to Caterham as were Algy's.

One day he came in earlier than usual, and looking less serenely happy than his wont. Lord Caterham, lying on his sofa, observed this, but said nothing, waiting until Algy should allude to it, as he was certain to do, for he had not the smallest power of reticence.

"Caterham, my dear old boy, how goes it this morning? I am seedy, my friend! The sage counsel given by the convivial bagman, that the evening's diversion should bear

the morning's reflection, has not been followed by me.
Does the cognac live in its usual corner, and is there yet
soda-water in the land?"

"You'll find both in the sideboard, Algy. What were
you doing last night to render them necessary?"

"Last night, my dear Caterham, I did what England
expected me to do—my duty, and a most horrible nuisance
that doing one's duty is. I dined with an old fellow named
Huskisson, a friend of my governor's, who nearly poisoned
me with bad wine. The wine, sir, was simply infamous;
but it was a very hot night, and I was dreadfully thirsty,
so what could I do but drink a great deal of it? I had
some very fiery sherry with my soup, and some hock.
Yes; 'nor did my drooping memory shun the foaming
grape of eastern France;' only this was the foaming goose-
berry of Fulham Fields. And old Huskisson, with great
pomp, told his butler to bring ' the Hermitage.' What an
awful swindle!"

"What was it like?"

"Well, dear old boy, minds innocent and quiet may take
that for a Hermitage if they like; but I, who have drunk
as much wine, good and bad, as most men, immediately
recognised the familiar Beaujolais, which we get at the club
for a shilling a pint. So that altogether I'm very nearly
poisoned; and I think I shouldn't have come out if I had
not wanted to see you particularly."

"What is it, Algy? Some of that tremendously important business which always takes up so much of your
time?"

"No, no; now you're chaffing, Caterham. 'Pon my word
I really do a great deal in the course of the day, walking
about, and talking to fellows, and that sort of thing: there
are very few fellows who think what a lot I get through;
but I know myself."

"Do you? then you've learned a great thing—'know
thyself,' one of the great secrets of life;" and Caterham
sighed.

"Yes, dear old boy," said Algy; "'know thyself, but
never introduce a friend;' that I believe to be sterling
philosophy. This is a confoundedly back-slapping age;
every body is a deuced sight too fond of every body else;

there is an amount of philanthropy about which is quite terrible."

"Yes, and you're about the largest-hearted and most genial philanthropist·in the world ; you know you are."

"I, dear old boy ? I am Richard Crookback ; I am the uncle of the Babes in the Wood; I am Timon the Tartar of Athens, or whatever his name was ; I am a ruthless hater of all my species, when I have the *vin triste*, as I have this morning. O, that reminds me—the business I came to see you about. What a fellow you are, Caterham ! always putting things out of fellows' heads !"

"Well, what is it now ?"

"Why, old Ampthill is dead at last. Died last night; his man told my man this morning."

"Well, what then ?"

"What then ? Why, don't you recollect what we talked about ? about his leaving his money to dear old Lionel ?"

"Yes," said Caterham, looking grave, " I recollect that."

"I wonder whether any good came of it ? It would be a tremendously jolly thing to get dear old Lionel back, with plenty of money, and in his old position, wouldn't it ?"

"Look here, my dear Algy," said Lord Caterham; "let us understand each other once for all on this point. You and I are of course likely to differ materially on such a subject. You are a man of the world, going constantly into the world, with your own admirable good sense influenced by and impressed with the opinions of society. Society, as you tell me, is pleased to think my brother's— · well, crime—there's no other word !—my brother's crime a venial one, and will be content to receive him back again, and to instal him in his former position, if he comes back prepared to sacrifice to Society by spending his time and money on it !"

"Pardon me, my dear old Caterham,—just two words !" interrupted Algy. "Society—people, you know, I mean— would shake their heads at poor old Lionel, and wouldn't have him back perhaps, and all that sort of thing, if they knew exactly what he'd done. But they don't. It's been kept wonderfully quiet, poor dear old fellow."

"That may or may not be; at all events, such are Society's views, are they not ?" Barford inclined his head.

"Now, you see, mine are entirely different. This sofa, the bed in the next room, that wheel-chair, form my world; and these," pointing to his bookshelves, "my society. There is no one else on earth to whom I would say this; but you know that what I say is true. Lionel Brakespere never was a brother to me, never had the slightest affection or regard for me, never had the slightest patience with me. As a boy, he used to mock at my deformity; as a man, he has perseveringly scorned me, and scarcely troubled himself to hide his anxiety for my death, that he might be Lord Beauport's heir—"

"Caterham! I say, my dear, dear old boy Arthur—" and Algy Barford put one hand on the back of Lord Caterham's chair, and rubbed his own eyes very hard with the other.

"You know it, Algy, old friend. He did all this; and God knows I tried to love him through it all, and think I succeeded. All his scorn, all his insult, all his want of affection, I forgave. When he committed the forgery which forced him to fly the country, I tried to intercede with my father; for I knew the awful strait to which Lionel must have been reduced before he committed such an act: but when I read his letter, which you brought me, and the contents of which it said you knew, I recognised at last that Lionel was a thoroughly heartless scoundrel, and I thanked God that there was no chance of his further disgracing our name in a place where it had been known and respected. So you now see, Algy, why I am not enchanted at the idea of his coming back to us."

"Of course, of course, I understand you, dear fellow; and—hem!—confoundedly husky; that filthy wine of old Huskisson's! better in a minute—there!" and Algy cleared his throat and rubbed his eyes again. "About that letter, dear old boy! I was going to speak to you two or three times about that. Most mysterious circumstance, by Jove, sir! The fact is that—"

He was interrupted by the opening of the door and the entrance of Stephens, Lord Caterham's servant, who said that Lady Beauport would be glad to know if his master could receive her.

It was a bad day for Caterham to receive any one except his most intimate friends, and assuredly his mother was not included in that category. He was any thing but well bodily, and the conversation about Lionel had thoroughly unstrung his nerves; so that he was just about to say he must ask for a postponement of the visit, when Stephens said, "Her ladyship asked me if Mr. Barford wasn't here, my lord, and seemed particularly anxious to see him." Lord Caterham felt the colour flush in his cheeks as the cause of his mother's visit was thus innocently explained by Stephens; but the moment after he smiled, and sent to beg that she would come whenever she pleased.

In a very few minutes Lady Beauport sailed into the room, and, after shaking hands with Algy Barford in, for her, quite a cordial manner, she touched her son's forehead with her lips and dropped into the chair which Stephens had placed for her near the sofa.

"How are you, Arthur, to day?" she commenced. "You are looking quite rosy and well, I declare. I am always obliged to come myself when I want to know about your health; for they bring me the most preposterous reports. That man of yours is a dreadful kill-joy, and seems to have inoculated the whole household with his melancholy, where you are concerned. Even Miss Maurice, who is really quite a cheerful person, and quite pleasant to have about one,— equable spirits, and that sort of thing, you know, Mr. Barford; so much more agreeable than those moping creatures who are always thinking about their families and their fortunes, you know,—even Miss Maurice can scarcely be trusted for what I call a reliable report of Caterham."

"It's the interest we take in him, dear Lady Beauport, that keeps us constantly on the *qui vive*. He's such a tremendously lovable old fellow, that we're all specially careful about him;" and Algy's hand went round to the back of Caterham's sofa and his eyes glistened as before.

"Of course," said Lady Beauport, still in her hard dry voice. "With care, every thing may be done. There's Alice Wentworth, Lady Broughton's grand-daughter, was sent away in the autumn to Torquay, and they all declared she could not live. And I saw her last night at the French embassy, well and strong, and dancing away as hard as any girl in the room. It's a great pity you couldn't have gone to the embassy last night, Arthur; you'd have enjoyed it very much."

"Do you think so, mother?" said Caterham with a sad

smile. " I scarcely think it would have amused me, or that they would have cared much to have me there."

" O, I don't know ; the Duchess de St. Lazare asked after you very kindly, and so did the Viscomte, who is—" and Lady Beauport stopped short.

" Yes, I know—who is a cripple also," said Caterham quietly. " But he is only lame ; he can get about by himself. But if I had gone, I should have wanted Algy here to carry me on his back."

"Gad, dear old boy, if carrying you on my back would do you any good, or help you to get about to any place you wanted to go to, I'd do it fast enough ; give you a regular Derby canter over any course you like to name."

" I know you would, Algy, old friend. You see every one is very kind, and I am doing very well indeed, though I'm scarcely in condition for a ball at the French embassy.—By the way, mother, did you not want to speak to Barford about something ?"

" I did, indeed," said Lady Beauport. " I have heard just now, Mr. Barford, that old Mr. Ampthill died last night ?"

" Perfectly true, Lady Beauport. I myself had the same information."

" But you heard nothing further ?"

" Nothing at all, except that the poor old gentleman, after a curious eccentric life, made a quiet commonplace end, dying peacefully and happily."

" Yes, yes ; but you heard nothing about the way in which his property is left, I suppose ?"

" Not one syllable. He was very wealthy, was he not ?"

" My husband says that the Boxwood property was worth from twelve to fifteen thousand a-year ; but I imagine this is rather an under-estimate. I wonder whether there is any chance for—what I talked to you about the other day."

" Impossible to say, dear Lady Beauport," said Algy, with an awkward glance at Caterham, which Lady Beauport observed.

" O, you needn't mind Caterham one bit, Mr. Barford.— Any thing which would do good to poor Lionel I'm sure you'd be glad of, wouldn't you, Arthur ?"

" Any thing that would do him good, yes."

" Of course ; and to be Mr. Ampthill's heir would do him a great deal of good. It is that Mr. Barford and I are dis-

cussing.   Mr. Barford was good enough to speak to me some
time ago, when it was first expected that Mr. Ampthill's
illness would prove dangerous, and to suggest that, as poor
Lionel had always been a favourite with the old gentleman,
something might be done for him, perhaps, there being so
few relations.   I spoke to your father, who called two or
three times in Curzon Street, and always found Mr. Ampthill
very civil and polite, but he never mentioned Lionel's
name.

"That did not look particularly satisfactory, did it?"
asked Algy.

"Well, it would have looked bad in any one else; but
with such an extremely eccentric person as Mr. Ampthill, I
really cannot say I think so.   He was just one of those
oddities who would carefully refrain from mentioning the
person about whom their thoughts were most occupied.—I
cannot talk to your father about this matter, Arthur; he is
so dreadfully set against poor Lionel, that he will not listen
to a word.—But I need not tell you, Mr. Barford, I myself
am horribly anxious."

Perfectly appreciating Lord Beauport's anger; conscious
that it was fully shared by Caterham; with tender recollections
of Lionel, whom he had known from childhood; and with a
desire to say something pleasant to Lady Beauport, all
Algy Barford could ejaculate was, "Of course, of course."

"I hear that old Mr. Trivett the lawyer was with him two
or three times about a month ago, which looks as if he had
been making his will.   I met Mr. Trivett at the Dunsinanes
in the autumn, and at Beauport's request was civil to him.
I would not mind asking him to dine here one day this
week, if I thought it would be of any use."

Caterham looked very grave; but Algy Barford gave a
great laugh, and seemed immensely amused.   "How do you
mean 'of any use,' Lady Beauport?   You don't think you
would get any information out of old Trivett, do you?   He's
the deadest hand at a secret in the world.   He never lets
out any thing.   If you ask him what it is o'clock, you have
to dig the information out of him with a ripping-chisel.   O,
no; it's not the smallest use trying to learn anything from
Mr. Trivett."

"Is there, then, no means of finding out what the will
contains?"

"No, mother," interrupted Caterham; "none at all. You must wait until the will is read, after the funeral; or perhaps till you see a *résumé* of it in the illustrated papers."

"You are very odd, Arthur," said Lady Beauport; "really sometimes you would seem to have forgotten the usages of society.—I appeal to you, Mr. Barford. Is what Lord Caterham says correct? Is there no other way of learning what I want to know?"

"Dear Lady Beauport, I fear there is none."

"Very well, then; I must be patient and wait. But there's no harm in speculating how the money could be left. Who did Mr. Ampthill know now? There was Mrs. Macraw, widow of a dissenting minister, who used to read to him; and there was his physician, Sir Charles Dumfunk: I shouldn't wonder if he had a legacy."

"And there was Algernon Barford, commonly known as the Honourable Algernon Barford, who used to dine with the old gentleman half-a-dozen times every season, and who had the honour of being called a very good fellow by him."

"O, Algy, I hope he has left you his fortune," said Caterham warmly. "There's no one in the world would spend it to better purpose."

"Well," said Lady Beauport, "I will leave you now.—I know I may depend upon you, Mr. Barford, to give me the very first news on this important subject."

Algy Barford bowed, rose, and opened the door to let Lady Beauport pass out. As she walked by him, she gave him a look which made him follow her and close the door behind him.

"I didn't like to say any thing before Caterham," she said, "who is, you know, very odd and queer, and seems to have taken quite a singular view of poor Lionel's conduct. But the fact is, that, after the last time you spoke to me, I—I thought it best to write to Lionel, to tell him that—" and she hesitated.

"To tell him what, Lady Beauport?" asked Algy, resolutely determined not to help her in the least.

"To tell him to come back to us—to me—to his mother!" said Lady Beauport, with a sudden access of passion. "I cannot live any longer without my darling son! I have told Beauport this. What does it signify that he has been unfortunate—wicked if you will! How many others have been the same ! And our influence could get him something somewhere, even if this inheritance should not be his. O my God ! only to see him again ! My darling boy ! my own darling handsome boy !"

Ah, how many years since Gertrude, Countess of Beauport, had allowed real, natural, hot, blinding tears to course down her cheeks ! The society people, who only knew her as the calmest, most collected, most imperious woman amongst them, would hardly recognise this palpitating frame, those tear-blurred features. The sight completely finishes Algy Barford, already very much upset by the news which Lady Beauport has communicated, and he can only proffer a seat, and suggest that he should fetch a glass of sherry. Lady Beauport, her burst of passion over, recovers all her usual dignity, presses Algy's hand, lays her finger on her lip to enjoin silence, and sails along as unbending as before. Algy Barford, still dazed by the tidings he has heard, goes back to Caterham's room, to find his friend lying with his eyes half-closed, meditating over the recent discussion. Caterham scarcely seemed to have noticed Algy's absence ; for he said, as if in continuance of the conversation : "And do *you* think this money will come to Lionel, Algy ?"

"I can scarcely tell, dear old boy. It's on the cards, but the betting is heavily against it. However, we shall know in a very few days."

In a very few days they did know. The funeral, to which Earl Beauport and Algy Barford were invited, and which they attended, was over, and Mr. Trivett had requested them to return with him in the mourning-coach to Curzon Street. There, in the jolly little dining-room, which had so often enshrined the hospitality of the quaint, eccentric, warm-hearted old gentleman whose earthly remains they had left behind them at Kensal Green, after some cake and wine, old Mr. Trivett took from a blue bag, which had been left there for him by his clerk, the will of the deceased, and putting on his blue-steel spectacles, commenced reading it aloud. The executors appointed were George Earl Beauport and Algernon Barford, and to each of them was bequeathed a legacy of a thousand pounds. To Algernon Barford, "a good fellow, who, I know, will spend it like a gentleman," was also left a thousand pounds. There were legacies of five hundred pounds each "to John Saunders, my faithful valet, and to Rebecca, his wife, my cook and housekeeper." There was a legacy of one hundred pounds to the librarian of the Minerva Club, "to whom I have given much trouble." The library of books, the statues, pictures, and curios were bequeathed to "my cousin Arthur, Viscount Caterham, the only member of my family who can appreciate them;" and "the entire residue of my fortune, my estate at Boxwood, money standing in the funds and other securities, plate, wines, carriages, horses, and all my property, to Anna, only daughter of my second cousin, the late Ralph Ampthill Maurice, Esq., formerly of the Priory, Willesden, whom I name my residuary legatee."

CHAPTER X.

LADY BEAUPORT'S PLOT.

YES; little Annie Maurice, Lady Beauport's companion, was the heiress of the rich and eccentric Mr. Ampthill, so long known in society. The fact was a grand thing for the paragraph-mongers and the diners-out, all of whom distorted it in every possible way, and told the most inconceivable lies about it. That Annie was Mr. Ampthill's natural daughter, and had been left on a door-step, and was adopted by Lady Beauport, who had found her in an orphan-asylum; that Mr. Ampthill had suddenly determined upon leaving all his property to the first person he might meet on a certain day, and that Annie Maurice was the fortunate individual; that the will had been made purposely to spite Lady Beauport, with whom Mr. Ampthill, when a young man, had been madly in love—all these rumours went the round of the gossip-columns of the journals and of Society's dinner-parties. Other stories there were, perhaps a little nearer to truth, which explained that it was not until after Lionel Brakespere's last escapade he had been disinherited; indeed, that Parkinson of Thavies Inn and Scadgers of Berners Street had looked upon his inheritance as such a certainty, that they had made considerable advances on the strength of it, and would be heavily hit; while a rumour,

traceable to the old gentleman's housekeeper, stated that
Annie Maurice was the only one of Mr. Ampthill's connections who had never fawned on him, flattered him, or in
any way intrigued for his favour.

Be this as it might, the fact remained that Annie was now
the possessor of a large fortune, and consequently a person
of great importance to all her friends and acquaintance—a
limited number, but quite sufficient to discuss her rise in life
with every kind of asperity. They wondered how she would
bear it ; whether she would give herself airs ; how soon, and
to what member of the peerage, she would be married.
How *did* she bear it ? When Lord Beauport sent for her to
his study, after Mr. Ampthill's funeral, and told her what he
had heard, she burst into tears ; which was weak, but not
unnatural. Then, with her usual straightforward common-
sense, she set about forming her plans. She had never seen
her benefactor, so that even Mrs. Grundy herself could
scarcely have called on Annie to affect sorrow for his loss ;
and indeed remarks were made by Mr. Ampthill's old butler
and housekeeper (who, being provided with mourning out of
the estate, were as black and as shiny as a couple of old
rooks) about the very mitigated grief which Annie chose to
exhibit in her attire.

Then as to her mode of life. For the present, at least,
she determined to make no change in it. She said so at
once to Lord Beauport, expressing an earnest hope that she
should be allowed to remain under his roof, where she had
been so happy, until she had settled how and where she
should live ; and Lord Beauport replied that it would give
him—and he was sure he might speak for Lady Beauport—
the greatest pleasure to have Miss Maurice with them. He
brought a message to that effect from Lady Beauport, who
had one of her dreadful neuralgic attacks, and could see no
one, but who sent her kind love to Miss Maurice, and her
heartiest congratulations, and hoped that Miss Maurice would
remain with them as long as she pleased. The servants of
the house, who heard of the good fortune of "the young
lady," rejoiced greatly at it, and suggested that miss would go
hout of this at once, and leave my lady to grump about in
that hold carriage by herself. They were greatly astonished,
therefore, the next morning to find Annie seated at the nine-
o'clock breakfast-table, preparing Lady Beauport's chocolate,

and dressed just as usual. They had expected that the first sign of her independence would be lying in bed till noon, and then appearing in a gorgeous wrapper, such as the ladies in the penny romances always wore in the mornings; and they could only account for her conduct by supposing that she had to give a month's warning and must work out her time. Lady Beauport herself was astonished when, the necessity for the neuralgic attack being over, she found Annie coming to ask her, as usual, what letters she required written, and whether she should pay any calls for her ladyship. Lady Beauport delicately remonstrated; but Annie declared that she would infinitely prefer doing exactly as she had been accustomed to, so long as she should remain in the house.

So long as she should remain in the house! That was exactly the point on which Lady Beauport was filled with hope and dread. Her ladyship had been cruelly disappointed in Mr. Ampthill's will. She had suffered herself to hope against hope, and to shut her eyes to all unfavourable symptoms. The old gentleman had taken so much notice of Lionel when a boy, had spoken so warmly of him, had made so much of him, that he could not fail to make him his heir. In vain had Lord Beauport spoken to her more plainly than was his wont, pointing out that Lionel's was no venial crime; that Mr. Ampthill probably had heard of it, inasmuch as he never afterwards mentioned the young man's name; that however his son's position might be reinstated before the world, the act could never be forgotten. In vain Algy Barford shook his head, and Caterham preserved a gloomy silence worse than any speech. Lady Beauport's hopes did not desert her until she heard the actual and final announcement. Almost simultaneously with this came Lord Beauport with Annie's request that she should be permitted to continue an inmate of the house; and immediately Lady Beauport conceived and struck out a new plan of action. The heritage was lost to Lionel; but the heiress was Annie Maurice, a girl domiciled with them, clinging to them; unlikely, at least for the few ensuing months, to go into the world, to give the least chance to any designing fortune-hunter. And Lionel was coming home! His mother was certain that the letter which she had written to him on the first news of Mr. Ampthill's illness would induce him, already sick of exile, to start for England. He would arrive soon, and then the season would be over; they would all go away to Homershams, or one of Beauport's places; they would not have any company for some time, and Lionel would be thrown into Annie Maurice's society; and it would be hard if he, with his handsome face, his fascinating manners, and his experience of women and the world, were not able to make an easy conquest of this simple quiet young girl, and thus to secure the fortune which his mother had originally expected for him.

Such was Lady Beauport's day-dream now, and to its realisation she gave up every thought, in reference to it she planned every action. It has already been stated that she had always treated Annie with respect, and even with regard: so that the idea of patronage, the notion of behaving to her companion in any thing but the spirit of a lady, had never entered her mind. But now there was an amount of affectionate interest mingled with her regard which Annie could not fail to perceive and to be gratified with. All was done in the most delicate manner. Lady Beauport never forgot the lady in the *intrigante;* her advances were of the subtlest kind; her hints were given and allusions were made in the most guarded manner. She accepted Annie's assistance as her amanuensis, and she left to her the usual colloquies on domestic matters with the housekeeper, because she saw that Annie wished it to be so; and she still drove out with her in the carriage, only insisting that Annie should sit by her side instead of opposite on the back-seat. And instead of the dignified silence of the employer, only speaking when requiring an answer, Lady Beauport would keep up a perpetual conversation, constantly recurring to the satisfaction it gave her to have Annie still with her. " I declare I don't know what I should have done if you had left me, Annie!" she would say. " I'm sure it was the mere thought of having to be left by myself, or to the tender mercies of somebody who knew nothing about me, that gave me that last frightful attack of neuralgia. You see I am an old woman now; and though the Carringtons are proverbially strong and long-lived, yet I have lost all my elasticity of spirit, and feel I could not shape myself to any person's way now. And poor Caterham too! I cannot think how he would ever get on without you. You seem now to be an essential part of his life.

Poor Caterham! Ah, how I wish you had seen my other son, my boy Lionel! Such a splendid fellow; so handsome! Ah, Lord Beauport was dreadfully severe on him, poor fellow, that night,—you recollect, when he had you and Caterham in to tell you about poor Lionel; as though young men would not be always young men. Poor Lionel!" Poor Lionel! that was the text of Lady Beauport's discourse whenever she addressed herself to Annie Maurice.

It was not to be supposed that Annie's change of fortune had not a great effect upon Lord Caterham. When he first heard of it—from Algy Barford, who came direct to him from the reading of the will—he rejoiced that at least her future was secure; that, come what might to him or his parents, there would be a provision for her; that no chance of her being reduced to want, or of her having to consult the prejudices of other people, and to perform a kind of genteel servitude with any who could not appreciate her worth could now arise. But with this feeling another soon mingled. Up to that time she had been all in all to him—to him; simply because to the outside world she was nobody, merely Lady Beauport's companion, about whom none troubled themselves; now she was Miss Maurice the heiress, and in a very different position. They could not hope to keep her to themselves; they could not hope to keep her free from the crowd of mercenary adorers always looking out for every woman with money whom they might devour. In her own common sense lay her strongest safe-guard; and that, although reliable on all ordinary occasions, had never been exposed to so severe a trial as flattery and success. Were not the schemers already plotting? even within the citadel was there not a traitor? Algy Barford had kept his trust, and had not betrayed one word of what Lady Beauport had told him; but from stray expressions dropped now and again, and from the general tenor of his mother's behaviour, Lord Caterham saw plainly what she was endeavouring to bring about. On that subject his mind was made up. He had such thorough confidence in Annie's goodness, in her power of discrimination between right and wrong, that he felt certain that she could never bring herself to love his brother Lionel, however handsome his face, how-ever specious his manner; but if, woman-like, she should give way and follow her inclination rather than her reason, then he determined to talk to her plainly and openly, and to do every thing in his power to prevent the result on which his mother had set her heart.

There was not a scrap of selfishness in all this. However deeply Arthur Caterham loved Annie Maurice, the hope of making her his had never for an instant arisen in his breast. He knew too well that a mysterious decree of Providence had shut him out from the roll of those who are loved by woman, save in pity or sympathy; and it was with a feeling of relief, rather than regret, that of late—within the last few months—he had felt an inward presentiment that his commerce with Life was almost at an end, that his connection with that Vanity Fair, through which he had been wheeled as a spectator, but in the occupation or amusement of which he had never participated, was about to cease. He loved her so dearly, that the thought of her future was always before him, and caused him infinite anxiety. Worst of all, there was no one of whom he could make a confidant amongst his acquaintance. Algy Barford would do any thing; but he was a bachelor, which would incapacitate him, and by far too easy-going, trouble-hating, and unimpressive. Who else was there? Ah, a good thought!—that man Ludlow, the artist; an old friend of Annie's, for whom she had so great a regard. He was not particularly strong-minded out of his profession; but his devotion to his child-friend was undoubted; and besides, he was a man of education and common sense, rising, too, to a position which would insure his being heard. He would talk with Ludlow about Annie's future; so he wrote off to Geoffrey by the next post, begging him to come and see him as soon as possible. Yes, he could look at it all quite steadily now. Heaven knows, life to him had been no such happiness as to make its surrender painful or difficult. It was only as he neared his journey's end, he thought, that any light had been shed upon his path, and when that should be extinguished he would have no heart to go further. No: let the end come, as he knew it was coming, swiftly and surely; only let him think that *her* future was secured, and he could die more than contented—happy.

Her future secured! ah, that he should not live to see! It could not, must not be by a marriage with Lionel. His mother had never broached that subject openly to him, and therefore he had hitherto felt a delicacy in alluding to it in conversation with her; but he would before—well, he would in time. Not that he had much fear of Annie's succumbing to his brother's fascinations; he rated her too highly for that. It was not—and he took up a photographic album which lay on his table, as the idea passed through his mind—it was not that careless reckless expression, that easy insolent *pose*, which would have any effect on Annie Maurice's mental constitution. Those who imagine that women are enslaved through their eyes—true women—women worth winning at least—are horribly mistaken, he thought, and—And then at that instant he turned the page and came upon a photograph of himself, in which the artist had done his best so far as arrangement went, but which was so fatally truthful in its display of his deformity, that Lord Caterham closed the book with a shudder, and sunk back on his couch.

His painful reverie was broken by the entrance of Stephens, who announced that Mr. and Mrs. Ludlow were waiting to see his master. Caterham, who was unprepared for a visit from Mrs. Ludlow, gave orders that they should be at once admitted. Mrs. Ludlow came in leaning on her husband's arm, and looking so pale and interesting, that Caterham at once recollected the event he had seen announced in the *Times*, and began to apologise.

" My dear Mrs. Ludlow, what a horrible wretch I am to have asked your husband to come and see me, when of course he was fully occupied at home attending to you and the baby !" Then they both laughed; and Geoff said :

" This is her first day out, Lord Caterham; but I had promised to take her for a drive; and as you wanted to see me, I thought that—"

" That the air of St. Barnabas Square, the fresh breezes from the Thames, and the cheerful noise of the embankment-people, would be about the best thing for an invalid, eh ?"

" Well—scarcely ! but that as it was only stated that my wife should go for a quiet drive, I, who have neither the time nor the opportunity for such things, might utilise the occasion by complying with the request of a gentleman who has proved himself deserving of my respect."

" A hit ! a very palpable hit, Mr. Ludlow !" said Caterham. " I bow, and—as the common phrase goes—am sorry I spoke. But we must not talk business when you have brought Mrs. Ludlow out for amusement."

"O, pray don't think of me, Lord Caterham," said Margaret; "I can always amuse myself."

"O, of course; the mere recollection of baby would keep you sufficiently employed—at least, so you would have us believe. But I'm an old bachelor, and discredit such things. So there's a book of photographs for you to amuse yourself with while we talk.—Now, Mr. Ludlow, for our conversation. Since we met, your old friend Annie Maurice has inherited a very large property."

"So I have heard, to my great surprise and delight. But I live so much out of the world that I scarcely knew whether it was true, and had determined to ask you the first time I should see you."

"O, it's thoroughly true. She is the heiress of old Mr. Ampthill, who was a second cousin of her father's. But it was about her future career, as heiress of all this property, that I wanted to speak to you, you see.—I beg your pardon, Mrs. Ludlow, what did you say?"

Her face was dead white, her lips trembled, and it was with great difficulty she said any thing at all; but she did gasp out, "Who is this?"

"That,". said Lord Caterham, bending over the book; "O, that is the portrait of my younger brother, Lionel Brakespere; he—" but Caterham stopped short in his explanation, for Mrs. Ludlow fell backward in a swoon.

And every one afterwards said that it was very thoughtless of her to take such a long drive so soon after her confinement.

CHAPTER XI.

CONJECTURES.

MISS MAURICE was not in the house when Geoffrey Ludlow and his wife made that visit to Lord Caterham which had so plainly manifested Margaret's imprudence and inexperience. The housekeeper and one of the housemaids had come to the assistance of the gentlemen, both equally alarmed and one at least calculated to be, of all men living, the most helpless under the circumstances. Geoffrey was "awfully frightened," as he told her afterwards, when Margaret fainted.

"I shall never forget the whiteness of your face, my darling, and the dreadful sealed look of your eyelids. I thought in a moment that was how you would look if you were dead; and what should I do if I ever had to see *that* sight!"

This loving speech Geoffrey made to his wife as they drove homewards,—she pale, silent, and coldly abstracted; he full of tender anxiety for her comfort and apprehension for her health,—sentiments which rendered him, to say the truth, rather a trying companion in a carriage; for he was constantly pulling the glasses up and down, fixing them a button-hole higher or lower, rearranging the blinds, and giving the coachman contradictory orders. These proceedings were productive of no apparent annoyance to Margaret, who lay back against the cushions with eyes open and moody, and her underlip caught beneath her teeth. She maintained unbroken silence until they reached home, and then briefly telling Geoffrey that she was going to her room to lie down, she left him.

"She's not strong," said Geoffrey, as he proceeded to disembarrass himself of his outdoor attire, and to don his "working-clothes,"—"she's not strong; and it's very odd she's not more cheerful. I thought the child would have made it all right; but perhaps it will when she's stronger." And Geoff sighed as he went to his work, and sighed again once or twice as he pursued it.

Meanwhile Lord Caterham was thinking over the startling incident which had just occurred. He was an observant man naturally, and the enforced inaction of his life had increased this tendency; while his long and deep experience of physical suffering and weakness had rendered him acutely alive to any manifestations of a similar kind in other people. Mrs. Ludlow's fainting-fit puzzled him. She had been looking so remarkably well when she came in; there had been nothing feverish, nothing suggestive of fictitious strength or over-exertion in her appearance; no feebleness in her manner or languor in the tone of her voice. The suddenness and completeness of the swoon were strange,—were so much beyond the ordinary faintness which a drive undertaken a little too soon might be supposed to produce,—and the expression of Margaret's face, when she had recovered her consciousness, was so remarkable, that Lord Caterham felt instinctively the true origin of her illness had not been that assigned to it.

"She looked half-a-dozen years older," he thought; "and the few words she said were spoken as if she were in a dream. I must be more mistaken than I have ever been, or there is something very wrong about that woman. And what a good fellow he is!—what a simple-hearted blundering kind fellow! How wonderful his blindness is! I saw in a moment how he loved her, how utterly uninterested she is in him and his affairs. I hope there may be nothing worse than lack of interest; but I am afraid, very much afraid for Ludlow."

And then Lord Caterham's thoughts wandered away from the artist and his beautiful wife to that other subject which occupied them so constantly, and with which every other cogitation or contemplation contrived to mingle itself in an unaccountable manner, on which he did not care to reason, and against which he did not attempt to strive. What did it matter now? He might be ever so much engrossed, and no effort at self-control or self-conquest would be called for; the feelings he cherished unchecked could not harm any one—could not harm himself now. There was great relief, great peace in that thought,—no strife for him to enter on, no struggle in which his suffering body and weary mind must engage. The end would be soon with him now; and while he waited for it, he might love this bright young girl with all the power of his heart.

So Lord Caterham lay quite still upon the couch on which they had placed Margaret when she fainted, and thought over all he had intended to say to Geoffrey, and must now seek another opportunity of saying, and turned over in his mind sundry difficulties which he began to foresee in the way of his cherished plan, and which would probably arise in the direction of Mrs. Ludlow. Annie and Margaret had not hitherto seen much of each other, as has already appeared; and there was something ominous in the occurrence of that morning which troubled Lord Caterham's mind and disturbed his preconcerted arrangements. If trouble—trouble of some unknown kind, but, as he intuitively felt, of a serious nature—were hanging over Geoffrey Ludlow's head, what was to become of his guardianship of Annie in the future,—that future which Lord Caterham felt was drawing so near; that future which would find her without a friend, and would leave her exposed to countless flatterers. He was pondering upon these things when Annie entered the room, bright and blooming, after her drive in the balmy summer air, and carrying a gorgeous bouquet of crimson roses.

She was followed by Stephens, carrying two tall Venetian glasses. He placed them on a table, and then withdrew.

"Look, Arthur," said Annie; "we've been to Fulham, and I got these fresh cut, all for your own self, at the nursery-gardens. None of those horrid formal tied-up bouquets for you, or for me either, with the buds stuck on with wires, and nasty fluffy bits of cotton sticking to the leaves. I went round with the man, and made him cut each rose as I pointed it out; and they're such beauties, Arthur! Here's one for you to wear and smell and spoil; but the others I'm going to keep fresh for ever so long."

She went over to the couch and gave him the rose, a rich crimson full-formed flower, gorgeous in colour and exquisite in perfume. He took it with a smile and held it in his hand.

"Why don't you put it in your button-hole, Lord Caterham?" said Annie, with a pretty air of pettishness which became her well.

"Why?" said Lord Caterham. "Do you think I am exactly the style of man to wear posies and breast-knots, little Annie?" His tone was sad through its playfulness.

"Nonsense, Arthur," she began; "you—" Then she looked at him, and stopped suddenly, and her face changed. "Have you been worse to-day? You look very pale. Have you been in pain? Did you want me?"

"No, no, my child," said Lord Caterham; "I am just as usual. Go on with your flowers, Annie,—settle them up, lest they fade. They are beautiful indeed, and we'll keep them as long as we can."

She was not reassured, and she still stood and gazed earnestly at him.

"I am all right, Annie,—I am indeed. My head is even easier than usual. But some one has been ill, if I haven't. Your friends the Ludlows were here to-day. Did no one tell you as you came in?"

Q

"No, I did not see any one; I left my bonnet in the ante-room and came straight in here. I only called to Stephens to bring the flower-glasses. Was Mrs. Ludlow ill, Arthur? Did she come to see me?"

"I don't think so—she only came, I think, because I wanted to see Ludlow, and he took advantage of the circumstance to have a drive with her. Have you seen her since the child was born?"

"No, I called, but only to inquire. But was she ill? What happened?"

"Well, she was ill—she fainted. Ludlow and I were just beginning to talk, and, at her own request, leaving her to amuse herself with the photographs and things lying about—and she had just asked me some trifling question, something about Lionel's portrait—whose it was, I think —when she suddenly fainted. I don't think there could be a more complete swoon; she really looked as though she were dead."

"What did you do? was Geoffrey frightened?"

"Yes, we were both frightened. Stephens came, and two of the women. Ludlow was terrified; but she soon recovered, and she would persist in going home, though I tried to persuade her to wait until you returned. But she would not listen to it, and went away with Ludlow in a dreadful state of mind; he thinks he made her take the drive too soon, and is frightfully penitent."

"Well but, Arthur," said Annie, seriously and anxiously, " I suppose he did. It must have been that which knocked her up. She has no mother or sister with her, you know, to tell her about these things."

"My dear Annie," said Lord Caterham, "she has a doctor and a nurse, I suppose ; and she has common-sense, and knows how she feels, herself—does she not? She looked perfectly well when she came in, and handsomer than when I saw her before—and I don't believe the drive had any thing to do with the fainting-fit."

Miss Maurice looked at Lord Caterham in great surprise. His manner and tone were serious, and her feelings, easily roused when her old friend was concerned, were excited now to apprehension. She left off arranging the roses; she dried her finger-tips on her handkerchief, and placing a chair close beside Caterham's couch, she sat down and asked him anxiously to explain his meaning.

" I can't do that very well, Annie," he said, "for I am not certain of what it is; but of this I am certain, my first impression of Mrs. Ludlow is correct. There is something wrong about her, and Ludlow is ignorant of it. All I said to you that day is more fully confirmed in my mind now. There is some dark secret in the past of her life, and the secret in the present is, that she lives in that past, and does not love her husband."

" Poor Geoffrey," said Annie, in whose eyes tears were standing—" poor Geoffrey, and how dearly he loves her !"

" Yes," said Lord Caterham, "that's the worst of it ; that, and his unsuspiciousness,—he does not see what the most casual visitor to their house sees ; he does not perceive the weariness of spirit that is the first thing, next to her beauty, which every one with common perception must recognise. She takes no pains—she does not make the least attempt to hide it. Why, to-day, when she recovered, when her eyes opened—such gloomy eyes they were !— and Ludlow was kneeling here,"—he pointed down beside the couch he lay on—"bending over her,—did she look up at him ?—did she meet the gaze fixed on her and smile, or try to smile, to comfort and reassure him ? Not she : I was watching her ; she just opened her eyes and let them wander round, turned her head from him, and let it fall against the side of the couch as if she never cared to lift it more."

" Poor Geoffrey !" said Annie again ; this time with a sob.

" Yes, indeed, Annie," he went on ; "I pity him, as much as I mistrust her. He has never told you any thing about her antecedents, has he ?—and I suppose she has not been more communicative ?"

" No," replied Annie ; "I know nothing more than I have told you. She has always been the same when I have seen her—trying, I thought, to seem and be happier than at first, but very languid still. Geoffrey said sometimes that she was rather out of spirits, but he seemed to think it was only delicate health—and I hoped so too, though I could not help fearing you were right in all you said that day. O, Arthur, isn't it hard to think of Geoffrey loving her so much, and working so hard, and getting so poor a return ?"

" It is indeed, Annie," said Lord Caterham, with a strange

wistful look at her; "it is very hard. But I fear there are harder things than that in store for Ludlow. He is not conscious of the extent of his misfortune, if even he knows of its existence at all. I fear the time is coming when he must know all there is to be known, whatever it may be. That woman has a terrible secret in her life, Annie, and the desperate weariness within her—how she let it show when she was recovering from the swoon!—will force it into the light of day before long. Her dreary quietude is the calm before the storm."

"I suppose I had better write this evening and inquire for her," said Annie, after a pause; "and propose to call on her. It will gratify Geoffrey."

"Do so," said Lord Caterham; "I will write to Ludlow myself."

Annie wrote her kind little letter, and duly received a reply. Mrs. Ludlow was much better, but still rather weak, and did not feel quite able to receive Miss Maurice's kindly-proffered visit just at present.

"I am very glad indeed of that, Annie," said Lord Caterham, to whom she showed the note; "you cannot possibly do Ludlow any good, my child; and something tells me that the less you see of her the better."

For some days following that on which the incident and the conversation just recorded took place, Lord Caterham was unable to make his intended request to Geoffrey Ludlow that the latter would call upon him, that they might renew their interrupted conversation. One of those crises in the long struggle which he maintained with disease and pain, in which entire prostration produced a kind of truce, had come upon him; and silence, complete inaction, and almost a suspension of his faculties, marked its duration. The few members of the household who had access to him were familiar with this phase of his condition; and on this occasion it attracted no more notice than usual, except from Annie, who remarked additional gravity in the manner of the physician, and who perceived that the state of exhaustion of the patient lasted longer, and when he rallied was succeeded by less complete restoration to even his customary condition than before. She mentioned these results of her close observation to Lady Beauport; but the countess paid very little attention to the matter, assuring Annie that she knew Caterham much too well to be frightened; that he would do very well if there were no particular fuss made about him; and that all doctors were alarmists, and said dreadful things to increase their own importance. Annie would have called her attention to the extenuating circumstance that Lord Caterham's medical attendant had not said any thing at all, and that she had merely interpreted his looks; but Lady Beauport was so anxious to tell her something illustrative of "poor Lionel's" beauty, grace, daring, or dash—no matter which or what—that Annie found it impossible to get in another word.

A day or two later, when Lord Caterham had rallied a good deal, and was able to listen to Annie as she read to him, and while she was so engaged, and he was looking at her with the concentrated earnestness she remarked so frequently in his gaze of late,—Algy Barford was announced. Algy had been constantly at the house to inquire for Lord Caterham; but to-day Stephens had felt sure his master would be able and glad to see Algy. Every body liked that genial soul, and servants in particular—a wonderful test of popularity and its desert. He came in very quietly, and he and Annie exchanged greetings cordially. She liked him also. After he had spoken cheerily to Caterham, and called him "dear old boy" at least a dozen times in as many sentences, the conversation was chiefly maintained between him and Miss Maurice. She did not think much talking would do for Arthur just then, and she made no movement towards leaving the room, as was her usual custom. Algy was a little subdued in tone and spirits: it was impossible even to him to avoid seeing that Caterham was looking much more worn and pale than usual; and he was a bad hand at disguising a painful impression, so that he was less fluent and discursive than was his wont, and decidedly ill at ease.

"How is your painting getting on, Miss Maurice?" he said, when a pause became portentous.

"She has been neglecting it in my favour," said Lord Caterham. "She has not even finished the portrait you admired so much, Algy."

"O!—ah!—'The Muse of Painting,' wasn't it? It is a pity not to finish it, Miss Maurice. I think you would never succeed better than in that case,—you admire the original so much."

"Yes," said Annie, with rather an uneasy glance towards Caterham, "she is really beautiful. Arthur thinks her quite as wonderful as I do; but I have not seen her lately— she has been ill. By the bye, Arthur, Geoffrey Ludlow wrote to me yesterday inquiring for you; and only think what he says!—'I hope my wife's illness did not upset Lord Caterham; but I am afraid it did.'" Annie had taken a note from the pocket of her apron, and read these words in a laughing voice.

"Hopes his wife's illness did not upset Lord Caterham!" repeated Algy Barford in a tone of whimsical amazement. "What may that mean, dear old boy? Why are you supposed to be upset by the peerless lady of the unspeakable eyes and the unapproachable hair?"

Annie laughed, and Caterham smiled as he replied, "Only because Mrs. Ludlow fainted here in this room very suddenly, and very 'dead,' one day lately; and as Mrs. Ludlow's fainting was a terrible shock to Ludlow, he concludes that it was also a terrible shock to me,—that's all."

"Well, but," said Algy, apparently seized with an unaccountable access of curiosity, "why did Mrs. Ludlow faint? and what brought her here to faint in your room?"

"It was inconsiderate, I confess," said Caterham, still smiling; "but I don't think she meant it. The fact is, I had asked Ludlow to come and see me; and he brought his wife; and—and she has not been well, and the drive was too much for her, I suppose. At all events, Ludlow and I were talking, and not minding her particularly, when she said something to me, and I turned round and saw her looking deadly pale, and before I could answer her she fainted."

"Right off?" asked Algy, with an expression of dismay so ludicrous that Annie could not resist it, and laughed outright.

"Right off, indeed," answered Caterham; "down went the photograph-book on the floor, and down she would have gone if Ludlow had been a second later, or an inch farther away! Yes; it was a desperate case, I assure you. How glad you must feel that you wer'n't here, Algy,— eh? What would you have done now? Resorted to the bellows, like the Artful Dodger, or twisted her thumbs, according to the famous prescription of Mrs. Gamp?"

But Algy did not laugh, much to Lord Caterham's amusement, who believed him to be overwhelmed by the horrid picture his imagination conjured up of the position of the two gentlemen under the circumstances.

"But," said Algy, with perfect gravity, "why did she faint? What did she say? People don't tumble down in a dead faint because they're a little tired, dear old boy—do they?"

"Perhaps not in general, Algy, but it looks like it in Mrs. Ludlow's case. All I can tell you is, that the faint was perfectly genuine and particularly 'dead,' and that there was no cause for it, beyond the drive and the fatigue of looking over the photographs in that book. I am very tired of photographs myself, and I suppose most people are the same, but I haven't quite come to fainting over them yet."

Algy Barford's stupefaction had quite a rousing effect on Lord Caterham, and Annie Maurice liked him and his odd ways more than ever. He made some trifling remark in reply to Caterham's speech, and took an early opportunity of minutely inspecting the photograph-book which he had mentioned.

"So," said Algy to himself, as he walked slowly down St. Barnabas Square; "she goes to see Caterham, and faints at sight of dear old Lionel's portrait, does she? Ah, it's all coming out, Algy; and the best thing you can do, on the whole, is to keep your own counsel,—that's about it, dear old boy!"

CHAPTER XII.

GATHERING CLOUDS.

"MY younger brother Lionel Brakespere;" those were Lord Caterham's words. Margaret had heard them distinctly before consciousness left her; there was no mistake, no confusion in her mind,—"my younger brother Lionel Brakespere." All unconsciously, then, she

had been for months acquainted and in occasional communication with *his* nearest relatives !　Only that day she had
been in the house where he had lived ; had sat in a room
all the associations of which were doubtless familiar to him ;
had gazed upon the portrait of that face for the sight of
which her heart yearned with such a desperate restless
longing !

Lord Caterham's brother !　Brother to that poor sickly
cripple, in whom life's flame seemed not to shine, but to
flicker merely,—her Lionel, so bright and active and handsome !　Son of that proud, haughty Lady Beauport—yes,
she could understand that ; it was from his mother that
he inherited the cool bearing, the easy assurance, the never-
absent *hauteur* which rendered him conspicuous even in
a set of men where all these qualities were prized and
imitated.　She had not had the smallest suspicion the name
she had known him by was assumed, or that he had an
earl for his father and a viscount for his brother.　He had
been accustomed to speak of "the governor—a good old
boy ;" but his mother and his brother he never mentioned.

They knew him there, knew him as she had never known
him—free, unrestrained, without that mask which, to a
certain extent, he had necessarily worn in her presence.
In his intercourse with them he had been untrammelled,
with no lurking fear of what might happen some day ; no
dodging demon at his side suggesting the end, the separation that he knew must unavoidably come.　And she had
sat by, ignorant of all that was consuming their hearts'
cores, which, had she been able to discuss it with them,
would have proved to be her own deepest, most cherished,
most pertinacious source of thought.　They?—who were
they?　How many of them had known her Lionel?—how
many of them had cared for him?　Lady Beauport and
Lord Caterham, of course—but of the others?　Geoffrey
himself had never known him.　No ; thank God for that !
The comparison between her old lover and her husband
which she had so often drawn in her own mind had never,
could never have occurred to him.　Geoffrey's only connection with the Beauport family had been through Annie
Maurice.　Ah ! Annie Maurice !—the heiress now, whose
sudden acquisition of wealth and position they were all
talking of,—she had not seen Lionel in the old days ; and

even if she had, it had been slight matter. But Margaret's knowledge of the world was wide and ample, and it needed very little experience—far less indeed than she had had—to show her what might have been the effect had those two met under the existent different circumstances.

For Margaret knew Lionel Brakespere, and read him like a book. All her wild infatuation about him,—and her infatuation about him was wilder, madder than it had ever been before—all the length of time since she lost him,—all the long, weary, deadening separation, had not had the smallest effect on her calm matured judgment. She knew that he was at heart a scoundrel; she knew that he had no stability of heart, no depth of affection. Had not her own experience of him taught her that? had not the easy, indifferent, heartless way in which he had slipped out of her knotted arms, leaving her to pine and fret and die, for all he cared, shown her that? She had a thorough appreciation of his worship of the rising sun,—she knew how perfectly he would have sold himself for wealth and position; and yet she loved him, loved him through all!

This was her one consolation in the thought of his absence —his exile. Had he been in England, how readily would he have fallen into those machinations which she guessed his mother would have been only too ready to plot! She knew he was thousands of miles away; and the thought that she was freed from rivalry in a great measure reconciled her to his absence. She could hold him in her heart of hearts as her own only love; there was no one, in her thoughts, to dispute her power over him. He was hers,— hers alone. And he had obtained an additional interest in her eyes since she had discovered his identity. Now she would cultivate that acquaintance with his people,— all unknowingly she should be able to ally herself more closely to him. Casual questions would bring direct answers —all bearing on the topic nearest her heart : without in the smallest degree betraying her own secret, she would be able to feed her own love-flame,—to hear of, to talk of him for whom every pulse of her heart throbbed and yearned.

Did it never occur to her to catechise that heart, to endeavour to portray vividly to herself the abyss on the brink of which she was standing,—to ask herself whether she was prepared to abnegate all sense of gratitude and duty, and to persevere in the course which—not recklessly, not in a moment of passion, but calmly and unswervingly— she had begun to tread? Yes; she had catechised herself often, had ruthlessly probed her own heart, had acknowledged her baseness and ingratitude, yet had found it impossible to struggle against the pervading thrall. Worse than all, the sight of the man to whom she owed everything—comfort, respectability, almost life itself,—the sight of him patiently labouring for her sake had become oppressive to her; from calmly suffering it, she had come to loathe and rebel against it. Ah, what a contrast between the present dull, dreary, weary round and the bright old days of the past! To her, and to her alone, was the time then dedicated. She would not then have been left to sit alone, occupying her time as best she might, but every instant would have been devoted to her; and let come what might on the morrow, that time would have been spent in gaiety.

Was there no element of rest in the new era of her life? Did not the child which lay upon her bosom bring some alleviating influence, some new sphere for the absorption of her energies, some new hope, in the indulgence in which she might have found at least temporary forgetfulness of self? Alas, none! She had accepted her maternity as she had accepted her wifehood,—calmly, quietly, without even a pretence of that delicious folly, that pardonable self-satisfaction, that silly, lovable, incontrovertible, charming pride which nearly always accompanies the first experience of motherhood. Old Geoff was mad about his first-born— would leave his easel and come crooning and peering up into the nursery,—would enter that sacred domain in a half-sheepish manner, as though acknowledging his intrusion, but on the score of parental love hoping for forgiveness,— would say a few words of politeness to the nurse, who, inexorable to most men, was won over by his genuine devotion and his evident humility,—would take up the precious bundle, at length confided to him, in the awkwardest manner, and would sit chirrupping to the little putty face, or swing the shapeless mass to and fro, singing meanwhile the dismallest of apparently Indian dirges, and all the while be experiencing the most acute enjoyment.

Geoff was by nature a heavy sleeper; but the slightest cry of the child in the adjoining chamber would rouse him; the inevitable infantile maladies expressed in the inevitable peevish whine, so marvellously imitated by the toy-baby manufacturers, would fill him with horror and fright, causing him to lie awake in an agony of suspense, resting on his elbow and listening with nervous anxiety for their cessation or their increase; while Margaret, wearied out in mental anxiety, either slept tranquilly by his side or remained awake, her eyes closed, her mind abstracted from all that was going on around her, painfully occupied with retrospect of the past or anticipation of the future. She did not care for her baby? No—plainly no! She accepted its existence as she had accepted the other necessary corollaries of her marriage; but the grand secret of maternal love was as far removed from her as though she had never suffered her travail and brought a man-child into the world. That she would do her duty by her baby she had determined,—much in the same spirit that she had decided upon the strict performance of her conjugal duty; but no question of love influenced her. She did not dislike the child,—she was willing to give herself up to the inconveniences which its nurture, its care, its necessities occasioned her; but that was all.

If Margaret did not "make a fuss" with the child, there were plenty who did; numberless people to come and call; numberless eyes to watch all that happened,—to note the *insouciance* which existed, instead of the solicitude which should have prevailed; numberless tongues to talk and chatter and gossip,—to express wonderment, to declare that their owners "had never seen the like," and so on. Little Dr. Brandram found it more difficult than ever to get away from his lady-patients. After all their own disorders had been discussed and remedies suggested, the conversation was immediately turned to his patient at Elm Lodge; and the little medico had to endure and answer a sharp fire of questions of all kinds. Was it really a fine child? and was it true that Mrs. Ludlow did not care about it? She was nursing it herself; yes: that proved nothing; every decent woman would do that, rather than have one of those dreadful creatures in the house—pints of porter every hour, and doing nothing but sit down and abuse every one, and wanting so much waiting on, as though they were duchesses. But *was* it true? Now, doctor, you must know all these stories about her not caring for the child? Caring!—well, you ought to know, with all your experience, what the phrase meant. People would talk, you know, and that was what they said; and all the doctor's other patients wanted to know was whether it was really true. He did his best, the little doctor—for he was a kindly-hearted little creature, and Margaret's beauty had had its usual effect upon him,—he did his best to endow the facts with a roseate hue; but he had a hard struggle, and only partially succeeded. If there was one thing on which the ladies of Lowbar prided themselves, it was on their fulfilment of their maternal duties; if there was one bond of union between them, it was a sort of tacitly recognised consent to talk of and listen to each other's discussion of their children, either in existence or in prospect. It was noticed now that Margaret had always shirked this inviting subject; and it was generally agreed that it was no wonder, since common report averred that she had no pride in her first-born. A healthy child too, according to Dr. Brandram—a fine healthy well-formed child. Why, even poor Mrs. Ricketts, whose baby had spinal complaint, loved it, and made the most of it; and Mrs. Moule, whose little Sarah had been blind from her birth, thought her offspring unmatchable in the village, and nursed and tended it night and day. No wonder that in a colony where these sentiments prevailed, Margaret's reputation, hardly won, was speedily on the decline. It may be easily imagined too that to old Mrs. Ludlow's observant eyes Margaret's want of affection for her child did not pass unnoticed. By no one was the child's advent into the world more anxiously expected than by its grandmother, who indeed looked forward to deriving an increased social status from the event, and who had already discussed it with her most intimate friends. Mrs. Ludlow had been prepared for a great contest for supremacy when the child was born—a period at which she intended to assert her right of taking possession of her son's house and remaining its mistress until her daughter-in-law was able to resume her position. She had expected that in this act she would have received all the passive opposition of which Margaret was capable—opposition with which Geoff, being indoctrinated, might have been in a great measure successful. But, to her intense surprise, no opposition was made. Margaret received the announcement of Mrs. Ludlow's intended visit and Mrs. Ludlow's actual arrival with perfect unconcern; and after her baby had been born, and she had bestowed on it a very calm kiss, she suffered it to be removed by her mother-in-law with an expression which told even more of satisfaction than resignation. This behaviour was so far different from any thing Mrs. Ludlow had expected, that the old lady did not know what to make of it; and her daughter-in-law's subsequent conduct increased her astonishment. This astonishment she at first tried to keep to herself; but that was impossible. The feeling gradually vented itself in sniffs and starts, in eyebrow-upliftings for the edification of the nurse, in suggestive exclamations of "Well, my dear?" and "Don't you think, my love?" and such old-lady phraseology. Further than these little ebullitions Mrs. Ludlow made no sign until her daughter came to see her; and then she could no longer contain herself, but spoke out roundly.

"What it is, my dear, I can't tell for the life of me; but there's something the matter with Margaret. She takes no more notice of the child than if it were a chair or a table;—just a kiss, and how do you do? and nothing more."

"It's because this is her first child, mother. She's strange to it, you know, and—"

"Strange to it, my dear! Nonsense! Nothing of the sort. You're a young girl, and can't understand these things. But not only that,—one would think, at such a time, she would be more than ever fond of her husband. I'm sure when Geoff was born I put up with more from your father than ever I did before or since. His 'gander-month,' he called it; and he used to go gandering about with a parcel of fellows, and come home at all hours of the night—I used to hear him, though he did creep upstairs with his boots off—but he never had a cross word or look from me."

"Well, but surely, mother, Geoff has not had either cross words or cross looks from Margaret?"

"How provoking you are, Matilda! That seems to be my fate, that no one can understand me. I never said he had, did I? though it would be a good thing for him if he had, poor fellow, I should say—any thing better than what he has to endure now."

"Don't be angry at my worrying you, dear mother; but for Heaven's sake tell me what you mean—what Geoff has to endure?"

"I am not angry, Til; though it seems to be my luck to be imagined angry when there's nothing further from my thoughts. I'm not angry, my dear—not in the least."

"What about Geoff, mother?"

"O, my dear, that's enough to make one's blood boil! I've never said a word to you before about this, Matilda—being one of those persons who keep pretty much to themselves, though I see a great deal more than people think for,—I've never said a word to you before about this; for, as I said to myself, what good could it do? But I'm perfectly certain that there's something wrong with Margaret."

"How do you mean, mother? Something wrong!—is she ill?"

"Now, my dear Matilda, as though a woman would be likely to be well when she's just had—— Bless my soul, the young women of the present day are very silly! I wasn't speaking of her health, of course."

"Of what then, mother?" said Til, with resignation.

"Well, then, my dear, haven't you noticed,—but I suppose not: no one appears to notice these things in the way that I do,—but you might have noticed that for the last few weeks Margaret has seemed full of thought, dreamy, and not caring for any thing that went on. If I've pointed out once to her about the mite of a cap that that Harriet wears, and all her hair flying about her ears, and a crinoline as wide as wide, I've spoken a dozen times; but she's taken no notice; and now the girl sets me at defiance, and tells me I'm not her mistress, and never shall be! That's one thing; but there are plenty of others. I was sure Geoffrey's linen could not be properly aired—the colds he caught were so awful; and I spoke to Margaret about it, but she took no notice; and yesterday, when the clothes came home from the laundress, I felt them myself, and you might have wrung the water out of them in pints. There are many other little things too that I've noticed; and I'll tell you what it is, Matilda—I'm certain she has got something on her mind."

" O, I hope not, poor girl, poor dear Margaret !"

" Poor dear fiddlestick ! What nonsense you talk, Matilda ! If there's any one to be pitied, it's Geoffrey, I should say ; though what he could have expected, taking a girl for his wife that he'd known so little of, and not having any wedding-breakfast, or any thing regular, I don't know !"

" But why is Geoffrey to be pitied, mother ?"

" Why? Why, because his wife doesn't love him, my dear ! Now you know it !"

" O, mother, for Heaven's sake don't say such a thing ! You know you're—you won't mind what I say, dearest mother,—but you're a little apt to jump at conclusions, and—"

" O yes, I know, my dear ; I know I'm a perfect fool !—I know that well enough ; and if I don't, it's not for want of being reminded of it by my own daughter. But I know I'm right in what I say ; and what's more, my son shall know it before long."

" O, mother, you would never tell Geoff !—you would never—"

" If a man's eyes are not open naturally, my dear, they must be opened for him. I shall tell Geoffrey my opinion about his wife ; and let him know it in pretty plain terms, I can tell you !"

CHAPTER XIII.

MR. STOMPFF'S DOUBTS.

IT is not to be supposed that because Geoffrey Ludlow's married life offered no very striking points for criticism, it was left uncriticised by his friends. Those, be they married or single, quiet or boisterous, convivial or misanthropical, who do not receive discussion at the hands of their acquaintance, are very few in number. There can be nothing more charmingly delightful, nothing more characteristic of this chivalrous age, than the manner in which friends speak of each other behind, as the phrase goes, "each other's backs." To two sets of people, having a third for common acquaintance, this pastime affords almost inexpressible delight, more especially if the two sets present have been made acquainted with each other through the medium of the absent third. It is rather dangerous ground at first, because neither of the two sets present can tell whether the other may not have some absurd scruples as to the propriety of canvassing the merits or demerits of their absent friend; but a little tact, a little cautious dealing with the subject, a few advances made as tentatively as those of the elephant on the timber bridge, soon show that the discussion will not be merely endured, but will be heartily welcome; and straightway it is plunged into with the deepest interest. How they manage to keep that carriage,—that's what we've always wanted to know! O, you've noticed it too. Well, is it rouge, or enamel, or what? That's what I've always said to George—how that poor man can go on slaving and slaving as he does, and all the money going in finery for her, is what I can't understand! What a compliment to our opinion of our powers of character-reading to find all our notions indorsed by others, more especially when those notions have been derogatory to those with whom we have for some time been living on terms of intimacy! To be sure there is another side to the medal, when we find that those who have known our dear absents a much shorter time than we have, claim credit for being far more sharp-sighted than we. They marked at once, they say, all the shortcomings which we had taken so long to discover; and they lead the chorus of depreciation, in which we only take inferior parts.

It was not often that Mr. Stompff busied himself with the domestic concerns of the artists who formed his staff. It was generally quite enough for him provided they "came up to time," as he called it, did their work well, and did not want too much money in advance. But in Geoffrey Ludlow Mr. Stompff took a special interest, regarding him as a man out of whom, if properly worked, great profit and fame were to be made. He had paid several visits to Elm Lodge, ostensibly for the purpose of seeing how the Brighton-Esplanade picture was progressing; but with this he combined the opportunity of inspecting the domestic arrangements, and noting whether they were such as were likely to "suit his book." No man more readily understood the dispiriting influence of a slattern wife or a disorderly home upon the work that was to be done.

"I've seen 'em," he used to say, "chock-full of promise, and all go to the bad just because of cold meat for dinner, or the house full of steam on washing-days. They'd rush away, and go off—public-house or any where—and then good-bye to my work and the money they've had of me! What I like best 's a regular expensive woman,—fond of her dress and going about, and all that,—who makes a man stick to it to keep her going. That's when you get the work out of a cove. So I'll just look-up Ludlow, and see how he's goin' on."

He did "look-up" Ludlow several times; and his sharp eyes soon discovered a great deal of which he did not approve, and which did not seem likely to coincide with his notions of business. He had taken a dislike to Margaret the first time he had seen her, and his dislike increased on each subsequent visit. There was something about her which he could scarcely explain to himself,—a "cold stand-offishness," he phrased it,—which he hated. Margaret thought Mr. Stompff simply detestable, and spite of Geoff's half-hints, took no pains to disguise her feelings. Not that she was ever demonstrative—it was her calm quiet *insouciance* that roused Mr. Stompff's wrath. "I can't tell what to make of that woman," he would say; "she never gives Ludlow a word of encouragement, but sits there yea-nay, by G—, lookin' as though she didn't know he was grindin' his fingers off to earn money for her! She don't seem to take any notice of what's goin' on; but sits moonin' there, lookin' straight before her, and treatin' me and her husband as if we was dirt! Who's she, I should like to know, to give herself airs and graces like that? It was all very well when Ludlow wanted a model for that Skyllar picture; but there's no occasion for a man to marry his models, that I've heard of —leastways it ain't generally done. She don't seem to know that it's from me all the money comes, by the way she treats me. She don't seem to think that that pretty house and furniture, and all the nice things which she has, are paid for by my money. She's never a decent word to say to me. Damme, I hate her!"

And Mr. Stompff did not content himself by exploding in this manner. He let off this safety-valve of self-communion

R

to keep himself from boiling over; but all the cause for his wrath still remained, and he referred to it, mentally, not unfrequently. He knew that Geoffrey Ludlow was one of his greatest cards; he knew that he had obtained a certain mastery over him at a very cheap rate; but he also knew that Ludlow was a man impressible to the highest degree, and that if he were preoccupied or annoyed, say by domestic trouble for instance—and there was nothing in a man of Geoffrey's temperament more destructive to work than domestic trouble —he would be incapable of earning his money properly. Why should there be domestic trouble at Elm Lodge? Mr. Stompff had his ears wider open than most men, and had heard a certain something which had been rumoured about at the time of Geoff's marriage; but he had not paid much attention to it. There were many *ateliers* which he was in the habit of frequenting,—and the occupants of which turned out capital pictures for him,—where he saw ladies playing the hostess's part whose names had probably never appeared in a marriage-register; but that was nothing to him. Most of them accepted Mr. Stompff's compliments, and made themselves agreeable to the great *entrepreneur*, and laughed at his coarse story and his full-flavoured joke, and were only too delighted to get them, in conjunction with his cheque. But this wife of Ludlow's was a woman of a totally different stamp; and her treatment of him so worried Mr. Stompff that he determined to find out more about her. Charley Potts was the most intimate friend of Ludlow's available to Mr. Stompff, and to Charley Potts Mr. Stompff determined to go.

It chanced that on the morning which the great picture-dealer had selected to pay his visit, Mr. Bowker had strolled into Charley Potts's rooms, and found their proprietor hard at work. Mr. Bowker's object, though prompted by very different motives from those of Mr. Stompff, was identically the same. Old William had heard some of those irrepressible rumours which, originating no one knows how, gather force and strength from circulation, and had come to talk to Mr. Potts about them. "Dora in the Cornfield" had progressed so admirably since Bowker's last visit, that after filling his pipe he stood motionless before it, with the unlighted lucifer in his hand.

"'Pon my soul, I think you'll do something some day,

young 'un!" were his cheering words. "That's the real thing! Wonderful improvement since I saw it; got rid of the hay-headed child, and come out no end. Don't think the sunlight's *quite* that colour, is it? and perhaps no reason why those reaping-parties shouldn't have noses and mouths as well as eyes and chins. Don't try scamping, Charley,— you're not big enough for that; wait till you're made an R.A., and then the critics will point out the beauties of your outline; at present you must copy nature. And now"— lighting his pipe—"how are you?"

"O, I'm all right, William," responded Mr. Potts; "all right, and working like any number of steam-engines. Orson, sir—if I may so describe myself—Orson is endowed with reason. Orson has begun to find out that life is different from what he imagined, and has gone in for something different."

"Ha!" said old Bowker, eyeing the young man kindly as he puffed at his pipe; "it's not very difficult to discover what's up now, then."

"O, I don't want to make any mystery about it," said Charley. "The simple fact is, that having seen the folly of what is called a life of pleasure—"

"At thirty years of age!" interrupted Bowker.

"Well, what then?—at thirty years of age! One does not want to be a Methuselah like you before one discovers the vanity, the emptiness, the heartlessness of life."

"Of course not, Charley?" said Bowker, greatly delighted. "Go on!"

"And I intend to—to—to cut it, Bowker, and go in for something better. It's something, sir, to have something to work for. I have an end in view, to—"

"Well, but you've always had that. I thought that your ideas were concentrated on being President of the Academy, and returning thanks for your health, proposed by the Prime Minister."

"Bowker, you are a ribald. No, sir; there is a spur to my ambition far beyond the flabby presidentship of that collection of dreary old parties—"

"Yes, I know; and the spur is marked with the initials M. L. That it, Master Charley?"

"It may be, Bowker, and it may be not. Meanwhile, my newly-formed but unalterable resolutions do not forbid the

R 2

discussion of malt-liquor, and Caroline yet understands the signal-code."

With these words, Mr. Potts proceeded to make his ordinary pantomimic demonstration at the window, and, when the beer arrived, condescended to give up work for a time ; and, lighting a pipe and seating himself in his easy-chair, he entered into conversation with his friend.

"And suppose the spur were marked with M. L.," said he, reverting to the former topic, after a little desultory conversation,—"suppose the spur were marked with M. L., what would be the harm of that, Bowker?"

"Harm!" growled old Bowker; "you don't imagine when you begin to speak seriously of such a thing that I, of all people, should say there was any harm in it? I thought you were chaffing at first, and so I chaffed ; but I'm about the last man in the world to dissuade a young fellow with the intention and the power to work from settling himself in life with a girl such as I know this one to be. So far as I have seen of her, she has all our Geoff's sweetness of disposition combined with an amount of common-sense and knowledge of the world which Geoff never had and never will have."

"She's A 1, old boy, and that's all about it; but we're going a-head rather too quickly. I've not said a word to her yet, and I scarcely know whether—"

"Nonsense, Charley! A man who is worth any thing knows right well whether a woman cares for him or not; and knows in what way she cares for him too. On this point I go back to my old ground again, and say that Geoffrey Ludlow's sister could not be dishonest enough to flirt and flatter and play the deuce with a man. There's too much honesty about the family; and you would be in a very different state of mind, young fellow, if you thought there was any doubt as to how your remarks would be received in that quarter, when you chose to speak."

Mr. Potts smiled, and pulled his moustache, triumphantly now, not doubtfully as was his wont. Then his face settled into seriousness, as he said :

"You're right, William, I think. I hope so, please God! I've never said so much as this to any one, as you may guess; but I love that girl with all my heart and soul, and if only the dealers will stick by me, I intend to tell her that same very shortly. But what you just said has turned my thoughts into another channel—our Geoff."

"Well, what about our Geoff?" asked Mr. Bowker, twisting round on his seat, and looking hard at his friend.

"You must have noticed, Bowker—probably much more than I have, for you're more accustomed to that sort of thing—that our Geoff's not right lately. There's something wrong up there at Elm Lodge, that I can't make out,—that I daren't think of. You remember our talks both before and after Geoff's marriage? Well, I must hark back upon them. He's not happy, William—there, you have the long and the short of it! I'm a bad hand at explaining these matters, but Geoff's not happy. He's made a mistake; and though I don't think he sees it himself—or if he does, he would die sooner than own it—there can be no doubt about it. Mrs. Ludlow does not understand,—does not appreciate him; and our Geoff's no more like our crony of old days than I'm like Raffaelle. There, that's it, as clear as I can put it!"

Bowker waited for an instant, and then he said :

" I've tried hard enough, God knows !—hard enough to prevent myself from thinking as you think, Charley ; but all to no purpose. There is a cloud over Geoff's life, and I fear it springs from——Some one knocking. Keep 'em out, if possible ; we don't want any one boring in here just now."

But the knocker, whoever he was, seemed by no means inclined to be kept out. He not only obeyed the regular directions and "tugged the trotter," but he afterwards gave three distinct and loud raps with his fist on the door, which was the signal to the initiated ; and when the door was opened and the knocker appeared in the person of Mr. Stompff, further resistance was useless.

The great man entered the room with a light and airy step and a light and airy address. "Well, Charley, how are you? Come to give you a look-up, you see. Hallo ! who's this?—Mr. Bowker, how do you do, sir?" in a tone which meant, "What the devil do you do here?"—"how are you, sir?—Well, Charley, what are you at? Going to the bad, you villain,—going to the bad !"

" Not quite that, I hope, Mr. Stompff—"

" Working for Caniche, eh ? That's the same thing, just

the same thing! I've heard all about it. You've let that miserable Belgian get old of you, ch? This is it, is it? Gal in a cornfield and mowers? what you call 'em—reapers? That's it! reapers, and a little child. Some story, eh? O, ah! Tennyson; I don't know him—not bad, by Jove! not half bad! it's Caniche's?"

"Yes; that's Caniche's commission."

"Give you fifty more than he's given to make it over to me. You won't, of course not, you silly feller! it's only my joke. But look here, mind you give me the refusal of the next. I can do better for you than Caniche. He's a poor paltry chap. I go in for great things,—that's my way, Mr. Bowker."

"Is it?" growled old William over his pipe; "then you go in also for great pay, Mr. Stompff, I suppose?"

"Ask your friend Ludlow about that. He'll tell you whether I pay handsomely or not, sir.—By the way, how is your friend Ludlow, Potts?"

"He's all right, I believe."

"And his wife, how's she?"

There was something in his tone and in the expression of his eyes which made Mr. Potts say:

"Mrs. Ludlow is going on very well, I believe," in a tone of seriousness very unusual with Charley.

"That's all right," said Mr. Stompff. "Going on very well, eh? Every body will be glad to hear that, and Ludlow in partickler. Going on very well—in a regular domestic quiet manner, eh? That's all right. Hasn't been much used to the domestic style before her marriage, I should think, eh?"

"Whatever you may think, I should advise you not to say much, Mr. Stompff," said Bowker. "I don't think Geoff would much like hearing those things said of his wife; I'm sure I should not of mine."

"N-no; but you have not a wife; I—I mean living, Mr. Bowker," said Stompff with a sneer.

William Bowker swallowed down a great lump rising in his throat, and forcibly restrained the involuntary clenching of his fists, as he replied, "No, you're right there, Mr. Stompff; but still I repeat my advice."

"O, I shall say nothing. People will talk, you know, whether I'm silent or not, and people will want to know who

Mrs. Ludlow was before she married Ludlow, and why she's so silent and preoccupied, and why she never goes into society, and why she faints away when she looks at photograph-books, and so on. But I didn't come here to talk of Mrs. Ludlow. Now, Potts, *mon brave*, let us discuss business."

When the great man took his departure, after proposing handsome terms to Charley Potts for a three years' engagement, Bowker said: "There's more in what we were saying when that blatant ruffian came in than I thought for, Charley. The news of Geoff's domestic trouble has got wind."

"I'm afraid so. But what did Stompff mean about the fainting and the photograph-book?"

"God knows! probably an invention and a lie. But when people like Stompff begin to talk in that way, it's bad for those they talk about, depend upon it."

CHAPTER XIV.

THREATENING.

GEOFFREY LUDLOW felt considerable anxiety about his wife after the day of their inauspicious visit to Lord Caterham; and as anxiety was quite a foreign element in Geoff's placid temperament, it did not sit well upon him, and it rendered him idle and desultory. He could not make up his mind as to the true source of his anxiety,—the real spring of his discomfort. Margaret's health was very good; her naturally fine *physique* shook off illness easily and rapidly, and her rare beauty was once more irradiated with the glow of health and strength. Yet Geoffrey's inquietude was not lessened. He loved this strange woman—this woman who compelled admiration, indeed, from others, but won love only from him with passionate and intense devotion. But he was ill at ease with her, and he began to acknowledge to himself that it was so. He knew, he felt, that there was some new element, some impalpable power in their lives, which was putting asunder those who had never been very closely united in real bonds of sympathy and confidence, with an irresistible, remorseless hand,—invisible and sure as that of Death.

There are no words to tell what this good fellow suffered in his kindly, unselfish, simple way, as day by day the conviction forced itself upon him that the woman he had so loved, the woman for whom he lived, and worked, and thought, and hoped, was more and more divided from him by some barrier—all the more impassable because he could not point to it and demand an explanation of its presence, or utter a plea for its removal. He would sit in his painting-room quite idle, and with a moody brow—unlike the Geoff Ludlow of old times—and think and puzzle himself about his wife; he would sometimes work, in short desultory fits of industry, desperately, as though putting thought from him by main force; and then he would meet Margaret, at meals or other times of association, with so indifferent an assumption of being just as usual, that it was wonderful she did not notice the change in her husband. But Geoffrey did not interest her, and Margaret did not observe him with any curiosity. The state of mind of this ill-assorted pair at this time was very curious, had there been any one to understand and analyse it.

"What can it be?" Geoffrey would ask himself. "I cannot make it out. She does not take any interest in any thing. I thought all women loved their children at least, and the coldest warmed to their infants; but she does not."

Geoffrey had ceased to wonder at Margaret's coldness to him. She had always been cold, and latterly her reserve and silence had increased. She made no effort to hide the *ennui* which wholly possessed her; she made no attempt to simulate the interest in his occupations which she had never felt in more than a lukewarm degree. His perceptions were not very quick; but when he did see a thing, he was apt to understand and reason upon it, and he reasoned upon this now; he pondered upon it and upon his marriage, and he wondered when he remembered the joy and hope with which he had entered upon the pretty, comfortable new home and the quiet industrious life. What had come to it all? What had changed it, and yet left it the same? He had not failed in any duty to this woman; he had not given her less, but more than he had promised; for he was much better off than he had hoped to be, and she had the command of every shilling he earned. Never had an unkind word, a negligent act, a failure in the tenderest of household kindnesses, recorded itself in her memory against this man, who was her preserver, her protector, her husband. Surprise, trouble, vague apprehension, above all, the bewilderment of inexplicable wrong, were in Geoffrey's mind; but not a touch of bitterness against her. He remembered the story she had told him, and the promise he had pledged to her, and his generous heart rested in the assurance she had then given him, and sought no farther. His was not the nature which would count up the items in the bargain between them, and set down the large balance that really existed on his side. What had he given her? To answer this question aright, knowledge must have been had of her whole life, and all its depths of suffering, of actual physical want sounded; all her love of luxury, all her incapacity to bear privation, all her indolence, her artistic sensuousness, her cultivated power of enjoyment, must have been known and weighed.

He had given her ease, security, respectability,—a name, a home which was comfortable to the verge of luxury, which included all that any woman could reasonably desire who had voluntarily accepted a life upon the scale which it implied—a home to which his industry and his love constantly added new comforts and decorations. Geoffrey never thought of these things,—he did not appraise them; nor did his generous heart dwell upon the sacrifice he had made, the risk he had incurred, in short, upon the extraordinary imprudence of his marriage. His nature was too magnanimous, and not sufficiently practical for such considerations; he thought of nothing but the love he had given her,—the love she did not seem to understand, to care for,—and he wondered, in his simple way, why such love, so deep and quiet, so satisfied with home and her, could not make her more happy and cheerful. Poor Geoffrey, calm and peace were the conditions of life in which alone he could find or imagine happiness, and they were just those which were detestable to Margaret. It is possible that, had she been caught from the depths of her degradation and despair in the grasp of a nature stronger and more violent than her own, the old thrall might have fallen from her, and she might have been swayed by the mingled charm and authority, the fierceness, the delight, the fear of a great passion, so preoccupying that she would have had no time for retrospect, so entrancing that she would have been forced to live in the present. But the hand that had raised her from the abyss was only gentle and tender; it lacked the force which would have wrung submission from her afterwards, the power to imply that it could wound as well as caress,—and its touch had no potency for that perverted nature. What had she given him? Just her beauty,—nothing more. She was his wife, and she cared for him no more than she cared for the furniture of her rooms and the trinkets in her jewel-case (poor things, she thought, which once would have been unworthy of her wearing, but chosen with all Geoff's humble science, and bought with the guerdon of many a day of Geoff's hard work); he was her child's father; and the child bored her a little more unendurably than all the rest. Indeed, all the rest was quiet—which at least was something—but the child was not quiet; and Geoffrey made a fuss about it—a circumstance which lent a touch of impatience to her distaste. He talked about the infant,—he wanted to know if she thought her boy's eyes were like her own? and whether she would like him to be an artist like his father? He talked about the boy's eyes, and Lionel's electric glances were haunting her troubled soul; he babbled about the boy's future, when she was enduring the tortures of Tantalus in her terrible longing for the past.

The child throve, and Geoffrey loved the little creature with a vigilant affection curious and beautiful to see. When he felt that the hopes he had built upon the infant, as a new and strong tie between himself and Margaret, as a fresh source of interest, something to awaken her from her torpidity, were not destined to be realised, he turned, in the intensity of his disappointment and discomfiture, to the child itself, and sought—unconsciously it may be, at least unavowedly to himself—to fill up the void in his heart, to restore the warmth to his home, through the innocent medium of the baby. The child did not resemble his mother, even after the difficult-to-be-discovered fashion of likenesses in babyhood. When he opened his eyes, in the solemn and deliberate way in which young children look out upon the mysterious world, they did not disclose violet tints nor oval-shaped heavy lids; they were big brown eyes, like Geoffrey's, and the soft rings of downy hair, which the nurse declared to be " the beautifullest curls she ever see on an 'ead at 'is age," were not golden but dark brown. Geoffrey held numerous conferences with the nurse about her charge, and might be found many times in the day making his way with elaborate caution, and the noiseless step which is a characteristic of big men, up the nursery stair; and seen by the curious, had there been any to come there, gazing at the infant lying in his cradle, or on his nurse's knee, with a wistful rueful expression, and his hands buried in the pockets of his painting-coat.

He never found Margaret in the nursery on any of these occasions, and she never evinced the slightest interest in the nursery government, or responded to any of his ebullitions of feeling on the subject. Of course the servants were not slow to notice the indifference of the mother, and to comment upon it with unreserved severity. Margaret was not a favourite at any time—"master" being perfection in their minds—and her cold reserve and apathy impressing the domestics, who could not conceive that "a good home" could be despicable in even the most beautiful eyes, very unfavourably.

Margaret was arraigned before the domestic tribunal, unknown to herself; though, had she known it, the circumstance would have made no impression upon her. Her cold pride would at all times have rendered her indifferent to opinion; and now that indifference, weariness, and distaste had entire possession of her, she had not even cared to hide the dreary truth from her husband's mother and sister. What had become of her resolutions with regard to them? Where were her first impulses of gratitude? Gone—sunk in the Dead Sea of her overmastering passion—utterly lost beneath the tide of her conscienceless selfishness. She could not strive, she could not pretend, she could not play any part longer. Why should she, to whom such talk was twaddle of the trashiest description, try to appear interested because she had given birth to Geoffrey's child? Well, there was the child; let them make much of it, and talk nonsense to it and about it. What was Geoffrey's child to her, or Geoffrey's mother, or—she had gone very near to saying Geoffrey himself either, but something dimly resembling a pang of conscience stopped her. He was very good, very honest, very kind; and she was almost sorry for him,—as nearly sorry as she could be for any but herself; and then the tide of that sorrow for herself dashed over and swept all these trifling scraps of vague regret, of perhaps elementary remorse, away on its tumultuous waves.

She was cursed with such keen memory, she was haunted with such a terrible sense of contrast! Had it been more dreadful, more agonising, when she was a wanderer in the pitiless streets,—starving, homeless, dying of sheer want; when the bodily suffering she endured was so great that it benumbed her mind, and deadened it to all but craving for food and shelter? The time of this terrible experience lay so far in the past now, that she had begun to forget the reality of the torture; she had begun to undervalue its intensity, and to think that she had purchased rescue too dear. Too dear!—she, whose glance could not fall around her without resting on some memorial of the love she had won; she, whose daily life was sheltered from every breath of ill and care! She had always been weary; now she was growing enraged. Like the imprisoned creatures of the desert and the jungle, in whom long spells of graceful apathetic repose are succeeded by fierce fits of rebellious struggle, she strove and fought with the gentle merciful fate which had brought her into this pretty prison and supplied her with dainty daily fare. It had all been bearable—at least until now—and she had borne it well, and never turned upon her keeper. But the wind had set from the lands of sun and fragrance, from the desert whose sands were golden, whose wells were the sparkling waters of life and love, and she had scented the old perfume in the breeze. All the former instincts revived, the slight chain of formal uncongenial habit fell away, and in the strength of passion and beauty she rebelled against her fate. Perhaps the man she loved and longed for, as the sick long for health or the shipwrecked for a sail, had never seen her look so beautiful as she looked one day, when, after Mrs. Ludlow and her daughter, who had come to lunch at Elm Lodge, had gone away, and Geoffrey, puzzled and mortified more than ever, had returned to his painting-room, she stood by the long window of the drawing-room, gazing out over the trim little space which bloomed with flowers and glowed in the sunshine, with eyes which seemed indeed as if their vision cleft distance and disdained space. Her cheeks, usually colourless, were touched with a faint rose-tinge; and the hurry and excitement of her thoughts seemed to pervade her whole frame, which was lighted by the rays of the afternoon sun, from the rich coils of her red-gold hair to the restless foot which tapped the carpet angrily. As she stood, varying expressions flitted over her face like clouds; but in them all there was an intensity new to it, and which would have told an observer that the woman who looked so was taking a resolution.

Suddenly she lifted her hands above her head to the full extent of her arms, then tore the twisted fingers asunder with a moan, as if of pain or hunger, and letting them fall by her side, flung herself into a chair.

"Have you heard any thing of Lord Caterham lately?" asked Mrs. Geoffrey Ludlow of her husband, a few days after his mother's visit, just as Geoffrey, having breakfasted, was about to retire to his painting-room. She asked the question in the most careless possible manner, and without removing her eyes from the *Times*, which she was reading; but Geoffrey was pleased that she should have asked it at all, —any sign of interest on Margaret's part in any one for whom he cared being still precious to Geoffrey, and becoming rarer and more rare.

"No, dear," he replied; "Annie said she would write as soon as Lord Caterham should be well enough to see me. I suppose I may tell her, then, that she may come and see you. You are quite well now, Margaret?"

"O yes, quite well," she replied; and then added, with the faintest flicker of colour on her cheek, "Lord Caterham's brother is not at home, I believe. Have you ever seen him?"

"Captain Brakespere? No, not I. There's something wrong about him. I don't understand the story, but Annie just mentioned that Lord Caterham had been in great distress about him. Well, Margaret, I'm off now to the Esplanade."

He looked wistfully at her; but she did not speak or lift up her eyes, and he went out of the room.

If there was trouble of the silent and secret kind in Geoffrey's home, there was also discontent of the outspoken sort at his mother's cheerful house in Brompton.

Mrs. Ludlow was wholly unprepared to find that Margaret cared so little for her child. It was with no small indignation that she commented upon Margaret's demeanour, as she and her daughter sat together; and deeper than her indignation lay her anxiety, and a vague apprehension of evil in store for her darling son.

"She is sulky and discontented,—that's what she is," repeated Mrs. Ludlow; "and what she can want or wish for that she has not got passes my comprehension."

Miss Ludlow said that perhaps it was only accidental. She would be sorry to think Margaret had such faults of temper to any confirmed degree. It would be dreadful for dear old Geoff, who was so sweet-tempered himself, and who never could understand unamiable persons. But she added she did not think Geoff perceived it. She was sure he would never think that Margaret was not fond of the child.

"O yes, he does perceive it," said Mrs. Ludlow; "I can see that very plainly; I saw it in his face when he came up to the nursery with us, and she never offered to stir; and did you not notice, Til, that when I asked her what the doctor said about vaccinating baby, she looked at me quite vacantly, and Geoffrey answered? Ah, no; he knows it well enough, poor fellow; and how ever he is to get through life with a woman with a bad temper and no heart, I'm sure I can't tell."

Geoffrey had never relaxed in his attention to his mother. In the early days of his marriage, when he had persuaded himself that there was nothing in the least disappointing in Margaret's manner, and that he was perfectly happy; in those days to which he looked back now, in the chill dread and discomfort of the present, as to vanished hours of Paradise, he had visited his mother, sent her presents, written short cheery notes to her and Til, and done every thing in his power to lesson their sense of the inevitable separation which his marriage had brought about. His love and his happiness had had no hardening or narrowing effect upon Geoffrey Ludlow. They had quickened his perceptions and added delicacy to his sympathies. But there was a difference now. Geoffrey felt unwilling to see his mother and sister; he fe t that their perception of Margaret's conduct had been distinct, and their disapproval complete; and he shrank from an interview which must include avoidance of the subject occupying all their minds. He would not willingly have had Margaret blamed, even by implication, by others; though there was something more like anger than he had ever felt or thought he could feel towards her in his gentle heart, as he yielded to the conviction that she had no love for her child.

Thus it happened that Geoffrey did not see his mother and sister for a week just at this time, during which interval there was no change in the state of affairs at home. He wrote, indeed, to Til, and made cheery mention of the boy and of his picture, which was getting on splendidly, and at which he was working so hard that he could not manage to get so far as Brompton for a day or two yet, but would go very soon; and Margaret sent her love. So Geoffrey made out a letter which might have been written by a blundering schoolboy—a letter over which his mother bent sad and boding looks, and Til had a "good cry." Though Geoffrey had not visited them lately, the ladies had not been altogether deprived of the society of men and artists. The constancy with which Charley Potts paid his respects was quite remarkable; and it fell out that, seeing Matilda rather out of spirits, and discerning that something was going wrong, Charley very soon extracted from Til what that something was, and they proceeded to exchange confidences on the subject of Geoffrey and his beautiful wife. Charley informed Matilda that none of "our fellows" who had been introduced to Mrs. Geoffrey liked her; and as for Stompff, "he hates her all out, you know," said the plain-spoken Charley; "but I don't mind that, for she's a lady, and Stompff—he—he's a beast, you know."

When Geoffrey could no longer defer a visit to his mother without the risk of bringing about questions and expostulations which must make the state of things at home openly known, and place him in the embarrassing position of being obliged to avow an estrangement for which he could assign no cause, he went to Brompton. The visit was not a pleasant one, though the mother and sister were even more demonstrative in their affectionate greeting than usual, and though they studiously avoided any reference to the subject in their minds and in his. But this was just what he dreaded; they *did* studiously avoid it; and by doing so they confirmed all his suspicions, they realised all his fears. Geoffrey did not even then say to himself that his marriage was a mistake, and his mother and sister had discovered it; but had his thoughts, his misgivings been put into words, they must have taken some such shape. They talked energetically about the child, and asked Geoff all sorts of feminine questions, which it would have affected a male listener rather oddly to have heard Geoff answer with perfect seriousness, and a thorough acquaintance with details. He had several little bits of news for them; how Mr. Stompff, reminiscent of his rather obtrusive promise, had sent the clumsiest, stumpiest, ugliest lump of a silver mug procurable in London as a present to the child, but had not presented himself at Elm Lodge; how Miss Maurice had been so delighted with the little fellow, and had given him a beautiful embroidered frock, and on Lord Caterham's behalf endowed him with a salver "big enough to serve himself up upon, mother," said Geoff, with his jolly laugh: "I put him on it, and carried him round the room for Annie to see."

Beyond the inevitable inquiries, there was no mention made of Margaret; but when his mother kissed him at parting, and when Til lingered a moment longer than usual, with her arms round his neck, at the door, Geoffrey felt the depth and bitterness of the trouble that had come into his life more keenly, more chillingly than he had felt it yet.

"This shall not last," he said, as he walked slowly towards home, his head bent downwards, and all his features clouded with the gloom that had settled upon him. "This shall not last any longer. I have done all I can; if she is unhappy, it is not my fault; but I must know why. I cannot bear it; I have not deserved it. I will keep silence no longer. She must explain what it means."

CHAPTER XV.

LADY BEAUPORT'S PLOT COLLAPSES.

ALTHOUGH the flame of life, at its best a feeble flicker, now brightened by a little gust of hope, now deadened by an access of despair,—had begun steadily to lessen in Lord Caterham's breast, and he felt, with that consciousness which never betrays, that his interest in this world, small as it had been, was daily growing less, he had determined to prevent the execution of one act which he knew would be terribly antagonistic to the welfare of her whom his heart held dearest. We, fighting the daily battle of life, going forth each morning to the encounter, returning each eve with fresh dints on our harness, new notches in our swords, and able to reckon up the cost and the advantages gained by the day's combat, are unable to appreciate the anxieties and heart-burnings, the longings and the patience of those whom we leave behind us as a *corps de réserve*, apparently inactive, but in reality partaking of all the worst of the contest without the excitement of sharing it. The conflict that was raging amongst the Beauport family was patent to Caterham; he saw the positions taken up by the contending parties, had his own shrewd opinion as to their being tenable or the reverse, calmly criticised the various points of strategy, and laid his plans accordingly. In this it was an advantage to him that he was out of the din and the shouting and the turmoil of the battle ; nobody thought of him, any more than any one in the middle of an action thinks of the minister in his office at home, by whom the despatches are written, and who in reality pulls the strings by which the man in scarlet uniform and gold-laced cocked-hat is guided, and to whom he is responsible. Lord Caterham was physically unfitted for the conduct of strategic operations, but he was mentally qualified for the exercise of diplomacy in the highest degree ; and diplomacy was required in the present juncture.

In his solitary hours he had been accustomed to recal his past life in its apparently insignificant, but to him important ramifications ;—the red south wall is the world to the snail that has never known other resting-place ;—and in these days of illness and languor he reverted more and more to his old means of passing the time. A dull retrospect—a weary going over and over again of solitude, depression, and pain. Thoughts long since forgotten recurred to him as in the silence of the night he passed in review the petty incidents of his uneventful career. He recollected the burning shame which had first possessed him at the knowledge of his own deformity ; the half envy, half wonder, with which he had gazed at other lads of his own age ; the hope that had dawned upon him that his parents and friends might feel for him something of the special love with which Tiny Tim was regarded in that heartfullest of all stories, *The Christmas Carol;* how that wondrous book had charmed him, when, a

s

boy of ten or twelve years old, he had first read it; how, long before it had been seen by either his father or mother, he had studied and wept over it; how, prompted by a feeling which he could not analyse, he had induced Lord Beauport to read it, how he knew—intuitively, he was never told—that it had been shown to his mother; and how that Christmastide he had been treated with consideration and affection never before accorded to him—had been indeed preferred to Lionel, greatly to that young gentleman's astonishment and disgust. It did not last long, that halcyon time; the spells of the romancer held the practical father and the fashionable mother in no lengthened thrall; and when they were dissipated, there was merely a crippled, deformed, blighted lad as their eldest hope and the heir to their honours. Tiny Tim borne aloft on his capering father's shoulders; Tiny Tim in his grave,—these were images to wring the heart not unpleasantly, and to fill the eyes with tears of which one was rather proud, as proof of how easily the heart was wrung: but for a handsome couple—one known as a *beau garçon*, the other as a beauty—to have to face the stern fact that their eldest son was a cripple was any thing but agreeable.

Untrusted—that was it. Never from his earliest days could he recollect what it was to have trust reposed in him. He knew—he could not help knowing—how superior he was in ability and common-sense to any in that household; he knew that his father at least was perfectly aware of this; and yet that Lord Beauport could not disconnect the idea of bodily decrepitude and mental weakness; and therefore looked upon his eldest son as little more than a child in mind. As for Caterham's mother, the want of any feeling in common between them, the utter absence of any maternal tenderness, the manifest distaste with which she regarded him, and the half-wearied, half-contemptuous manner in which she put aside the attempts he made towards a better understanding between them, had long since begun to tell upon him. There was a time when, smarting under her lifelong neglect, and overcome by the utter sense of desolation weighing him down, he had regarded his mother with a feeling bordering on aversion; then her presence, occasionally bestowed upon him—always for her own purposes—awakened in him something very like disgust. But he had

long since conquered that : he had long since argued himself
out of that frame of mind. Self-commune had done its
work ; the long, long days and nights of patient reflexion and
self-examination, aided by an inexplicable sense of an overhanging great change, had softened and subdued all that
had been temporarily hard and harsh in Lord Caterham's
nature ; and there was no child, kneeling at its little bedside,
whose " God bless dear papa and mamma !" was more
tenderly earnest than the blessing which the crippled man
constantly invoked on his parents.

He loved them in a grave, steady, reverential, dutiful
way—loved them even with greater warmth, with more
complete fondness than he had done for years; but his
love never touched his instinct of justice—never warped his
sense of what was right. He remembered how, years
before, he had been present, a mere boy, sitting perched up
in his wheelchair, apparently forgotten, in an obscure corner
of his father's study at Homershams, while Lord Beauport
administered a terrific " wigging," ending in threats of gaols
and magistrates, to an unlucky wretch accused of poaching
by the head-keeper; and he recollected how, when the man
had been dismissed with a severe warning, he had talked to
and argued with his father, first on the offence, and then on
Lord Beauport's administration of justice, with an air of
grave and earnest wisdom which had amused his father
exceedingly. He had held the same sentiments throughout
his dreary life—he held them now. He knew that a plot
was formed by his mother to bring his brother Lionel back
to England, with a view to his marriage with Annie Maurice,
and he was determined that that plot should not succeed.
Why ? He had his reasons, as they had theirs. To his own
heart he confessed that he loved Annie with all the depth
of his soul; but that was not what prompted him in this
matter. He should be far removed from the troubling
before that ; but he had his reason, and he should keep it to
himself. They had not trusted in him, though they had
been compelled to take allies from the outside—dear old
Algy Barford, for instance—but they had not trusted him,
and he would not reveal his secret. Was Lionel to marry
Annie Maurice, eh ? No ; that should never be. He
might not be there himself to prevent it ; but he would leave
behind him instructions with some one, which would—

Ah! he had hit upon the some one at once,—Geoffrey Ludlow, Annie's oldest and dearest friend, honest as the day, brave and disinterested; not a clever business man perhaps, but one who, armed with what he could arm him with, must, with his sheer singleness of purpose, carry all before him. So far, so good; but there would be a first step which they would take perhaps before he could bring that weapon into play. His mother would contrive to get Lionel into the house, on his return, to live with them, so that he might have constant opportunities of access to Annie. That was a point in which, as he gleaned, she placed the greatest confidence. If her Lionel had not lost all the fascinating qualities which had previously so distinguished him; if he preserved his looks and his address, this young girl—so inexperienced in the world's ways, so warm-hearted and impressible—would have no choice but to succumb.

Caterham would see about that at once. Lionel should never remain *en permanence* in that house again. Lady Beauport would object of course. She had, when she had set her mind upon an object, a steady perseverance in its accomplishment; but neither her patience nor her diplomacy were comparable to his, when he was equally resolved, as she should find. No; on that point at least he was determined. His darling, his treasure, should not even be compelled to run the gauntlet of such a sin-stained courtship as his brother Lionel's must necessarily be. What might be awaiting her in the future, God alone knew: temptations innumerable; pursuit by fortune-hunters: all those trials which beset a girl who, besides being pretty and rich, has no blood-relative on whom to reckon for counsel and aid. He would do his best to remedy this deficiency; he would leave the fullest instructions, the warmest adjurations to good Geoffrey Ludlow—ah! what a pity it was that Ludlow's wife was not more heartful and reliable!—and he would certainly place a veto upon the notion that Lionel, on his return, should become an inmate of the house. He knew that this must be done quickly, and he determined to take the first opportunity that presented itself. That opportunity was not long in coming; within ten days after Margaret's fainting-fit, Lady Beauport paid one of her rare maternal visits, and Lord Caterham saw that his chance had arrived.

There was an extra glow of geniality in Lady Beauport's

manner that morning, and the frosty peck which she had made at her son's cheek had perhaps a trifle more warmth in it than usual. She seated herself instead of standing, as was her wont, and chatted pleasantly.

"What is this I hear about your having a lady fainting in your room, Arthur?" said she, with one of her shiniest smiles. (What calumny they spread about enamel! Lady Beauport smiled perpetually, and her complexion never cracked in the slightest degree.) "You must not bring down scandal on our extremely proper house. She did faint, didn't she?"

"O, yes, mother, she did faint undoubtedly—went what you call regularly 'off,' I believe."

"Ah! so Stephens told Timpson. Well, sir, don't you think that is reprehensible enough? A lady comes to call on a bachelor, and is discovered fainting! Why? Heaven knows—" and her ladyship gave an unpleasantly knowing chuckle.

"Well, I must admit that no one knows, or ever will know why, save that the lady was probably over-fatigued, having only just recovered from a serious illness. But then, you know, the lady's husband was with her, so that—"

"O, yes, I heard all about that. You are a most prudent swain, Caterham! The lady's husband with her, indeed! Most prudent! You always remind me of the play—I don't know what it's called—something about a French milliner and a screen—"

"'The School for Scandal,' you mean?"

"Very likely. I've forgotten the name, but I know I recollect seeing Farren and Miss Foote and all of them in it. And I so often think of the two brothers: you so quiet and reserved, like one; and the other so rackety and buoyant, so full of high spirits and gaiety, like our Lionel. Ah me!" and Lady Beauport heaved a deep sigh and clasped her hands sadly in front of her.

Caterham smiled—rather a sad dreary smile—as he said, "Let us trust that quiet and reserve don't always have the effect which they produced on the gentleman to whom you are alluding, mother. But I may as well let you know the real story of Mrs. Ludlow's fainting-fit, which seems to have become rather warped in its journey. I had asked her husband to call upon me on a matter of business; and he

foolishly brought her—only just out of her confinement—
with him. The consequence was, that, as we were talking,
and she was looking through a book of photographs, she
fainted away."

"Ay! I heard something of that sort. She must be a
curious person to be so easily affected, or it was thoughtless
of her husband to bring her out too soon. He is an odd
kind of man though, is he not? Absent, and that kind of
thing?"

"Ye-es; his heart is in his work, and he is generally
thinking about it."

"So I had imagined. What odd people you know, Arthur!
Your acquaintances all seem such strange people—so different from your father's and mine!"

"Yes, mother," said Caterham, with a repetition of the
sad smile; "perhaps you're right. generally. Your friends
would scarcely care for me, and I am sure I do not care
for them. But Geoffrey Ludlow became known to me
through his old intimacy with Annie—our Annie."

"Ye-es. I scarcely know why 'our Annie,' though. You
see, both your father and I have many blood-relations, more
or less distant, on either side; and it would not be particularly convenient if the mere fact of their being blood-
relations compelled us to acknowledge them as 'ours.' Not
that I've any thing to say against Miss Maurice, though; on
the contrary, she's a very charming girl. At one time I
thought that—However, let that pass. She holds quite a
different position now; and I think every one will allow
that my treatment of her is what it should be."

"Of course, mother. No one would dream of doubting it."

"Well, perhaps not, Arthur; but you're such a recluse,
you know, that you're scarcely a judge of these things—one
does not know what people won't say. The world is so full
of envy and jealousy, and all that, I'm sure my position in
regard to the matter is any thing but an agreeable one.
Here I am, having to act *chaperon* to this girl, who is known
now as an heiress; and all kinds of men paying her attention,
simply on account of her wealth. What I suffer when we're
out together, you can't conceive. Every night, wherever we
may be, there is a certain set of men always hanging about
her, waiting for an introduction—persons whose acquaintance
cannot do her the slightest good, and with whom she is yet

quite as willing to talk or to dance as she is with the most available *parti* in London."

Caterham smiled again. " You forget, mother, that she's not accustomed to the kind of life—"

" No ; I don't forget anything of the kind, Arthur. It is her not being accustomed to it that is my greatest trouble. She is as raw as a child of seventeen after her first drawing-room. If she had any *savoir faire*, any knowledge of society, I should be perfectly at ease. A girl of any appreciation would know how to treat these people in an instant. Why, I know myself, that when I was far younger than Miss Maurice, I should have felt a kind of instinctive warning against two-thirds of the men with whom Annie Maurice is as talkative and as pleasant as though they were really persons whose acquaintance it was most desirable that she should make."

" And yet Annie is decidedly a clever girl."

" So much the worse, Arthur,—so much the worse. The more reason that she is utterly unlikely to possess or to be able readily to acquire the peculiar knowledge which would fit her to act under the circumstances of which I am speaking. Your clever people—such at least as are called clever by you and those whom you cultivate—are precisely the people who act idiotically in worldly affairs, who either know nothing or who set at defiance the *convenances* of society, and of whom nothing can be made. That man—no, let me give you an example—that man who dined here last Thursday on your invitation—Professor Somebody, wasn't he ?—I've heard of him at that place where they give the scientific lectures in Albemarle Street—was any thing ever seen like his cravat, or his shoes, or the way in which he ate his soup ?—he trod on my dress twice in going down to dinner, and I heard perfectly plainly what Lady Clanronald said to that odious Mr. Beauchamp Hogg about him."

" My father spoke to me in the highest terms about—"

" Of course he did ; that's just it. Your father knows nothing about this sort of thing. It all falls upon me. If Annie Maurice were to make a *mésalliance*, or, without going so far as that, were to permit herself to be engaged to some penniless fortune-hunter, and were to refuse—as she very likely would, for she has an amount of obstinacy in her composition, I am inclined to think, which one very seldom finds

—to listen to the remonstrances of those whose opinion ought to have weight with her, it is I, not your father, who would be blamed by the world.'"

"Your troubles certainly seem greater, mother, than I, in my bachelor ignorance, could have imagined."

"They are not comprehensible, even after my explanation, Arthur, by those who have not to undergo them. There is scarcely any thing in my married life which has given me such pleasure as the thought that, having no daughters, I should be relieved of all duties of chaperonage; that I should not be compelled to go to certain places unless I wished; and that I should be able to leave others at what hours I liked. And now I find this very duty incumbent upon me."

"Well, but, my dear mother, surely Annie is the very last girl in the world for whom it is necessary to make any such sacrifices. She does not care about going out; and when out, she seems, from all she says to me, to have only one anxiety, and that is—to get home again as soon as possible."

"Ay, from all she says to you, Arthur; but then you know, as I've said before, you are a regular old bachelor, without the power of comprehending these things, and to whom a girl certainly would not be likely to show her real feelings. No; there's only one way to relieve me from my responsibility."

"And that is—"

"And that is by getting her married."

"A-ah!" Caterham drew a long breath—it was coming now.

"Married," continued Lady Beauport, "to some one whom we know, and in whom we could trust; some one who would keep her near us, so that we could still keep up an interest in her; and you—for I know how very much attached you are to her, Arthur—could see her constantly, without trouble to yourself. That is the only manner in which I can see a conclusion to my anxiety on Annie's account."

Lady Beauport endeavoured to speak in the same tone in which she had commenced the conversation; but there was a quiver in her voice and a tremulous motion in her hands which showed Caterham plainly that she was ill at ease.

" And do you think that such a husband would be easily found for Annie, mother?" said he, looking up at her with one of his steady piercing glances from under his eyebrows.

" Not easily, of course ; but still to be found, Arthur."

" From your manner, you seem to have already given the subject some attention. May I ask if you have any one in prospect who would fulfil all the conditions you have laid down in the first place, and in the second would be likely to be acceptable to Annie ?"

" How very singular you are, Arthur ! You speak in a solemn tone, as if this were the most important matter in the world."

" It is sufficiently important to Annie at least. Would you mind answering me ?"

Lady Beauport saw that it was useless fighting off the explanation any further. Her project must be disclosed now, however it might be received by her eldest son ; and she determined to bring her stateliest and most dignified manner to its disclosure : so she composed her face to its usual cold statuesque calmness, folded her wandering hands before her, and in a voice in which there was neither break nor tremor, said :

" No : I will answer you quite straightforwardly. I think that it would be an admirable thing for all parties if a marriage could be arranged between Annie Maurice and your brother Lionel. Lionel has position, and is a distinguished-looking man, of whom any woman might be proud ; and the fortune which Mr. Ampthill so oddly left to Miss Maurice will enable him to hold his own before the world, and—how strangely you look, Caterham !—what is the matter ?—what were you about to say ?"

" Only one thing, mother—that marriage must never be."

" Must never be !"

" Never. Hear me out. I have kept accurate account of all you have said, and will judge you in the first place simply out of your own mouth. Your first point was that Miss Maurice should be married to some one whom we knew, and whom we could trust. Could we trust Lionel ? Could we trust the man whose father's head was bowed to the dust, whose mother's eyes were filled with tears at the mere recital of his deeds of sin and shame ? Could we trust the man who was false to his friend, and who dragged down into the dirt not merely himself, but all who bore his name? You spoke of his position—what is that, may I ask? Are we to plume ourselves on our relationship with an outcast? or are we to hold out as an inducement to the heiress the fact that her intended husband's liberty is at the mercy of those whom he has swindled and defrauded?"

"Caterham! Arthur! you are mad—you—"

"No, mother, I am simply speaking the truth. I should not even have insisted on that in all its bitterness, had I not been goaded to it by your words. You talk of devoting the fortune which Annie Maurice has inherited to setting Lionel right before the world, and you expect me to sit quietly by! Why, the merest instincts of justice would have made me cry out against such a monstrous proposition, even if Lionel had not long since forfeited, as Annie has long since won, all my love."

"A-h!" said Lady Beauport, suddenly pausing in her tears, and looking up at him,—"long since won all your love, eh? I have often suspected that, Caterham; and now you have betrayed yourself. It is jealousy then,—mere personal jealousy,—by which all your hatred of your younger brother is actuated!"

Once more the dreary smile came over Lord Caterham's face. "No, mother," said he, "it is not that. I love Annie Maurice as I love the sun, as I love health, as I love rest from pain and weariness; and with about as much hope of winning either. You could confer on me no greater happiness than by showing me the man deserving of her love; and the thought that her future would have a chance of being a happy one would relieve my life of its heaviest anxiety. But marry Lionel she shall not; nay, more, she shall not be exposed to the chance of communication with him, so long as I can prevent it."

"You forget yourself, Lord Caterham! You forget not merely whose house you are in, but to whom you are speaking."

"I trust not, mother. I trust I shall never—certainly not now, at this time—forget my duty to you and to my father; but I know more than I can ever divulge even to you. Take for granted what I tell you; let what you know of Lionel's ways and conduct suffice to prove that

a marriage between him and Annie is impossible,—that
you would be culpable in lending yourselves to such a
scheme."

"I have not the least idea of what you are talking about,
Arthur," said Lady Beauport after a minute's pause. "You
appear to have conceived some ridiculous idea about your
brother Lionel, into the discussion of which you must really
excuse my following you. Besides, even if you had good
grounds for all you say, you are too late in making the
remonstrance. Lionel arrived in England the day before
yesterday."

Lord Caterham started, and by the help of his stick raised
himself for a moment.

"Lionel returned! Lionel in England, mother! After
all his promises, after the strict conditions on which my
father purchased for him immunity from the penalties of
his crime! How is this? Does Lord Beauport know it?"

Lady Beauport hesitated. She had been betrayed by her
vexation into saying more than she had intended, and had
placed Lionel in his brother's power. Lord Caterham, she
had hoped, would have received her confidence in a different
spirit,—perhaps she had calculated on his being flattered by
its novelty,—and would assist her in breaking the fact of
the prodigal's return to his father, and winning him over
to her way of thinking. She had by no means forgotten
the painful solemnity with which the Earl had renounced
Lionel, and the formal sentence of exclusion which had
been passed against him; but Lady Beauport understood
her husband well, and had managed him with tolerable
success for many years. He had forbidden all mention
of their son to her, as to every other member of the family;
but Lady Beauport had been in the habit of insinuating
an occasional mention of him for some time past; and it
had not been badly received. Perhaps neither the father
nor the mother would have acknowledged to themselves
or to each other the share in this change of feeling which
belonged to the unmistakable daily decline of Lord Caterham's health. They never alluded to the future, but they
saw it, and it influenced them both. Lady Beauport had
not looked for Lionel's return so soon; she had expected
more patience—it might have been appropriately called
more decency—from him; she had thought her difficulties

would be much lessened before his return; but he had neglected her injunctions, and forestalled her instructions : he had arrived,—there was no help for it; she must meet the difficulty now. She had been meeting difficulties, originating from the same source, for many years ; and though Caterham's manner annoyed her deeply, she kept her courage up. Her first instinct was to evade her son's last question, by assuming an injured tone in reference to his first. So she said,

"O, it's all very well to talk about his promises, Arthur ; but, really, how you could expect Lionel to remain in Australia I cannot understand."

"I did not, and I do not, form any expectations whatever concerning Lionel, mother," her son replied, in a steady voice, and without releasing her from his gaze; "that is beside the question. Lionel has broken his pledged word to my father by returning here,—you know he has,—and he has not given any career a fair trial. I can guess the expectations with which he has returned," he continued in a bitter tone; "and God knows I trust they are not unfounded. But my place is not vacant *yet;* and he has forfeited his own. You cannot restore it to him. Why has he returned ?"

Lady Beauport did not dare to say, "Because I wrote to him, and told him to come home, and marry Annie Maurice, and buy the world's fickle favour over again with her money, while waiting for yours ;" but her silence said it for her ; and Caterham let his eyes drop from her face in disgust, as he coldly said,

"Once more, madam, I ask you, is my father aware that Lionel is in London ?"

"No," she replied boldly, seeing things were at the worst; "he is not. I tell you, Caterham, if you tell him, before I have time and opportunity to break it to him, and set your father against him, and on keeping his word just as a point of pride, I will never forgive you. What good could it do you ? What harm has Lionel done you ? How could he stay in that horrid place ? He's not a tradesman, I should think ; and what could he *do* there ? nor an Irishman, I hope ; so what could he *be* there ? The poor boy was perfectly miserable ; and when I told him to come home, I thought you'd help me, Arthur,—I did indeed."

A grave sad smile passed over Lord Caterham's worn face. Here was his proud mother trying to cajole him for the sake of the profligate son who had never felt either affection or respect for her. Had a less object been at stake he might have yielded to the weakness which he rather pitied than despised ; yielded all the more readily that it would not be for long. But Annie's peace, Annie's welfare was in danger, and his mother's weakness could meet with no toleration at his hands.

"Listen to me, mother," he said ; "and let this be no more mentioned between us. I am much exhausted to-day, and have little strength at any time ; but my resolve is unshaken. I will not inform my father of Lionel's return, if you think you can manage to tell him, and to induce him to take it without anger more successfully than I can. But while I live Lionel Brakespere shall never live in the same house with Annie Maurice ; and whether I am living or dead, I will prevent his ever making her his wife. This is her proper home ; and I will do my best to secure her remaining in it ; but how long do you suppose she would stay, if she heard the plans you have formed ?" Lady Beauport attempted to speak, but he stopped her. "One moment more, mother," he said, "and I have done. Let me advise you to deceive my father no more for Lionel. He is easily managed, I have no doubt, by those whom he loves and admires ; but he is impatient of deceit, being very loyal himself. Tell him without delay what you have done ; but do not, if even he takes it better than you hope, and that you think such a suggestion would be safe,—do not suggest that Lionel should come here. Let me, for my little time, be kept from any collision with my father. I ask this of you, mother." O, how the feeble voice softened, and the light in the eyes deepened ! "And my requests are neither frequent nor hard to fulfil, I think."

He had completely fathomed her purpose ; he had seen the projects she had formed, even while he was speaking the first sentences ; and had defeated them. By a violent effort she controlled her temper,—perhaps she had never made so violent an effort, even for Lionel, before,—and answered,—

"I hardly understand you, Arthur ; but perhaps you are

right. At all events, you agree to say nothing to **your** father,—to leave it to me?"

"Certainly," said Caterham. He had won the day; but his mother's manner had no sign of defeat about it, no more than it had sign of softening. She rose, and bade him good-morning. He held her hand for a moment, and his eyes followed her wistfully, as she went out of his room.

As she passed through the passage, just outside her son's door she saw a stout keen-looking man sitting on the bench, who rose and bowed as she passed.

When Stephens answered the bell, he found his master lying back, bloodless and almost fainting. After he had administered the usual restoratives, and when life seemed flowing back again, the valet said,

"Inspector Blackett, my lord, outside."

Lord Caterham made a sign with his hand, and the stout man entered.

"The usual story, Blackett, I suppose?"

"Sorry to say so, my lord. No news. Two of my men tried Maidstone again yesterday, and Canterbury, thinking they were on the scent there; but no signs of her."

"Very good, Blackett," said Caterham faintly; "don't give in yet."

Then, as the door closed behind the inspector, the poor sufferer looked up heavenward and muttered, "O Lord, how long—how long?"

𝔅𝔬𝔬𝔨 𝔱𝔥𝔢 𝔗𝔥𝔦𝔯𝔡.

CHAPTER I.

THE WHOLE TRUTH.

NO one who knew Geoffrey Ludlow would have recognised him in the round-shouldered man with the prone head, the earth-seeking eyes, the hands plunged deeply in his pockets, plodding home on that day on which he had determined that Margaret should give him an explanation of her conduct towards him. Although Geoff had never been a roisterer, had never enlisted in that army of artists whose members hear "the chimes o' midnight," had always been considered more or less slow and steady, and was looked upon as one of the most respectable representatives of the community, yet his happy disposition had rendered him a general favourite even amongst those ribalds, and his equable temper and kindly geniality were proverbial among all the brethren of the brush. Ah, that equable temper, that kindly geniality,—where were they now? Those expanded nostrils, those closed lips, spoke of very different feelings; that long steady stride was very different from the joyous step which had provoked the cynicism of the City-bound clerks; that puckered brow, those haggard cheeks, could not be recognised as the facial presentments of the Geoffrey Ludlow of a few short months since.

In good sooth he was very much altered. The mental worrying so long striven against in silence had begun to tell upon his appearance; the big broad shoulders had become rounded; the gait had lost its springy elasticity, the face was lined, and the dark-brown hair round the temples and the long full beard were dashed with streaks of silver. These changes troubled him but little. Never, save perhaps during the brief period of his courtship of Margaret, had he given the smallest thought to his personal appearance; yellow soap and cold water had been his cosmetics, and his greatest sacrifice to vanity had been to place himself at rare intervals under the hairdresser's scissors. But there were other changes to which, try as he might, he could not blind himself. He knew that the very source and fount of his delight was troubled, if not sullied; he knew that all his happiness, so long wished for, so lately attained, was trembling in the balance; he felt that indefinable, indescribable sensation of something impending, something which would shatter his roof-tree and break up that home so recently established. As he plunged onward through the seething streets, looking neither to the right nor to the left, he thought vaguely of the events of the last few months of his life—thought of them, regarding them as a dream. How long was it since he was so happy at home with his old mother and with Til? when the monthly meeting of the Titians caused his greatest excitement, and when his hopes of fame were yet visionary and indistinct? How long was it since he had met *her* that fearful night, and had drunk of the beauty and the witchery which had had such results? He was a man now before the world with a name which people knew and respected, with a wife whose beauty people admired; but, ah! where was the quietude, the calm unpretending happiness of those old days?

What could it mean? Had she a wish ungratified? He taxed his mind to run through all the expressions of her idle fancy, but could think of none with which he had not complied. Was she ill? He had made that excuse for her before her baby was born; but now, not merely the medical testimony, but his own anxious scrutiny told him that she was in the finest possible health. There was an odd something about her sometimes which he could not make out—an odd way of listening vacantly, and not replying to direct questions, which he had noticed lately, and only lately; but that might be a part of her idiosyncrasy. Her appetite too was scarcely as good as it used to be; but in all other respects she seemed perfectly well. There might have been some difficulty with his mother and sister, he had at first imagined; but the old lady had been wonderfully complaisant; and Til and Margaret, when they met, seemed to get on excellently together. To be sure his mother had assumed the reins of government during Margaret's confinement, and held them until the last moment compatible with decency; but her *régime* had been over long since; and Margaret was the last person to struggle for power so long as all trouble was taken off her hands. Had the neighbours slighted her, she might have had some cause for complaint; but the neighbours were every thing that was polite, and indeed at the time of her illness had shown her attention meriting a warmer term. What could it mean? Was there— No; he crushed out the idea as soon as it arose in his mind. There could not be any question about—any one else—preying on her spirits? The man, her destroyer—who had abandoned and deserted her—was far away; and she was much too practical a woman not to estimate all his conduct at its proper worth. No amount of girlish romance could survive the cruel schooling which his villany had subjected her to; and there was no one else whom she had seen who could have had any influence over her. Besides, at the first, when he had made his humble proffer of love, she had only to have told him that it could not be, and he would have taken care that her future was provided for—if not as it had been, at all events far beyond the reach of want. O, no, that could not be.

So argued Geoff with himself—brave, honest, simple old Geoff, with the heart of a man and the guilelessness of a child. So he argued, determining at the same time that he would pluck out the heart of the mystery at once, whatever might be at its root; any thing would be better than this suspense preying on him daily, preventing him from doing his work, and rendering him moody and miserable.

But before he reached his home his resolution failed, and his heart sunk within him. What if Margaret were silent and preoccupied? what if the occasional gloom upon her face became more and more permanent? Had not her life been full of sorrow? and was it wonderful that the remembrance of it from time to time came over her? She had fearlessly confided her whole story to him; she had given him time to reflect on it before committing himself to her; and would it be generous, would it be even just, to call her to account now for freaks of behaviour engendered doubtless in the memory of that bygone time? After all, what was the accusation against her? None. Had there been the smallest trace of levity in her conduct, how many eyebrows were there ready to be lifted—how many shoulders

T

waiting to be shrugged! But there was nothing of the kind; all that could be said about her was that,—all that could be said about her—now he thought it over, nothing was said about her; all that was hinted was that her manner was cold and impassable; that she took no interest in what was going on around her, and that therefore there must be something wrong. There is always something to be complained of. If her manner had been light and easy, they would have called her a flirt, and pitied him for having married a woman so utterly ill-suited to his staid habits. He knew so little of her when he married her, that he ran every kind of risk as to what she might really prove to be; and on reflection he thought he had been exceedingly lucky. She might have been giddy, vulgar, loud, presuming, extravagant; whereas she was simply reserved and unde-monstrative,—nothing more. He had been a fool in thinking of her as he had done during the last few weeks; he had,—without her intending it doubtless, for she was an excellent woman,—he had taken his tone in this matter from his mother, with whom Margaret was evidently no favourite, and—there, never mind—it was at an end now. She was his own darling wife, his lovely companion, merely to sit and look at whom was rapturous delight to a man of his keen appreciation of the beauty of form and colour; and as to her coldness and reserve, it was but a temporary man-nerism, which would soon pass away.

So argued Geoffrey Ludlow with himself,—brave, honest, simple old Geoff, with the heart of a man, and the guile-lessness of a child.

So happy was he under the influence of his last thought, that he longed to take Margaret to his heart at once, and without delay to make trial of his scheme for dissipating her gloom; but when he reached home, the servant told him that her mistress had gone out very soon after he himself had left that morning, and had not yet returned. So he went through into the studio, intending to work at his picture; but when he got there he sunk down into a chair, staring vacantly at the lay-figure, arranged as usual in a preposterous attitude, and thinking about Margaret. Rousing himself, he found his palette, and commenced to set it; but while in the midst of this task, he suddenly fell a-thinking again, and stood there mooning, until the hope of doing any work was past, and the evening shadows were falling on the landscape. Then he put up his palette and his brushes, and went into the dining-room. He walked to the window, but had scarcely reached it, when he saw a cab drive up. The man opened the door, and Margaret descended, said a few hasty words to the driver, who touched his hat and fastened on his horse's nosebag, and approached the house with rapid steps.

From his position in the window, he had noticed a strange light in her eyes which he had never before seen there, a bright hectic flush on her cheek, a tight compression of her lips. When she entered the room he saw that in his first hasty glance he had not been deceived; that the whole expression of her face had changed from its usual state of statuesque repose, and was now stern, hard, and defiant.

He was standing in the shadow of the window-curtain, and she did not see him at first; but throwing her parasol on the table, commenced pacing the room. The lamp was as yet unlit, and the flickering firelight—now glowing a deep dull red, now leaping into yellow flame—gave an additiona! weirdness to the set intensity of her beautiful face. Gazing at her mechanically walking to and fro, her head supported by one hand, her eyes gleaming, her hair pushed back off her face, Geoffrey again felt that indescribable sinking at his heart; and there was something of terror in the tone in which, stepping forward, he uttered her name— "Margaret!"

In an instant she stopped in her walk, and turning towards the place whence the voice came, said, "You there, Geoffrey?"

"Yes, darling,—who else? I was standing at the window when the cab drove up, and saw you get out. By the way, you've not sent away the cab, love; is he paid?"

"No, not yet,—he will—let him stay a little."

"Well, but why keep him up here, my child, where there is no chance of his getting a return-fare? Better pay him and let him go. I'll go and pay him!" and he was leaving the room.

"Let him stay, please," said Margaret in her coldest tones; and Geoffrey turned back at once. But as he turned he saw a thrill run through her, and marked the manner in which she steadied her hand on the mantelpiece on which she was leaning. In an instant he was by her side.

"You are ill, my darling?" he exclaimed. "You have done too much again, and are over-fatigued—"

"I am perfectly well," she said; "it was nothing—or whatever it was, it has passed. I did not know you had returned. I was going to write to you."

"To write to me!" said Geoff in a hollow voice,—"to write to me!"

"To write to you. I had something to tell you—and—and I did not know whether I should ever see you again!"

For an instant the table against which Geoffrey Ludlow stood seemed to spin away under his touch, and the whole room reeled. A deadly faintness crept over him, but he shook it off with one great effort, and said in a very low tone, "I scarcely understand you—please explain."

She must have had the nature of a fiend to look upon that large-souled loving fellow, stricken down by her words as by a sudden blow, and with his heart all bleeding, waiting to hear the rest of her sentence. She had the nature of a fiend, for through her set teeth she said calmly and delibe-rately:

"I say I did not know whether I should ever see you again. That cab is detained by me to take me away from this house, to which I ought never to have come—which I shall never enter again."

Geoff had sunk into a chair, and clutching the corner of the table with both hands, was looking up at her with a helpless gaze.

"You don't speak!" she continued; "and I can under-stand why you are silent. This decision has come upon you unexpectedly, and you can scarcely realise its meaning or its origin. I am prepared to explain both to you. I had intended doing so in a letter, which I should have left behind me; but since you are here, it is better that I should speak."

The table was laid for dinner, and there was a small decanter of sherry close by Geoff's hand. He filled a glass from it and drank it eagerly. Apparently involuntarily, Margaret extended her hand towards the decanter; but she instantly withdrew it, and resumed:

"You know well, Geoffrey Ludlow, that when you asked

me to become your wife, I declined to give you any answer until you had heard the story of my former life. When I noticed your growing interest in me—and I noticed it from its very first germ—I determined that before you pledged yourself to me—for my wits had been sharpened in the school of adversity, and I read plainly enough that love from such a man as you had but one meaning and one result,—I determined that before you pledged yourself to me you should learn as much as it was necessary for you to know of my previous history. Although my early life had been spent in places far away from London, and among persons whom it was almost certain I should never see again, it was, I thought, due to you to explain all to you, lest the gossiping fools of the world might some day vex your generous heart with stories of your wife's previous career, which she had kept from you. Do you follow me?"

Geoffrey bowed his head, but did not speak.

"In that story I told you plainly that I had been deceived by a man under promise of marriage ; that I had lived with him as his wife for many months ; that he had basely deserted me and left me to starve,—left me to die—as I should have died had you not rescued me. You follow me still ?"

She could not see his face now,—it was buried in his hands; but there was a motion of his head, and she proceeded :

"That man betrayed me when I trusted him, used me while I amused him, deserted me when I palled upon him. He ruined, you restored me ; he left me to die, you brought me back to life ; he strove to drag me to perdition, you to raise me to repute. I respected, I honoured you ; but I loved him ! yes, from first to last I loved him ; infatuated, mad as I knew it to be, I loved him throughout ! Had I died in those streets from which you rescued me, I should have found strength to bless him with my last breath. When I recovered consciousness, my first unspoken thought was of him. It was that I would live, that I would make every exertion to hold on to life, that I might have the chance of seeing him again. Then dimly, and as in a dream, I saw you and heard your voice, and knew that you were to be a portion of my fate. Ever since, the image of that man has been always present before me ; his soft words of love have been always ringing in my ears; his gracious presence has been always at my side. I have striven and striven against the infatuation. Before Heaven I swear to you that I have prayed night after night that I might not be led into that awful temptation of retrospect which beset me; that I might be strengthened to love you as you should be loved, to do my duty towards you as it should be done. All in vain, all in vain! That one fatal passion has sapped my being, and rendered me utterly incapable of any other love in any other shape. I know what you have done for me—more than that, I know what you have suffered for me. You have said nothing; but do you think I have not seen how my weariness, my coldness, the impossibility of my taking interest in all the little schemes you have laid for my diversion, have irked and pained you? Do you think I do not know what it is for a full heart to beat itself into quiet against a stone? I know it all; and if I could have spared you one pang, I swear I would have done so. But I loved this man; ah, how I loved him! He was but a memory to me then; but that memory was far, far dearer than all reality! He is more than a memory to me now; for he lives, and he is in London, and I have seen him!"

Out of Geoffrey Ludlow's hands came, raised up suddenly, a dead white face, with puckered lips, knit brows, and odd red streaks and indentations round the eyes.

"Yes, Geoffrey Ludlow," she continued, not heeding the apparition, "I have seen him,—now, within this hour,—seen him, bright, well, and handsome—O, so handsome!—as when I saw him first; and that has determined me. While I thought of him as perhaps dead; while I knew him to be thousands of miles away, I could bear to sit here, to drone out the dull monotonous life, striving to condone the vagrancy of my thoughts by the propriety of my conduct,—heart-sick, weary, and remorseful. Yes, remorseful, so far as you are concerned; for you are a true and noble man, Geoffrey. But now that he is here, close to me, I could not rest another hour,—I must go to him at once. Do you hear, Geoffrey,—at once?"

He tried to speak, but his lips were parched and dry, and he only made an inarticulate sound. There was no mistaking the flash of his eyes, however. In them Margaret had never seen such baleful light; so that she was scarcely astonished when, his voice returning, he hissed out "I know him!"

"You know him?"

"Yes; just come back from Australia—Lord Caterham's brother! I had a letter from Lord Caterham to-day,—his brother—Lionel Brakespere!"

"Well," she exclaimed, "what then? Suppose it be Lionel Brakespere, what then, I ask—what then?"

"Then!" said Geoffrey, poising his big sinewy arm— "then, let him look to himself; for, by the Lord, I'll kill him!"

"What!" and in an instant she had left her position against the mantelpiece, and was leaning over the table at the corner where he sat, her face close to his, her eyes on his eyes, her hot breath on his cheeks—"You dare to talk of killing him, of doing him the slightest injury! You dare to lift your hand against my Lionel! Look here, Geoffrey Ludlow: you have been good and kind and generous to me,—have loved me, in your fashion—deeply, I know; and I would let us part friends; but I swear that if you attempt to wreak your vengeance on Lionel Brakespere, who has done you no harm—how has he injured you?—I will be revenged on you in a manner of which you little dream, but which shall break your heart and spirit, and humble your pride to the dust. Think of all this, Geoffrey Ludlow— think of it. Do nothing rashly, take no step that will madden me, and drive me to do something that will prevent your ever thinking of me with regret, when I am far away."

There was a softness in her voice which touched a chord in Geoffrey Ludlow's breast. The fire faded out of his eyes; his hands, which had been tight-clenched, relaxed, and spread out before him in entreaty; he looked up at Margaret through blinding tears, and in a broken voice said,

"When you are far away! O, my darling, my darling, you are not going to leave me? It cannot be,—it is some horrible dream. To leave me, who live but for you, whose existence is bound up in yours! It cannot be. What have I done?—what can you charge me with? Want of affection, of devotion to you? O God, it is hard that I should have to suffer in this way! But you won't go, Margaret darling? Tell me that—only tell me that."

She shrank farther away from him, and seemed for a moment to cower before the vehemence and anguish of his appeal; but the next her face darkened and hardened, and as she answered him, the passion in her voice was dashed with a tone of contempt.

"Yes, I will leave you," she said,—"of course I will leave you. Do you not hear me? Do you not understand me? I have seen him, I tell you, and every thing which is not him has faded out of my life. What should I do here, or any where, where he is not? The mere idea is absurd. I have only half lived since I lost him, and I could not live at all now that I have seen him again. Stay here! not leave *you!* stay *here!*" She looked round the room with a glance of aversion and avoidance, and went on with increasing rapidity: "You have never understood me. How should you? But the time has come now when you must try to understand me, for your own sake; for mine it does not matter—nothing matters now."

She was standing within arm's-length of him, and her face was turned full upon him : but she did not seem to see him. She went on as though reckoning with herself, and Geoffrey gazed upon her in stupefied amazement; his momentary rage quenched in the bewilderment of his anguish.

"I don't deny your goodness—I don't dispute it—I don't think about it at all; it is all done with, all past and gone; and I have no thought for it or you, beyond these moments in which I am speaking to you for the last time. I have suffered in this house torments which your slow nature could neither suffer nor comprehend—torments wholly impossible to endure longer. I have raged and rebelled against the dainty life of dulness and dawdling, the narrow hopes and the tame pleasures which have sufficed for you. I must have so raged and rebelled under any circumstances; but I might have gone on conquering the revolts, if I had not seen him. Now, I tell you, it is no longer possible, and I break with it at once and for ever. Let me go quietly, and in such peace as may be possible : for go I must and I will. You could as soon hold a hurricane by force or a wave of the sea by entreaty."

Geoffrey Ludlow covered his face with his hands, and groaned. Once again she looked at him—this time **as if** she saw him—and went on:

"Let me speak to you, while I can, of yourself—while I can, I say, for his face is rising between me and all the world beside, and I can hardly force myself to remember any thing, to calculate any thing, to realise any thing which is not him. You ask me not to leave you; you would have me stay! Are you mad, Geoffrey Ludlow? Have you lived among your canvases and your colours until you have ceased to understand what men and women are, and to see facts? Do you know that I love him, though he left me to what you saved me from, so that all that you have done for me and given me has been burdensome and hateful to me, because these things had no connection with him, but marked the interval in which he was lost to me? Do you know that I love him so, that I have sickened and pined in this house, even as I sickened and pined for hunger in the streets you took me from, for the most careless word he ever spoke and the coldest look he ever gave me? Do you know the agonised longing which has been mine, the frantic weariness, the unspeakable loathing of every thing that set my life apart from the time when my life was his? No, you don't know these things! Again I say, how should you? Well, I tell them to you now, and I ask you, are you mad that you say, 'Don't leave me'? Would you have me stay with *you* to think of *him* all the weary hours of the day, all the wakeful hours of the night? Would you have me stay with you to feel, and make you know that I feel, the tie between us an intolerable and hideous bondage, and that with every pang of love for him came a throb of loathing for you? No, no! you are nothing to me now,—nothing, nothing! My thoughts hurry away from you while I speak; but if any thing so preposterous as my staying with you could be possible, you would be the most hateful object on this earth to me."

"My God!" gasped Geoffrey. That was all. The utter, unspeakable horror with which her words, poured out in a hard ringing voice, which never faltered, filled him over-powered all remonstrance. A strange feeling, which was akin to fear of this beautiful unmasked demon, came over him. It was Margaret, his wife, who spoke thus! The knowledge and its fullest agony were in his heart; and yet a sense of utter strangeness and impossibility were there too. The whirl within him was not to be correctly termed thought;

but there was in it something of the past, a puzzled remembrance of her strange quietude, her listlessness, her acquies-
cent, graceful, wearied, compliant ways ; and this was she,
—this woman whose eyes burned with flames of passion and
desperate purpose,—on those ordinarily pale cheeks two
spots of crimson glowed,—whose lithe frame trembled with
the intense fervour of the love which she was declaring for
another man ! Yes, this was she ! It seemed impossible ;
but it was true.

"I waste words," she said; "I am talking of things
beside the question, and I don't want to lie to you. Why
should I ? There has been nothing in my life worth having
but him, nothing bearable since I lost him, and there is
nothing else since I have found him again. I say, I must
leave you for your sake, and it is true ; but I would leave
you just the same if it was not true. There is nothing
henceforth in my life but him."

She moved towards the door as she spoke, and the action
seemed to rouse Geoffrey from the stupefaction which had
fallen upon him. She had her hand upon the door-handle
though, before he spoke.

"You are surely mad !" he said ! "I think so.—I hope so ;
but even mad women remember that they are mothers.
Have you forgotten your child, that you rave thus of leaving
your home ?"

She took her hand from the door and leaned back against
it—her head held up, and her eyes turned upon him, the
dark eyebrows shadowing them with a stern frown.

"I am not mad," she said; "but I don't wonder you
think me so. Continue to think so, if you needs must
remember me at all. Love is madness to such as you; but
it is life, and sense, and wisdom, and wealth to such as I
and the man I love. At all events it is all the sanity I ask
for or want. As for the child—" she paused for one
moment, and waved her hand impatiently.

"Yes," repeated Geoffrey hoarsely,—"the child !"

"I will tell you then, Geoffrey Ludlow," she said, in a
more deliberate tone than she had yet commanded,—"I
care nothing for the child ! Ay, look at me with abhorrence
now; so much the better for *you*, and not a jot the worse
for me. What is your abhorrence to me?—what was your
love? There are women to whom their children are all in

all. I am not of their number; I never could have been. They are not women who love as I love. Where a child has power to sway and fill a woman's heart, to shake her resolution, and determine her life, love is not supreme. There is a proper and virtuous resemblance to it, no doubt, but not love—no, no, not love. I tell you I care nothing for the child. Geoffrey Ludlow, if I had loved you, I should have cared for him almost as little; if the man I love had been his father, I should have cared for him no more, if I know any thing of myself. The child does not need me. I suppose I am not without the brute instinct which would lead me to shelter and feed and clothe him, if he did; but what has he ever needed from me? If I could say without a lie that any thought of him weighs with me— but I cannot—I would say to you, for the child's sake, if for no other reason, I must go. The child is the last and feeblest argument you can use with me—with whom indeed there are none strong or availing."

She turned abruptly, and once more laid her hand upon the door-handle. Her last words had roused Geoffrey from the inaction caused by his amazement. As she coldly and deliberately avowed her indifference to the child, furious anger once more awoke within him. He strode hastily towards her and sternly grasped her by the left arm. She made a momentary effort to shake off his hold; but he held her firmly at arm's-length from him, and said through his closed teeth :

"You are a base and unnatural woman—more base and unnatural than I believed any woman could be. As for me, I can keep silence on your conduct to myself; perhaps I deserved it, seeing where and how I found you." She started and winced. "As for the child, he is better motherless than with such a mother; but I took you from shame and sin, when I found you in the street, and married you; and you shall not return to them if any effort of mine can prevent it. You have no feeling, you have no conscience, you have no pride; you glory in a passion for a man who flung you away to starve! Woman, have you no sense of decency left, that you can talk of resuming your life of infamy and shame?"

The husband and wife formed a group which would have been awful to look upon, had there been any one to witness that terrible interview, as they stood confronting one another, while Geoffrey spoke. As his words came slowly forth, a storm of passion shook Margaret's frame. Every gleam of colour forsook her face; she was transformed into a fixed image of unspeakable wrath. A moment she stood silent, breathing quickly, her white lips dry and parted. Then, as a faint movement, something like a ghastly smile, crept over her face, she said:

"You are mistaken, Geoffrey Ludlow; I leave my life of infamy and shame in leaving *you !*"

"In leaving me! Again you are mad!"

"Again I speak the words of sanity and truth. If what I am going to tell you fills you with horror, I would have spared you; you have yourself to thank. I intended to have spared you this final blow,—I intended to have left you in happy ignorance of the fact—which you blindly urge me to declare by your taunts. What did I say at the commencement of this interview? That I wanted us to part friends. But you will not have that. You reproach me with ingratitude; you taunt me with being an unnatural mother; finally, you fling at me my life of infamy and shame; I repeat that no infamy, no shame could attach to me until I became—your mistress!"

The bolt had shot home at last. Geoffrey leapt to his feet, and stood erect before her; but his strength must have failed him in that instant; for he could only gasp, "My mistress!"

"Your mistress. That is all I have been to you, so help me Heaven!"

"My wife! my own—married—lawful wife!"

"No, Geoffrey Ludlow, no! In that wretched lodging to which you had me conveyed, and where you pleaded your love, I told you—the truth indeed, but not the whole truth. Had you known me better then,—had you known me as you—as you know me now, you might have guessed that I was not one of those trusting creatures who are betrayed and ruined by fair words and beaming glances, come they from ever so handsome a man. One fact I concealed from you, thinking, as my Lionel had deserted me, and would probably never be seen again, that its revelation would prevent me from accepting the position which you were about to offer me; but the day that I fled from my home at

Tenby I was married to Lionel Brakespere; and at this moment I am his wife, not merely in the sight of God, but by the laws of man!"

For some instants he did not speak, he did not move from the chair into which he had again fallen heavily during her speech : he sat gazing at her, his breathing thickened, impeded, gasping. At length he said :

" You're—you're speaking truth ?"

" I am speaking gospel-truth, Geoffrey Ludlow. You brought it upon yourself : I would have saved you from the knowledge of it if I could, but you brought it upon yourself."

" Yes—as you say—on myself;" still sitting gazing vacantly before him, muttering to himself rather than addressing her. Suddenly, with a wild shriek, " The child ! O God, the child !"

" For the child's sake, no less than for your own, you will hold your tongue on this matter," said Margaret, in her calm, cold, never-varying tone. "In this instance at least you will have sense enough to perceive the course you ought to take. What I have told you is known to none but you and me, and one other—who can be left with me to deal with. Let it be your care that the secret remains with us."

" But the child is a——"

" Silence, man !" she exclaimed, seizing his arm,—"silence now,—for a few moments at all events. When I am gone, proclaim your child's illegitimacy and your own position if you will, but wait till then. Now I can remain here no longer. Such things as I absolutely require I will send for. Good-bye, Geoffrey Ludlow."

She gathered her shawl around her, and moved towards the door. In an instant his lethargy left him ; he sprang up, rushed before her, and stood erect and defiant.

" You don't leave me in this way, Margaret. You shall not leave me thus. I swear you shall not pass !"

She looked at him for a moment with a half-compassionate, half-interested face. This assumption of spirit and authority she had never seen in him before, and it pleased her moment- arily. Then she said quietly :

" O yes, I shall. I am sure, Mr. Ludlow, you will not prevent my going to my husband !"

ı

When the servant, after waiting more than an hour for dinner to be rung for, came into the room to see what was the cause of the protracted delay, she found her master prostrate on the hearth-rug, tossing and raving incoherently. The frightened girl summoned assistance; and when Dr. Brandram arrived, he announced Mr. Ludlow to be in the incipient stage of a very sharp attack of brain-fever.

CHAPTER II.

THE REVERSE OF THE MEDAL.

IT was one of those cheerless days not unfrequent at the end of September, which first tell us that such fine weather as we have had has taken its departure, and that the long dreary winter is close at hand. The air was moist and "muggy;" there was no freshening wind to blow away the heavy dun clouds which lay banked up thick, and had seemed almost motionless for days; there was a dead faint depression over all things, which weighed heavily on the spirits, impeded the respiration, and relaxed the muscles. It was weather which dashed and cowed even the lightest-hearted, and caused the careworn and the broken to think self-destruction less extraordinary than they had hitherto considered it.

About noon a man was looking out of one of the upper-windows of Long's Hotel on the dreary desert of Bond Street. He was a tall man; who with straight-cut features, shapely beard, curling light hair, and clear complexion, would have been generally considered more than good-looking, notwithstanding that his eyes were comparatively small and his mouth was decidedly sensual. That he was a man of breeding and society one could have told in an instant—could have told it by the colour and shape of his hands, by his bearing, by the very manner in which he, leaving the window from time to time, lounged round the room, his hands plunged in his pockets or pulling at his tawny beard. You could have told it despite of his dress, the like of which had surely never been seen before on any visitor to that select hostelry; for he wore a thick jacket and trousers of

blue pilot-cloth, a blue flannel-shirt, with a red-silk handkerchief knotted round the collar, and ankle jack-boots.   When
he jumped out of the cab at the door on the previous day,
he had on a round tarpaulin-hat, and carried over his arm an
enormous pea-jacket with horn buttons; and as he brought
no luggage with him save a small valise, and had altogether
the appearance of the bold smugglers who surreptitiously
vend cigars and silk-handkerchiefs, the hall-porter at first
refused him admittance; and it was not until the proprietor
had been summoned, and after a close scrutiny and a whispered name had recognised his old customer, that the strange-
looking visitor was ushered upstairs.   He would have a
private room, he said; and he did not want it known that
he was back just yet—did Jubber understand?   If any body
called, that was another matter: he expected his mother and
one or two others; but he did not want it put in the papers,
or any thing of that kind.   Jubber did understand, and left
Captain Lionel Brakespere to himself.

Captain Lionel Brakespere, just at that time, could have
had no worse company.   He had been bored to death by
the terrible monotony of a long sea-voyage, and had found
on landing in England that his boredom was by no means at
an end.   He had heard from his mother that " that awkward
business had all been squared," as he phrased it; and that it
was desirable he should return home at once, where there
was a chance of a marriage by which " a big something was
to be pulled off," as he phrased it again.   So he had come
back, and there he was at Long's; but as yet he was by no
means happy.   He was doubtful as to his position in society,
as to how much of his escapade was known, as to whether
he would be all right with his former set, or whether he
would get the cold shoulder, and perhaps be cut.   He could
only learn this by seeing Algy Barford, or some other fellow
of the *clique;* and every fellow was of course out of town at
that infernal time of year.   He must wait, at all events, until
he had seen his mother, to whom he had sent word of his
arrival.   He might be able to learn something of all this from
her.   Meantime he had taken a private room; not that
there was much chance of his meeting any one in the coffee-
room, but some fellow might perhaps stop there for the night
on his way through town; and he had sent for the tailor,
and the hair-cutter fellow, and that sort of thing, and was

going to be made like a Christian again—not like the cad
he'd looked like in that infernal place out there.

He lounged round the room, and pulled his beard and
yawned as he looked out of the window ; pulling himself together afterwards by stretching out his hands and arms, and
shrugging his shoulders and shaking himself, as if endeavouring to shake off depression. He *was* depressed ; there was
no doubt about it. Out there it was well enough. He had
been out there just long enough to have begun to settle down
into his new life, to have forgotten old ties and old feelings ;
but here every thing jarred upon him. He was back in
England certainly, but back in England in a condition which
he had never known before. In the old days, at this time of
year, he would have been staying down at some country-
house, or away in some fellow's yatch, enjoying himself to
the utmost ; thoroughly appreciated and highly thought of,—
a king among men and a favourite among women. Now he
was cooped up in this deserted beastly place, which every
one decent had fled from, not daring even to go out and see
whether some old comrade, haply retained in town by duty,
were not to be picked up, from whom he could learn the
news, with whom he might have a game of billiards, or something to get through the infernally dragging wearisome time.
He expected his mother. She was his truest and stanchest
friend, after all, and had behaved splendidly to him all
through this terrible business. It was better that she should
come down there, and let him know exactly how the land
lay. He would have gone home, but he did not know what
sort of a reception he might have met with from the governor;
and from all he could make out from his mother's letters, it
was very likely that Caterham might cut up rough, and say
or do something confoundedly unpleasant. It was an infernal shame of Caterham, and just like his straightlaced
nonsense—that it was. Was not he the eldest son, and
what did he want more ? It was all deuced well for him to
preach and moralise, and all that sort of thing ; but his
position had kept him out of temptation, else he might not
be any better than other poor beggars, who had fallen
through and come to grief.

So he reasoned with himself as he lounged round and
round the room ; and at last began to consider that he was
a remarkably ill-used person. He began to hate the room

and its furniture, altered the position of the light and elegant little couch, flung himself into the arm-chair, drumming his heels upon the floor, and rose from it leaving the chintz covering all tumbled, and the anti-macassar all awry, drummed upon the window, stared at the prints already inspected—the " Hero and his Horse," which led him into reminiscences of seeing the old Duke with his white duck trousers and his white cravat, with the silver buckle gleaming at the back of his bowed head, at Eton on Montem days—glanced with stupid wonderment at Ward's " Dr. Johnson reading the Manuscript of the *Vicar of Wakefield*," which conveyed to him no idea whatsoever—looked at a proof of " Hogarth painting the Muse of Comedy," and wondered " who was the old cock with the fat legs, drawing." He watched the few people passing through the streets, the very few hansom-cabs with drivers listlessly creeping up and down, as though conscious that the chances of their being hired were dismally remote, the occasional four-wheelers with perambulators and sand-spades on the top, and bronzed children leaning out of the windows, talking of the brief holiday over and the work-a-day life about to recommence—he watched all this, and, watching, worked himself up to such a pitch of desperation that he had almost determined to brave all chances of recognition, and sally forth into the streets, when the door opened and a waiter entering, told him that a lady was waiting to speak with him.

His mother had come at last, then? Let her be shown up directly.

Of all things Lionel Brakespere abhorred a "scene ;" and this was likely to be an uncommonly unpleasant meeting. The Mater was full of feeling and that sort of thing, and would probably fling herself into his arms as soon as the waiter was gone, and cry, and sob, and all that sort of thing, and moan over him—make a fellow look so confoundedly foolish and absurd, by Jove ! Must get that over as soon as possible—all the hugging and that—and then find out how matters really stood. So he took up his position close to the door ; and as the footsteps approached, was a little astonished to hear his heart thumping so loudly.

The door opened, and passing. the bowing waiter, who closed it behind her, a lady entered. Though her veil was down, Lionel saw instantly that it was not his mother. A

U

taller, younger woman, with step graceful though hurried, an eager air, a strange nervous manner. As the door closed, she threw up her veil and stood revealed—Margaret !

He fell back a pace or two, and the blood rushed to his heart, leaving his face as pale as hers. Then, recovering himself, he caught hold of the table, and glaring at her, said hoarsely, " You here !"

There was something in his tone which jarred upon her instantly. She made a step forward, and held out her hand appealingly—" Lionel," she said, quite softly, " Lionel, you know me ?"

" Know you ?" he repeated. O yes—I—I have that honour. I know you fast enough—though what you do here I *don't* know. What do you do here ?"

" I came to see you."

" Devilish polite, I'm sure. But—now you have seen me —" he hesitated and smiled. Not a pleasant smile by any means : one of those smiles in which the teeth are never shown. A very grim smile, which slightly wrinkled the lips, but left the eyes hard and defiant ; a smile which Margaret knew of old, the sight of which recalled the commencement of scenes of violent passion and bitter upbraiding in the old times ; a smile at sight of which Margaret's heart sank within her, only leaving her strength enough to say : " Well !"

" Well !" he repeated—" having seen me—having fulfilled the intention of your visit—had you not better—go ?"

" Go !" she exclaimed—" leave you at once, without a look, without a word ! Go ! after all the long weary waiting, this hungering to see and speak with you, to pillow my head on your breast, and twine my arms round you as I used to do in the dear old days ! Go ! in the moment when I am repaid for O such misery as you, Lionel, I am sure, cannot imagine I have endured—the misery of absence from you ; the misery of not knowing how or where you were—whether even you were dead or alive ; misery made all the keener by recollection of joy which I had known and shared with you. Go ! Lionel, dearest Lionel, you cannot mean it ! Don't try me now, Lionel ; the delight at seeing you again has made me weak and faint. I am not so strong as I used to be. Lionel, dearest, don't try me too much."

Never had she looked more beautiful than now. Her arms were stretched out in entreaty, the rich tones of her voice were broken, tears stood in her deep-violet eyes, and the dead-gold hair was pushed off the dead-white brow. Her whole frame quivered with emotion—emotion which she made no attempt to conceal.

Lionel Brakespere had seated himself on the corner of the table, and was looking at her with curiosity. He comprehended the beauty of the picture before him, but he regarded it as a picture. On most other men in his position such an appeal from such a woman would have caused at least a temporary rekindling of the old passion ; on him it had not the slightest effect, beyond giving him a kind of idea that the situation was somewhat ridiculous and slightly annoying. After a minute's interval he said, with his hands in his pockets, and his legs swinging to and fro :

" It's deuced kind of you to say such civil things about me, and I appreciate them—appreciate them, I assure you. But, you see the fact of the matter is, that I'm expecting my mother every minute, and if she were to find you here, I should be rather awkwardly situated."

" O," cried Margaret, "you don't think I would compromise you, Lionel ? You know me too well for that. You know too well how I always submitted to be kept in the background—only too happy to live on your smiles, to know that you were fêted and made much of."

" O, yes," said Lionel, simply ; " you were always a deuced sensible little woman."

" And I sha'n't be in the way, and I sha'n't bore you. They need know nothing of my existence, if you don't wish it, any more than they used. And we shall lead again the dear old life—eh, Lionel ?"

" Eh !" repeated he in rather a high key,—"the dear old life !"

" Ah, how happy I was !" said Margaret. " You, whose intervening time has been passed in action, can scarcely imagine how I have looked back on those days,—how eagerly I have longed for the time to come when I might have them again."

" Gad !" said he, " I don't exactly know about my time being passed in action. It's been horribly ghastly and melancholy, and deuced unpleasant, if you mean that."

" Then we will both console ourselves for it now, Lionel. We will forget all the misery we have suffered, and—"

"Y-es!" said he, interrupting her, swinging his leg a little more slowly, and looking quietly up into her face; "I don't exactly follow you in all this."

"You don't follow me?"

"N-no! I scarcely think we can be on the same tack, somehow."

"In what way?"

"In all this about leading again the old life, and living the days over again, and consoling ourselves, and that kind of thing."

"You don't understand it?"

"Well, I don't know about understanding it. All I mean to say is, I'm not going to have it."

But for something in his tone, Margaret might not have entirely comprehended what he sought to convey in his words, so enraptured was she at seeing him again. But in his voice, in his look, there was a bravado that was unmistakable. She clasped her hands together in front of her; and her voice was very low and tremulous, as she said,

"Lionel, what do you mean?"

"What do I mean? Well, it's a devilish awkward thing to say—I can't conceive how it came about—all through your coming here, and that sort of thing; but it appears to me that, as I said before, you're on the wrong tack. You don't seem to see the position."

"I don't indeed. For God's sake speak out!"

"There, you see!—that's just it; like all women, taking the thing so much in earnest, and—"

"So much in earnest? Is what would influence one's whole life a thing to be lightly discussed or laughed over? Is—"

"There you are again! That's exactly what I complain of. What have I to do with influencing your life?"

"All—every thing!"

"I did not know it, then, by Jove,—that's all I've got to say. You're best out of it, let me tell you. My influence is a deuced bad one, at least for myself."

Once again the tone, reckless and defiant, struck harshly on her ear. He continued, "I was saying you did not seem to see the position. You and I were very good friends once upon a time, and got on very well together; but that would never do now."

She turned faint, sick, and closed her eyes; but remained silent.

"Wouldn't do a bit," he continued. "You know I've been a tremendous cropper — must have thought deuced badly of me for cutting off in that way; but it was my only chance, by Jove; and now I've come back to try and make all square. But I must keep deuced quiet and mind my p's and q's, or I shall go to grief again, like a bird."

She waited for a moment, and then she said faintly and slowly, "I understand you thoroughly now. You mean that it would be better for us to remain apart for some time yet?"

"For some time?—yes. Confound it all, Margaret!— you won't take a hint, and you make a fellow speak out and seem cruel and unkind, and all that kind of thing, that he does not want to. Look here. You ought never to have come here at all. It's impossible we can ever meet again."

She started convulsively; but even then she seemed unable to grasp the truth. Her earnestness brought the colour flying to her cheeks as she said hurriedly, "Why impossible, Lionel,—why impossible? If you are in trouble, who has such a right to be near you as I? If you want assistance and solace, who should give it you before me? That is the mistake you made, Lionel. When you were in your last trouble you should have confided in me: my woman's wit might have helped you through it; or at the worst, my woman's love would have consoled you in it."

She was creeping closer to him, but stopped as she saw his face darken and his arms clasp themselves across his breast.

"D—n it all!" said he petulantly; "you *won't* under-stand, I think. This sort of thing is impossible. Any sort of love, or friendship, or trust is impossible. I've come back to set myself straight, and to pull out of all the infernal scrapes I got myself into before I left; and there's only one way to do it."

"And that is—"

"Well, if you will have it, you must. And that is—by making a good marriage."

She uttered a short sharp cry, followed by a prolonged wail, such as a stricken hare gives. Lionel Brakespere looked up at her; but his face never relaxed, and his arms still remained tightly folded across his breast. Then she spoke, very quietly and very sadly :

"By making a good marriage! Ah! then I see it all. That is why you are annoyed at my having come to you. That is why you dread the sight of me, because it reminds you that I am in the way ; reminds you of the existence of the clog round your neck that prevents your taking up this position for which you long ; because it reminds you that you once sacrificed self to sentiment, and permitted yourself to be guided by love instead of ambition. That is what you mean ?"

His face was darker than ever as he said, " No such d—d nonsense. I don't know what you're talking about ; no more do you, I should think, by the way in which you are going on. What *are* you talking about ?"

He spoke very fiercely ; but she was not cowed or dashed one whit. In the same quiet voice she said : " I am talking about myself—your wife !"

Lionel Brakespere sprung from the corner of the table on which he had been sitting, and stood upright, confronting her.

"O, that's it, is it ?" in a hard low voice. "That's your game, eh ? I thought it was coming to that. Now, look here," shaking his fist at her,—" drop that for good and all ; drop it, I tell you, or it will be the worse for you. Let me hear of your saying a word about your being my wife, and, so help me God, I'll be the death of you ! That's plain, isn't it ? You understand that ?"

She never winced ; she never moved. She sat quietly under the storm of his rage ; and when he had finished speaking, she said :

"You can kill me, if you like,—you very nearly did, just before you left me,—but so long as I am alive I shall be your wife !"

"Will you, by George ?—not if there's law in the land, I can tell you. What have you been doing all this time ? How have you been living since I've been away ? How do you come here, dressed like a swell as you are, when I left you without money ? I shall want to know all that ; and I'll find out, you may take your oath. There are heaps of ways of discovering those things now, and places where a fellow has only to pay for it, and he may know any thing that goes on about any body. I don't think you would particularly care to have those inquiries made about *you*, eh?"

She was silent. He waited a minute; then, thinking from her silence that he had made a point, went on:

"You understand me at last, don't you? You see pretty plainly, I should think, that being quiet and holding your tongue is your best plan, don't you? If you're wise you'll do it; and then, when I'm settled, I may make you some allowance—if you want it, that's to say,—if your friends who've been so kind to you while I've been away don't do it. But if you open your mouth on this matter, if you once hint that you've any claim on me, or send to me, or write to me, or annoy me at all, I'll go right in at once, find out all you've been doing, and then see what they'll say to you in the Divorce Court. You hear?"

Still she sat perfectly silent. He was apparently pleased with his eloquence and its effect, for he proceeded:

"This is all your pretended love for me, is it? This is what you call gratitude to a fellow, and all that kind of thing? Turning up exactly when you're not wanted, and cooly declaring that you're going in to spoil the only game that can put me right and bring me home! And this is the woman who used to declare in the old days that she'd die for me, and all that! I declare I didn't think it of you, Madge!"

"Don't call me by that name!" she screamed, roused at last; "don't allude to the old days, in God's name, or I shall go mad! The recollection of them, the hope of their renewal, has been my consolation in all sorts of misery and pain. I thought that to hear them spoken of by you would have been sufficient recompense for all my troubles: now to hear them mentioned by your lips agonises and maddens me; I—"

"This is the old story," he interrupted; "you haven't forgotten that business, I see. This is what you used to do before, when you got into one of these states. It frightened me at first, but I got used to it; and I've seen a great deal too much of such things to care for it now, I can tell you. If you make this row, I'll ring the bell—upon my soul I will!"

"O, Lionel, Lionel!" said Margaret, stretching out her

hands in entreaty towards him—"don't speak so cruelly! You don't know all I have gone through for you—you don't know how weak and ill I am. But it is nothing to what I will do. You don't know how I love you, Lionel, my darling! how I have yearned for you; how I will worship and slave for you, so that I may only be with you. I don't want to be seen, or heard of, or known, so long as I am near you. Only try me and trust me, only let me be your own once more."

"I tell you it's impossible," said he petulantly. "Woman, can't you understand? I'm ruined, done, shut up, cornered, and the only chance of my getting through is by my marriage with some rich woman, who will give me her money in exchange for—There, d—n it all,—it's no use talking any more about it. If you can't see the position, I can't show it you any stronger; and there's an end of it. Only, look here!— keep your mouth shut, or it will be the worse for you. You understand that?—the worse for you."

"Lionel!" She sprang towards him and clasped her hands round his arm. He shook her off roughly, and moved towards the door.

"No more foolery," he said in a low deep voice. "Take my warning now, and go. In a fortnight's time you can write to me at the Club, and say whether you are prepared to accept the conditions I have named. Now, go."

He held the door open, and she passed by him and went out. She did not shrink, or faint, or fall. Somehow, she knew not how, she went down the stairs and into the street. Not until she had hailed a cab, and seated herself in it, and was being driven off, did she give way. Then she covered her face with her hands, and burst into a passionate fit of weeping, rocking herself to and fro, and exclaiming, "And it is for this that I have exiled myself from my home, and trampled upon a loving heart! O my God! my God; if I could only have loved Geoffrey Ludlow!—O, to love as I do, such a man as this!"

CHAPTER III.

GONE TO HIS REST.

THE last-mentioned interview between Lord Caterham and his mother, though productive of good in a certain way—for Lady Beauport, however bravely she succeeded in bearing herself at the time, was in reality not a little frightened at her son's determination—had a visibly bad effect on Caterham's health. The excitement had been too much for him. The physician had enjoined perfect rest, and an absence of all mental effort, in the same way in which they prescribe wine and nourishing food to the pauper, or Turkish baths to the cripple on the outskirts of Salisbury Plain. Perfect rest and absence of all mental effort were utterly impossible to Caterham, whose mind was on the rack, who knew that he had pitted himself against time for the accomplishment of his heart's desire, and who felt that he must either fulfil his earnest intention, or give up it and life simultaneously. Life was so thin and faint and feeble within him, that he needed all of it he could command to bear him up merely through "the fever called living,"—to keep him together sufficiently to get through the ordinary quiet routine of his ever-dull day. When there was an exceptional occasion—such as the interview with his mother, for instance, where he had gone through a vast amount of excitement—it left him exhausted, powerless, incapable of action or even of thought, to an extent that those accustomed only to ordinary people could never have imagined.

The next day he was too ill to leave his bed; but that made little difference to the rest of the household. Lord Beauport was away in Wales looking after some mines on one of his estates, which had suddenly promised to be specially productive. Lady Beauport, detained in town for the due carrying out of her plans with respect to Lionel, sent down her usual message of inquiry by Timpson, her maid, who communicated with Stephens, and gave the reply to her mistress. Lady Beauport repeated the message, "Very unwell indeed, eh?" and adding, "this weather is so horribly depressing," proceeded with her toilette. Miss

Maurice sent grapes and flowers and some new perfume to the invalid; and—it revived him more than any thing else— a little hurried note, bidding him not give way to depression, but rouse sufficiently to get into his easy-chair by the morrow, and she would spend all the day with him, and read to him, and play to him whatever he wanted.

He had strength enough to raise that little note to his lips so soon as he heard the door shut behind the outgoing Stephens; to kiss it over and over again, and to place it beneath his pillow ere he sunk into such imitation of rest as was vouchsafed to him. A want of sleep was one of the worst symptoms of his malady, and the doctors had all agreed that if they could only superinduce something like natural sleep, it might aid greatly in repairing the little strength which had been given to him originally, and which was so gradually and imperceptibly, and yet so surely, wearing away. But that seemed to be impossible. When he was first assisted to bed he was in a sufficiently drowsy state, partly from the fatigue of the day, partly from the effect of the wine, of which the doctors insisted on his taking a quantity which would have been nothing to an ordinary man, but was much to one feeble in frame, and unable to take any exercise to carry off its strength. Then, after a short slumber—heavy, stertorous, and disturbed—he would wake, bright and staring, without the smallest sign of sleep in his head or in his eye. In vain would he toss from side to side, and try all the known recipes for somnolence— none were of the slightest avail. He could not sleep, he could not compose himself in the least degree, he could not empty his mind as it were ; and the mind must be, or at all events must seem, empty before sleep will take possession of it. Lord Caterham's mind in the dead silence of the night was even more active than it was in the daytime. Before him rose up all the difficulties which he had to surmount, the dangers which he had to avoid, the hopes and fears and triumphs and vexations which made up the sum of his bitter life. They were not many now,— they never had been diffuse at any time ; so little had Caterham been a citizen of the world, that all his aspirations had lain within a very small compass, and now they centred in one person—Annie Maurice. To provide for her safety when he was not there to look after it in person ; to leave such records as would show what action he had taken in her behalf, and on what grounds that action had been undertaken; to arm some competent and willing person so thoroughly to bestir himself at the necessary juncture as to prevent the chance of the conspiracy against Annie's future being carried into effect:— these were the night-thoughts which haunted Caterham's couch, and rendered him sleepless.

Sleeplessness had its usual effect. The following day he was quite worn out in mind and body,—felt it, knew it, could not deny the fact when it was suggested to him mildly by Stephens, more firmly by his doctors,—but yet persevered in his intention of getting up. He was sure he should be so much better out of bed; he was certain that a change—were it only to his easy-chair—would do him so much good. He could be very positive—" obstinate " was the phrase by which the doctors distinguished it, arbitrary " was Stephen's phrase—when he chose; and so they let him have his way, wondering why he preferred to leave the calm seclusion of his bed. They little knew that the contents of that little note which the valet had seen protruding from the corner of his master's pillow when he went in to call him in the morning had worked that charm; they did not know that she had promised to spend the day with him, and read and play to him. But he did; and had he died for it, he could not have denied himself that afternoon of delight.

So he was dressed, and wheeled into his sitting-room, and placed by his desk and among his books. He had twice nearly fainted during the process; and Stephens, who knew his every look, and was as regardful of his master's health as the just appreciation of a highly-paid place could make him, had urged Lord Caterham to desist and return to his bed. But Caterham was obstinate; and the toilette was performed and the sitting-room gained, and then he desired that Miss Maurice might be told he was anxious to see her.

She came in an instant. Ah, how radiant and fresh she looked as she entered the room! Since the end of the season, she had so far assumed her heiress position as to have a carriage of her own and a saddle-horse; and instead of accompanying Lady Beauport in her set round of " airing," Annie had taken long drives into country regions, where she had alighted and walked in the fresh air, duly followed by the carriage; or on horseback, and attended by her groom, had galloped off to Hampstead and Highgate and Willesden and Ealing in the early morning, long before Lady Beauport had thought of unclosing her eyes. It was this glorious exercise, this enjoyment of heaven's light and air and sun, that had given the rose to Annie's cheeks and the brilliance to her eyes. She was freckled here and there; and there was a bit of a brown mark on her forehead, showing exactly how much was left unshaded by her hat. These were things which would have distressed most well-regulated Belgravian damsels; but they troubled Annie not one whit; and as she stood close by his chair, with her bright eyes and her pushed-off brown hair, and the big teeth gleaming in her fresh wholesome mouth, Caterham thought he had never seen her look more charming, and felt that the distance between her, brimming over with health, and him, gradually succumbing to disease, was greater than ever.

Annie Maurice was a little shocked when she first glanced at Caterham. The few days which had intervened since she had been to his room had made a great difference in his appearance. His colour had not left him—on the contrary, it had rather increased—but there was a tight look about the skin, a dull glassiness in his eyes, and a pinched appearance in the other features, which were unmistakable. Of course she took no notice of this : but coming in, greeted him in her usual affectionate manner. Nor was there any perceptible difference in his voice as he said :

" You see I have kept you to your word, Annie. You promised, if I were in my easy-chair, that you would play and read to me ; and here I am."

" And here I am to do your bidding, Arthur ! and too delighted to do it, and to see you sufficiently well to be here. You're not trying too much, are you, Arthur?"

" In what, Annie ?"

" In sitting up and coming into this room. Are you strong enough to leave your bed ?"

" Ah, I am so weary and wretched alone, Annie. I long so for companionship, for—" he checked himself and said, " for some one to talk, to read, to keep me company in all the long hours of the day. I'm not very bright just now, and even I have been stronger—which seems almost ridiculous—but I could keep away no longer, knowing you would come to lighten my dreariness."

Though his voice was lower and more faint than usual, there was an impassioned tone in it which she had never heard before, and which jarred ever so slightly on her ear. So she rose from her seat, and laughingly saying that she would go at once and perform part of her engagement, sat down at the piano, and played and sang such favourite pieces of his as he had often been in the habit of asking for. They were simple ballads,—some of Moore's melodies, Handel's "Harmonious Blacksmith," and some of Mendelssohn's *Lieder ohne Wörte*,—all calm, soft, soothing music, such as Caterham loved; and when Annie had been playing for some time he said:

"You don't know how I love to hear you, Annie! You're getting tired now, child."

"Not in the least degree, Arthur. I could go on singing all day, if it amused you."

"It does more than amuse me, Annie. I cannot describe to you the feeling that comes over me in listening to your singing; nothing else has such a calm, holy, sanctifying influence on me. Listening to you, all the petty annoyances, the carking cares of this world fade away, and—"

He ceased speaking suddenly; and Annie looking round, saw the tears on his cheek. She was about to run to him, but he motioned her to keep her seat, and said: "Annie dear, you recollect a hymn that I heard you sing one night when you first came here?—one Sunday night when they were out, and you and I sat alone in the twilight in the drawing-room? Ah, I scarcely knew you then, but that hymn made a great impression on me."

"You mean—

> Abide with me! fast falls the eventide
> The darkness deepens: Lord, with me abide!'"

"Yes, that is it. How lovely it is!—both words and music, I think."

"Yes, it is lovely. It was written by a Mr. Lyte, when he was—"

She checked herself, but he finished the sentence for her, —"When he was dying. Yes; I recollect your telling me so that night. Sing it for me, dear."

She turned to the piano at once, and in an instant the

rich deep tones of her voice were ringing through the room. Annie Maurice sang ballads sweetly, but she sang hymns magnificently. There was not the slightest attempt at ornamentation or *bravura* in her performance, but she threw her whole soul into her singing; and the result was rich and solemn melody. As she sang,.she seemed to embody the spirit of the composer, and her voice vibrated and shook with the fervour which animated her.

Half leaning on his stick, half reclining in his chair, Caterham watched her in rapt delight; then when she had finished, and ere the thrilling music of her voice had died away, he said: "Thanks, dear—again a thousand thanks! Now, once more a request, Annie. I shall not worry you much more, my child."

"Arthur,"—and in an instant she was by his side,—" if you speak like that, I declare I will not sing to you."

"O yes, you will, Annie dear!—O yes, you will. You know as well as I do that—Well, then"—obedient to a forefinger uplifted in warning—" I'll say no more on that point. But I want you now to sing me the old-fashioned Evening Hymn. I've a very ancient love for dear old Bishop Ken, and I don't like to think of his being set aside for any modern hymnologist,—even for such a specimen as that you have just sung. Sing me 'Glory to Thee,' Annie,—that is, if you are old-fashioned enough to know it."

She smiled, and sang. When she ceased, finding that he remained speechless and motionless, she went up to him, fearing that he had fainted. He was lying back in his chair perfectly quiet, with his eyes closed. When she touched him, he opened them dreamily, saying, " 'That I may dread the grave as little as my bed.' Yes, yes!—Ah, Annie dear, you've finished!—and to think that you, a modern young lady, should be able to sing old Bishop Ken without book! Where did you learn him?"

"When I was a very little child,—at the Priory, Arthur. Geoffrey Ludlow—as I've told you, I think—used to come out to us every Sunday; and in the evening after dinner, before I went to bed, he used to ask for his little wife to sing to him. And then poor papa used to tell me to sit on Geoft's knee, and I used to sing the Evening Hymn."

"Ay," said Caterham in an absent manner, " Geoffrey Ludlow's little wife! Geoffrey Ludlow's little wife!—ay, ay!

'That so I may, rise glorious at Thine awful day!' in Thy mercy, in Thy mercy!" and saying this, he fainted away.

That evening Algy Barford, at Lord Dropmore's in Lincolnshire, on his return from shooting, found a telegram on his dressing-room table. It was from Annie Maurice, and begged his immediate return to town.

Lord Caterham was better the next day. Though still very weak, he insisted on being dressed and wheeled into his sitting-room. Once there, he had his despatch-box placed before him, and the writing-materials put ready to his hand. Of late he had occasionally been in the habit of employing an amanuensis. Annie Maurice had frequently written from his dictation; and when she had been engaged, a son of the old housekeeper, who was employed at a law-stationer's, and who wrote a hand which was almost illegible from its very clearness, had sometimes been pressed into the service. But now Lord Caterham preferred writing for himself. Annie had sent to beg him to rest; and in reply he had scrawled two lines, saying that he was ever so much better, and that he had something to do which must be done, and which when done would leave him much happier and easier in mind. So they left him to himself; and Stephens, looking in from time to time, as was his wont, reported to the servants'-hall that his master was "at it as hard as ever— still a-writin'!" They wondered what could thus occupy him, those curious domestics. They knew exactly the state in which he was, the feeble hold that he had on life;—what do they not know, those London servants?—and they thought that he was making his will, and speculated freely among themselves as to what would be the amount of Stephens's inheritance; and whether it would be a sum of money "down," or an annuity; and whether Stephens would invest it after the usual fashion of their kind—in a public-house, or whether, from excessive gentility, he was not "a cut above that." Lord Caterham would not hold out much longer, they opined; and then Mr. Lionel would come in for his title; and who Mr. Lionel was—inquired about by the new servants, and the description of Mr. Lionel by the old servants —and mysterious hints as to how, in the matter of Mr. Lionel, there had been a "screw loose" and a "peg out;" how he was a "regular out-and-out fast lot," and had had to "cut it;"—all this occasioned plenty of talk in the servants'-

hall, and made the dreary autumn-day pass quite pleasantly. And still the sick man sat at his desk, plying his pen, with but rare intervals of rest—intervals during which he would clasp his poor aching head, and lift his shrivelled attenuated hands in earnest silent prayer.

The Beauport household was sunk in repose the next morning, when a sharp ring at the bell, again and again repeated, aroused the young lady who as kitchen-maid was on her preferment, and whose dreams of being strangled by the cook for the heaviness of her hand in an omelette were scared by the shrill clanging of the bell which hung immediately over her head. The first notion of "fire" had calmed down into an idea of "sweeps" by the time that she had covered her night-attire with a dingy calico robe known to her as her "gownd;" and she was tottering blindly down stairs before she recollected that no sweeps had been ordered, and thought that it was probably a "runaway." But lured perhaps by a faint idea that it might be the policeman, she descended; and after an enormous amount of unbolting and unchaining, found herself face-to-face with a fresh-coloured, light-bearded, cheery gentleman, who wore a Glengarry cap, had a travelling-rug in his hand, was smoking a cigar, and had evidently just alighted from a hansom-cab which was standing at the door, and the driver of which was just visible behind a big portmanteau and a gun-case. The fresh-coloured gentleman was apparently rather startled at the apparition of the kitchen-maid, and exclaimed, apparently involuntarily, "Gad !" in a very high key. Recovering himself instantly, he asked how Lord Caterham was. Utterly taken aback at discovering that the visitor was not the policeman, the kitchen-maid was floundering about heavily for an answer, when she was more than ever disconcerted at seeing the fresh-coloured gentleman tear off his Glengarry-cap and advance up the steps with outsretched hand. These demonstrations were not made in honour of the kitchen-maid, but of Annie Maurice, who had been aroused from her usual light sleep by the ring, and who, guessing at the visitor, had come down in her dressing-gown to see him.

They passed into the dining-room, and then he took her hand and said : "I only got your telegram at dinner-time last night, my dear Miss Maurice, and came off just as I was.

Dropmore—deuced civil of him—drove me over to the station himself hard as he could go, by Jove ! just caught mail-train, and came on from King's Cross in a cab. It's about Caterham, of course. Bad news,—ay, ay, ay ! He—poor—I can't say it—he's in danger, he—" And brave old Algy stopped, his handsome jolly features all tightened and pinced in his anxiety.

"He is very, very ill, dear Mr. Barford,—very ill ; and I wanted you to see him. I don't know—I can't tell why—but I think he may possibly have something on his mind—something which he would not like to tell me, but which he might feel a relief in confiding to some one else ; and as you, I know, are a very dear and valued friend of his, I think we should all like you to be that some one. That was what made me send for you."

"I'm—I'm not a very good hand at eloquence, Miss Maurice—might put pebbles in my mouth and shout at the sea-shore and all that kind of thing, like the—the celebrated Greek person, you know—and wouldn't help me in getting out a word ; but though I can't explain, I feel very grateful to you for sending for me, to see—dear old boy !" The knot which had been rising in Algy Barford's throat during this speech had grown nearly insurmountable by this time, and there were two big tears running down his waistcoat. He tried to pull himself together as he said : " If he has any thing to say, which he would like to say to me—of course—I shall—any thing that would—God bless him, my dear old boy !—good, patient, dear darling old boy, God bless him !" The thought of losing his old friend flashed across him in all its dread heart-wringing dreariness, and Algy Barford fairly broke down and wept like a child. Recovering himself after a moment, he seized Annie's hand, and muttering something to the effect that he would be back as soon as he had made himself a little less like an Esquimaux, he dashed into the cab and was whirled away.

You would scarcely have thought that Algy Barford had had what is called sleep, but what really is a mixture of nightmare and cramp in a railway-carriage, had you seen him at eleven o'clock, when he next made his appearance at St. Barnabas Square, so bright and fresh and radiant was he. He found Annie Maurice awaiting his arrival, and had with her a short earnest conversation as to Caterham's state.

X

From that he learned all. The doctors had a very bad opinion of their patient's state : it was—hum—ha !—Yes—you know !—general depression—a want of vitality, which—just now—looking at his normal lack of force, of what we call professionally *vis vitæ*, might—eh ? Yes, no doubt, serious result. Could not be positively stated whether he would not so far recover—pull through, as it is called—rally, as we say, as to—remain with us yet some time ; but in these cases there was always—well, yes, it must be called a risk. This was the decision which the doctors had given to Annie, and which she, in other words, imparted to Algy Barford, who, coupling it with his experience of the guarded manner in which fashionable physicians usually announced their opinions, felt utterly hopeless, and shook his head mournfully. He tried to be himself, to resume his old smile and old confident buoyant way ; he told his dear Miss Maurice that she must hope for the best ; that these doctor-fellows, by Jove, generally knew nothing ; half of them died suddenly themselves, without even having anticipated their own ailments ; "physician, heal thyself," and all that sort of thing ; that probably Caterham wanted a little rousing, dear old boy ; which rousing he would go in and give him. But Annie marked the drooping head and the sad despondent manner in which he shrugged his shoulders and plunged his hands into his pockets when he thought she had retired—marked also how he strove to throw elasticity into his step and light into his face as he approached the door of Caterham's room.

It had been arranged between Algy and Annie Maurice that his was to have the appearance of a chance visit, so that when Stephens had announced him, and Lord Caterham had raised his head in wonder, Algy, who had by this time pulled himself together sufficiently, said : " Ah, ha ! Caterham !—dear old boy !—thought you had got rid of us all out of town, eh ?—and were going to have it all to yourself ! Not a bit of it, dear boy ! These doctor-fellows tell you one can't get on without ozone. Don't know what that is—daresay they're right. All I know is, I can't get on without a certain amount of chimney-pot. Country, delicious fresh air, turf, heather, peat-bog, stubble, partridge, snipe, grouse—all deuced good ! cows and pigs, and that kind of thing ; get up early, and go to bed and snore ; get red face and double-chin and awful weight—then chimney-pot required. I

always know, bless you! Too much London season, get
my liver as big as Strasburg goose's, you know—*foie gras* and
feet nailed to a board, and that kind of thing; too much
country, tight waistcoat, red face—awfully British, in point
of fact. Then, chimney-pot. I'm in that state now; and
I've come back to have a week's chimney-pot and blacks
and generally cabbage-stalky street—and then I shall go away
much better."

"You keep your spirits, Algy, wherever you are." The
thin faint voice struck on Algy Barford's ear like a knell.
He paused a minute and took a short quick gulp, and then
said: "O yes, still the same stock on hand, Caterham. I
could execute country orders, or supply colonial agencies
even, with promptitude and despatch, I think. And you,
Arthur—how goes it with you?"

"Very quietly, Algy,—very, very quietly, thank God! I've
had no return of my old pain for some time, and the head-
ache seems to have left me."

"Well, that's brave! We shall see you in your chair out
on the lawn at the hunt-breakfast at Homershams again this
winter, Arthur. We shall—"

"Well, I scarcely think that. I mean, not perhaps as
you interpret me; but—I scarcely think—However, there's
time enough to think of that. Let's talk of nearer subjects.
I'm so glad you chanced to come to town, Algy—so very
glad. Your coming seems predestined; for it was only
yesterday I was wishing I had you here."

"Tremendously glad I came, dear old boy! Chimney-
pot attack fell in handy this time, at all events. What did
you want, Arthur, old fellow? Not got a new leaning
towards dogginess, and want me to go up to Bill George's?
Do you recollect that Irish deerhound I got for you?"

"I recollect him well—poor old Connor. No, not a dog
now. I want you to—just raise me a bit, Algy, will you?—
a little bit: I am scarcely strong enough to—that's it. Ah,
Algy, old fellow, how often in the long years that we have
been chums have you lifted this poor wretched frame in your
strong arms!"

It was a trial for a man of Algy Barford's big heart; but
he made head against it even then, and said in a voice
harder and drier than usual from the struggle, "How often

have I brought my bemuddled old brains for you to take
them out and pick them to pieces and clean them, and put
them back into my head in a state to be of some use to me!
—that's the question, dear old boy. How often have you
supplied the match to light the tow inside my head—I've got
deuced little outside now—and sent me away with some
idea of what I ought to do when I was in a deuce of a knot!
Why, I recollect once when Lionel and I—what is it, dear
old boy?"

"You remind me—the mention of that name—I want to
say something to you, Algy, which oddly enough had—just
reach me that bottle, Algy; thanks!—which—"

"Rest a minute, dear old boy; rest. You've been exert-
ing yourself too much."

"No; I'm better now—only faint for a minute. What
was I saying?—O, about Lionel. You recollect a letter
which—" his voice was growing again so faint that Algy took
up the sentence.

"Which I brought to you; a letter from Lionel, after he
had, you know, dear old boy—board ship and that kind of
thing?"

"Yes, that is the letter I mean. You—you knew its
contents, Algy?"

"Well, Arthur, I think I did—I—you know Lionel was
very fond of me, and—used to be about with him, you know,
and that kind of thing—"

"You knew his—his wife?"

"Wife, Gad, did he say?—Jove! Knew you were—dear
me!—charming person—lady. Very beautiful—great friend
of Lionel's; but not his wife, dear old boy—somebody
else's wife."

"Somebody else's wife?"

"Yes; wonderful story. I've wanted to tell you, and,
most extraordinary thing, something always interrupted.
Friend of yours too; tall woman, red hair, violet eyes—wife
of painter-man—Good God, Arthur!"

Well might he start; for Lord Caterham threw his hands
wildly above his head, then let them fall helplessly by his
side. By the time Algy Barford had sprung to his chair, and
passed his arms around him, the dying man's head had drooped
on to his right shoulder, and his eyes were glazing fast.

"Arthur! dear Arthur! one instant! Let me call for help."

"No, Algy; leave us so; no one else. Only one who could—and she—better not—bless her! better not. Take my hand, Algy, old friend—tried, trusted, dear old friend—always thoughtful, always affectionate—God bless you—Algy! Yes, kiss my forehead again. Ah, so happy! where the wicked cease from troubling and the—Yes, Lord, with me abide, with me abide!—the darkness deepens: Lord, with me abide!"

And as the last words fell faintly on Algy Barford's ears, the slight form which was lying in Algy Barford's arms, and on which the strong man's tears were falling like rain, slipped gradually out of his grasp—dead.

CHAPTER IV.

THE PROTRACTED SEARCH.

ANNIE MAURICE was aroused from the brooding loneliness in which she had sought refuge, in the first bewilderment and stupefaction of her grief, by a communication from Lord Beauport. All was over now; the last sad ceremonial had taken place; and the place which had known Arthur, in his patient suffering, in his little-appreciated gentleness and goodness, should know him no more for ever. The crippled form was gone, and the invalid-chair which had for so long supported it had been removed, by order of the housekeeper, to a receptacle for discarded articles of use or ornament. Lord and Lady Beauport were not likely to notice the circumstance, or to object to it if they did. The blinds were decorously drawn; the rooms were scrupulously arranged; every thing in them in its place, as though never to be used or handled any more. The books, the objects of art, the curious things which the dead man alone of all the house had understood and valued, had a staring lifeless look about them in the unaccustomed precision of their distribution; the last flowers which Annie had placed in the Venetian glasses had withered, and been thrown away by the notable housemaids. A ray

of sunlight crept in at one side of the blind, and streamed
upon the spot where Arthur's head had fallen back upon
his friend's arm,—ah, how short a time ago!—and yet
all looked strange and changed, not only as if he had gone
away for ever, but as if he had never been there at all.
Annie had not gone into the rooms since he had left them
for the last time; she had an instinctive feeling of how
it would be, and she could not bear it yet; she knew that
in nothing would there be so sharp a pang as in seeing
the familiar things which had been so like him, grown so
unlike. So, when her maid told her that Lord Beauport
wished to see her immediately, she asked nervously where
he was.

"In the library, Miss Annie," said her maid, and looked
very pityingly at the purple eyelids and white face.

" Alone ?"

No, his lordship was not alone; one of the lawyer gentlemen and her ladyship were with him.

Annie went slowly and reluctantly to the library. She
did not think for a moment that Lord and Lady Beauport
were indifferent to the death of their eldest son; on the
contrary, she knew that the event had come upon them
with a mighty shock, and that they had felt it, if not deeply,
at least violently and keenly. But she had the faculty
of vivid perception, and she used it intuitively; and in this
case it told her that shame, self-detection, and remorse,—
the vague uneasiness which besets all who cannot reckon
with themselves to the full in the daylight of conscience,
but, like the debtor called to an account, kept something
back,—mingled largely with their grief. It was not whole-
hearted, lavish, sacred, like hers; it was not the grief which
takes the spontaneous form of prayer, and chastens itself
into submission, elevating and sanctifying the mind and
character of the mourner. Annie knew, by that keen un-
reasoning instinct of hers, that while her sole and earnest
desire was to keep the memory of her dead cousin green,
recalling his words, his counsels, his wishes,—dwelling on
his views of life and its duties, and preserving him in her
faithful heart, for ever near her, as a living friend,—while
her chosen thoughts would be of him, and her best consolation in memory,—his father and mother would forget him
if they could. They mourned for him, but it was with

captious impatient grief; there was a sting in every remembrance, every association, which they could not yet
escape from, but would have put away if they had had the
power. To them, sorrow for the dead was as a haunting
enemy, to be outwitted and left behind as speedily as might
be; to her it was a friend, cherished and dear, solemnly
greeted, and piously entertained.

When Annie entered the library, she found that the
"lawyer gentleman," whom her maid had mentioned, was
the family solicitor, Mr. Knevitt, who was well known to
her, and for whom Caterham had had much liking and
respect. Lord Beauport and he were standing together
beside a long table, strewn with papers, and on which stood
a large despatch-box open, and, as she saw while she walked
up the room, also full of papers. At some distance from
the table, and in the shade, Lady Beauport was seated,
her hands clasped together in her lap, and her figure leaning
completely back in the deep arm-chair she occupied. She
looked very pale and worn, and her deep mourning was
not becoming to her. Sharp contention of thought and
feeling was going on under that calm exterior,—bitter pangs,
in which vexation had a large share, as well as regret, and
a sense that she was to be baffled in the future as she had
been defeated in the past. Ay, the future,—she had begun
to think of it already, or rather she had begun (when had
she ever ceased?) to think of *him*. Lionel was the future
to her. What if there were more trouble and opposition
in store for her? What if Arthur (ah, poor fellow! he had
never understood young men different from himself, and
he was always hard on Lionel) had left any communication
for his father, had written any thing touching the particulars
of Lionel's career which he knew, and had warned her not
to ask? Hitherto nothing of the sort had been found in
the examination of Lord Caterham's papers instituted by
Lord Beauport and Mr. Knevitt. There was a packet
for Annie Maurice, indeed; they had found it an hour ago,
and Lord Beauport had just sent for Annie in order to
hand it over to her. Lady Beauport had, however, no
apprehensions connected with this matter; the virtues of
the dead and the vices of the living son (though she would
not have given them their true name) secured her from
feeling any. Whatever Lionel had done she felt convinced

was not of a nature to be communicated to Annie, and Caterham would have guarded her with the utmost caution from hearing any thing unfit for her ears. No, no; there was no danger in that quarter. Had she not felt sure, before this "dreadful thing"—as she called Lord Caterham's death to herself—happened, that the scrupulous delicacy of her son, where Annie was concerned, would be her best aid and defence against his defeat of her projects? The letter, the packet—whatever it might be called—was probably an effusion of feeling, a moral lecture on life, or a posthumous guide to studies, in which Arthur had desired to see his gentle and interesting cousin proficient.

So Lady Beauport looked at the packet as it lay on the table, close to the despatch-box, without the least anxiety, and fixed her impatient attention on the further investigation of the papers, continued by Lord Beauport and Mr. Knevitt. It was not until they had concluded as much of their melancholy task as they proposed to undertake that day, that the Earl sent the summons which brought Annie to the library.

He took up the packet as she drew near, and said, very sadly:

"This is for you, my dear."

"From—from Arthur?" she asked, in a trembling voice.

"Yes, Annie,—we found it among his papers."

She took it from him, looked at it, and sat down in a chair beside the table, but made no attempt to break the seal. Lady Beauport did not speak. The Earl resumed his conversation with Mr. Knevitt, and Annie sat still and silent for a few minutes, Then she interrupted Lord Beauport by asking him if he required her for any thing further.

"No, my dear," he said kindly; "you may go away if you like. How weary you look!" he added, with a deep sigh. Still Lady Beauport spoke no word; but her keen unsympathetic eyes followed the girl's graceful figure and drooping head as she left the library.

Arrived at her own room, Annie opened the packet, which she felt was a sacred thing. Her departed friend had written to her, then, words which he intended her to read only when he should be no more; solemn counsel, very precious affection, a priceless legacy from the dead would no doubt be in the letter, whose folds felt so thick and heavy in her hand. She removed the outer cover, placing it carefully by her side, and found an enclosure directed to Geoffrey Ludlow, and merely a few lines to herself, in which the writer simply directed her to place the accompanying letter in Geoffrey's hands *herself*, and privately, as soon after it came into hers as possible.

Surprise and disappointment were Annie's first feelings. She looked forlornly enough at the meagre scrap of writing that was her share, and with some wonder at the letter—no doubt voluminous—which was Geoffrey's. What could it be about? Arthur and Ludlow had been good friends, it is true, and had entertained strong mutual respect; but she could not account for this solemn communication, implying so strange and absolute a confidence. She turned the letter over in her hands, she scrutinised the address, the paper, the seal; then she rose and locked it carefully away, together with the note to herself in which it had been enclosed. "Give this letter *privately* to Ludlow," were Arthur's words; then, if he did not wish its delivery to be known, it was plain he wished to conceal its existence. If Lady Beauport should question her as to the contents of the packet? Well, she must either give an evasive answer, or refuse to answer at all; the alternative should be decided by the terms of the question. She could venture to refuse an answer to a question of Lady Beauport's now; her heiress-ship had secured her many immunities, that one among the rest.

Lord Beauport was right; Annie was weary, and looking so. The sickness and dreariness of a great grief were upon her, and she was worn out. The stillness of the great house was oppressive to her; and yet she shrank from the knowledge that that stillness was soon to pass away, that life would resume its accustomed course, and the dead be forgotten. By all but her; to her his memory should be ever precious, and his least wish sacred. Then she debated within herself how she should fulfil his last request. There were difficulties in the way. She could not tell Geoffrey to call on her yet, nor could she go to his house. Then she remembered that he had not written to her. She had forgotten, until then, that there had been no answer

to the letter in which she told Geoffrey Ludlow of Caterham's
death. Could a letter have come, and been overlooked?
She rang for her maid and questioned her, but she was
positive no letter had been mislaid or forgotten. Several
papers lay on her writing-table ; she turned them over, to
satisfy herself, though nothing could be more improbable
than that she should have overlooked a letter from her dear
old friend. There was no such thing. Puzzled and vaguely
distressed, Annie stood looking at the heap of notes, with
her hands pressed on her throbbing temples ; and her maid
entreated her to lie down and rest, commenting, as Lord
Beauport had done, upon her appearance. Annie complied ;
and the girl carefully darkened the room and left her. For
a while she lay still, thinking how she was to convey the
letter to Geoffrey, without delay, "as soon as possible,"
Arthur had said ; but she soon dropped into the dull heavy
sleep of grief and exhaustion.

It was late in the evening when she awoke, and she again
eagerly inquired for letters. There were none, and Annie's
surprise grew into uneasiness. She resolved to write to
Ludlow again, to tell him that she had something of importance to communicate, without indicating its character.
"He may tell Margaret, or not, as he pleases," she thought—
"that is for him to decide. I daresay, if she sees my note,
she will not feel any curiosity or interest about it. Poor
Geoffrey !" And then the girl recalled all that Arthur had
said of his suspicion and distrust of Ludlow's beautiful wife,
and thought sorrowfully how large was his share in the loss
they had sustained of such a friend. Something must be
wrong, she thought, or Geoffrey would surely have written.
In her sore grief she yearned for the true and ready sympathy
which she should have from him, and him alone. Stay ; she
would not only write, she would send her maid to inquire
for Geoffrey, and Margaret, and the child. She could go
early next morning in a cab, and be back before breakfast-
hour. So Annie made this arrangement, wrote her note,
got through a short hour or two in the great dreary drawing-
room as best she could, and once more cried herself to the
merciful sleep which in some degree strengthened her for
the intelligence which awaited her in the morning.

She was aroused by her maid, who came hurriedly to her

bedside, holding in her hand Annie's note to Ludlow. She started up, confused, yet sufficiently awake to be startled at the look in the girl's face.

"What is it?" she said faintly.

"O Miss Annie, dreadful, dreadful news! Mrs. Ludlow has gone away, nobody knows where, and Mr. Ludlow is raving mad, in brain-fever!"

Lord Caterham's letter lay for many days undisturbed in the receptacle in which Annie Maurice had placed it. Not yet was the confidence of the dead to be imparted to the living. He was to read that letter in time, and to learn from it much that the writer had never dreamed it could convey. Little had the two, who had lived in so near and pleasant an intimacy, dreamed of the fatal link which really, though unseen, connected them. This was the letter which, in due time, Annie Maurice deposited in Geoffrey's hands :

"My dear Ludlow,—I have felt for some time that for me 'the long disease called life' is wearing toward its cure. Under this conviction I am 'setting my house in order;' and to do so thoroughly, and enjoy peace of mind for the brief space which will remain to me when that is done, I must have recourse to your honest and trusty friendship. I have to bequeath to you two services to be done for me, and one confidence to be kept, until your discretion shall judge it expedient that it should be divulged. These two services are distinct, but cognate; and they concern one who is the dearest of all living creatures to me, and for whom I know you entertain a sincere and warm affection— I allude to Annie Maurice. The confidence concerns my unworthy brother, Lionel Brakespere.

"In the fortune left her by Mr. Ampthill, Annie has security against material ills, and is safe from the position of dependence, in which I never could bear to feel she must remain. This is an immense relief to my mind ; but it has substituted a source of uneasiness, though of considerably less dimensions, for that which it has removed. When I wrote to you lately, asking you to come to me, it was with the intention of speaking to you on this subject ; but as our interview has been accidentally prevented, I made up my mind to act in the matter myself, as long as I live, and to bequeath action after my death to you, as I am now doing. My brother is as worthless a man as there is on the face of the earth—heartless, depraved, unprincipled to an almost incredible degree, considering his early association with men and women of character. You have, I daresay, heard vaguely of certain disgraceful circumstances which forced him to leave the country, and which brought immeasurable distress upon us all.

"I need not enter into these matters : they have little to do with the thing that is pressing on my mind. If Lionel's vices had been hidden from society ever so discreetly, I was sufficiently aware of their existence to have shrunk with as much horror as I feel now from the idea of his becoming Annie's husband. Let me preface what I am about to say by assuring you that I do not entertain any such fear. I know Annie ; and I am perfectly assured that for her pure, upright, intelligent, and remarkably clear-sighted nature such a man as Lionel,— whose profound and cynical selfishness is not to be hidden by external polish, and whose many vices have left upon him the *cachet* which every pure woman feels instinctively, even though she does not understand theoretically,—will never have any attraction. She knows the nature of the transaction which drove him from England; and such a knowledge would be sufficient protection for her, without the repulsion which I am satisfied will be the result of association with him. I would protect her from such association if I could, and while I live I do not doubt my power to do so. It will be painful to me to use it ; but I do not mind pain for Annie's benefit. A sad estrangement always existed between Lionel and me ; an estrangement increased on his side by contempt and dislike — which he expressed in no measured terms—but on my part merely passive. The power which I possess to hinder his return to this house was put into my hands by himself—more, I believe, to wound me, and in the wanton malice and daring of his evil nature, than for the reason he assigned ; but it is effectual, and I shall use it, as I can, without explanation. When I am gone, it needs be, some one must be enabled to use this power in my stead ; and that person, my dear Ludlow, is you. I choose you for Annie's sake, for yours, and for my own. My mother designs to marry Lionel to Annie, and thus secure to him by marriage the fortune which his misconduct lost him by inheritance. With this purpose in view, she has summoned Lionel to England, and she proposes that he should return to this house. She and I have had a painful explanation, and I have positively declared that it cannot and shall not be. In order to convince her of the necessity of yielding the point, I have told her that I am in possession of particulars of Lionel's conduct, unknown to her and my father, which perfectly justify me in my declaration ; and I have entreated her, for the sake of her own peace of mind, not to force me, by an attempt which can have no issue but failure, to communicate the disgraceful particulars. Lady Beauport has been forced to appear satisfied for the present ; and matters are in a state of suspense.

" But this cannot last, and with my life it will come to an end. Lionel will return here, in my place, and bearing my name—the heir to an earldom ; and the follies and crimes of the younger son will be forgotten. Still Annie Maurice will be no less a brilliant match, and my mother will be no less anxious to bring about a marriage. I foresee misery to Annie—genteel persecution and utter friendlessness—unless you, Ludlow, come to her aid. With all its drawbacks, this is her fitting home ; and you must not propose that she should leave it without very grave cause. But you must be in a position to preserve her from Lionel ; you must hold the secret in your hand, as I hold it, which makes all schemes for such an accursed marriage vain—the secret which will keep the house she will adorn free from the pollution of his presence. When you hear that Lionel Brakespere is paying attention to Annie under his father's roof, go to Lord Beauport, and tell him that Lionel Brakespere is a married man.

" And now, my dear Ludlow, you know one of the services you are to do me when I am gone ; and you are in possession of the confidence I desire to repose in you. To explain the other, I must give you particulars. When my brother left England, he sent me, by the hands of a common friend, a letter which he had written at Liverpool, and which, when I have made you acquainted with its contents, I shall destroy. I do not desire to leave its low ribaldry, its coarse contempt, its cynical wickedness, to shock my poor father's eyes, or to testify against my brother when I am gone.

"I enable you to expose him, in order to prevent unhappiness to one dear to us both; but I have no vindictive feeling towards him, and no eyes but mine must see the words in which he taunts me with the physical afflictions to which he chooses to assign my 'notions of morality' and 'superiority to temptation.' Enough—the facts which the letter contains are these: As nearly as I can make out, four years ago he met and tried to seduce a young lady, only eighteen years old, at Tenby. Her virtue, I hope—he says her ambition—foiled him, and he ran away with the girl and married her. He called himself Leonard Brookfield; and she never knew his name or real position. He took her abroad for a time; then brought her to London, where she passed for his mistress among the men to whom he introduced her, and who were aware that she had no knowledge of his identity. He had left the army then, or of course she would have discovered it. When the crash came, he had left her, and he coolly told me, as he had next to nothing for himself, he had nothing for her. His purpose in writing to me was to inform me, as especially interested in the preservation of the family, that not only was there a wife in the case, but, to the best of his belief, a child also, to be born very soon; and as no one could say what would become of him, it might be as well to ascertain where the heir of the Beauports might be found, if necessary. He supposed I would keep the matter a secret, until it should become advisable, if ever, to reveal it. Mrs. Brakespere had no knowledge of her rights, and could not, therefore, make herself obnoxious by claiming them. If I chose to give her some help, I should probably be rewarded by the consciousness of charity; but he advised me to keep the secret of our relationship for my own sake: she was perfectly well known as his mistress; and as they were both under a cloud at present, the whole thing had better be kept as dark as possible. I read this letter with the deepest disgust; the personal impertinence to myself I could afford to disregard, and was accustomed to; but the utter baseness and villany of it sickened me. This was the man who was to bear my father's name and fill my father's place. I determined at once to afford assistance to the wretched forsaken wife, and to wait and consider when and how it would be advisable to bring about the acknowledgment of the truth and her recognition. I thought of course only of simple justice. The circumstances of the marriage were too much against the girl to enable me to form any favourable opinion of her. I turned to the letter to find her name and address; they were not given: of course this was only an oversight; he must have intended to subjoin them. My perplexity was extreme. How was I to discover this unhappy woman? I knew too well the code of honour, as it is called, among men, to hope for help from any of his dissolute friends; they would keep his evil secret—as they believed it—faithfully.

"Algy Barford had brought me the letter, and on that occasion had referred to his being 'no end chums' with Lionel. But he had also declared that he knew nothing whatever of the contents of the letter. Still he might know something of her. I put a question or two to him, and found he did not. He had known a woman who lived with Lionel for a short time, he believed, but she was dead. Clearly this was another person. Then I determined to have recourse to the professional finders-out of secrets, and I sent for Blackett. You have often seen him leaving me as you came in, or waiting for me as you went out. The day Mrs. Ludlow fainted, you remember, he was in the hall as you took her to the carriage, and he asked me so many questions about her, that I was quite amused at the idea of a detective being so enthusiastic. The materials he had to work on were sparing indeed, and the absence of all clue by name was very embarrassing. He went to work skilfully, I am sure, though he failed. He went to Tenby, and there he ascertained the name of the girl who had deserted her widowed mother for Leonard Brookfield. The mother had been many months dead. This was little help, for she had doubtless discarded the Christian name; and the personal description was probably coloured by the indignation her conduct had excited. Blackett learned that she was handsome, with red hair and blue eyes,—some said black. He could get no certain information on that point.

"But I need not linger over these details. No efforts were spared, yet our search proved vain. When some time had elapsed, their direction changed, and a woman and child were sought for : in every part of London where destitution hides, in all the abodes of flaunting sin, in hospitals, in refuges, in charitable institutions,— in vain. Sometimes Blackett suggested that she might have taken another protector and gone abroad ; he made all possible inquiry. She had never communicated with her home, or with any one who had formerly known her. I began to despair of finding her ; and I had almost made up my mind to relinquish the search, when Blackett came to me one day, in great excitement for him, and told me he was confident of finding her in a day or two at the farthest. 'And the child ?' I asked. No, he knew nothing of the child ; the woman he had traced, and whom he believed to be my brother's deserted wife, had no child, had never had one, within the knowledge of the people from whom he had got his information ; nevertheless he felt sure he was right this time, and the child might have died before she came across them. She must have suffered terribly. Then he told me his information came through a pawnbroker, of whom he had frequent occasion to make inquiries. This man had shown him a gold locket, which had evidently held a miniature, on the inside of which was engraved 'From Leonard to Clara,' and which had been pawned by a very poor but respectable person, whose address, in a miserable lane at Islington, he now gave to Blackett. He went to the place at once and questioned the woman, who was only too anxious to give all the information in her power in order to clear herself. She had received the locket in the presence of two persons, from a young woman who had lodged with her, and who had no other means of paying her. The young woman had gone away a week before, she did not know where ; she had no money, and only a little bundle of clothes—a handkerchief full. She had no child, and had never said any thing about one. The woman did not know her name. She had taken a picture out of the locket. She had red hair and dark eyes. This was all. I shall never forget the wretched feeling which came over me as I thought of the suffering this brief story implied, and of what the wretched woman might since have undergone. I remember so well, it was in January,— a dirty, wet, horrible day,—when Blackett told me all this ; and I was haunted with the idea of the woman dying of

cold and want in the dreadful streets. Blackett had no
doubt of finding her now; she had evidently fallen to the
veriest pauperism, and out of the lowest depths she would
be drawn up, no doubt. So he set to work at once, but all
in vain. Dead or living, no trace of her has ever been
found; and the continuous search has been abandoned.
Blackett only 'bears it in mind' now. Once he suggested
to me, that as she was no doubt handsome, and not over
particular, she might have got a living by sitting to the
painters, and 'I'll try that lay,' he said; but nothing came
of that either. I thought of it the day Annie and I met you
first, at the Private View, and if I had had the opportunity,
would have asked you if you knew such a face as the one
we were only guessing at, after all; but you were hurried,
and the occasion passed; and when we met again, Blackett
had exhausted all sources of information in that direction,
and there was nothing to be learned.

" This is the story I had to tell you, Ludlow, and to leave
to your discretion to use when the time comes. Within the
last week Blackett has made further attempts, and has again
failed. Lionel is in London; but while I live he does not
enter this house. I shall, after a while, when I am able,
which I am not now, let him know that search has been
unsuccessfully made for his wife, and demand that he shall
furnish me with any clue in his possession, under the threat
of immediate exposure. This, and every other plan, may
be at any moment rendered impossible by my death; therefore I write this, and entreat you to continue the search
until this woman be found, dead or living. So only can
Annie's home be made happy and reputable for her when I
shall have left it for ever. You will receive this from Annie's
hands; a packet addressed to her will not be neglected or
thrown aside; and if it becomes necessary for you to act for
her, she will have the knowledge of the confidence I repose
in you to support her in her acceptance of your interference
and obedience to your advice. I confide her to you, my
dear Ludlow—as I said before—as the dearest living thing
in all the world to me.—Yours ever,

"CATERHAM."

Y

CHAPTER V

DISMAY.

MRS. LUDLOW and Til had concluded the meal which is so generally advanced to a position of unnatural importance in a household devoid of the masculine element *en permanence;* and, the tea-things having been removed, the old lady, according to the established order, was provided with a book, over which she was expected to fall comfortably asleep. But she did not adhere to the rule of her harmless and placid life on this particular occasion. The "cross" was there—no doubt about it; and it was no longer indefinite in its nature, but very real, and beginning to be very heavy. Under the pressure of its weight Geoffrey's mother was growing indifferent to, even unobservant of, the small worries which had formerly occupied her mind, and furnished the subject-matter of her pardonable little querulousness and complaints—a grievance in no way connected with the tradespeople, and uninfluenced by the "greatest plagues in life"—which no reduction of duties involving cheap groceries, and no sumptuary laws restraining servant-gal-ism within limits of propriety in respect of curls and crinoline, had any power to assuage,—had taken possession of her now, and she fidgeted and fumed no longer, but was haunted by apprehension and sorely troubled.

A somewhat forced liveliness on Til's part, and a marked avoidance of the subject of Geoffrey, of whom, as he had just left them, it would have been natural that the mother and daughter should talk, bore witness to the embarrassment she felt, and increased Mrs. Ludlow's depression. She sat in her accustomed arm-chair, but her head drooped forward and her fingers tapped the arms in an absent manner, which showed her pre-occupation of mind. Til at length took her needle-work, and sat down opposite her mother, in a silence which was interrupted after a considerable interval by the arrival of Charley Potts, who had not altogether ceased to offer clumsy and violently-improbable explanations of his visits. though such were rapidly coming to be unnecessary.

On the present occasion Charley floundered through the preliminaries with more than his usual impulsive awkwardness, and there was that in his manner which caused Til (a quick observer, and especially so in his case) to divine that he had something particular to say to her. If she were right in her conjecture, it was clear that the opportunity must be waited for,—until the nap, in which Mrs. Ludlow invariably indulged in the evening, should have set in. The sooner the conversation settled into sequence, the sooner this desirable event might be expected to take place ; so Til talked vigorously, and Charley seconded her efforts. Mrs. Ludlow said little, until, just as Charley began to think the nap was certainly coming, she asked him abruptly if he had seen Geoffrey lately. Miss Til happened to be looking at Charley as the question was put to him, and saw in a moment that the matter he had come to speak to her about concerned her brother.

"No, ma'am," said Charley ; "none of us have seen Geoff lately. Bowker and I have planned a state visit to him ; he's as hard to get at as a swell in the Government—with things to give away—what do you call it ?—patronage ; but we're not going to stand it. We can't do without Geoff. By the bye, how's the youngster, ma'am ?"

"The child is very well, I believe," said Mrs. Ludlow, with a shake of the head, which Charley Potts had learned to recognise in connection with the "cross," but which he saw with regret on the present occasion. "I'm afraid they've heard something," he thought. "But," continued the old lady querulously, "I see little of him, or of Geoffrey either. Things are changed; I suppose it's all right, but it's not easy for a mother to see it ; and I don't think any mother would like to be a mere visitor at her own son's house,—not that I am even much of that now, Mr. Potts ; for I am sure it's a month or more since ever I have darkened the doors of Elm Lodge,—and I shouldn't so much mind it, I hope, if it was for Geoffrey's good ; but I can't think it's that—" Here the old lady's voice gave way, and she left off with a kind of sob, which went to Charley's soft heart and filled him with inexpressible confusion. Til was also much taken aback, though she saw at once that her mother had been glad of the opportunity of saying her little say, under the influence of the mortification she had felt at Geoffrey's silence on the subject of her future visits to Elm Lodge. He had, as we have seen, made himself as delightful as possible in every other respect; but he had been strictly reticent about Margaret, and he had not invited his mother and sister to his house. She had been longing to say all this to Til; and now she had got it out, in the presence of a third party, who would "see fair" between her justifiable annoyance and Til's unreasonable defence of her brother. Til covered Charley's embarrassment by saying promptly, in a tone of extreme satisfaction,

"Geoffrey was here to-day; he paid us quite a long visit."

"Did he?" said Charley; "and is he all right?"

"O yes," said Til, "he is very well; and he told us all about his pictures; and, do you know, he's going to put baby and the nurse into a corner group, among the people on the Esplanade,—only he must wait till baby's back is stronger, and his neck leaves off waggling, so as to paint him properly, sitting up nice and straight in nurse's arms." And then Miss Til ran on with a great deal of desultory talk, concerning Geoffrey, and his description of the presents, and what he had said about Lord Caterham and Annie Maurice. Charley listened to her with more seriousness than he usually displayed; and Mrs. Ludlow sighed and shook her head at intervals, until, as the conversation settled into a dialogue, she gradually dropped asleep. Then Til's manner changed, and she lowered her voice, and asked Charley anxiously if he had come to tell her any bad news.

"If you have," she said, "and that it can be kept from mamma, tell it at once, and let me keep it from her."

With much true delicacy and deep sympathy, Charley then related to Til the scene which had taken place between himself, Bowker, and Stompff,—and told her that Bowker had talked the matter over with him, and they had agreed that it was not acting fairly by Geoffrey to allow him to remain in ignorance of the floating rumours, injurious to his wife's character, which were rife among their friends. How Stompff had heard of Margaret's having fainted in Lord Caterham's room, Charley could not tell; that he had heard it, and had heard a mysterious cause assigned to it, he knew. That he could have known any thing about an incident apparently so trivial proved that the talk had become tolerably general, and was tending to the injury of Geoffrey, not only in his self-respect and in his feelings, but in his prospects. Charley was much more alarmed and uneasy, and much more grieved for Geoffrey, than even Bowker; for he had reason to fear that no supposition derogatory to Margaret's antecedents could surpass the reality. He alone knew where and how the acquaintance between Geoffrey and Margaret had begun, and he was therefore prepared to estimate the calamity of such a marriage correctly. He did not exactly know what he had intended to say to Matilda Ludlow; he had come to the house with a vague idea that something ought to be done;—that Til ought to speak to her sister-in-law,—a notion which in itself proved Charley Potts to be any thing but a wise man,—ought to point out to her that her indifference to her husband was at once ungrateful to him and short-sighted to her own interest; and that people, notably his employer, were talking about it. Charley Potts was not exactly an adept in reading character, and the real Margaret was a being such as he could neither have understood nor believed in; therefore the crudity, wildness, and inapplicability of this scheme were to be excused.

A very few words on his part served to open the susceptible heart of Miss Til, especially as they had spoken on the subject, though generally, before; and they were soon deep in the exchange of mutual confidences. Til cried quietly, so as not to wake her mother; and it distressed Charley very keenly to see her tears and to hear her declare that her sister-in-law had not the slightest regard for her opinion; that though perfectly civil to her, Margaret had met all her attempts at sisterly intimacy with most forbidding coldness; and that she felt sure any attempt to put their relation on a more familiar footing would be useless.

"She must have been very badly brought up, I am sure," said Til. "We don't know anything about her family; but I am sure she never learned what the duties of a wife and mother are."

Charley looked admirably at Til as she sadly uttered this remark, and his mind was divided between a vision of Til realising in the most perfect manner the highest ideal of conjugal and maternal duty, and speculating upon what might have been the polite fiction presented by Geoffrey to his mother and sister as an authentic history of Margaret's parentage and antecedents.

"Did Geoffrey seem cheerful and happy to-day?" he asked, escaping off the dangerous ground of questions which he could have answered only too completely.

"Well," replied Til, "I can't say he did. He talked and laughed, and all that; but I could see that he was uneasy and unhappy. How much happier he was when we were all together, in the days which seem so far off now!"

At this point the conversation became decidedly senti-mental; for Charley, while carefully maintaining that true happiness was only to be found in the married state, was equally careful to state his opinion that separation from Til must involve a perfectly incomparable condition of misery; and altogether matters were evidently reaching a climax. Matilda Ludlow was an unaffected honest girl: she knew perfectly well that Charley loved her, and she had no par-ticular objection to his selecting this particular occasion on which to tell her so. But Til and Charley were not to part that evening in the character of affianced lovers; for in one of those significant pauses which precede important words, cab-wheels rolled rapidly up to the little gate, hurried foot-steps ran along the flagged path, and a loud knock and ring at the door impatiently demanded attention.

Mrs. Ludlow awoke with a violent start: Charley and Til looked at each other. The door was opened, and a moment later the cook from Elm Lodge was in the room, and had replied to Charley's hurried question by the statement that her master was very ill, and she had been sent to fetch Miss Ludlow.

"Very ill! has any accident happened?" they all questioned the woman, who showed much feeling—all his dependents loved Geoffrey—and the confusion was so great, that it was some minutes before they succeeded in learning what actually had happened. That Geoffrey had returned home as usual; had gone to the nursery, and played with the child and talked to the nurse as usual; had gone to his painting-room; and had not again been seen by the servants, until the housemaid had found him lying on the hearth-rug an hour before, when they had sent for Dr. Brandram, and that gentleman had despatched the cook to bring Miss Ludlow.

" Did Mrs. Ludlow tell you to come ?" asked Til.

To this question the woman replied that her mistress was not at home. She had been out the greater part of the day, had returned home some time later than Mr. Ludlow, and had kept the cab waiting for an hour ; then she had gone away again, and had not returned when the cook had been sent on her errand. Charley Potts exchanged looks of undisguised alarm with Til at this portion of the woman's narrative, and, seeing that reserve would now be wholly misplaced, he questioned her closely concerning Mrs. Ludlow. She had nothing to tell, however, beyond that the housemaid had said her master and mistress had been together in the dining-room, and, surprised that dinner had not been ordered up, she had gone thither ; but hearing her mistress speaking " rather strangely," she had not knocked at the door. The servants had wondered at the delay, she said, not understanding why their master should go without his dinner because Mrs. Ludlow was not at home, and had at length found him as she described.

" Did Mrs. Ludlow often go out in this way?" asked Mr. Potts.

" No, sir, never," said the woman. " I never knew my mistress leave my master alone before, sir ; and I am afraid something has took place between them."

The distress and bewilderment of the little party were extreme. Manifestly there was but one thing to be done ; Til must obey the doctor's summons, and repair immediately to her brother's house. He was very ill indeed, the cook said, and quite " off his head ;" he did not talk much, but what he did say was all nonsense ; and Dr. Brandram had said it was the beginning of brain-fever. Charley and Til were both surprised at the firmness and collectedness manifested by Mrs. Ludlow under this unexpected trial. She was very pale and she trembled very much, but she was quite calm and quiet when she told Til that she must put up such articles of clothing as she would require for a few days, as it was her intention to go to her son and to remain with him.

" I am the fittest person, my dear," said the old lady. "If it be only illness that ails him, I know more about it than you do; if it is sorrow also, and sorrow of the kind I suspect, I am fitter to hear it and act in it than you."

It was finally agreed that they should both go to Geoffrey's house and that Til should return home in the morning ; for even in this crisis Mrs. Ludlow could not quite forget her household gods, and to contemplate them bereft at once of her own care and that of Til would have been too grievous ; so they started—the three women in the cab, and Charley Potts on the box, very silent, very gloomy, and not even in his inmost thoughts approaching the subject of a pipe.

It was past ten when Geoffrey Ludlow's mother and sister reached the house which had seen such terrible events since they had visited it last. Already the dreary neglected air which settles over every room in a dwelling invaded by serious illness, except the one which is the scene of suffering, had come upon it. Four hours earlier all was bright and cheerful, well cared for and orderly ; now, though the disarray was not material, it was most expressive. Mrs. Geoffrey Ludlow had not returned ; the doctor had gone away, but was coming back as soon as possible, having left one of the servants by Geoffrey's bedside, with orders to apply wet linen to his temples without intermission. Geoffrey was quiet now—almost insensible, they thought. Mrs. Ludlow and Til went to the sick-room at once, and Charley Potts turned disconsolately into the dining-room, where the cloth was still laid, and the chairs stood about in disorder—one, which Geoffrey had knocked down, lay unheeded on the ground. Charley picked it up, sat down upon it, and leaned his elbows disconsolately on the table.

" It's all up, I'm afraid," said he to himself ; " and she's off with the other fellow, whoever he is. Well, well, it will either kill Geoff outright or break his heart for the rest of his life. At all events, there couldn't have been much good in her if she didn't like Til."

After some time Dr. Brandram arrived, and Charley heard him ask the servant whether Mrs. Ludlow had returned, and heard her reply that her mistress was still absent, but Mrs. Ludlow and her daughter had come, and were in her master's room. The doctor went upstairs immediately, and Charley still waited in the parlour, determined to waylay him has he came down.

Geoffrey was dangerously ill, there was no doubt of that, though his mother's terror magnified danger into hopeless-ness, and refused to be comforted by Dr. Brandram's assurance that no living man for certain could tell how things would be. She met the doctor's inquiry about Margaret with quiet reserve : she did not expect her daughter-in-law's return that evening, she said ; but she and Miss Ludlow were prepared to remain. It was very essential that they should do so, Dr. Brandram assured her ; and on the following day he would procure a professional nurse. Then he made a final examination of his patient, gave the ladies their instructions, observed with satisfaction the absence of fuss, and the quiet self-subduing alacrity of Til, and went downstairs, shaking his head and wondering, to be pounced upon in the little hall by the impulsive Charley, who drew him into the dining-room, and poured out a torrent of questions. Dr. Brandram was disposed to be a little reserved at first, but unbent when Charley assured him that he and Geoffrey were the most intimate friends— "Brothers almost," said Mr. Potts in a conscious tone, which did not strike the doctor. Then he told his anxious interlocutor that Geoffrey was suffering from brain-fever, which he supposed to be the result of a violent shock, but of what kind he could form no idea ; and then he said something, in a hesitating sort of way, about "domestic affairs."

"It is altogether on the mind, then," said Charley. "In that case, no one can explain any thing but himself."

"Precisely so," said Dr. Brandram ; "and it may, it most probably will, be a considerable time before he will be able to give us any explanation of any thing, and before it would be safe to ask him for any. In the mean time,—but no doubt Mrs. Ludlow will return, and—"

"I don't think she will do any thing of the kind," said Charley Potts in a decisive tone ; "and, in fact, doctor, I think it would be well to say as little as possible about her."

Dr. Brandram looked at Mr. Potts with an expression intended to be knowing, but which was in reality only puzzled, and assuring him of his inviolable discretion, departed. Charley remained at Elm Lodge until after midnight, and then, finding that he could be of no service to the watchers, sorrowfully wended his way back to town on foot.

Wearily dragged on the days in the sick man's room,

where he lay racked and tormented by fever, and vaguely oppressed in mind.. His mother and sister tended him with unwearied assiduity, and Dr. Brandram called in further medical advice. Geoffrey's life hung in the balance for many days—days during which the terror his mother and Til experienced are not to be told. The desolate air of the house deepened; the sitting-rooms were quite deserted now. All the bright pretty furniture which Geoff had bought for the delectation of his bride, all the little articles of use and ornament peculiarly associated with Margaret, were dust-covered, and had a ghostly seeming. Charley Potts—who passed a great deal of his time moping about Elm Lodge, too thankful to be permitted on the premises, and occasionally to catch a glimpse of Til's figure, as she glided noiselessly from the sick-room to the lower regions in search of some of the innumerable things which are always being wanted in illness and are never near at hand—occasionally strolled into the painting-room, and lifting the cover which had been thrown over it, looked sadly at "The Esplanade at Brighton," and wondered whether dear old Geoff would ever paint baby's portrait among that group in the left-hand corner.

The only member of the household who pursued his usual course of existence was this same baby. Unconscious alike of the flight of his mother and the illness, nigh unto death, of his father, the child throve apace, and sometimes the sound of his cooing, crowing voice, coming through the open doors into the room where his grandmother sat and looked into the wan haunted face of her son, caused her unspeakable pangs of sorrow and compassion. The child "took to" Til wonderfully, and it is impossible to tell the admiration with which the soul of Charley Potts was filled, as he saw the motherly ways of the young lady towards the little fellow, happily unconscious that he did not possess a mother's love.

Of Margaret nothing was heard. Mrs. Ludlow and Til were utterly confounded by the mystery which surrounded them. She made no sign from the time she left the house. Their ignorance of the circumstances of her departure was so complete, that they could not tell whether to expect her to do so or not. Her dresses and ornaments were all undisturbed in the drawers in the room where poor Geoffrey lay, and they did not know whether to remove them or not. She had said to Geoffrey, "Whatever I actually require I will send for;" but they did not know this, and she never had sent. The centre of the little system—the chief person in the household—the idolised wife—she had disappeared as utterly as if her existence had been only a dream. The only person who could throw any light on the mystery was, perhaps, dying—at all events, incapable of recollection, thought, or speech. It "got about" in the neighbourhood that Mr. Ludlow was dangerously ill, and that his mother and sister were with him, but his beautiful wife was not; whereat the neighbourhood, feeling profoundly puzzled, merely looked unutterably wise, and had always thought there was something odd in that quarter. Then the neighbourhood called to enquire and to condole, and was very pointed in its hopes that Mrs. Geoffrey Ludlow was "bearing up well," and very much astonished to receive for answer, "Thank you ma'am; but missis is not at home." Mrs. Ludlow knew nothing of all this, and Til, who did know, cared nothing; but it annoyed Charley Potts, who beard and saw a good deal from his post of vantage in the dining-room window, and who relieved his feelings by swearing under his breath, and making depreciatory comments upon the personal appearance of the ladies as they approached the house, with their faces duly arranged to the sympathetic pattern.

It chanced that, on one occasion, when Geoffrey had been about ten days ill, Til came down to the dining-room to speak to the faithful Charley, carrying the baby on one arm, and in her other hand a bundle of letters. Charley took the child from her as a matter of course; and the youthful autocrat graciously sanctioning the arrangement, the two began to talk eagerly of Geoffrey. Til was looking very pale and weary, and Charley was much moved by her appearance.

"I tell you what it is," he said, "you'll kill yourself, whether Geoffrey lives or dies." He spoke in a tone suggestive of feeling himself personally injured, and Til was not too far gone to blush and smile faintly as she perceived it.

"O no, I sha'n't," she said. "I'm going to lie down all

this afternoon in the night-nursery. Mamma is asleep now, and Geoffrey is quite quiet, though the nurse says she sees no change for the better, no real change of any kind indeed. And so I came down to ask you what you think I had better do about these letters." She laid them on the table as she spoke. "I don't think they are business letters, because you have taken care to let all Geoffrey's professional friends know, haven't you, Charley?"

Charley thrilled; she had dropped unconsciously, in the intimacy of a common sorrow, into calling him by his Christian name, but the pleasure it gave him had by no means worn off yet.

"Yes," he said; "and you have no notion what a state they are all in about dear old Geoff. I assure you they all envy me immensely, because I can be of some little use to you. They don't come here, you know, because that would be no use—only making a row with the door-bell, and taking up the servants' time; but every day they come down to my place, or write me notes, or scribble their names on the door, with fat notes of interrogation after them, if I'm not at home. That means, 'How's dear old Geoff? send word at once.' Why, there's Stompff—I told you he was a beast, didn't I? Well, he's not half a beast, I assure you; he is in such a way about Geoff; and, upon my word, I don't think it's all because he is worth no end of money to him,—I don't indeed. He is mercenary, of course, but not always and not altogether; and he really quite got over me yesterday by the way he talked of Geoffrey, and wanted to know if there was any thing in the world he could do. Any thing in the world, according to Stompff, meant any thing in the way of money, I suppose; an advance upon the 'Esplanade,' or something of that sort."

"Yes, I suppose it did," said Til; "but we don't want money. Mamma has plenty to go on with until—" here her lip quivered,—"until Geoffrey can understand and explain things. It's very kind of Mr. Stompff, however, and I'm glad he's not quite a beast," said the young lady simply. "But, Charley, about these letters; what should I do?"

At this point the baby objected to be any longer

unnoticed, and was transferred to Til, who walked up and down the room with the injured innocent, while Charley turned over the letters, and looked at their superscriptions.

"You are sure there is no letter from his wife among these?" said Charley.

"O no!" replied Til; "I know Magaret's hand well; and I have examined all the letters carefully every day. There has never been one from her."

"Here are two with the same monogram, and the West-end district mark; I think they must be from Miss Maurice. If these letters can be made out to mean any thing, they are A.M. And see, one is plain, and one has a deep black edge."

Til hurried up to the table. "I hope Lord Caterham is not dead," she said! "I have heard Geoffrey speak of him with great regard; and only the day he was taken ill, he said he feared the poor fellow was going fast."

"I think we had better break the seal and see," said Charley; "Geoff would not like any neglect in that quarter."

He broke the seal as he spoke, and read the melancholy note which Annie had written to Geoffrey when Arthur died, and which had never received an answer.

Charley Potts and Til were much shocked and affected at the intelligence which the note contained.

"I haven't cared about the papers since Geoff has been ill, or I suppose I should have seen the announcement of Lord Caterham's death, though I don't particularly care for reading about the swells at any time," said Charley. "But how nicely she writes to Geoffrey, poor girl! I am sure she will be shocked to hear of his illness, and you must write to her,—h'm,—Til. What do you say to writing, and letting me take your letter to-morrow myself? Then she can ask me any questions she likes, and you need not enter into any painful explanations."

Til was eminently grateful for this suggestion, which she knew was dictated by the sincerest and most disinterested wish to spare her; for to Charley the idea of approaching the grandeur of St. Barnabas Square, and the powdered pomposity of the lordly flunkeys, was, as she well knew, wholly detestable. So it was arranged that Charley should fulfil this mission early on the following day, before he presented himself at Elm Lodge. The baby was sent upstairs, Til wrote her note, and Charley departed very reluctantly, stipulating that Til should at once fulfil her promise of lying down in the nursery.

When, on the ensuing morning, Miss Maurice's maid reached Elm Lodge, the servants communicated to her the startling intelligence, which she roused Annie from her sleep to impart to her, without any reference to Mrs. Ludlow and Til, who were not aware for some time that Miss Maurice had sent to make inquiries. On his arrival at St. Barnabas Square, Charley Potts was immediately admitted to Annie's presence, and the result of the interview was that she arrived at Elm Lodge escorted by that gentleman, whose embarrassment under the distinguished circumstances was extreme, before noon. She knew from Charley's report that it would be quite in vain to take Caterham's letter with her; that it must be long ere it should meet the eyes for which it was written, if ever it were to do so, and it remained still undisturbed in her charge. So Annie Maurice shared the sorrow and the fear of Geoffrey's mother and sister, and discussed the mystery that surrounded the calamities which had befallen them, perfectly unconscious that within reach of her own hand lay the key to the enigma.

CHAPTER VI.

A CLUE.

WRITTEN by a dying hand, the letter addressed by Lord Caterham to Geoffrey Ludlow was read when the doctors would scarcely have pronounced its recipient out of the jaws of death. Gaunt, wan, hectic; with great bistre-rings round his big eyes, now more prominent than ever; with his shapely white hands now almost transparent in their thinness; with his bushy beard dashed here and there with gray patches; and with O such a sense of weariness and weakness,—old Geoff, stretched supine on his bed, demanded news of Margaret. They had none to give him: told him so—at first gently, then reiterated it plainly; but he would not believe it. They must know something of her movements; some one must have been there to tell him where she was; something must have been heard of her. To all these questions negative answers. Then, as his brain cleared and his strength increased—for, except under both of these conditions, such a question would not have occurred to him— he asked whether, during his illness, there had been any communication from Lord Beauport's house. A mystery then—a desire to leave it over, until Miss Maurice's next call, which happened the next day, when Caterham's letter, intact, was handed to him.

That letter lay on a chair by Geoffrey's bedside the whole of that afternoon. To clutch it, to look at it, to hold it, with its seal yet unbroken, before his eyes, he had employed such relics of strength as remained to him; but he dared not open it. He felt that he could give no explanation of his feelings; but he felt that if he broke that seal, and read what was contained in that letter, all his recent tortures would return with tenfold virulence: the mocking demons that had sat on his bed and sneered at him; the fiery serpents that had uncoiled themselves between him and the easel on which stood the picture which urgent necessity compelled him to work at; the pale fair form, misty and uncertain generally, yet sometimes with Margaret's hair and eyes, that so constantly floated across his vision, and as constantly eluded his outstretched arms,—all these phantasms of his fevered brain would return again. And yet, in it, in that sheet of paper lying so temptingly near to his pillow, there was news of her! He had but to stretch out his hand, and he should learn how far, at least, her story was known to the relatives of him who——The thought in itself was too much; and Geoffrey swooned off. When he recovered, his first thought was of the letter; his first look to assure himself that it had not been removed. No, there it lay! He could resist the temptation no longer; and, raising himself on his elbow, he opened and read it.

The effect of the perusal of that letter on Geoffrey Ludlow none knew but himself. The doctors found him "not quite so well" for the succeeding day or two, and thought that his "tone" was scarcely so good as they had been led to anticipate; certain it was that he made no effort to rouse himself, and that, save occasionally, when spoken to by Til, he remained silent and preoccupied. On the third day he asked Til to write to Bowker, and beg him to come to him at once. Within twenty-four hours that worthy presented himself at Elm Lodge.

After a few words with Til downstairs, Mr. Bowker was shown up to Geoffrey's room, the door of which Til opened, and, when Mr. Bowker had entered, shut it behind him. The noise of the closing door roused Geoffrey, and he turned in his bed, and, looking up, revealed such a worn and haggard face, that old Bowker stopped involuntarily, and drew a long breath, as he gazed on the miserable appearance of his friend. There must have been something comical in the rueful expression of Bowker's face, for old Geoff smiled feebly, as he said,

"Come in, William; come in, old friend! I've had a hard bout of it, old fellow, since you saw me; but there's no danger now—no infection, I mean, or any thing of that kind."

Geoff spoke haphazard; but what he had said was the best thing to restore Mr. Bowker to himself.

"Your William's fever-proof," he growled out in reply, "and don't fear any nonsense of that kind; and if he did, it's not that would keep him away from a friend's bedside. I should have been here—that is, if you'd have let me; and, oddly enough, though I'm such a rough old brute in general, I'm handy and quiet in times of sickness,—at least so I've been told;" and here Bowker stifled a great sigh. "But the first I heard of your illness was from your sister's letter, which I only got this morning."

"Give me your hand, William; I know that fast enough. But I didn't need any additional nursing. Til and the old lady—God bless them!—have pulled me through splendidly, and—But I'm beyond nursing now, William; what I want is—" and Geoff's voice failed him, and he stopped.

Old Bowker eyed him with tear-blurred vision for a moment, and then said, "What you want is—"

"Don't mind me just now, William; I'm horribly weak, and girlish, and trembling, but I shall get to it in time. What I want is, some man, some friend, to whom I can talk openly and unreservedly,—whose advice and aid I can seek, in such wretchedness as, I trust, but few have experienced.

It was a good thing that Geoffrey's strength had in some

degree returned, for Bowker clutched his hand in an iron grip, as in a dull low voice, he said, " Do you remember my telling you the story of my life ? Why did I tell you that ? Not for sympathy, but for example. I saw the rock on to which you were drifting, and hoped to keep you clear. I exposed the sadness of my life to you when the game was played out and there was no possibility of redemption. I can't tell what strait you may be in ; but if I can help you out of it, there is no mortal thing I will not do to aid you.

As well as he could Geoff returned the pressure ; then, after a moment's pause, said, " You know, of course, that my wife has left me ?"

Bowker bowed in acquiescence.

" You know the circumstances ?"

" I know nothing, Geoff, beyond the mere fact. Whatever talk there may be among such of the boys as I drop in upon now and then, if it turned upon you and your affairs, save in the matter of praising your art, it would be certain to be hushed as soon as I stepped in amongst them. They knew our intimacy, and they are by far too good fellows to say any thing that would pain me. So that beyond the mere fact which you have just stated, I know nothing."

Then in a low weak voice, occasionally growing full and powerful under excitement, and subsiding again into its faint tone, Geoffrey Ludlow told to William Bowker the whole history of his married life, beginning with his finding Margaret on the door-step, and ending by placing in his friend's hands the posthumous letter of Lord Caterham. Throughout old Bowker listened with rapt attention to the story, and when he came back from the window, to which he had stepped for the perusal of the letter, Geoffrey noticed that there were big tears rolling down his cheeks. He was silent for a minute or two after he had laid the letter on Geoffrey's bed ; when he spoke, he said, " We're a dull lot, the whole race of us ; and that's the truth. We pore over our own twopenny sorrows, and think that the whole army of martyrs could not show such a specimen as ourselves. Why, Geoff, dear old man, what was my punishment to yours ! What was,—but, however, I need not talk of that. You want my services— say how."

" I want your advice first, William. I want to know how

z

to—how to find my wife—for, O, to me she is my wife;
how to find Margaret. You'll blame me probably, and tell
me that I am mad—that I ought to cast her off altogether,
and to—But I cannot do that, William; I cannot do that;
for I love her—O my God, how I love her still!" And
Geoffrey Ludlow hid his face in his arms, and wept like a
child.

"I shan't blame you, Geoff, nor tell you any thing of the
kind," said old Bowker, in a deep low voice. "I should
have been very much surprised if—However, that's neither
here nor there. What we want is to find her now. You
say there's not been the slightest clue to her since she left
this house?"

"Not the slightest."

"She has not sent for any thing—clothes, or any thing?"

"For nothing, as I understand."

"She has not sent,—you see, one must understand these
things, Geoff; all our actions will be guided by them,—she
has not sent to ask about the child?"

Geoff shuddered for an instant, then said, "She has not."

"That simplifies our plans," said Bowker. "It is plain
now that we have only one chance of discovering her
whereabouts."

"And that is—"

"Through Blackett the detective, the man mentioned in
Lord Caterham's letter. He must be a sharp fellow; for
through the sheer pursuance of his trade, and without the
smallest help, he must have been close upon her trail, even
up to the night when you met her and withdrew her from
the range of his search. If he could learn so much unaided,
he will doubtless be able to strike again upon her track with
the information we can give him."

"There's no chance of this man—this Captain Brakespere,
having—I mean—now he's back, you know—having taken
means to hide her somewhere—where—one couldn't find
her, you know?" said Geoffrey, hesitatingly.

"If your William knows any thing of the world," replied
Bowker, "there's no chance of Captain Thingummy having
taken the least trouble about her. However, I'll go down to
Scotland Yard and see what is to be made of our friend
Inspector Blackett. God bless you, old boy! You know if
she is to be found, I'll do it."

They are accustomed to odd visitors in Scotland Yard; but the police-constables congregated in the little stone hall stared the next day when Mr. Bowker pushed open the swing-door, and calmly planting himself among them, ejaculated "Blackett." Looking at his beard, his singular garb, and listening to his deep voice, the sergeant to whom he was referred at first thought he was a member of some foreign branch of the force; then glancing at the general wildness of his demeanour, had a notion that he was one of the self-accused criminals who are so constantly forcing themselves into the grasp of justice, and who are so impatient of release; and finally, comprehending what he wanted, sent him, under convoy of a constable, through various long corridors, into a cocoa-nut-matted room furnished with a long green-baize-covered table, on which were spread a few sheets of blotting-paper, and a leaden inkstand, and the walls of which were adorned with a printed tablet detailing the disposition of the various divisions of the police-force, and the situation of the fire-escapes in the metropolis, and a fly-blown Stationers' Almanac. Left to himself, Mr. Bowker had scarcely taken stock of these various articles, when the door opened, and Mr. Inspector Blackett, edging his portly person through the very small aperture which he had allowed himself for ingress, entered the room, and closed the door stealthily behind him.

"Servant, sir," said he, with a respectful bow, and a glance at Bowker, which took in the baldness of his head, the thickness of his beard, the slovenliness of his apparel, and the very shape of his boots,—"servant, sir. You asked for me?"

"I did, Mr. Blackett. I've come to ask your advice and assistance in a rather delicate manner, in which you've already been engaged—Lord Caterham's inquiry."

"O, beg pardon, sir. Quite right. Friend of his lordship's, may I ask, sir?"

"Lord Caterham is dead, Mr.—"

"Quite right, sir; all right, sir. Right to be cautious in these matters; don't know who you are, sir. If you had not known that fact, must have ordered you out, sir. Imposter, of course. All on the square, Mr.—beg pardon; didn't mention your name, sir."

"My name is Bowker. To a friend of mine, too ill now

to follow the matter himself, Lord Caterham on his death-bed wrote a letter, detailing the circumstances under which he had employed you in tracing a young woman. That friend has himself been very ill, or he would have pursued this matter sooner. He now sends me to ask whether you have any news?"

"Beg pardon, sir; can't be too cautious in this matter. What may be the name of that friend?"

"Ludlow—Mr. Geoffrey Ludlow."

"Right you are, sir! Know the name well; have seen Mr. Ludlow at his lordship's; a pleasant gentleman too, sir, though not given me the idea of one to take much interest in such a business as this. However, I see we're all square on that point, sir; and I'll report to you as exactly as I would to my lord, if he'd been alive,—feeling, of course, that a gentleman's a gentleman, and that an officer's trouble will be remunerated—"

"You need not doubt that, Mr. Blackett."

"I don't doubt it, sir; more especially when you hear what I have got to tell. It's been a wearing business, Mr. Bowker, and that I don't deny; there have been many cases which I have tumbled-to quicker, and have been able to lay my finger upon parties quicker; but this has been a long chase; and though other members of the force has chaffed me, as it were, wanting to know when I shall be free for any thing else, and that sort of thing, there's been that excite-ment in it that I've never regretted the time bestowed, and felt sure I should hit at it last. My ideas has not been wrong in that partic'ler, Mr. Bowker; I *have* hit it at last!"

"The devil you have!"

"I have indeed, sir; and hit it, as has cur'ously happened in my best cases, by a fluke. It was by the merest fluke that I was at Radley's Hotel in Southampton and nobbled Mr. Sampson Hepworth, the absconding banker of Lombard Street, after Daniel Forester and all the city-men had been after him for six weeks. It was all a fluke that I was eatin' a Bath-bun at Swindon when the clerk that did them Post-office robberies tried to pass one of the notes to the refresh-ment gal. It was all a fluke that I was turning out of Grafton Street, after a chat with the porter of the Westminster Club,—which is an old officer of the G's and a pal of mine, —into Bond Street, when I saw a lady that I'd swear to, if

description's any use, though I never see her before, comin'
out of Long's Hotel."

" A lady !—Long's Hotel !"

" A lady a-comin' out of Long's Hotel. A lady with—not
to put too fine a point upon it—red hair and fine eyes and
a good figure ; the very moral of the description I got at
Tenby and them other places. I twigged all this before she
got her veil down ; and I said to myself, ' Blackett, that's
your bird, for a hundred pound.'"

" And were you right ? Was it—"

" Wait a minute, sir : let's take the things in the order in
which they naturally present themselves. She hailed a cab
and jumped in, all of a tremble like, as I could see. I
hailed another—hansom mine was ; and I give the driver the
office, which he tumbled-to at once—most of the West-enders
knows me ; and we follows the other until he turned up a
little street in Nottin' 'Ill, and I, marking where she got out,
stopped at the end of it. When she'd got inside, I walked up
and took stock of the house, which was a little milliner's and
stay-shop. It was cur'ous, wasn't it, sir," said Mr. Blackett,
with a grave professional smile, " that my good lady should
want a little job in the millinery line done for her just then,
and that she should look round into that very shop that
evening, and get friendly with the missis, which was a communicative kind of woman, and should pay her a trifle in
advance, and should get altogether so thick as to be asked
in to take a cup of tea in the back-parlour, and get a-talking
about the lodger? Once in, I'll back my old lady against
any ferret that was ever showed at Jemmy Welsh's. She
hadn't had one cup of tea before she know'd all about the
lodger; how she was the real lady, but dull and lonesome
like; how she'd sit cryin' and mopin' all day; how she'd no
visitors and no letters ; and how her name was Lambert, and
her linen all marked M. L. She'd only been there a day or
two then, and as she'd scarcely any luggage, the milliner was
doubtful about her money. My good lady came back that
night, and told me all this, and I was certain our bird was
caged. So I put one of our men regular to sweep a crossin'
during the daytime, and I communicated with the sergeant
of the division to keep the house looked after at night. But,
Lor' bless you, she's no intention of goin' away. Couldn't
manage it, I think, if she had ; for my missis, who's been up

several times since, says the milliner says her lodger's in a queer way, she thinks."

" How do you mean in a queer way ?" interrupted Bowker; " ill ?"

"Well, not exactly ill, I think, sir. I can't say exactly how, for the milliner's rather a stupid woman ; and it wouldn't do for my missis—though she'd find it out in a minute—to see the lady. As far as I can make out, it's a kind of fits, and she seems to have had 'em pretty bad—off her head for hours at a time, you know. It's rather cornered me, that has, as I don't exactly know how to act in the case ; and I went round to the Square to tell his lordship, and then found out what had happened. I was thinking of asking to see the Hearl—"

" The what, Mr. Blackett ?"

" The Hearl—Hearl Beauport, his lordship's father. But now you've come, sir, you'll know what to do, and what orders to give me."

" Yes, quite right," said Bowker, after a moment's consideration. " You must not see Lord Beauport; he's in a sad state of mind still, and any further worry might be dangerous. You've done admirably, Mr. Blackett,—admirably indeed ; and your reward shall be proportionate, you may take my word for that ; but I think it will be best to leave matters as they are until—at all events, until I have spoken to my friend. The name was Lambert, I think you said ; and what was the address ?"

" No. 102, Thompson Street, just beyond Nottin'-'Ill Gate; milliner's shop, name of Chapman. Beg your pardon, sir, but this is a pretty case, and one as has been neatly worked up ; you won't let it be spoilt by any amatoors ?"

" Eh ?—by what ? I don't think I understand you."

" You won't let any one go makin' inquiries on their own hook ? So many of our best cases is spoilt by amatoors shovin' their oars in."

" You may depend on that, Mr. Blackett ; the whole credit of the discovery is justly due to you, and you shall have it. Now good day to you; I shall find you here, I suppose, when next I want you ?"

Mr. Blackett bowed, and conducted his visitor through the hollow-sounding corridors, and bade him a respectful farewell at the door. Then, when William Bowker was alone, he stopped, and shook his head sorrowfully, muttering, " A bad job, a bad job ! God help you, Geoff, my poor fellow ! there's more trouble in store for you—more trouble in store !"

———◆◆———

CHAPTER VII.

TRACKED.

THE news which Mr. William Bowker had heard from Inspector Blackett troubled its recipient considerably, and it was not until he had thought it over deeply and consumed a large quantity of tobacco in the process, that he arrived at any settled determination as to what was the right course to be pursued by him. His first idea was to make Geoffrey Ludlow acquainted with the whole story, and let him act as he thought best; but a little subsequent reflection changed his opinion on this point. Geoff was very weak in health, certainly in no fit state to leave his bed ; and yet if he heard that Margaret was found, that her address was known, above all that she was ill, Bowker knew him well enough to be aware that nothing would prevent him at once setting out to see her, and probably to use every effort to induce her to return with him. Such a course would be bad in every way, but in the last respect it would be fatal. For one certain reason Bowker had almost hoped that nothing more might ever be heard of the wretched woman who had fallen like a curse upon his friend's life. He knew Geoffrey Ludlow root and branch, knew how thoroughly weak he was, and felt certain that, no matter how grievous the injury which Margaret had done him, he had but to see her again— to see her more especially in sickness and misfortune—to take her back to his heart and to his hearth, and defy the counsel of his friends and the opinion of the world. That would never do. Geoff had been sufficiently dragged down by this unfortunate infatuation ; but he had a future which should be independent of her, undimmed by any tarnish accruing to him from those wondrous misspent days. So old Bowker firmly believed ; and to accomplish that end he determined that none of Inspector Blackett's news should find its way to Geoffrey's ears, at all events until he, Bowker, had personally made himself acquainted with the state of affairs.

It must have been an impulse of the strongest friendship and love for Geoff that induced William Bowker to undertake this duty; for it was one which inspired him with aversion, not to say horror. At first he had some thoughts of asking Charley Potts to do it; but then he bethought him that Charley, headstrong, earnest, and impulsive as he was, was scarcely the man to be intrusted with such a delicate mission. And he remembered, moreover, that Charley was now to a great extent *lié* with Geoff's family, that he had been present at Geoff's first meeting with Margaret, that he had always spoken against her, and that now, imbued as he was likely to be with some of the strong feelings of old Mrs. Ludlow, he would be certain to make a mess of the mission, and, without the least intention of being offensive, would hurt some one's feelings in an unmistakable and unpardonable manner. No; he must go himself, horribly painful as it would be to him. His had been a set gray life for who should say how many years; he had not been mixed up with any woman's follies or griefs in ever so slight a degree, he had heard no woman's voice in plaintive appeal or earnest confession, he had seen no woman's tears or hung upon no woman's smile, since— since when? Since the days spent with *her*. Ah, how the remembrance shut out the present and opened up the long, long vistas of the past! He was no longer the bald-headed, grizzle-bearded, stout elderly man; he was young Bowker, from whom so much was expected; and the common tavern-parlour in which he was seated, with its beer-stained tables and its tobacco-reek faded away, and the long dusty roads of Andalusia, the tinkling bells of the mules, the cheery shouts of the sunburnt *arrieros*, the hard-earned pull at the *bota*, and the loved presence, now vanished for ever, rose in his memory.

When his musings were put to flight by the entrance of the waiter, he paid his score, and summoning up his resolution he went out into the noisy street, and mounting the first omnibus was borne away to his destination. He found the place indicated to him by Blackett—a small but clean and decent street—and soon arrived at Mrs. Chapman's house. There, at the door, he stopped, undecided what to do. He had not thought of any excuse for demanding an interview with Mrs. Chapman's lodger, and, on turning the subject over in his mind, he could not imagine any at all likely to be readily received. See Margaret he must; and to do that, he thought he must take her unprepared and on a sudden: if he sent up his name, he would certainly be refused admittance. His personal appearance was far too Bohemian in its character to enable him to pass himself off as her lawyer, or any friend of her family; his only hope was to put a bold front on it, to mention her name, and to walk straight on to her room, leaving it to chance to favour his efforts.

He entered the shop—a dull dismal little place, with a pair of stays lying helplessly in the window, and a staring black-eyed torso of a female doll, for cap-making purposes, insanely smiling on the counter. Such a heavy footfall as Mr. Bowker's was seldom heard in those vestal halls; such a grizzly-bearded face as Mr. Bowker's was seldom seen in such close proximity to the cap-making dummy; and little Mrs. Chapman the milliner came out "all in a tremble," as she afterwards expressed it, from her inner sanctum, which was about as big and as tepid as a warm-bath, and in a quavering voice demanded the intruder's business. She was a mild-eyed, flaxen-haired, quiet, frightened little woman, and old Bowker's heart softened towards her, as he said, " You have a friend of mine lodging with you, ma'am, I think—Mrs. Lambert?"

"O, dear; then, if you're a friend of Mrs. Lambert's, you're welcome here, I can assure you, sir !" and the little woman looked more frightened than ever, and held up her hands half in fear, half in relief.

"Ah, she's been ill, I hear," said Bowker, wishing to have it understood that he was thoroughly *en rapport* with the lodger.

" Ill !—I'm thankful you've come, sir !—no one, unless they saw her, would credit how ill she is—I mean to be up and about, and all that. She's better to-day, and clearer; but what she have been these few days past, mortal tongue cannot tell—all delirium-like, and full of fancies, and talking of things which set Hannah—the girl who does for me— and me nearly out of our wits with fright. So much so, that six-and-sixpence a-week is—well, never mind, poor thing ; it's worse for her than for us ; but I'm glad, at any rate, some friend has come to see her."

" I'll go and do so at once, Mrs. Chapman," said Bowker. " I know my way ; the door straight opposite to the front of the stairs, isn't it ? Thank you ; I'll find it ;" and with the last words yet on his tongue, Mr. Bowker had passed round the little counter, by the little milliner, and was making the narrow staircase creak again with his weight.

He opened the door opposite to him, after having knocked and received no answer, and peered cautiously in. The daylight was fading, and the blind of the window was half down, and Bowker's eyesight was none of the best now, so that he took some little time before he perceived the outline of a figure stretched in the white dimity-covered easy-chair by the little Pembroke table in the middle of the room. Although some noise had been made by the opening of the door, the figure had not moved ; it never stirred when Bowker gave a little premonitory cough to notify his advent ; it remained in exactly the same position, without stirring hand or foot, when Bowker said, "A friend has come to see you, Mrs.—Lambert." Then a dim un-defined sense of terror came upon William Bowker, and he closed the door silently behind him, and advanced into the room. Immediately he became aware of a faint sickly smell, a cloying, percolating odour, which seemed to fill the place ; but he had little time to think of this, for immediately before him lay the form of Margaret, her eyes closed, her features rigid, her long red hair falling in all its wild luxuriance over her shoulders. At first William thought she was dead ; but, stooping close over her, he marked her slow laboured breathing, and noticed that from time to time her hands were unclenched, and then closed again as tightly as ever. He took a little water from a tumbler on the table and sprinkled it on her face, and laid his finger on her pulse ; after a minute or two she opened her eyes, closing them again immediately, but after a time opening them again, and fixing them on Bowker's face with a long wistful gaze.

"Are you one of them also ?" she asked, in a deep hushed voice. "How many more to come and gibber and point at me ; or, worse than all, to sit mutely staring at me with pitiless unforgiving eyes! How many more? You are the latest. I have never seen you before."

"O yes you have," said Bowker quietly, with her hand in his, and his eyes steadfastly fixed on hers—"O yes you have : you recollect me, my dear Mrs. Ludlow."

He laid special stress on the name, and as he uttered the words, Margaret started, a new light flashed into her beautiful eyes, and she regarded him attentively.

"What was that you said?" she asked; "what name did you call me?"

"What name? Why, your own, of course; what else should I call you, my dear Mrs. Ludlow?"

She started again at the repetition, then her eyes fell, and she said dreamily,

"But that is not my name—that is not my name."

Bowker waited for a moment, and then said,

"You might as well pretend to have forgotten me and our talk at Elm Lodge that day that I came up to see Geoffrey."

"Elm Lodge! Geoffrey!—ah, good God, now I remember all!" said Margaret, in a kind of scream, raising herself in the chair, and wringing Bowker's hand.

"Hush, my dear Madam; don't excite yourself; I thought you would remember all; you—"

"You are Mr. Bowker!" said Margaret, pressing her hand to her head; "Mr. Bowker, whose story Geoff told me : Geoff! ah, poor, good Geoff! ah, dear, good Geoff! But why are you here? he hasn't sent you? Geoffrey has not sent you?"

"Geoffrey does not know I am here. He has been very ill; too ill to be told of all that has been going on; too ill to understand it, if he had been told. I heard by accident that you were living here, and that you had been ill; and I came to see if I could be of any service to you."

While he had been speaking, Margaret had sat with her head tightly clasped between her hands. When he finished, she looked up with a slightly dazed expression, and said, with an evident attempt at controlling her voice, "I see all now; you must pardon me, Mr. Bowker, for any incoherence or strangeness you may have noticed in my manner; but I have been very ill, and I feel sure that at times my mind wanders a little. I am better now. I was quite myself when you mentioned about **your having** heard of my illness, and offering me service ; and I thank you very sincerely for your kindness."

Old William looked at her for a minute, and then said,

" I am a plain-spoken man, Mrs. Ludlow—for you are Mrs. Ludlow to me—as I daresay you may have heard, if you have not noticed it yourself; and I tell you plainly that it is out of no kindness to you that I am here now, but only out of love for my dear old friend."

" I can understand that," said Margaret ; " and only respect you the more for it ; and now you are here, Mr. Bowker, I shall be very glad to say a few words to you,— the last I shall ever say regarding that portion of my life which was passed in—at—You know what I would say ; you have heard the story of the commencement of my acquaintance with Geoffrey Ludlow ?"

Bowker bowed in acquiescence.

" You know how I left him—why I am here ?"

Then William Bowker—the memory of all his friend's trouble and misery and crushed hopes and wasted life rising up strongly within him—set his face hard, and said, between his clenched teeth, " I know your history from two sources. Yesterday, Geoffrey Ludlow, scarce able to raise himself in his bed, so weak was he from the illness which your conduct brought upon him, told me, as well as he could, of his first meeting with you, his strange courtship, his marriage,—at which I was present,—of his hopes and fears, and all the intricacies of his married life ; of the manner in which, finally, you revealed the history of your previous life, and parted from him. Supplementing this story, he gave me to read a letter from Lord Caterham, the brother of the man you call your husband. This man, Captain Brakespere, flying from the country, had written to his brother, informing him that he had left behind him a woman who was called his mistress, but who was in reality his wife. To find this woman Lord Caterham made his care. He set the detectives to work, and had her tracked from place to place ; continually getting news of, but never finding her. While he lived, Lord Caterham never slackened from the pursuit ; finding his end approaching—"

" His end approaching !—the end of his life do you mean ?"

"He is dead. But before he died, he delegated the duty of pursuit, of all men in the world, to Geoffrey Ludlow,—to Geoffrey Ludlow, who, in his blind ignorance, had stumbled upon the very woman a year before, had saved her from a miserable death, and, all unknowingly, had fondly imagined he had made her his loving wife."

"Ah, my God, this is too much! And Geoffrey Ludlow knows all this?"

"From Geoffrey Ludlow's lips I heard it not twenty-four hours since."

Margaret uttered a deep groan and buried her face in her hands. When she raised her head her eyes were tear-blurred, and her voice faltered as she said, "I acknowledge my sin, and—so far as Geoffrey Ludlow is concerned—I deeply, earnestly repent my conduct. It was prompted by despair; it ended in desperation. Have those who condemned me—and I know naturally enough I am condemned by all his friends—have those who condemned me ever known the pangs of starvation, the grim tortures of house-lessness in the streets? Have they ever known what it is to have the iron of want and penury eating into their souls, and then to be offered a comfortable home and an honest man's love? If they have, I doubt very much whether they would have refused it. I do not say this to excuse myself. I have done Geoffrey Ludlow deadly wrong; but when I listened to his proffered protestations, I gave him time for reflection; when I said 'Yes' to his repeated vows, I thought that the dead past had buried its dead, and that no ghost from it would arise to trouble the future. I vowed to myself that I would be true to that man who had so befriended me; and I was true to him. The life I led was inexpressibly irksome and painful to me; the dead solemn monotony of it goaded me almost to madness at times; but I bore it—bore it all out of gratitude to him—would have borne it till now if *he* had not come back to lure me to destruction. I do not say I did my duty; I am naturally undomestic and unfitted for household management; but I brought no slur on Geoffrey Ludlow's name in thought or deed until that man returned. I have seen him, Mr. Bowker; I have spoken to him, and he spurned me from him; and yet I love him as I loved him years ago. He need only raise his finger, and I would fly to him and fawn upon him, and be grateful if he but smiled upon me in return. They cannot understand this—they cannot understand my disregard of the respectabilities by flinging away the position and the name and the repute, and all that which they had fitted to me, and which clung to me, ah, so irritatingly; but if all I have heard be true, you can understand it, Mr. Bowker,—you can.—Is Geoffrey out of danger?"

The sudden change in the tone of her voice, as she uttered the last sentence, struck on Bowker's ear, and looking up, he noticed a strange light in her eyes.

"Geoffrey is out of danger," he replied; "but he is still very weak, and requires the greatest care."

"And requires the greatest care!" she repeated. "Well, he'll get it, I suppose; but not from me. And to think that I shall never see him again! Poor Geoffrey! poor, good Geoffrey! How good he was, and how grave!—with those large earnest eyes of his, and his great head, and rough curling brown hair, and—the cruel cold, the pitiless rain, the cruel, cruel cold!" As she said these words, she crept back shivering into her chair, and wrapped her dress round her. William Bowker bent down and gazed at her steadily; but after an instant she averted her face, and hid it in the chair. Bowker took her hand, and it fell passively into his own; he noticed that it was burning.

"This will not do, Mrs. Ludlow!" he exclaimed; "you have over-excited yourself lately. You want rest and looking after—you must—" he stopped; for she had turned her head to him again and was rocking herself backwards and forwards in her chair, weeping meanwhile as though her heart would break. The sight was too much for William to bear unaided, and he opened the door and called Mrs. Chapman.

"Ah, sir," said the good little woman when she entered the room, "she's off again, I see. I knew she was, for I heard that awful sobbing as I was coming up the stairs. O, that awful sobbing that I've laid awake night after night listening to, and that never seemed to stop till daylight, when she was fairly wore out. But that's nothing, sir, compared to the talk when she's beside herself. Then she'd go on and say—"

"Yes, yes, no doubt, Mrs. Chapman," interrupted Bowker, who did not particularly wish to be further distressed by the narration of Margaret's sadness; "but this faintness, these weeping fits, are quite enough to demand the instant attention of a medical man. If you'll kindly look to her now, I'll go off and fetch a doctor; and if there's a nurse required —as I've little doubt there will be—you won't mind me intruding further upon you? No; I knew you'd say so. Mrs. Lambert's friends will ever be grateful to you; and here's something just to carry you on, you know, Mrs. Chapman—rent and money paid on her account, and that sort of thing." The something was two sovereigns, which had lain in a lucifer-match box used by Mr. Bowker as his bank, and kept by him in his only locked drawer for six weeks past, and which had been put aside for the purchase of a "tweed wrapper" for winter wear.

Deliberating within himself to what physician of eminence he should apply, and grievously hampered by the fact that he was unable to pay any fee in advance, Bowker suddenly bethought him of Dr. Rollit, whose great love of art and its professors led him, "in the fallow leisure of his life," to constitute himself a kind of honorary physician to the brotherhood of the brush. To him Bowker hastened, and, without divulging Margaret's identity, explained the case, and implored the doctor to see her at once. The doctor hesitated for a moment, for he was at his easel and in a knot. He had "got something that would not come right," and he scarcely seemed inclined to move until he had conquered his difficulty; but after explaining the urgency of the case, old Bowker took the palette and sheaf of brushes from the physician's hand and said, "I think we can help each other at this moment, doctor: go you and see the patient, and leave me to deal with this difficulty. You'll find me here when you come back, and you shall then look at your canvas."

But when Dr. Rollit, after a couple of hours' absence, returned, he did not look at his picture—at least on his first entry. He looked so grave and earnest that William Bowker, moving towards him to ask the result of his visit, was frightened, and stopped.

"What is the matter?" he asked; "you seem—"

"I'm a little taken aback—that's all, old friend," said the doctor; "you did not prepare me to find in my patient an old acquaintance—you did not know it, perhaps?"

"By Jove! I remember now: Charley Potts said—What an old ass I am!"

"I was called in by Potts and Ludlow, or rather called out of a gathering of the Titians, to attend Mrs. Lambert, as the landlady called her, nearly two years ago. She is not much altered—outwardly—since I left her convalescent."

"You lay a stress on 'outwardly'—what is the inner difference?"

"Simply that her health is gone, my good fellow; her whole constitution utterly shattered; her life not worth a week's purchase."

"Surely you're wrong, doctor. Up to within the last few weeks her health has been excellent."

"My dear William Bowker, I, as an amateur, meddle with your professional work; but what I do is on the surface, and the mistakes I make are so glaring, that they are recognisable instantly. You might meddle, as an amateur, with mine, and go pottering on until you'd killed half a parish, without any body suspecting you. The disease I attended Mrs.— there! it's absurd our beating about the bush any longer—Mrs. Ludlow for was rheumatic fever, caught from exposure to cold and damp. The attack I now find left behind it, as it generally does, a strong predisposition to heart-disease, which, from what I learn from her, seems to have displayed itself in spasms and palpitations very shortly afterwards."

"From what you learn from her? She was sensible, then, when you saw her?"

"She was sensible before I left her; ay, and that's the deuce of it. Partly to deaden the pain of these attacks, partly, as she said herself just now, to escape from thought, she has had recourse to a sedative, morphia, which she has taken in large quantities. I smelt it the instant I entered her room, and found the bottle by her side. Under this influence she is deadened and comatose; but when the reaction comes — Poor creature! poor creature!" and the kind-hearted doctor shook his head sadly.

"Do you consider her in absolute danger?" asked Bowker, after a pause.

"My dear fellow it is impossible to say how long she may last; but—though I suppose that's out of the question now, eh?—people will talk, you know, and I've heard rumours;—

but if her nusband wished to see her, I should say fetch him at once."

" If her husband wished to see her!" said old Bowker to himself, as he walked away towards his lodgings,--"if her husband wished to see her! He don't—at least the real one don't, I imagine; and Geoff mustn't; though, if he knew it, nothing would keep him away. But that other—Captain Brakespere—he ought to know the danger she's in; he ought to have the chance of saying a kind word to her before—He must be a damned villain!" said old William, stopping for an instant, and pondering over the heads of the story; " but he deserves that chance, and he shall have it."

Pursuant to his determination, Mr. Bowker presented himself the next day at Long's Hotel, where he recollected Mr. Blackett had informed him that Captain Brakespere was stopping. The porter, immediately divining from Mr. Bowker's outward appearance that he meditated a raid upon coats, hats, or any thing that might be lying about the coffee-room, barricaded the entrance with his waistcoat, and parleyed with the visitor in the hall. Inquiring for Captain Brakespere, Mr. Bowker was corrected by the porter, who opined " he meant Lord Catrum." The correction allowed and the inquiry repeated, the porter replied that his "lordship had leff," and referred the inquirer to St. Barnabas Square.

To St. Barnabas Square Mr. Bowker adjourned, but there learned that Lord Caterham had left town with Mr. Barford, and would not be back for some days.

And meanwhile the time was wearing by, and Margaret's hold on life was loosening day by day. Would it fail altogether before she saw the man who had deceived her so cruelly? would it fail altogether before she saw the man whom she had so cruelly deceived?

CHAPTER VIII.

IN THE DEEP SHADOW.

IN the presence of the double sorrow which had fallen upon her, Annie Maurice's girlhood died out. Arthur was gone, and Geoffrey in so suffering a condition of body

2 A

and mind that it would have been easier to the tender-hearted girl to know that he was at rest, even though she had to face all the loneliness which would then have been her lot. Her position was very trying in all its aspects at this time; for there was little sympathy with her new sorrow at the great house which she still called home, and where she was regarded as decidedly "odd." Lady Beauport considered that Caterham had infected her with some of his strange notions, and that her fancy for associating with "queer" people, removed from her own sphere not more by her heiress-ship than by her residence in an earl's house and her recognition as a member of a noble family, was charge-able to the eccentric notions of her son. Annie came and went as she pleased, free from comment, though not from observation; but she was of a sensitive nature; she could not assert herself, and she suffered from the consciousness that her grief, her anxiety, and her constant visits to Lowbar were regarded with mingled censure and contempt. Her pre-occupation of mind prevented her noticing many things which otherwise could not have escaped her attention; but when Geoffrey's illness ceased to be actively dangerous, and the bulletin brought her each morning from Til by the hands of the faithful Charley contained more tranquillising but still sad accounts of the patient, she began to observe an air of mystery and preparation in the household. The few hours which she forced herself to pass daily in the society of Lady Beauport had been very irksome to her since Arthur died, and she had been glad when they were curtailed by Lady Beauport's frequent plea of "business" in the evenings, and her leaving the drawing-room for her own apartments. Every afternoon she went to Elm Lodge, and her presence was eagerly hailed by Mrs. Ludlow and Til. She had seen Geoffrey frequently during the height of the fever; but since the letter she had kept in such faithful custody had reached his hands she had not seen him. Though far from even the vaguest conjecture of the nature of its contents, she had dreaded the effect of receiving a communication from his dead friend on Geoffrey Ludlow, and had been much relieved when his mother told her, on the following day, that he was very calm and quiet, but did not wish to see any one for a few days. Bowker and he had fully felt the embarrassment of the position in which Lord Caterham's revelation had placed Geoffrey with regard to Annie Maurice, and the difficulties which the complications produced by Margaret's identity with Lionel Brakespere's wife added to Ludlow's fulfilment of Caterham's trust. They had agreed—or rather Bowker had suggested, and Geoffrey had acquiesced, with the languid assent of a mind too much enfeebled by illness and sorrow to be capable of facing any difficulty but the inevitable, immediate, and pressing—that Annie need know nothing for the present.

"She could hardly come here from the Beauports, Geoff," Bowker had said; "it's all nonsense, of course, to men like you and me, who look at the real, and know how its bitterness takes all the meaning out of the rubbish they call rules of society; but the strongest woman is no freer than Gulliver in his fetters of packthread, in the conventional world she lives in. We need not fret her sooner than it must be done, and you had better not see her for the present."

So Annie came and went for two or three days and did not see Geoffrey. Mrs. Ludlow, having recovered from the sudden shock of her son's illness and the protracted terror of his danger, had leisure to feel a little affronted at his desire for seclusion, and to wonder audibly why *she* should be supposed to do him more harm than Mr. Bowker.

"A big blundering fellow like that, Til," she said; "and I do assure you, Miss Maurice, he quite forgot the time for the draught when he was shut up there with him the other day—and talk of *he's* doing Geoffrey no harm! All I can say is, if Geoffrey had not been crying when I went into his room, and wasn't trembling all over in his bed, I never was so mistaken before."

Then Til and Annie looked blankly at each other, in mute wonder at this incomprehensible sorrow — for the women knew nothing but that Margaret had fled with a former lover — so much had been necessarily told them, under Bowker's instructions, by Charley Potts; and Annie, after a little, went sorrowfully away.

That day at dinner Lord Beauport was more than usually kind in his manner to her; and Annie considered it due to him, and a fitting return for some inquiries he had made for "her friend," which had more of warmth and less of condescension than usual in their tone, to rouse herself into greater cheerfulness than she had yet been able to assume.

2 A 2

Lady Beauport rose sooner than usual; and the two ladies had hardly seated themselves in the dreary drawing-room when the Earl joined them. There was an air of preparation in Lord Beauport's manner, and Annie felt that something had happened.

The thing which had happened was this—Lady Beauport had not miscalculated her experienced power of managing her husband. She had skilfully availed herself of an admission made by him that Lionel's absence, at so great a distance just then was an unfortunate complication; that the necessary communications were rendered difficult and tedious; and that he wished his "rustication" had been nearer home. The Countess caught at the word 'rustication:' then not expulsion, not banishment, was in her husband's mind. Here was a commutation of her darling's sentence; a free pardon would follow, if she only set about procuring it in the right way. So she resorted to several little expedients by which the inconvenience of the heir's absence was made more and more apparent: having once mentioned his name, Lord Beauport continued to do so;—perhaps he was in his secret heart as much relieved by the breaking of the ban as the mother herself;—and at length, on the same day which witnessed William Bowker's visit to Lionel Brakespere's deserted wife, Lady Beauport acknowledged to her husband that their son was then in London, and that she had seen him. The Earl received her communication in frowning silence; but she affected not to observe his manner, and expatiated, with volubility very unusual to her, upon the fortunate concurrence of circumstances which had brought Lionel to England just as his improved position made it more than ever probable he would be perfectly well received.

"That dear Mr. Barford," she said—and her face never changed at the name of the man in whose arms her son had died so short a time before—"assures me that every one is delighted to see him. And really, George, he mustn't stay at Long's, you know—it looks so bad—for every one knows he's in town; and if we don't receive him properly, that will be just the way to rake up old stories. I'm sure they're old enough to be forgotten; and many a young man has done worse than Lionel, and—"

"Stop, Gertrude," said Lord Beauport sternly; "stick to

the truth, if you please. I hope very few young men in our
son's position have disgraced it and themselves as he has
done. The truth is, that we have to make the best of a
misfortune. He has returned; and by so doing has added
to the rest a fresh rascality by breaking his pledged word.
Circumstances oblige me to acquiesce,—luck is on his side,
— his brother's death—" Lord Beauport paused for a
moment, and an expression, hitherto unfamiliar, but which
his wife frequently saw in the future, flitted over his face—
"his brother's death leaves me no choice. Let us say as
little as possible on this subject. He had better come here,
for every reason. For appearances' sake it is well; and he
will probably be under some restraint in this house." Here
the Earl turned to leave the room, and said slowly as he
walked towards the door, "Something tells me, Gertrude,
that in Arthur's death, which we dreaded too little and
mourn too lightly, we have seen only the beginning of evils."

Lady Beauport sat very still and felt very cold after he
left her. Conscience smote her dumbly,—in days to come
it would find a voice in which to speak,—and fear fell upon
her. "I will never say any thing to him about Annie
Maurice," she said to herself, as the first effect of her
husband's words began to pass away; "I do believe he
would be as hard on Lionel as poor Arthur himself, and
warn the girl against him."

How relieved she felt as she despatched a note to Lionel
Brakespere, telling him she had fulfilled her task, and
inviting him to return to his father's house when he pleased!

Assuredly the star of the new heir was in the ascendant;
his brother was dead, his place restored to him, and society
ready to condone all his "follies,"—which is the fashionable
synonym for the crimes of the rich and the great. If Lionel
Brakespere could have seen "that cursed woman"—as in
his brutal anger he called his wife a hundred times over, as
he fretted and fumed over the remembrance of their interview
—as William Bowker saw her that day,—he would have
esteemed himself a luckier fellow still than he did when he
lighted his cigar with his mother's note, and thought how
soon he would change that "infernal dull old hole" from
what it was in Caterham's time, and how he would have
every thing his own way now.

Such, as far as his knowledge of them extended, **and**

without any comment or expression of opinion of his own, were the circumstances which Lord Beauport narrated to Annie. She received his information with an indescribable pang, compounded of a thousand loving remembrances of Arthur and a keen resuscitation by her memory of the scene of Lionel's disgrace, to which she and her lost friend had been witnesses. She could hardly believe, hardly understand it all; and the clearest thought which arose above the surging troubled sea within her breast was, that the place which knew Arthur no more would be doubly empty and desolate when Lionel should fill it.

The tone in which Lord Beauport had spoken was grave and sad, and he had confined himself to the barest announcement. Annie had listened in respectful silence; but though she had not looked directly at her, she was conscious of Lady Beauport's reproachful glances, addressed to her husband, as he concluded by saying coldy,

"You were present, Annie, by my desire, when I declared that that which is now about to happen should never be, and I have thought it necessary to explain to you a course of conduct on my part which without explanation would have appeared very weak and inconsistent. As a member of *my* family you are entitled to such an explanation; and indeed, as an inmate of this house, you are entitled to an apology."

"Thank you, my lord," said Annie, in a voice which, though lower than usual, was very firm.

This was more than Lady Beauport's pride could bear. She began, fiercely enough,

"Really, Lord Beauport, I cannot see—"

But at that moment a servant opened the door and announced

"Lord Caterham."

The group by the fireside stood motionless for a moment, as Lionel, dressed in deep mourning, advanced towards them with well-bred ease and perfect unconcern. Then Lady Beauport threw herself into his arms; and Annie, hardly noticing that Lord Beauport had by an almost involuntary movement stretched out his hand to the handsome prodigal, glided past the three, hurried to her own room, and, having locked the door, sank down on her knees beside her bed in an agony of grief.

Three days elapsed, during which events marched with a
steady pace at Elm Lodge and at the lodging were the
woman who had brought such wreck and ruin within that
tranquil-looking abode was lying contending with grief and
disease, dying the death of despair and exhaustion. When
Bowker returned from his unsuccessful quest for Lionel
Brakespere, he found that she had passed into another phase
of her malady,—was quiet, dreamy, and apparently forgetful
of the excitement she had undergone. She was lying quite
still on her bed, her eyes half closed, and a faint unmeaning
smile was on her lips.

" I have seen her so for hours and hours, sir," said the
gentle little landlady ; " and it's my belief it's what she takes
as does it."

So Bowker concluded that Margaret had found means to
avail herself of the fatal drug from which she had sought
relief so often and so long, in the interval of depression
which had succeeded the delirium he had witnessed. He
was much embarrassed now to know how to proceed. She
required better accommodation and careful nursing, and he
was determined she should have both,—but how that was
to be managed was the question ; and Bowker, the most
helpless man in the world in such matters, was powerless
to answer it. He had never imagined, as he had turned the
probabilities over and over in his mind, that such a complication as severe physical illness would arise ; and it routed
all his plans, besides engaging all his most active sympathies.
William Bowker had an extreme dread, indeed a positive
terror, of witnessing bodily suffering in women and children;
and had his anger and repulsion towards Margaret been far
greater than they were, they would have yielded to pain and
pity as he gazed upon the rigid lines of the pale weary face,
from which the beauty was beginning to fade and drop away
in some mysterious manner of vanishing, terrible to see and
feel, but impossible to describe. He made the best pro-
visional arrangements within his power, and went away,
promising Mrs. Chapman that he would return on the
following day to meet the doctor, and turned his steps in
much mental bewilderment towards the abode of Charley
Potts, purposing to consult him in the emergency, previous
to their proceeding together to Lowbar.

" I can't help it now," he thought ; " the women cannot

possibly be kept out of the business any longer. If she were
let to want any thing, and had not every care taken of her,
dear old Geoff would never forgive any of us ; and it could
not be hidden from him.   I am sure she's dying ; and—I'm
glad of it: glad for her sake, poor wretched creature ; and O
so glad for his ! He will recover her death—he *must;* but I
doubt whether he would recover her life.   He would be for
ever hankering after her, for ever remembering the past, and
throwing away the remainder of his life, as he has thrown
away too much of it already.   No, no, dear old Geoff, this
shall not be, if your William can save you.   I know what a
wasted life means ; and you shall put yours out at good
interest, Geoff, please God."

Charley was at home ; and he received Mr. Bowker's
communication with uncommon gravity, and immediately
bestowed his best attention upon considering what was to
be done.   He was not in the least offended by discovering
that it had not been his William's intention to tell him
any thing about it.   " Quite right too," he observed.   " I
should have been of no use, if every thing had not been
capsized by her illness ; and I don't like to know any thing
I'm not to tell to Til.   Not that she's in the least inquisitive,
you know,—don't make any mistake about that,—but things
are in such an infernally mysterious mess ; and then they
only know enough to make them want to know more ; and
I shouldn't like, under these circumstances—it would seem
hypocritical, don't you see—and every thing must come out
sometime, eh ?"

" O yes, I see," said Bowker drily ; "but I have to tell
you *now*, Charley ; for what the devil's to be done ? You
can't bring her here and nurse her ; and I can't bring her to
my place and nurse her,—yet she must be taken somewhere
and nursed ; and we must be prepared with a satisfactory
account of every thing we have done, when Geoff gets well ;
and what are we to do ?"

Mr. Potts did not answer for a few moments, but handed
over the beer in an absent manner to Mr. Bowker; then,
starting up from the table on which he had been sitting, he
exclaimed,

" I have it, William.   Let's tell the women—Til, I mean,
and Miss Maurice.   They'll know all about it, bless you,"
said Charley, whose confidence in female resources was

unbounded. "It's all nonsense trying to keep things dark, when they've got to such a pass as this. If Mrs. Ludlow's in the state you say, she will not live long ; and then Geoff's difficulty, if not his trouble, will be over. Her illness alters every thing. Come on, Bowker; let's get on to Elm Lodge; tell Til, and Miss Maurice, if she's there ; and let them make proper arrangements."

"But, Charley," said Bowker, much relieved, in spite of his misgivings, by the suggestion, "you forget one important point. Miss Maurice is Brakespere's cousin, and she lives in his father's house. It won't do to bring her in."

"Never you mind that, William," replied the impetuous Charley. Til can't act alone ; and old Mrs. Ludlow is nervous, and would not know what to do, and must not be told ; and I am sure Miss Maurice doesn't care a rap about her cousin—the ruffian—why should she? And I know she would do any thing in the world, no matter how painful to herself, and no matter whether he ever came to know it or not, that would serve or please Geoff."

"Indeed !" said Bowker, in a tone half of inquiry, half of susprise, and looking very hard at Charley ; "and how do you know that, eh, Charley?"

"O, bother," answered that gentleman, "I don't know how I know it ; but I do know it ; and I am sure the sooner we act on my knowledge the better. So come along."

So saying, Mr. Potts made his simple out-door toilet ; and the two gentlemen went out, and took their way towards the resort of omnibuses, eagerly discussing the matter in hand as they went, and Mr. Bowker finding himself unexpectedly transformed from the active into the passive party.

It was agreed between them that Geoffrey should not be informed of Bowker's presence in the house, as he would naturally be impatient to learn the result of the mission with which he had intrusted him ; and that result it was their present object to conceal.

Fortune favoured the wishes of Bowker and Charley. Mrs. Ludlow was with her son ; and in the drawing-room, which was resuming somewhat of its former orderly and pleasant appearance, they found Miss Maurice and Til. The two girls were looking sad and weary, and Til was hardly brightened up by Charley's entrance, for he looked so much more grave than usual, that she guessed at once he had heard something new and important. The little party were too vitally interested in Geoffrey and his fortunes, and the occasion was too solemn for any thing of ceremony ; and when Charley Potts had briefly introduced Bowker to Annie Maurice, he took Til's hand in his, and said,

"Til, Geoffrey's wife has been found—alone, and very ill —dying, as we believe !"

"You are quite sure, William ?"

"I am quite sure, Geoffrey. Do you think I would deceive you, or take any thing for granted myself, without seeing and hearing what is so important to you ? She is well cared for in every respect. Your own care, when she needed it before, was not more tender or more effective. Be satisfied, dear old Geoff; be content."

"You saw her—you really saw her ; and she spoke kindly of me ?" asked Geoffeey with a pitiable eagerness which pained Bowker to witness.

"I did. Yes, have I not told you again and again—" Then there was a moment's silence ; and Bowker thought, if she were not dying, how terrible this tenderness towards her would be, how inexplicable to all the world but him, how ruinous to Geoffrey ; but as it was, it did not matter: it would soon be only the tenderness of memory, the pardon of the grave.

Geoffrey was sitting in an arm-chair by the bedroom window which overlooked the pretty flower-garden and the lawn. He was very weak still, but health was returning, and with it the power of acute mental suffering, which severe bodily illness mercifully deadens. This had been a dreadful day to him. When he was able to sit up and look around the room from which all the graceful suggestive traces of a woman's presence had been carefully removed; when he saw the old home look upon every thing before his eyes (for whom the idea of home was for ever desecrated and destroyed), the truth presented itself to him as it had never before done, in equal horror and intensity, since the day the woman he loved had struck him a blow by her words which had nearly proved mortal. Would it had been so ! he thought, as his large brown eyes gazed wearily out upon the lawn and the flower-beds, and then were turned upon the familiar objects in the chamber, and closed with a shudder. His large frame look gaunt and worn, and his hands rested listlessly upon the sides of his chair. He had requested them to leave him alone for a little, that he might rest previous to seeing Bowker.

From the window at which Geoffrey sat he could see the nurse walking monotonously up and down the gravel-walk which bounded his little demesne with the child in her arms. Sometimes she stopped to pluck a flower and give it to the baby, who would laugh with delight and then throw it from him. Geoffrey watched the pair for a little, and then turned his head wearily away and put his question to Bowker, who was seated beside him, and who looked at him furtively with glances of the deepest concern.

"You shall hear how she is, Geoff,—how circumstanced, how cared for, and by whom, from one who can tell you the story better than I can. Your confidence has not been misplaced." Geoffrey turned upon him the nervous anxious gaze which is so touching to see in the eyes of one who has lately neared the grave, and still seems to hover about its brink. William Bowker proceeded: "You have not asked for Miss Maurice lately. I daresay you felt too much oppressed by the information in Lord Caterham's letter, too uncertain of the future, too completely unable to make up your mind what was to be done about her, to care or wish to see her. She has been here as usual, making herself as useful as possible, and helping your mother and sister in every conceivable way. But she has done more for you than that, Geoff; and if you are able to see her now, I think you had better hear it all from herself."

With these words Bowker hurried out of the room; and in a few minutes Annie Maurice, pale, quiet, and self-possessed, came in, and took her seat beside Geoffrey.

What had she come to tell him? What had she been doing for the help and service of her early friend,—she, this young girl so unskilled in the world's ways, so lonely, so dependent hitherto,—who now looked so womanly and sedate,—in whose brown eyes he saw such serious thought, such infinite sweetness and pity,—whose deep mourning dress clothed her slender figure with a sombre dignity new to it, and on whom a nameless change had passed, which Geoffrey had eyes to see now, and recognised even in that moment of painful emotion with wonder.

Calmly, carefully subduing every trace of embarrassment for his sake, and in a business-like tone which precluded the necessity for any preliminary explanation, Annie told Geoffrey Ludlow that she had been made aware of the circumstances which had preceded and caused his illness. She touched lightly upon her sorrow and her sympathy, but passed on to the subject of Caterham's letter. Geoffrey listened to her in silence, his head turned away and his eyes covered with his hand. Annie went on :

"I little thought, Geoffrey, when I was so glad to find that you were well enough to read Arthur's letter, and when I only thought of fulfilling so urgent a request as soon as I could, and perhaps diverting your mind into thoughts of our dear dead friend, that I was to be the means of making all this misery plain and intelligible. But it was so, Geoffrey; and I now see that it was well. Why Arthur should have selected you to take up the search after his death I cannot tell,—I suppose he knew instinctively your fidelity and true-heartedness; but the accident was very fortunate, for it identified your interests and mine, it made the fulfilment of his trust a sacred duty to me, and enabled me to do with propriety what no one else could have done, and what she— what Margaret—would not have accepted from another."

Geoffrey started, let his hand fall from his face, and caught hers. "Is it you, then, Annie?"

"Yes, yes," she said, "it is I, Geoffrey; do not agitate yourself, but listen to me. When Mr. Bowker found Margaret, as you know he did, she was very ill, and—she had no protector and no money. What could he do? He did the best thing; he told me, to whom Arthur's wishes were sacred, who would have done the same had you never existed—you know I am rich and free; and I made all the needful arrangements for her at once. When all was ready for her reception—it is a pretty house at Sydenham, Geoffrey, and she is as well cared for as any one can be—I went to her, and told her I was come to take her home."

"And she—Margaret—did she consent? Did she think it was I who—"

"Who sent me?" interrupted Annie. "No,—she would not have consented; for her feeling is that she has so wronged you that she must owe nothing to you any more. In this I know she is quite wrong; for to know that she was

in any want or suffering would be still worse grief to you,—
but that can never be,—and I did not need to contradict
her. I told her I came to her in a double character; that
of her own friend—though she had not had much friendship
for me, Geoffrey; but that is beside the question—and—and
—" here she hesitated for a moment, but then took courage
and went on, "that of her husband's cousin." Geoffrey
ground his teeth, but said never a word. She continued,
with deepening light in her eyes and growing tenderness in
her voice, " I told her how Arthur, whom I loved, had
sought for her,—how a strange fatality had brought them in
contact, neither knowing how near an interest each had in
the other. She knew it the day she fainted in his room, but
he died without knowing it, and so dying left her, as I told
her I felt she was, a legacy to me. She softened then,
Geoffrey, and she came with me."

Here Annie paused, as if expecting he would speak, but
he did not. She glanced at him, but his face was set and
rigid, and his eyes were fixed upon the walk, where the
nurse and child still were.

"She is very ill, Geoffrey," Annie went on ; "very weak
and worn, and weary of life. I am constantly with her, but
sometimes she is unable or unwilling to speak to me. She
is gloomy and reserved, and suffers as much in mind as in
body, I am sure."

Geoffrey said slowly, "Does she ever speak to you of
me ?"

Annie replied, "Not often. When she does, it is always
with the greatest sorrow for your sorrow, and the deepest
sense of the injury she has done you. I am going to her to-
day, Geoffrey, and I should like to take to her an assurance
of your forgiveness. May I tell Margaret that you forgive
her ?"

He turned hastily, and said with a great gasp, "O Annie,
tell her that I love her !"

"I will tell her that," the girl said gently and sadly, and
an expression of pain crossed her face. She thought of
the love that had been wasted, and the life that had been
blighted.

"What is she going to do ?" asked Geoffrey ; "how is it
to be in the future ?" This was a difficult question for
Annie to answer : she knew well what lay in the future ; but

she dreaded to tell Geoffrey, even while she felt that the wisest, the easiest, the best, and the most merciful solution of the terrible dilemma in which a woman's ungoverned passion had placed so many innocent persons was surely and not slowly approaching.

"I don't know, Geoffrey," she said; "I cannot tell you. Nothing can be decided upon until she is better, and you are well enough to advise and direct us. Try and rest satisfied for the present. She is safe, no harm can come to her; and I am able and willing to befriend her now as you did before. Take comfort, Geoffrey; it is all dreadful; but if we had not found her, how much worse it would have been!"

At this moment the nurse carried her charge out of their sight, as she came towards the house, and Annie, thinking of the more than motherless child, wondered at the no-meaning of her own words, and how any thing could have been worse than what had occurred.

She and Geoffrey had spoken very calmly to each other, and there had been no demonstration of gratitude to her on his part; but it would be impossible to tell the thankfulness which filled his heart. It was a feeling of respite which possessed him. The dreadful misfortune which had fallen upon him was as real and as great as ever; but he could rest from the thought of it, from its constant torture, now that he knew that she was safe from actual physical harm; now that no awful vision of a repetition of the destitution and misery from which he had once rescued her, could come to appal him. Like a man who, knowing that the morrow will bring him a laborious task to do, straining his powers to the utmost, inexorable and inevitable in its claims, covets the deep rest of the hours which intervene between the present and the hour which must summon him to his toil, Geoffrey, in the lassitude of recent illness, in the weakness of early convalescence, rested from the contemplation of his misery. He had taken Annie's communication very quietly; he had a sort of feeling that it ought to surprise him very much, that the circumstances were extraordinary, that the chain of events was a strangely-wrought one—but he felt little surprise; it was lurking somewhere in his mind, he would feel it all by and by, no doubt; but nothing beyond relief was very evident to him in his present state. He wondered, indeed, how it was with Annie herself; how the brave, devoted, and unselfish girl had been able, trammelled as she was by the rules and restrictions of a great house, to carry out her benevolent designs, and dispose of her own time after her own fashion. There was another part of the subject which Geoffrey did not approach even in his thoughts. Bowker had not told him of Margaret's entreaties that she might see Lionel Brakespere; he had not told him that the young man had returned to his father's house; and he made no reference to him in his consideration of Annie's position. He had no notion that the circumstances in which Lord Caterham had entreated his protection for Annie had already arisen.

"How is it that you can do all this unquestioned, Annie?" he asked; "how can you be so much away from home?"

She answered him with some embarrassment. "It was difficult—a little—but I knew I was right, and I did not suffer interference. When you are quite well, Geoffrey, I want your advice for myself. I have none else, you know, since Arthur died."

"He knew that, Annie; and the purport of the letter which told me such a terrible story was to ask me in all things to protect and guide you. He little knew that he had the most effectual safeguard in his own hands; for, Annie, the danger he most dreaded for you was association with his brother."

"That can never be," she said vehemently. "No matter what your future course of action may be, Geoffrey, whether you expose him or not—in which, of course, you will consider Margaret only—I will never live under the same roof with him. I must find another home, Geoffrey, let what will come of it, and let them say what they will."

"Caterham would have been much easier in his mind, Annie," said Geoffrey, with a sad smile, "if he had known how baseless were his fears that his brother would one day win your heart."

"There never could have been any danger of that, Geoffrey," said Annie, with a crimson blush, which had not subsided when she took her leave of him.

CHAPTER IX.

CLOSING IN.

THE porter at Lord Beauport's mansion in St. Barnabas Square became so familiarised with Mr. Bowker's frequent visits as at length to express no surprise at the sight of the "hold cove," who daily arrived to inquire whether any tidings of Lord Caterham had been received. Although the porter's experience of life had been confined to London, his knowledge of the ways of men was great ; and he was perfectly certain that this pertinacious inquirer was no dun, no tradesman with an overdue account, no begging letter-writer or imposter of any kind. What he was the porter could not tell ; mentioned, in casual chat with the footman waiting for the carriage to come round, that he could not "put a name" to him, but thought from his "rum get-up" that he was either in the picture-selling or the money-lending line.

"Undeterred by, because ignorant of, the curiosity which his presence excited—and indeed it may be assumed that, had he been aware of it, his actions would have been very little influenced thereby—old William Bowker attended regularly every day at the St. Barnabas-Square mansion, and having asked his question and received his answer, adjourned to the nearest tavern for his lunch of bread-and-cheese and beer, and then puffing a big meerschaum pipe, scaled the omnibus which conveyed him to London Bridge, whence he took the train for the little house at Sydenham. They were always glad to see him there, even though he brought no news ; and old Mrs. Ludlow especially found the greatest comfort in pouring into his open ears the details of the latest experience of her "cross." William Bowker to such recitals was a splendid listener ; that is to say, he could nod his head and throw in an " Indeed !" or a " Really !" exactly at the proper moment, while all the time his thoughts were far away, occupied with some important matter. He saw Til occasionally, and sometimes had flying snatches of talk with Annie Maurice in the intervals of her attendance on the invalid. Bowker did not meet Charley Potts very frequently, although that gentleman was a regular visitor at

Sydenham whenever Mrs. Ludlow and Til were there ; but it was not until the evening that Mr. Potts came, for he was diligently working away at his commissions and growing into great favour with Mr. Caniche ; and besides, he had no particular interest in Miss Maurice ; and so long as he arrived in time to escort Miss Til and her mother back to London Bridge and to put them into the Lowbar omnibus, he was content, and was especially grateful for the refreshing sleep which always came upon old Mrs. Ludlow in the train.

At length, when many weary days had worn themselves away, and Geoffrey was beginning to feel his old strength returning to him, and with it the aching void which he had experienced on regaining consciousness daily increasing in intensity, and when Margaret's hold on life had grown very weak indeed, old William Bowker, making his daily inquiry of Lord Beauport's porter, was informed that Lord Caterham had returned the previous afternoon, and was at that moment at breakfast. Then, with great deliberation, Mr. Bowker unbuttoned his coat and from an inner breast-pocket produced an old. leather pocket-book, from which, among bits of sketches and old envelopes, he took a card, and pencilling his name thereon, requested the porter to give it to Lord Caterham.

The porter looked at the card, and then said jocosely, " You ain't wrote your business on it, then ? 'Spose you couldn't do that, eh ? Well, you are a plucked 'un, you are, and I like you for it, never givin' in and comin' so reg'lar ; and I'll let him have your card just for that reason. He disappeared as he said these words, but came back speedily, remarking, " He'll see you, he says, though he don't know the name. Do you know the way ? Same rooms which his brother used to have,—straight afore you. Here, I'll show you."

The friendly porter, preceding Mr. Bowker down the passage, opened the door of what had been poor Arthur's sitting-room, and ushered in the visitor. The bookcases, the desk, the pictures and nicnacks, were all as they had been in the old days ; but there was a table in the middle of the room, at which was seated the new Lord Caterham finishing his late breakfast. Bowker had never seen the Lionel Brakespere of former days ; if he had, he would have noticed the change in the man before him,—the boldness of bearing, the calm unflinching regard, the steadiness of voice, the assurance of manner,—all of which, though characteristic of Lionel Brakespere in his earliest days, had deserted him, only to reappear with his title.

"You wished to see me, Mr. ——. I don't know your name," said Lionel, stiffly returning the stiff bow which Bowker gave him on entering.

"You have my card, my lord," said old Bowker quietly.

"Ah, yes, by the way, I have your card," said Lionel, taking it up. "Mr. Bowker—Mr.—Bowker! Now that does not convey to me any idea whatever?"

"I daresay not. You never heard it before—you never saw me before; and you would not see me now, if I did not come on business of the greatest importance."

"Business of the greatest importance! Dear me, that's what they all come on. Of the greatest importance to yourself, of course?"

"Of the greatest importance to you. Except in a very minor degree, I've nothing to do in the matter."

"Of the greatest importance to me! O, of course—else it would not have been worth while your coming, would it? Now, as my time is valuable, be good enough to let me know what this business is."

"You shall know in as few words as I can tell you. I come to you from a woman—"

Lionel interrupted him with a cynical laugh.

"The deuce you do !" he said. "From a woman? Well, I thought it was cigars, or a blue diamond, or a portrait of some old swell whom you had made out to be an ancestor of mine, or—"

"I would advise you not to be funny on the subject until you've heard it explained, Lord Caterham," said Mr. Bowker grimly. "I scarcely imagine you'll find it so humorous before I'm done."

"Sha'n't I? Well, at all events, give me the chance of hearing," said Lionel. He was in a splendid temper. He had come back, after a pleasant run with Algy Barford, to enjoy all the advantages of his new position. On the previous night he and his mother had had a long talk about Miss Maurice—this heiress whom he was to captivate so easily. The world lay straight and bright before him, and he could spare a few minutes to this old fellow—who was either a lunatic or a swindler—for his own amusement.

"I come to you, Lord Caterham, from a woman who claims to be your wife."

In an instant the colour died out of Lionel's face; his brows were knit, and his mouth set and rigid. "O, ho!" said he through his clenched teeth, after a moment's pause; "you do, do you? You come to me from *that* woman? That's your line of country, is it? O yes—I guessed wrong about you, certainly—you don't look a bit like a bully!"

"A bully!" echoed William Bowker, looking very white.

"A bully!" repeated Lionel—"the woman's father, brother, former husband—any thing that will give you a claim to put in an appearance for her. And now look here. This game won't do with me—I'm up to it; so you had better drop it at once, and get out."

Old Bowker waited for a minute with set teeth and clenched fists, all the gray hair round his mouth bristling with fury. Only for a minute. Then he resumed the seat which he had quitted, and said,

"I'm not quite so certain of myself nowadays, as I've been a long time out of practice; but it strikes me that during your long career of gentlemanly vice, my Lord Caterham, you never were nearer getting a sound drubbing than you have been within the last five minutes. However, let that pass. You have been good enough to accuse me of being a bully, by which term I imagine you mean a man sent here by the unfortunate lady of whom we have spoken to assert her rights. I may as well start by telling you that she is utterly ignorant of my intention to call on you."

"Of course;—O yes, of course. Didn't give you my address, did she?"

"She did not."

"She didn't? O, then you've come on your own hook, being some relation or friend of hers, to see what you could bounce me out of."

"I am no relation of hers. I have not seen her half a dozen times in the course of my life."

"Then what the deuce brings you here?"

"I'll tell you as shortly as I can. When you deserted this woman—not caring what became of her; leaving her to sink or swim as best she might—she slipped from one point

of wretchedness to another, until, at the bottom of her
descent, she was discovered by a very old friend of mine
perishing of cold and hunger—dying in the streets !"

Lionel, whose face when Bowker commenced speaking
had been averted, turned here, and gave a short sharp
shudder, fixing his eyes on Bowker as he proceeded.

"Dying in the streets ! My friend rescued her from this
fate, had her nursed and attended, and finally—ignorant
of the chief fact of her life, though she had confided to him
a certain portion of her story—fell so desperately in love
with her as to ask her to become his wife."

"To become his wife !" cried Lionel; "and she consented ?"

"She did."

"And they were married ?"

"They were. I was present."

"*Bravissimo !*" said Lionel in a low voice. "You've
done me a greater service than you think for, Mr.—what's-
your-name. She'll never trouble me again."

"Only once more, my lord," said old Bowker solemnly.

"What the devil do you mean, sir ?"

"Simply this, my lord. I understand your exclamation
of delight at seeing your way legally to rid yourself of this
woman, who is now nothing to you but an incumbrance.
But you need not fear; you will not even have the trouble
of consulting your lawyer in the matter. There is one who
breaks up marriage-ties more effectually even than the
Divorce Court, and that one is—Death !"

"Death !"

"Death. The woman of whom we have been speaking
lies in the jaws of death. Her recovery, according to all
human experience, is impossible. Dying,—and knowing
herself to be dying,—she wishes to see you."

"To see me !" said Lionel scornfully; "O no, thank
you ; I won't interfere in the family party. The gentleman
who has married her might object to my coming."

"The gentleman who married her in all noble trust and
honour, she deserted directly she heard of your return.
Overwhelmed by her cruelty, and by the full details of
her story, which he heard from your brother, the then
Lord Caterham, at the same time, he fell, smitten with an
illness from which he is barely recovering. She is in another

house far away from his, and on her death-bed she calls for you."

"She may call," said Lionel, after a moment's pause, frowning, thrusting his hands into his pockets, and settling himself back into his chair; "she may call; I shall not go."

"You will not?"

"I will not—why should I?"

"If you can't answer that question for yourself, Lord Caterham, upon my soul I can't for you," said Bowker gruffly. "If you think you owe no reparation to the woman, your wife, whom you left to be rescued by strangers' charity from starvation, I cannot convince you of it: if you decline to accede to her dying request, I cannot enforce it."

"Why does not the—the gentleman who was so desperately in love with her, and whom she—she accepted—why does not he go to her?" said Lionel. He did not care for Margaret himself, but the thought that she had been something to any one else grated upon his pride.

"Ah, my God," said old Bowker, "how willingly would he; but it is not for him she asks—it is for you. You boast of your experience of women, and yet you know so little of them as to expect gratitude of them. Gratitude from a woman—gratitude—and yet, God knows, I ought not to say that—I ought not to say that."

"You seem to have had a singular experience, Mr. Bowker," said Lionel, "and one on which you can scarcely make up your mind. Where is this lady whom you wish me to see?"

"At Sydenham—within an hour's drive."

Lionel rang the bell. "'Tell them to get the brougham round," said he to the servant who answered it. Now, look here, Mr. Bowker; I am going with you thoroughly depending on your having told me the exact truth."

"You may depend on it," said old Bowker simply. And they started together.

That was a strange ride. At starting Lionel lit a cigar, and puffed fiercely out of the window; idly looking at the Parliament-houses and other familiar objects which met his gaze as they drove over Westminster Bridge, the passing populace, the hoardings blazing with placards, the ordinary

bustle and turmoil of every-day life. He was angry and
savage; savage with Margaret for the annoyance she had
brought upon him, savage with Bowker for having found
him out, savage with himself for having allowed himself,
in the impulse of a moment, to be betrayed into this expedition. Then, as the houses became fewer, and the open
spaces more frequent; as they left behind them the solid
blocks of streets and rows and terraces, dull wretched
habitations for ninth-rate clerks, solemn old two-storied
edifices where the shipping agents and Baltic merchants
of a past generation yet lingered in their retirement, frowsy
dirty little shops with a plentiful sprinkling of dirtier and
frowsier taverns, imbued as was the whole neighbourhood
with a not-to-be explained maritime flavour,—as they slipped
by these and came into the broad road fringed by pretty
gardens, in which stood trim villas stuccoed and plate-
glassed, with the "coach-house of gentility" and every other
sign of ease and wealth; then leaving these behind, emerged
into country lanes with wide-spreading meadows on either
side, green uplands, swelling valleys, brown shorn fields
whence the harvest had been carried,—as they passed
through all these the cruel thoughts in Lionel's mind softened, and he began to think of the scene to which he was
being hastened, and of his own share in bringing about
that scene. As he flung away the butt-end of his cigar,
there rose in his mind a vision of Margaret as he had first
seen her, walking on the Castle Hill at Tenby with some of
her young companions, and looking over the low parapet
at the boiling sea raging round Catherine's Rock. How
lovely she looked, glowing with youth and health! What
a perfectly aristocratic air and *tournure* she had, visible
in the careless grace of her hat, the sweeping elegance
of her shawl, the fit of her boots and gloves! How completely he had been taken aback by the apparition! how
he had raved about her! had never rested until he had
obtained an introduction, and—ah, he remembered at that
moment distinctly the quivering of her eyelids, the fluttering
of her young bosom under its simple gauze, her half hesitating timid speech. That was comparatively a short time
ago—and now in what condition was he to find her? He
was not all bad, this man—who is?—and the best part

of him was awakened now.   He crossed his arms, leaned back in the carriage, and was nearer repentance than he had been since his childhood.

And old William Bowker, what was he thinking of? Indeed, he had fallen into his usual day-dream.   The comparison between Margaret and his own lost love, made when he first saw her, had always haunted him ; and he was then turning in his mind how, if such a complication as they were experiencing at that moment had been possible, it would have affected her and him.   From this his thoughts glided to the impending interview, and he wondered whether he had done right in bringing it about.   He doubted whether Margaret would have the physical strength to endure it ; and even if she had, whether any good—even so far as the arousing even a transient good in his companion—would result from it.   As he was pondering upon these things, Lionel turned quietly upon him and said in a hoarse voice,

" You said she was very ill ?"

" Very ill ; could hardly be worse—to be alive."

" It's—" and here he seemed to pull himself together, and nerve himself to hear the worst—" it's consumption, I suppose, caught from—damn it all, how my lip trembles ! —brought on by—want, and that."

" It originated in rheumatic fever, produced by cold and exposure, resulting in heart-disease and a complication of disorders."

" Has she had proper advice?—the best, I mean, that can be procured?"

" Yes ; she has been seen twice by —— and ——" said Bowker, naming two celebrated physicians, "and her own doctor sees her every day."

" And their opinions agree?"

" They all agree in saying that—"

" Hush," said Lionel, seizing him by the arm ; "your face is quite enough.   I'd rather not hear it again, please." And he plunged his hands into his pockets, and sunk back shuddering into the corner of the brougham.

Bowker was silent ; and they drove on without interchanging a word until William stopped the coachman at a small gate in a high garden-wall.   Then Lionel looked up with a strange frightened glance, and asked, " Is this the place ?"

"It is," said Bowker; "she has been here for some little time now. You had better let me go in first, I think, and prepare for your coming."

And all Lionel answered was, "As you please," as he shrunk back into his corner again. He was under a totally new experience. For the first time in his life he found himself suffering under a conscience-pang; felt disposed to allow that he had acted badly towards this woman now lying so stricken and so helpless; had a kind of dim hope that she would recover, in order that he might—vaguely, he knew not how—make her atonement. He felt uncomfortable and fidgetty. Bowker had gone, and the sun-blistered damp-stained garden-door had been closed behind him, and Lionel sat gazing at the door, and wondering what was on the other side of it, and what kind of a house it was, and where she was, and who was with her. He never thought he should have felt like this. He had thought of her—half a dozen times—when he was out there; but he knew she was a clever girl, and he always had a notion that she would fall upon her legs, and outgrow that first girlish smite, and settle down comfortably, and all that kind of thing. And so she would now. They were probably a pack of nervous old women about her—like this fellow who had brought him here—and they exaggerated danger, and made mountains of mole-hills. She was ill—he had little doubt of that; but she would get better, and then he'd see what could be done. Gad! it was a wonderful thing to find any woman caring for a fellow so; he might go through life without meeting another; and after all, what the deuce did it matter? He was his own master, wasn't he? and as for money—well, he should be sure to have plenty some day: things were all altered now, since poor old Arthur's death; and—— And at that moment the door opened; and behind William Bowker, who was pale and very grave, Lionel saw the house with all its blinds drawn down. And then he knew that his better resolutions had come too late, and that Margaret was dead.

Yes, she was dead; had died early that morning. On the previous day she had been more than usually restless and uncomfortable, and towards evening had alarmed the nurse—who thought she was asleep, and who herself was dozing—by breaking out into a shrill cry, followed by a deep long-drawn lamentation. Annie Maurice at the sound rushed hastily into the room, and never left it again until all was over. She found Margaret dreadfully excited. She had had a horrible dream, she said—a dream in which she went through all the miseries of her days of penury and starvation, with the added horror of feeling that they were a just punishment on her for her ingratitude to Geoffrey Ludlow. When she was a little quieted, she motioned Annie to sit by her ; and holding her hand, asked her news of Geoffrey. Annie started, for this was the first time that, in her calm senses, Margaret had mentioned him. In her long ravings of delirium his name was constantly on her lips, always coupled with some terms of pity and self-scornful compassion ; but hitherto, during her brief intervals of reason, she had talked only of Lionel, and of her earnest desire to see and speak to him once again. So Annie, pleased and astonished, said,

"He is getting better, Margaret ; much better, we trust."

"Getting better ! Has he been ill, then ?"

" He has been very ill—so ill that we at one time feared for his life. But he is out of danger now, thank God."

" Thank God !" repeated Margaret. " I am grateful indeed that his death is not to be charged to my account ; that would have been but a bad return for his preservation of my life ; and if he had died, I know his death would have been occasioned by my wickedness. Tell me, Miss Maurice —Annie—tell me, has he ever mentioned my name ?"

"Ah, Margaret," said Annie, her eyes filling with tears, "his talk is only of you."

"Is it?" said Margaret, with flushing cheeks and brightening eyes ; "is it ? That's good to hear—O how good ! And tell me, Annie—he knows I shall not trouble him long—has he, has he forgiven me ?"

"Not that alone," said Annie quietly. "Only yesterday he said, with tears in his eyes, how he loved you still."

There was silence for a moment, as Margaret covered her eyes with her hands. Then, raising her head, in a voice choked with sobs she said, with a blinding rush of tears, "O Annie, Annie, I can't be *all* bad, or I should never have won the love of that brave, true-hearted man."

She spoke but little after this ; and Lionel's name never

passed her lips—she seemed to have forgotten all about him and her desire to see him. From time to time she mentioned Geoffrey—no longer, as in her delirium, with pity, but with a kind of reverential fondness, as one speaks of the dead. As the night deepened, she became restless again, tossing to and fro, and muttering to herself; and bending down, Annie heard her, as she had often heard her before, engaged in deep and fervent prayer. Then she slept; and, worn out with watching, Annie slept also.

It was about four o'clock in the morning when Annie felt her arm touched; and at once unclosing her eyes, saw Margaret striving to raise herself on her elbow. There was a bright weird look in her face that was unmistakable.

"It's coming, Annie," she said, in short thick gasps; "it's coming, dear—the rest, the peace, the home! I don't fear it, Annie. I've—I've had that one line running in my brain, 'What though my lamp was lighted late, there's One will let me in.' I trust in His mercy, Annie, who pardoned Magdalen; and—God bless you, dear; God in His goodness reward you for all your love and care of me; and say to Geoffrey that I blessed him too, and that I thanked him for all his—your hand, Annie—so bless you both!—lighted late, there's One will—"

And the wanderer was at rest.

CHAPTER X.

AFTER THE WRECK.

THEY looked to Bowker to break the news to Geoffrey; at least so Charley Potts said, after a hurried conference with Til and her mother, at which Annie Maurice, overwhelmed by the reaction from excessive excitement, had not been present. They looked to Bowker to perform this sad duty—to tell Geoffrey Ludlow that the prize which had been so long in coming, and which he had held in his arms for so short a time, was snatched from him for ever. "For ever," said old William: "that's it. He bore up wonderfully, so long as he thought there was any chance of seeing her again. He hoped against hope, and strove against what he knew to be right and just, and would have made any sacrifice—ay, to the extent of bowing his head to his own shame, and taking her back to his home and his heart. If she had recovered ; and even if she would have shown herself willing to come back—which she never would —I could have faced Geoff, and told him what his duty was, and fought it out with him to the last. It would have rather done me good, such a turn as that; but I can't bear this job ;—I can't bear to see my old friend, to have to tell him that it's all over, that the light of his life has died out, that— Upon my soul," said old William energetically, " I think they might have got some one else to do this. And yet I don't know," said he, after a moment's pause : "the women couldn't be expected to do it. As for Charley, he'd have bungled it, safe. No, I'll go and do it myself ; but I'll wait till to-morrow, I think : there's no good adding another day's anguish to the dear fellow's life."

This was on the second day after Margaret's death, and Bowker yet postponed the execution of his task. On the third day, however, he set out for Elm Lodge, and found Geoffrey in the dining-room. The servant who admitted Mr. Bowker said, in reply to his inquiry, that "master was better certainly, but poor and peaky; did not take much notice of what went on, and were quite off his food." Geoffrey's looks certainly bore out the handmaiden's account. His cheeks were thin and hollow ; there were great circles round his eyes ; his flesh was tight and yellow ; his hands so fallen away that they looked like mere anatomical preparations. He looked up as Bowker entered, and the ghost of his old smile hovered round his lips.

"So you've come at last, William, after failing in your troth these three days, eh ?" said he. " What kept you, old friend ?"

Bowker was not prepared for any questions. He had gone through all this scene in his mind more than once ; but in his rehearsal it was always he who commenced the subject ; and this order not being followed, he was rather taken aback.

"I have been particularly engaged," he said. "You know, Geoff, that I should not have missed coming to you otherwise ; but—it was impossible."

"Was it?" said Geoffrey, raising his head quietly, and

stedfastly regarding him with his bright eyes; "was it on my business that you were engaged?"

"It was," said Bowker. He knew at that moment that his friend had guessed the truth.

"Then," said Geoffrey, "Margaret is dead!" He said it without altering the inflection of his voice, without removing his eyes from his friend's face. Scarcely inquiringly he said it, apparently convinced of the fact; and he took Bowker's silence for an affirmative, and rose and walked towards the window, supporting himself by the wall as he went. Bowker left him there by himself for a few minutes, and then, going up to him and laying his hand affectionately on his shoulder, said, "Geoff!"

Geoff's head was averted, but his hand sought Bowker's, and pressed it warmly.

"Geoff, dear old Geoff,—my old friend of many happy years,—you must bear up in this hour of trial. Think of it, dear old fellow. God knows, I'm one of the worst in the world to preach content and submission, and all that; but think of it: it is the—you know I wouldn't hurt your feelings Geoff—the best thing that, under all the circumstances, could have occurred."

"I've lost her, William—lost her whom I loved better than my heart's blood, whom I so prized and cherished and worshipped—lost her for ever—ah, my God, for ever!" And the strong man writhed in his agony, and burying his head in his arms, burst into tears.

"But, Geoff," said old Bowker, with a great gulp, "you could never have been any thing to her again; you have nothing to reproach yourself with in your conduct to her. It was her misfortune, poor soul, that she did not value you as she should have done; and yet before she died she spoke very, very affectionately of you, and your name was the last on her lips."

"Tell me about that, William," said Geoffrey, raising his head; "tell me what she said about me." He was comparatively calm even then, and sat quite quietly to listen to the details which Bowker had heard from Annie Maurice, and which he now poured into Geoff's eager ears. When he had finished, Geoff thanked him, and said he felt much easier and more relieved than he had been for some days past, but that he was tired out, and would ask Bowker to excuse him then, and by all means to come the next day. Honest William, glad to have accomplished his mission under such apparently favourable circumstances, and with so little of a "scene," took his leave.

But the next day, when he arrived at Elm Lodge, he found Dr. Brandram's gig at the gate, and on entering the house was met by Dr. Brandram himself in the hall. "And a very fortunate man I esteem myself in meeting you, my dear Mr. Boucher—beg pardon, Bowker! Boucher—name of old friend of mine in Norfolk—very fortunate indeed. Let's step into the dining-room, eh?—no need to stand in the draught, eh? You see I speak without the least professional feeling—ha, ha." And the little doctor laughed, but very softly. "Now look here, my dear sir," he continued; "our friend upstairs—I advised his remaining upstairs to-day—this *won't* do, my dear sir—this *won't* do."

"I know it, doctor, almost as well as you," said old William gruffly; "but what I don't know, and what I suppose you do, is—what will?"

"Change, my dear sir—thorough and entire change; not merely of air and scene, but of thought, life, habits, surroundings. He has a splendid constitution, our friend; but if he remains much longer in this cage, from which all the—all the joys have flown—he'll beat himself to death against the bars." This was a favourite simile with Dr. Brandram; and after he had uttered it he leant back, as was his wont, and balanced himself on his heels, and looked up into the eyes of his interlocutor to see its effect. On this occasion he was not much gratified, for old Bowker had not troubled himself about the poetical setting, but was thinking over the sense of the doctor's remark.

"Change," he repeated, "thorough change; have you told him that yourself, doctor?"

"Fifty times, my dear sir; repeated it with all the weight of medical authority."

"And what does he say?"

"Always the same thing—that his duty keeps him here. He's an extraordinary man, our friend, a most estimable man; but it would be an excellent thing for him,—in fact, make all the difference in the length of his life,—if his duty would take him abroad for six months."

"It shall," said old Bowker, putting on his hat, and driving it down hard down on his head. "Leave that to me. I'll take care of that." And with these words he nodded at the doctor and departed, leaving the little medico more astonished at the "odd ways" of artists than ever.

When Mr. Bowker had once made up his mind to carry any thing out, he never rested until it was achieved; so that on quitting Elm Lodge he at once made his way to Mr. Stompff's "gallery of modern masters," which he entered, greatly to the surprise of the proprietor, who was hovering about the room like a great spider on the watch for flies. There had never been any thing like cordiality between the great *entrepreneur* and the rough old artist; and the former opened his eyes to their widest extent, and pulled his whisker through his teeth, as he bowed somewhat sarcastically and said, "This is an honour and no flies?" But before his visitor left, Mr. Stompff had occasion to rub his eyes very hard with a bright silk pocket-handkerchief, and to resort to a cupboard under the desk on which the catalogues stood, whence he produced a tapering flask, from which he and Mr. Bowker refreshed themselves—his last words being, as Mr. Bowker took his departure, "You leave it to me, old fellow—you leave it to me."

Carrying out apparently the arrangement herein entered upon, the next day the great Mr. Stompff's brougham stopped at Elm Lodge, and the great Mr. Stompff himself descended therefrom, exhibiting far less than his usual self-sufficiency, swagger, and noise. To the servant who opened the door in answer to his modest ring he gave a note which he had prepared; and Geoffrey coming down into the dining-room found him waiting there, apparently deep in a photographic album. He rose, as the door opened, and caught Geoffrey warmly by the hand.

"How are you, Ludlow? How are you, my dear fellow? It must have been pressing business that brought me here just now, worrying you when you're only just recovered from your illness, my boy; pressing business, you may take your oath of that." And all the time Mr. Stompff held Geoffrey's hand between his own, and looked into his eyes with a wavering unsettled glance.

"I'm better, thank you, Mr. Stompff, much better; so much better that I hope soon to be at work again," said Geoff nervously.

"That's right; that's the best hearing possible. Nothing like getting back to work to set a man straight and bring him to his bearings."

" You were getting nervous about the ' Esplanade,' " said Geoff with a sickly smile—"as well indeed you might, for it's been a long time about. But you need not be frightened about that; I've managed to finish it."

"Have you?" said Stompff, very dry and husky in the throat.

"Yes; if you'll step into the studio, I'll show it you." They went down the little steps which Margaret had traversed so oft; and Geoffrey, as he pulled the big easel round into the light, said, "It's not quite what I wished. I —circumstances, you know, were against me—and but—it can be altered, you know; altered in any manner you wish."

"Altered be—hanged !" cried Stompff, very nearly relapsing into the vernacular; "altered !" he repeated, gazing at it with delight; now approaching closely to the canvas, now stepping away and looking at it under the shade of his hand; "why, that's first chop, that is. You've done it up brown ! You've made reg'ler ten-strike, as the Yankees say. Altered ! I wouldn't have a brush laid upon that for a fifty-pun' note. By George, Ludlow, well or ill, you lick the lot in your own line. There's none of 'em can touch you, d'ye hear? Altered !—damme, it's splendid."

"I'm very glad you like it," said Geoff wearily, "very glad; more especially as it may be a long time before I paint again."

"What's that you say?" said Mr. Stompff, turning upon him sharply. "What's that you say?" he repeated in a gentler tone, laying his hand softly upon Geoffrey Ludlow's shoulder—"a long time before you paint again? Why, nonsense, my good fellow; you don't know what nonsense you're talking."

"No nonsense, Mr. Stompff, but plain, honest, simple fact. I seem to have lost all zest for my art; my spirit is broken, and—"

"Of course, my good fellow; I understand all that well enough; too much England,—that's what it is. Home of the free, and ruling the waves, and all that. Pickles ! Capital place to sell pictures; deuced bad place to paint 'em. Now look here. You've been good enough to say more than once that I've been your friend, eh? Not that I've ever done more than give a good price for good work, though that's more than some people do—some people, eh? we know who—never mind. Now, I want you to do *me* a turn, and I am sure you will."

Geoffrey bowed his head and said, "So long as you don't require a picture from me—"

"Picture! O no; of course not. A steam engine, or a hansom cab, or a stilton cheese—that's what I look for from you naturally, isn't it? Ludlow, my dear fellow, how can you talk such stuff? Now listen. The British public, sir, has had a sickener of British subjects. Little Dab and his crew have pretty nearly used up all the sentimental domesticity; and we've had such a lot of fancy fairs, and Hyde Parks, and noble volunteers, and archery fêtes, and gals playing at croky, that the B. P. won't stand it any longer. There'll be a reaction, you'll see; and the 'Cademy will be choke full of Charles the Seconds, and Nell Gwynns, and coves in wigs, and women in powder and patches, and all that business, just because the modern every-day gaff has been done to death. I shall have to give in to this; and I shall give in of course. There's lots of coves can do that trick for me well enough to sell. But I look for more from you;—and this is what I propose. You go straight away out of this; where, I don't care—so long as you remain away a year or so, and keep your eyes about you. You'll work hard enough,—I don't fear that; and whatever you do, send it home to me and I'll take it. Lor' bless you, there's rigs that the B. P. knows nothing about, and that would make stunnin' subjects for you—a *table-d'hôte* on the Rhine, a students' *kneipe* at Heidelberg, a *schützenfest* in Switzerland; and then you've never been to Italy yet, and though that game's been worked pretty often, yet any thing Italian from you would sell like mad." He paused for a moment and looked up at Geoffrey, whose eyes were fixed intently on him, and who seemed eager and excited.

"It's all one to me," said he; "I scarcely know what to say; it's very kind of you. I know you mean it well; but do you think I can do it? Do you really think so?"

"Think so! I know so," said Mr. Stompff. "See here!

I never take up a thing of this sort without carrying it
through. We said five hundred for the ' Esplanade,' didn't
we? You've had three on account—that's right! Now
here's the other two; and if you're as well pleased with
the bargain as me, no knife shall cut our love in two, as the
song says. Now you must leave this money behind for
the old lady and the little 'un, and that nice sister of yours
—O yes, by the way, what makes Charley Potts paint her
head in all his pictures, and why don't he sell to me instead
of Caniche?—and here's a hundred in circular notes. I
went round to my bank and got 'em this morning on purpose
for you to go abroad with. When they're done, you know
where to send for some more."

"You are very kind, Mr. Stompff, but—"

"No, I ain't. I'm a man of business, I am; and there
ain't many as is very fond of me. But I know what the
B. P wants, and I know a good fellow when I see one; and
when I do see one, I don't often let him slide. I ain't a
polished sort of cove," said Mr. Stompff reflectively; " I
leave that to Caniche, with his paw-paw bowins and scrapins;
but I ain't quite so black as some of the artists paint me.
However, this is a matter of business that I'm rather eager
about; and I should be glad to know if I may look upon it
as settled."

"Look here, Mr. Stompff," said Geoffrey Ludlow, turning
to his companion, and speaking in an earnest voice; " you
have behaved generously to me, and you deserve that I
should speak frankly with you. I should immensely like to
get away from this place for a while, to shake off the
memory of all that has passed within the last few months—
so far as it is possible for me to shake it off—to get into
new scenes, and to receive fresh impressions. But I very
much doubt whether I shall be able to undertake what you
wish. I feel as if all the little power I ever had were gone;
as if my brain were as barren to conceive as I know my
hand is impotent to execute; I feel—"

"I know," interrupted Mr. Stompff; " regularly sewed up;
feel as if you'd like somebody to unscrew your head, take
your brains out and clean 'em, and then put 'em back; feel
as if you didn't care for the world, and would like to try the
hermit dodge and eat roots and drink water, and cut society,
eh? Ah, I've felt like that sometimes; and then I've heard

2 C

of some pictures that was comin' to the hammer, and I've just looked in at Christie's, and, Lord, as soon as I heard the lots a-goin' up, and felt myself reg'ler in the swing of competition, I've given up all them foolish notions, and gone home and enjoyed a roast fowl and a glass of sham and Mrs. S.'s comp'ny, like a Christian! And so will you, Ludlow, my boy; you'll pull through, I'll pound it. You work just when you feel inclined, and draw upon me when you want the ready; I'll stand the racket, never fear."

The conspiracy between Mr. Stompff and old William Bowker had been carried out minutely in detail; one of the points insisted on being that, the position once carried, Geoff should have no time for retreat. Accordingly, while Mr. Stompff was proceeding to Elm Lodge, Mr. Bowker was indoctrinating the ladies (whom he knew he should find at Sydenham) as to the tenour of their advice; and scarcely had Mr. Stompff quitted Geoffrey when Mr. Bowker was announced. To his old friend, Geoffrey, now in a very excited state, told the whole story of Stompff's visit and of the proposition which he had made; and old William— whom no one would have given credit for possessing such control over his face—sat looking on with the greatest apparent interest. When Geoffrey came to an end of his narration, and asked his friend whether he had done right in partially acceding to what had been offered him, or whether —it was not too late—he should retract, Mr. Bowker was extremely vehement—more so than he had ever known himself to be—in insisting that it was the very best thing that could possibly have happened. When Mrs. Ludlow and Til returned, they unhesitatingly pronounced the same opinion; and so Geoff's departure was decided on.

He had a great deal to attend to before he could leave; and the mere bustle and activity of business seemed to do him good at once. Mrs. Ludlow was thoroughly happy in preparing his clothes for his journey; Mr. Bowker and Charley Potts were constantly at Elm Lodge, the latter gentleman finding his assistance usually required by Miss Til; and on the day before that fixed for Geoffrey's departure, Annie Maurice called to take farewell. It was an interview which had been dreaded by both of them, and was as brief as possible. Annie expressed her satisfaction at his having been persuaded to seek change, by which she was sure he would benefit, and extended her hand in ": good-bye."

Geoff took her hand, and holding it tenderly in his, said :

"Annie, some day I may be able—I am very far from being able now — to tell you how the knowledge of your kindness to—to one whom I have lost—has sustained me under my bitter sorrow. God bless you, my more than sister ! God bless you, my good angel !" And Geoffrey touched her forehead with his lips, and hurried from the room.

The authorities at the South-Eastern terminus at London Bridge thought that some distinguished exile must be about returning to France that night, there were so many curiously-hatted and bearded gentlemen gathered round the mail-train. But they were only some of our old friends of the Titians come to say "God speed" to Geoffrey Ludlow, whose departure had been made known to them by Mr. Stompff. That worthy was there in great force, and old Bowker, and Charley Potts, and little Dabb, and old Tom Wrigley, and many others ; and as the train wound out of the station, bearing Geoff along with it, there were rising tears and swelling knots in eyes and throats that were very unused to such manifestations of weakness.

———◆———

CHAPTER XI.

LAND AT LAST.

THE calm had come after the storm ; the great, hurrying, thundering waves had stilled into silence, and lay quiet over the shattered wreck of home, and happiness, and hope. The winter rain had beaten upon the pretty house, and the light snow had fallen and lain a while, and had then melted away upon the garden ground and the smooth green turf, within the walls which had made a prison to the restless spirit of Margaret, even as the rain had beaten and the snow had fallen upon her grave in Norwood Cemetery. Now the spring odours were abroad in the air, and the trees were breaking into leaf, and Elm Lodge was looking the very perfection of tranquillity, of well-ordered, tasteful comfort and domesticity; an appearance in which there was all the sadness of a great contrast, a terrible retrospect, and an irremediable loss. Yet this appearance was not altogether deceptive; for within the house which had witnessed so much misery, peace and resignation now reigned. Mrs. Ludlow's unacknowledged desire was now realised; she was the mistress of her son's house, of all the modest splendour which had come with poor Geoff's improved fortunes; she ruled now where she had been subordinate before, and in the nursery, where at best she had only enjoyed toleration, she found herself supreme. To be sure, the great element of enjoyment, her son's presence, was wanting; but she knew that Geoffrey was doing the best thing in his power to do, was taking the most effectual means for the establishment of his health and the alleviation of his sorrow; and the old lady — on whom the supineness which comes with years, and which takes the edge off the sword of grief and the bitterness out of its cup, was beginning to steal—was satisfied. Much that had occurred was only imperfectly known to her; and indeed she would have been unfitted, by the safe routine and happy inexperience of evil passions which had marked her own life, to understand the storm and conflict which had raged around her. That her son's beautiful wife had been utterly unworthy of him, and that she had deceived and left him, Mrs. Ludlow knew; but Margaret's death had come so soon to terminate the terrible and mysterious dilemma in which her conduct had placed them all, that it had imposed upon them the silence of compassion, and filled them with the sense of merciful relief; so that by mutual consent her name had not been mentioned in the house where she had been mistress for so long. Her son's illness, and the danger of losing him, had impressed Mrs. Ludlow much more vividly than his domestic calamity; and she had settled down with surprising ease and readiness to the routine of life at Elm Lodge.

That routine included a good deal of the society of Mr. Charley Potts; and as Mrs. Ludlow was almost as much attached to that warm-hearted and hot-headed gentleman as Miss Til herself, she acquiesced with perfect willingness in the state of affairs which brought him to Elm Lodge with regularity equalled only by that of the postman. The household was a quiet one; and the simple and unpretending women who walked along the shady paths at Lowbar in their deep-mourning dresses, or played with the little child upon the lawn, furnished but scanty food for the curiosity of the neighbourhood. Popular feeling was indeed somewhat excited on the subject of Charley Potts; but Dr. Brandram —a gallant gentleman in his way—set that matter at rest very quickly by announcing that Charley and Miss Ludlow were engaged, and were shortly to be married—information which was graciously received; as indeed the most distant tidings of a prospective wedding always are received by small communities in which the female element predominates. Dr. Brandram had done Geoffrey good service too, by his half-made, half-withheld communications respecting the beautiful mistress of Elm Lodge, whose disappearance had been so sudden. She had not recovered her confinement so well as he had hoped: the nervous system had been greatly shaken. He had ordered change: a temporary removal from home was frequently of great benefit. Yes, there had been a terrible scene with Mr. Ludlow—that was quite true: the non-medical mind was hard to convince in these matters sometimes; and Mr. Ludlow had been hard to manage. But a quarrel between *them?*—O dear no: quite a mistake. Mrs. Ludlow left home by herself?—O dear no: by her own consent, certainly. She perfectly comprehended the necessity of the change, and was ready to submit; while Ludlow could not be brought to see it—that was all. "I assure you, my dear madam," the doctor would say to each of his female catechists, "I never had a more interesting patient; and I never pitied a man more than Ludlow when she sank so rapidly and unexpectedly. I really feared for *his* reason then, and of course I sent *him* away immediately. A little change, my dear madam,— a little change in these cases produces a wonderful effect—quite wonderful!"

"But, doctor," the anxious inquirer would probably say, "Mr. Ludlow never saw her again after she was removed, did he?"

"Well, indeed, my dear madam,—you see I am telling professional secrets; but you are not like other women: you are so far above any vulgar curiosity, and I know I may rely so entirely on your discretion, that I make an exception in your case,—they never did meet. You see these **cases** are so uncertain; and cerebral disease developes itself so rapidly, that before any favourable change took place, the patient sunk."

"Dear me, how very sad! It was at an asylum, I suppose?"

"Well, my dear madam, it was under private care—under the very best circumstances, I assure you; but — you'll excuse me; this is entirely confidential. And now to return to your dear little boy."

So did kind-hearted Dr. Brandram lend his aid to the laying of the ghost of scandal at Elm Lodge; and gradually it became accepted that Mrs. Ludlow had died under the circumstances hinted at by Dr. Brandram.

"It is rather a disadvantage to the dear child, Charley, I fear," sapiently remarked Miss Til to the docile Mr. Potts as he was attending her on a gardening expedition, holding a basket while she snipped and weeded, and looking as if pipes and beer had never crossed the path of his knowledge or the disc of his imagination; "people will talk about his mother having died in a lunatic-asylum."

"Suppose they do?" asked Charley in reply. "That sort of thing does not harm a man; and "—here the honest fellow's face darkened and his voice fell—"it is better they should say that than the truth. I think that can always be hidden, Til. The poor woman's death has saved us all much; but it has been the greatest boon to her child; for now no one need ever know, and least of all the child himself, that he has no right to bear his father's name."

"It is well Geoff is not a rich man, with a great estate to leave to an eldest son," said Til, pulling at an obstinate tuft of groundsel, and very anxious to prevent any suspicion that her lover's words had brought tears to her eyes.

"Well," said Charley, with rather a gloomy smile, "I'm not so certain of that, Til: it's a matter of opinion; but I'm clear that it's a good thing he's not a great man—in the 'nob' sense of the word I mean—and that the world can afford to let him alone. Here comes the young shaver — let's go and talk to him." And Charley, secretly pining to get rid of the basket, laid down that obnoxious burden, and went across the grass-plat towards the nurse, just then making her appearance from the house.

"Charley is always right," said Til to herself as she eradicated the last obstinate weed in the flower-bed under inspection, and rejoined Mr. Potts; from which observation it is to be hoped that the fitness of Miss Til for undertaking that most solemn of human engagements—matrimony—will be fully recognised. There are women who practically apply to their husbands the injunctions of the Church Catechism, in which duty to God is defined; who "believe in, fear, trust, and love" them "with all their hearts, with all their minds, with all their souls, and with all their strength ;" and Matilda Ludlow, though a remarkably sensible girl, and likely enough to estimate other people at their precise value, was rapidly being reduced to this state of mind about Charley, who was at all events much less unworthy than most male objects of female devoteeism.

Mrs. Ludlow and her daughter heard pretty regularly from Geoff. Of course his letters were unsatisfactory; men's letters always are, except they be love-letters, when their meaning is tempered by their exclusiveness. He was eager for news of the child; but he never referred to the past in any other respect, and he said little in anticipation of the future. He described his travels, reported the state of his health, and expressed his anxiety for his mother's comfort; and that was about the sum-total of these literary productions, which no doubt were highly penitential performances to poor Geoffrey.

Spring was well advanced when Charley and Til began to discuss the propriety of naming a time for their marriage. The house at Brompton was still "on their hands," as Mrs. Ludlow was fond of saying, while in her secret heart she would have deeply regretted the turning-up of an eligible tenant; for who could answer for the habits and manners of strangers, or tell what damage her sacred furniture might receive ? Charley proposed to Til that they should become her mother's tenants, and urged that young lady to consent to a speedy marriage, from the most laudable economic principles, on the ground that under present circumstances he was idling dreadfully, but that he confidently expected that marriage would "settle his mind." The recent date of the family calamity Charley could not be brought to regard as a reasonable obstacle to his wishes.

"Look here, Til," he said; "it isn't as if we were swells, you know, with our names, ages, and weights in the *Morning*

Post, and our addresses in the *Red Book*. What need we care, if Geoff don't mind?—and he won't, God bless him!—the happier we are, the sooner he'll cease to be miserable; and who's to know or to care whether it's so many months sooner or later after that poor woman's death? Besides, consider this, Til; if we wait until Geoff comes home, a wedding and all that won't be pleasant for him: will it, now? Painful associations you know, and all that. I really think, for Geoff's sake, we had better get it over."

"Do you indeed, Master Charley?" said Til, with a smile full of pert drollery, which rendered her exasperatingly pretty. "How wonderfully considerate you are of Geoff; and how marvellously polite to describe marrying me as 'getting it over'! No, no, Charley," she continued, seriously; "it cannot be. I could not leave mamma to the responsibility of the house and the child—at least not yet. Don't ask me; it would not be right towards Geoff, or fair to my mother. You must wait, sir."

And the crestfallen Charley knew that he must wait, and acquiesced with a very bad grace; not but that Miss Til would have been horribly vexed had it been better.

An unexpected auxiliary was about this time being driven by fate towards Charley Potts in the person of Annie Maurice. She had been constant and regular in her visits to Elm Lodge, affectionate and respectful in her demeanour to Mrs. Ludlow, and sisterly in her confidence towards Til. The hour that had united the two girls in a tie of common responsibility towards Geoff and Margaret had witnessed the formation of a strong and lasting friendship; and though Annie's superior refinement and higher education raised her above the level of Matilda Ludlow, she was not more than her equal in true womanly worth. They passed many happy hours together in converse which had now become cheerful, and their companionship was strengthened by the bond of their common interest in Til's absent brother. Miss Ludlow, perhaps, did an unfair proportion of the talking on these occasions; for she was of the gushing order of girls, though she did not border even remotely on silliness. By common consent they did not speak of Margaret, and Til had never known Arthur; so that Annie rarely talked of him, always sacredly loved and remembered in her faithful heart, preserved as her friend and monitor — dead, yet speaking.

Annie had been more silent than usual lately, and had looked sad and troubled; and it chanced that on the day following that which witnessed Charley's luckless proposition, Miss Maurice arrived at Elm Lodge at an earlier hour than usual; and having gained a private audience of Til, made to her a somewhat startling revelation.

The conference between the girls lasted long, and its object took Til completely by surprise. Annie Maurice had resolved upon leaving Lord Beauport's house, and she had come to ask Mrs. Ludlow to receive her. She told Til her reasons, simply, honestly, and plainly

"I cannot live in the house with Lionel Brakespere," she said; "and I have no friends but you. Geoffrey and I were always friends, and my dear Arthur trusted him, and knew he would befriend me. I am sure if he were living now, he would counsel me to do what I am doing. I have often thought if he had had any idea that the end was so near, he would have told me, if any difficulty came in my way, to apply for aid to Geoffrey, and I am clear that I am doing right now. I have no friends, Til, though I am rich," Annie repeated, with a more bitter smile than had ever flitted over her bright face in former days; "and I have no 'position' to keep up. I cannot go and live in a big house by myself, or in a small one either, for that matter, and I want your mother to let me come and live with her while Geoffrey is away."

Til hesitated before she replied. She saw difficulties in the way of such an arrangement which Annie did not; difficulties arising from the difference in the social position of the friends Annie wished to leave, and those she wished to come to.

"I am sure, as far as we are concerned, every thing might be as you wish," she said; "but—Lady Beauport might not think it quite the thing."

"Lady Beauport knows I will not remain in her house, Til; and she will soon see as plainly as I do that it is well I should not. The choice is between me and her son, and the selection is not difficult. Lionel Brakespere (I cannot call him by Arthur's familiar name) and I are not on speaking terms. He knows that I am acquainted with his crimes; not only those known to his family, but those which he thought death had assisted him to hide. I might have concealed my knowledge from him, had he not dared to insult me by an odious pretence of admiration, which I resented with all my heart and soul. A few words made him understand that the safest course he could pursue was to abandon such a pretence, and the revelation filled him with such wrath and hatred as only such a nature could feel. Why he has adopted a line of behaviour which can only be described as down-right savage rudeness—so evidently intended to drive me out of the house, that Lord and Lady Beauport themselves see it in that light—I am unable to comprehend. I have sometimes fancied that he and his mother have quarrelled on the matter; but if so, he has had the best of it. However, there is no use in discussing it, Til; my home is broken up and gone from me; and if your mother will not take me under her charge until Geoffrey comes home, and advises me for the future, I must only set up somewhere with a companion and a cat."

Annie smiled, but very sadly; then she continued :

"And now, Til, I'll tell you how we will manage. First, we will get the mother's leave, and I will invite myself on a visit here, to act as your bridesmaid, you see, and—"

"Charley has been talking to you, Annie!" exclaimed Miss Til, starting up in mingled indignation and amusement; "I see it all now—you have been playing into each other's hands."

"No, indeed, Charley never said a word to me about it," replied Annie seriously; "though I am sure if he had, I should have done any thing he asked; but, Til, do let us be earnest,—I am serious in this. I don't want to make a scandal and a misery of this business of my removal from Lord Beauport's; and if I can come here to be your bridesmaid, in a quiet way, and remain with your mother when you have left her, it will seem a natural sort of arrangement, and I shall very soon, heiress though I am, drop out of the memory of the set in which I have lately moved. I am sure Geoffrey will be pleased; and you know that dear little Arthur is quite fond of me already."

It is unnecessary to report the conversation between the two girls in fuller detail. Mrs. Maurice carried her point; the consent of Mrs. Ludlow to the proposed arrangement was easily gained; and one day the fine carriage with the fine coronets, which had excited the admiration of the neighbourhood when Miss Maurice paid her first visit to Geoffrey Ludlow's bride, deposited that young lady and her maid at Elm Lodge. A few days later a more modest equipage bore away Mr. and Mrs. Potts on the first stage of their journey of life.

"And so, my dear Annie," wrote Geoffrey to his ex-pupil, "you are established in the quiet house in which I dreamed dreams once on a time. I continue the children's phrase, and say 'a long time ago.' I am glad to think of you there with my mother and my poor little child. If you were any one but Annie Maurice, I might fear that you would weary of the confined sphere to which you have gone; but, then, it is because you *are* Annie Maurice that you are there. Sometimes I wonder whether I shall ever see the place again, which, if ever I do see it, I must look upon with such altered eyes. God knows : it will be long first—for I am wofully weak still. But enough of me. My picture goes on splendidly. When it is finished and sent home to Stompff, I shall start for Egypt. I suppose many a one before me has tried to find the waters of Lethe between the banks of Nile."

Charley Potts and Til were comfortably settled in the house at Brompton, where Til guarded the household gods with pious care, and made Charley uncommonly comfortable and abnormally orderly. Mrs. Ludlow and her young guest led a tranquil life at Elm Lodge. Annie devoted herself to the old lady and the child with a skilful tenderness partly natural to her and partly acquired by the experiences of her life in her rural home, and within the scene of Caterham's lengthened and patient suffering. The child loved her and throve under her charge; and the old lady seemed to find her "cross" considerably less troublesome within the influence of Annie's tranquil cheerfulness, strong sense, and accommodating disposition. The neighbourhood had taken to calling vigorously and pertinaciously on Mrs. Ludlow and Miss Maurice. It approved highly of those ladies; for the younger was very pleasant, not alarmingly beautiful, reputed to be very rich, and acknowledged not to "give herself airs;" while the elder was intensely respectable—after the fashion dear to the heart of Lowbar ; and both went to church with scrupulous regularity. Dr. Brandram was even more cordial in his appreciation of Annie than he had been in his admiration of Margaret; and the star of Elm Lodge was quite in the ascendant. A few of the members of the great world whom she had met in the celestial sphere of St. Barnabas Square found Annie out even at Elm Lodge, and the apparition of other coronets than that of the Beauports was not unknown in the salubrious suburb. Lady Beauport visited Miss Maurice but rarely, and her advent seldom gave Annie pleasure. The girl's affectionate and generous heart was pained by the alteration which she marked more and more distinctly each time that she saw the cold and haughty Countess, on whose face care was fast making marks which time had failed to impress.

Sometimes she would be almost silent during her short visits, on which occasions Mrs. Ludlow was wont to disappear as soon as possible; sometimes she would find querulous fault with Annie—with her appearance and her dress, and her "throwing herself away." Sometimes Annie felt that she was endeavouring to turn the conversation in the direction of Lionel; but that she invariably resisted. It chanced one day, however, that she could not succeed in preventing Lady Beauport from talking of him. Time had travelled on since Annie had taken up her abode at Elm Lodge, and the summer was waning; the legislative labours of the Houses had come to an end, and Lord and Lady Beauport were about to leave town. This time the Countess had come to say good-bye to Annie, whom she found engaged in preparations for a general flitting of the Elm-Lodge household to the seaside for the autumn. Annie was in blooming health, and her usual agreeable spirits—a strong contrast to the faded, jaded, cross-looking woman who said to her complainingly,

"Really, Annie, I think you might have come with us, and left your friends here to find their autumnal amusements for themselves; you know how much Lord Beauport and I wished it."

"Yes," said Annie gently, "I know you are both very kind; but it cannot be. You saw that yourself, dear Lady Beauport, and consented to my entering on so different a life. You see I could not combine the two; and I have new duties now—"

"Nonsense, Annie!" said Lady Beauport angrily. "You

will not come because of Lionel,—that is the truth. Well, he is not to be at home at all; he is going away to a number of places : he likes any place better than home, I think. I cannot understand why you and he should disagree so much; ·but if it must be so, I suppose it must. However, you will not meet him now." And Lady Beauport actually condescended to reiterate her request ; but she had no success. Annie had resolutely broken with the old life, which had never suited her fresh, genial, simple tastes ; and she was determined not to renew the tie. She knew that she was not in any true sense necessary to Lady Beauport's happiness; she was not ungrateful for such kindness as she had received; but she was a sensible girl, and she made no mistake about her own value, and the true direction in which her duty, her vocation lay. So she steadily declined ; but so gently that no offence was taken ; and made inquiry for Lord Beauport. The worried expression which had gradually marred the high-bred repose of Lady Beauport's face increased as she replied, and there was a kind of involuntary confidence in her manner which struck Annie with a new and painful surprise. Lord Beauport was well, she said ; but he was not in good spirits. Things seemed to be wrong with them somehow and out of joint. Then the elder lady, seeing in the face of her young listener such true sympathy, thawed suddenly from her habitual proud reserve, and poured out the bitterness of her disappointment and vain regret. There was a tone of reproach against Annie mingled with her compliant, which the girl pityingly passed over. If Annie had but liked Lionel ; if she would but have tried to attract him, and keep him at home, all might have been well : but Annie had imbibed poor Arthur's prejudices; and surely never were parents so unfortunate as she and the Earl in the mutual dislike which existed between their children. Lady Beauport did not want to justify Lionel entirely—of course not : but she thought he might have had a better chance given him in the first instance. Now he had greatly deteriorated—she saw that : she could not deny it ; and her " granted prayer " for his return had not brought her happiness.

Annie listened to all this with a swelling heart. A vision floated before her tearful eyes of the lost son, who had been so little loved, so lightly prized ; whose place the brother preferred before him had taken and disgraced ; and a terrible sense of retribution came into her mind. Too late the father and mother were learning how true his judgment had been, and how valuable his silent influence. Time could only engrave that lesson more and more deeply on their hearts; experience could only embitter it—its sting was never to be withdrawn. They had chosen between the two, and their choice, like Esau's, was "profane." Lady Beauport spoke more and more bitterly as she proceeded. The softening touch of grief was not upon her—only the rankling of disappointment and mortification; only the sting of a son's ingratitude, of discovering that in return for the sacrifice of principle, self-respect, and dignity to which she had consented for Lionel's sake, she had not received even the poor return of a semblance of affection or consideration.

The hardness of Lionel's nature was shown in every thing his mother said of him—the utter want of feeling, the deadness of soul. Annie felt very sad as she listened to Lady Beauport's melancholy account of the life they had fallen into at the great house. She was oppressed by the sense of the strangeness of the events which had befallen, and in which the Countess had, all unconsciously, so deep an interest. It was very sad and strange to remember that she was detailing the conduct of the man whose baseness had enabled Margaret to lay Geoffrey's life in ruins under Geoffrey's own roof. It was terrible to Annie to feel that in her knowledge there was a secret which might so easily have been divulged at any moment, and which would have afflicted the vexed and mortified woman before her more deeply than any thing that had occurred. Lady Beauport was not tender-hearted; but she was a high-minded gentlewoman, and would have been shamed and stricken to the soul had she discovered the baseness of her son in this particular instance. She had fondly flattered herself into a belief that the crime which had been so inadequately punished was only a folly; but there was no possibility of such a reading of this one, and Annie was glad to think that at least the pang of this knowledge was spared to Lady Beauport. She could say nothing to comfort her. In her inmost heart she had an uneasy, unexplained sense that it was all the just retribution for the conduct of Arthur's parents towards him, and hopelessness for the future of a family of which Lionel formed a member took possession of her.

"He is so disagreeable, so selfish, Annie," continued Lady Beauport, "and O so slangy; and you know how his father hates that sort of thing."

"It is better that he should be away, then, for a little," said Annie, trying to be soothing, and failing lamentably.

"Well, perhaps it is," said Lady Beauport; "and yet that seems hard too, when I longed so much for his return, and when now he has every thing he wants. Of course, when he was only a second son, he had excuses for discontent; but now he has none, and yet he is never satisfied. I sometimes think he is ill at ease, and fancies people are thinking about the past, who don't even know any thing about it, and would not trouble themselves to resent it if they did. But his father does not agree with me, Annie: he will not give Lionel credit for any thing good. I cannot make out Lord Beauport: he is much more cold and stern towards Lionel than he need be, for he is not so careless and inconsiderate towards his father as he is towards me. He seems to have taken up poor Arthur's notions now, and to judge Lionel as severely as he did. He does not say much; but things are uncomfortable between them, and Lord Beauport is altered in every way. He is silent and dispirited; and do you know, Annie, I think he grieves for Arthur more than he did at first?"

Distress and perplexity were in Lady Beauport's face and voice, and they went to Annie's gentle heart.

"Try not to think so much of it," she said; "circumstances may alter considerably when Lionel gets more settled at home, and Lord Beauport has had time to get over the irritation which his return occasioned him."

"He resents your having left us more bitterly than any thing, Annie. He constantly speaks of you in the highest terms of praise, and wishes you back with us. And so do I, my dear, so do I."

Annie was amazed. Tears were in Lady Beauport's eyes, and a tremble in her voice. During all the period of Annie's residence in her house, the Countess had never shown so much feeling towards her, had never suffered her to feel herself of so much importance. The sterling merit of the girl, her self-denial, her companionable qualities, had never before met with so much recognition; and a thrill of gratification passed through her as she felt that she was missed and valued in the home whence Lionel's conduct had driven her.

"I am very glad," she said, "that Lord Beauport thinks and speaks so kindly of me—indeed, he was always kind to me, and I am very grateful to him and you."

"Then why will you not come to us, Annie? Why do you prefer these new friends to us?"

"I do not," she answered; "but as things have been, as they are, it is better I should not be in a position possibly to estrange the father and son still more. If I were in the house, it would only furnish him with an excuse to remain away, and cause Lord Beauport additional anxiety."

Annie knew that she must appear strangely obstinate to Lady Beauport; but it could not be helped; it was impossible that she could explain. The visit of the Countess was a long one; and Annie gathered from her further confidences that her dissatisfaction with Lionel was not her only trouble. The future was not bright before Lady Beauport. The charms of the world were fading in her estimation; society was losing its allurements, not under the chastening of a wholesome grief, but under the corroding, disenchanting influence of bitterness and disappointment. She looked aged and wearied; and before she and Annie parted that day, she had acknowledged to the girl that she dreaded the prospect before her, and had no confidence in her only son, or in his line of conduct towards her in the event of Lord Beauport's death. The Earl's words to his wife had been prophetic,—in Caterham's death there had been but the beginning of sorrow.

Annie stood sadly at the house-door, and watched the carriage as it rolled away and bore Lady Beauport out of her sight, as it bears her out of this history.

"This is the man," she thought, "whom she would have remorselessly made me marry, and been insensible to the cruel wrong she would have done to me. What a wonderful thing is that boundless, blind egotism of mothers! In one breath she confesses that he makes her miserable, and admits his contemptible, wretched nature, though she knows little of its real evil; in the next she complains that I did not tie myself to the miserable destiny of being his wife!"

Then Annie turned into the drawing-room, and went over to the window, through whose panes Margaret's wistful, weary gaze had been so often and so long directed. She leaned one round fair arm against the glass, and laid her sleek brown head upon it, musingly:

"I wonder when *home* will really come for me," she thought. "I wonder where I shall go to, and what I shall do, when I must leave this. I wonder if little Arthur will miss me very much when I go away, after Geoffrey comes back."

Geoffrey Ludlow's letters to his mother and sister were neither numerous nor voluminous, but they were explicit; and the anxious hearts at home gradually began to feel more at rest about the absent one so dear to them all. He had written with much kindness and sympathy on the occasion of Til's marriage, and they had all felt what a testimony to his unselfish nature and his generous heart his letter was. With what pangs of memory,—what keen revivals of vain longing love and cruel grief for the beautiful woman who had gone down into her grave with the full ardour of his passionate devotion still clinging around her,—what desperate struggles against the weariness of spirit which made every thing a burden to him,—Geoffrey had written the warm frank letter over which Til had cried, and Charley had glowed with pleasure, the recipients never knew. There was one who guessed them,—one who seemed to herself intuitively to realise them all, to weigh and measure every movement of the strong heart which had so much ado to keep itself from breaking, far away in the distant countries, until time should have had sufficient space in which to work its inevitable cure. Mrs. Potts showed her brother's letter to Annie Maurice with infinite delight, on that memorable day when she made her first visit, as a married woman, to Elm Lodge. The flutter and excitement of so special an occasion makes itself felt amid all the other flutters and excitements of that period which is the great epoch in a woman's life. The delights of "a home of one's own" are never so truly realised as when the bride returns, as a guest, to the home she has left for ever as an inmate. It may be much more luxurious, much more important, much more wealthy; but it is not hers, and, above all, it is not "his;" and the little sense of strangeness is felt to be an exquisite and a new pleasure. Til was just the sort of girl to feel this to the fullest, though her " own " house was actually her "old" home, and she had never been a resident at Elm Lodge: but the house at Brompton had a

2 D

thousand charms now which Til had never found in it before, and on which she expatiated eagerly to Mrs. Ludlow, while Annie Maurice was reading Geoffrey's letter. She was very pale when she handed it back to Til, and there were large tears standing in her full brown eyes.

"Isn't it a delightful letter, Annie?" asked Mrs. Potts; "so kind and genial; so exactly like dear old Geoff."

"Yes," Annie replied, very softly; "it is indeed, Til; it is very like Geoffrey."

Then Annie went to look after little Arthur, and left the mother and daughter to their delightful confidential talk.

When the party from Elm Lodge were at the seaside, after Til's marriage, Annie began to write pretty regularly to Geoffrey, who was then in Egypt. She was always thinking of him, and of how his mind was to be roused from its grief, and once more interested in life. She felt that he was labouring at his art for money, and because he desired to secure the future of those dear to him, in the sense of duty, but that for him the fame which he was rapidly winning was very little worth, and the glory was quite gone out of life,— gone down, with the golden hair and the violet eyes, into the dust which was lying upon them. Annie, who had never known a similar grief, understood his in all its intricacies of suffering, with the intuitive comprehension of the heart, which happily stands many a woman instead of intellectual gifts and the learning of experience; and knowing this, the girl, whose unselfish spirit read the heart of her early friend, but never questioned her own, sought with all her simple and earnest zeal how to "cure him of his cruel wound." His picture had been one of the gems of the Academy, one of the great successes of the year, and Annie had written to him enthusiastically about it, as his mother had also done; but she counted nothing upon this. Geoffrey was wearily pleased that they were pleased and gratified, but that was all. His hand did its work, but the soul was not there; and as he was now working amid the ruins of a dead world, and a nation passed away in the early youth of time, his mood was congenial to it, and he grew to like the select lapse of the sultry desert life, and to rebel less and less against his fate, in the distant land where every thing was strange, and there was no fear of a touch upon the torturing nerves of association. All this Annie Maurice divined, and turned con-

stantly in her mind ; and amidst the numerous duties to
which she devoted herself with the quiet steadiness which
was one of her strongest characteristics, she thought incessantly of Geoffrey, and of how the cloud was to be lifted
from him. Her life was a busy one, for all the real cares of
the household rested upon her. Mrs. Ludlow had been an
admirable manager of her own house, and in her own sphere,
but she did not understand the scale on which Elm Lodge
had been maintained even in Margaret's time, and that
which Miss Maurice established was altogether beyond her
reach. The old lady was very happy ; that was quite evident.
She and Annie agreed admirably. The younger lady studied
her peculiarities with the utmost care and forbearance, and
the " cross " sat lightly now. She was growing old ; and what
she did not see she had lost the faculty of grieving for ; and
Geoffrey was well, and winning fame and money. It seemed
a long time ago now since she had regarded her daughter-in-
law's furniture and dress with envy, and speculated upon
the remote possibility of some day driving in her son's
carriage.

Mrs. Ludlow had a carriage always at her service now, and
the most cheerful of companions in her daily drive ; for she,
Annie, and the child made country excursions every afternoon, and the only time the girl kept for her exclusive enjoyment was that devoted to her early-morning rides. Some of
the earliest among the loungers by the sad sea-waves grew
accustomed to observe, with a sense of admiration and
pleasure, the fresh fair face of Annie Maurice, as, flushed
with exercise and blooming like a rose in the morning air,
she would dismount at the door of her " marine villa," where
a wee toddling child always awaited her coming, who was
immediately lifted to her saddle, and indulged with a few
gentle pacings up and down before the windows, whence an
old lady would watch the group with grave delight. Mrs.
Ludlow wrote all these and many more particulars of her
happy life to her absent son ; and sometimes Annie wondered
whether those cheerful garrulous letters, in which the unconscious mother showed Geoffrey so plainly how little she
realised his state of mind, increased his sense of loneliness.
Then she bethought her of writing to Geoffrey constantly
about the child. She knew how he had loved the baby in
happier times, and she never wronged the heart she knew so

2 D ?

well by a suspicion that the disgrace and calamity which had befallen him had changed this deep-dwelling sentiment, or included the motherless child in its fatal gloom. She had not spoken of little Arthur in her earlier letters more than cursorily, assuring his father that the child was well and thriving; but now that time was going over, and the little boy's intellect was unfolding, she caught at the legitimate source of interest for Geoffrey, and consulted him eagerly and continuously about her little *protégé* and pupil.

The autumn passed and the winter came; and Mrs. Ludlow, her grandchild, and Annie Maurice were settled at Elm Lodge. Annie had 'taken anew to her painting, and Geoffrey's deserted studio had again an inmate. Hither would come Charley Potts—a genial gentleman still, but with much added steadiness and scrupulously-neat attire. The wholesome subjugation of a happy marriage was agreeing wonderfully with Charley, and his faith in Til was perfectly unbounded. He was a model of punctuality now; and when he "did a turn" for Annie in the painting-room, he brushed his coat before encountering the unartistic world outside with a careful scrupulousness, at which, in the days of Caroline and the beer-signals, he would have derisively mocked. Another visitor was not infrequent there, though he had needed much coaxing to induce him to come, and had winced from the sight of Geoff's ghostly easel on his first visit with keen and perceptible pain.

A strong mutual liking existed between William Bowker and Annie Maurice. Each had recognised the sterling value of the other on the memorable occasion of their first meeting; and the rough exterior of Bowker being less perceptible then than under ordinary circumstances, it had never jarred with Annie's taste or offended against her sensibilities. So it came to pass that these two incongruous persons became great friends; and William Bowker—always a gentleman in the presence of any woman in whom he recognised the soul of a lady—passed many hours such as he had never thought life could again give him in his dear old friend's deserted home. Miss Maurice had no inadequate idea of the social duties which her wealth imposed upon her, and she discharged them with the conscientiousness which lent her character its combined firmness and sweetness. But all her delight was in her adopted home, and in the

child, for whom she thought and planned with almost
maternal foresight and quite maternal affection. William
Bowker also delighted in the boy, and would have expended
an altogether unreasonable portion of his slender substance
upon indigestible eatables and curiously-ingenious and des-
tructible toys but for Annie's prohibition, to which he yielded
loyal obedience. Many a talk had the strangely-assorted
pair of friends as they watched the child's play; and they
generally ran on Geoffrey, or if they rambled off from him
for a while, returned to him through strange and tortuous
ways. Not one of Geoff's friends forgot him, or ceased to
miss him, and to wish him back among them. Not one of
"the boys" but had grieved in his simple uncultivated way
over the only half-understood domestic calamity which had
fallen upon "old Geoff;" but time has passed, and they had
begun to talk more of his pictures and less of himself. It
was otherwise with Bowker, whose actual associates were few,
though his spirit of *camaraderie* was unbounded. He had
always loved Geoffrey Ludlow with a peculiar affection, in
which there had been an unexplained foreboding; and its
full and terrible realisation had been a great epoch in the
life of William Bowker. It had broken up the sealed
fountains of feeling; it had driven him away from the grave
of the past; it had brought his strong sympathies and strong
sense into action, and had effected a moral revolution in the
lonely man, who had been soured by trouble only in appearance, but in whom the pure sweet springs of the life of the
heart still existed. Now he began to weary for Geoffrey.
He dreaded to see his friend sinking into the listlessness and
dreariness which had wasted his own life; and Geoffrey's
material prosperity, strongly as it contrasted with the poverty
and neglect which had been his own lot, did not enter into
Bowker's calculations with any reassuring effect.

"Does Geoffrey never fix any time for his return?" asked
William Bowker of Miss Maurice one summer evening
when they were slowly pacing about the lawn at Elm Lodge,
after the important ceremonial of little Arthur's *coucher* had
been performed.

"No," said Annie, with a quick and painful blush.

"I wish he would, then," said Bowker. "He has been
away quite long enough now; and he ought to come home
and face his duties like a man, and thank God that he has a

home, and duties which don't all centre in himself. If **they** did, the less he observed them the better." This with a touch of the old bitterness, rarely apparent now. Annie did not answer, and Bowker went on :

" His mother wants him, his child wants him, and for that matter Mrs. Potts's child wants him too. Charley talks some nonsense about waiting to baptize the little girl until Geoff comes home 'with water from the Jordan,' said Master Charley, being uncertain in his geography, and having some confused notion about some sacred river. However, if we could only get him home, he might bottle a little of the Nile for us instead. I really wish he'd come. I want to know how far he has really lived down his trouble ; I can't bear to think that it may conquer and spoil him."

" It has not done that ; it won't do that—no fear of it," said Annie eagerly ; " I can tell from his letters that Geoffrey is a strong man again,—stronger than he has ever been before."

" He needs to be, Miss Maurice," said William, with a short, kind, sounding laugh, " for Geoffrey's nature is not strong. I don't think I ever knew a weaker man but one—"

He paused, but Annie made no remark. Presently he fell to talking of the child and his likeness to Geoffrey, which was very strong and very striking.

" There is not a trace of the poor mother in him," said Bowker ; " I am glad of it. The less there is before Geoffrey's eyes when he returns to remind him of the past the better."

" And yet," said Annie in a low voice, and with something troubled in her manner, " I have often thought if he returned, and I saw his meeting with the child, how dreadful it would be to watch him looking for a trace of the dead in little Arthur's face, and not finding it, to know that he felt the world doubly empty."

Her face was half averted from Bowker as she spoke, and he looked at her curiously and long. He marked the sudden flush and pallor of her cheek, and the hurry in her words ; and a bright unusual light came into William Bowker's eyes. He only said,

" Ay—that would indeed be a pang the more." And a few minutes later he took his leave.

"Charley," said Mr. Bowker to Mr. Potts, three or four days afterwards, as he stood before that gentleman's easel, criticising the performance upon it with his accustomed science and freedom, "why don't you get your wife to write to Geoffrey, and make him come home? He ought to come, you know, and it's not for you or me to remonstrate with him. Women do these things better than men; they can handle sores without hurting them, and pull at heart-strings without making them crack. There's his mother, growing old, you know, and wanting to see him; and the child's a fine young shaver now, and his father ought to know something of him, eh, Charley, what do you think?"

"You're about right, old fellow, that's what I think. Til often talks about it, particularly since the baby was born, and wonders how Geoffrey can stay away; but I suppose if his own child won't bring him home, ours can't be expected to do it; eh, William? Til doesn't think of that, you see."

"I see," said Mr. Bowker, with a smile. "But, Charley, do you just get Til to write to Geoffrey, and tell him his mother is not as strong as she used to be, and that the care of her and the child is rather too much of a responsibility to rest upon Miss Maurice's shoulders, and I think Geoffrey will see the matter in the true light, and come home at once."

Charley promised to obey Mr. Bowker's injunction, premising that he must first "talk it over with Til." William made no objection to this perfectly proper arrangement, and felt no uneasiness respecting the result of the conjugal discussion. He walked away smiling, congratulating himself on having done "rather a deep thing," and full of visions in which Geoffrey played a part which would have considerably astonished him, had its nature been revealed to him.

Six weeks after the conversation between Mr. Bowker and Mr. Potts, a foreign letter in Geoffrey's hand reached Mrs. Ludlow. She hardly gave herself time to read it through, before she sought to impart its tidings to Annie. The young lady was not in the painting-room, not in the drawing-room, not in the house. The footman thought he had seen her on the lawn with the child, going towards the swing. Thither

Mrs. Ludlow proceeded, and there she found Annie; her hat flung off, her brown hair falling about her shoulders, and her graceful arms extended to their full length as she swung the delighted child, who shouted "higher, higher!" after the fashion of children.

"Geoffrey's coming home, Annie!" said Mrs. Ludlow, as soon as she reached the side of the almost breathless girl. "He's coming home immediately,—by the next mail. Is not that good news?"

The rope had dropped from Annie's hand at the first sentence. Now she stooped, picked up her hat, and put it on; and turning to lift the child from his seat, she said,

"Yes, indeed, Mrs. Ludlow, it is; but very sudden. Has any thing happened?"

"Nothing whatever, my dear. Geoffrey only says—stay, here's his letter; read for yourself. He merely says he feels it is time to come home; he has got all the good out of his captivity in Egypt in every way that he is likely to get— though why he should call it captivity when he went there of his own accord, and could have come away at any moment he liked, is more than I can understand. Well, well, Geoffrey always had queer sayings; but what matter, now that he is coming home!—Papa is coming home, Arty; —we shall see him soon."

"Shall we?" said the child. "Let me go, Annie; you are making my hand cold with yours;" and he slipped his little hand from her grasp, and ran on to the house, where he imparted the news to the household with an air of vast importance.

"Annie," said Geoffrey Ludlow one day when he had been about three weeks at home, and after he had passed some time in examining Miss Maurice's art-performances, "what has become of the drawing I once made of you, long ago, when you were a little girl? Don't you remember you laughed at it, and said, 'Grandmamma, grandmamma, what big eyes you've got!' to it? and the dear old Rector was so dreadfully frightened lest I should be offended."

"Yes, I remember," answered Annie; "and I have the picture. Why?"

"Because I want it, Annie. If you will let me have it, I

will paint a full-length portrait of you for the next Academy, in which every one shall recognise a striking likeness of the beautiful and accomplished Miss Maurice."

"Don't, Geoffrey," said Annie gravely. "I am not in the least more beautiful now than I was when you took my likeness long ago ; but you shall have the drawing, and you shall paint the picture, and it shall belong to Arthur, to remind him of me when I am gone abroad."

"Gone abroad!" said Geoffrey, starting up from his chair and approaching her. "You—gone abroad!"

"Yes," she said, with a very faint smile. "Is no one to see men and cities, and sand and sphinxes, and mummies and Nile boatmen, except yourself? Don't you remember how Caterham always wished me to travel and improve my mind?"

"I remember," said Geoff moodily; "but I don't think your mind wants improving, Annie. How selfish I am ! I really had a kind of fancy that this was your home ; different as it is from such as you might, as you may command, it was your own choice once. You see what creatures we men are. A woman like you sacrifices herself for one of us, to do him good in his adversity, and he takes it as a matter of course that the sacrifice is to continue—" Geoffrey turned to the window, and looked wearily out. From the dim corner in which she sat, Annie looked timidly at his tall figure—a true image of manliness and vigour. She could see the bronzed cheek, the full rich brown eye, the bushy beard with its mingled lines of brown and gray. There was far more strength in the face than in former days, and far more refinement, a deeper tenderness, and a loftier meaning. She thought so as she looked at him, and her heart beat hard and fast.

"It was no sacrifice to me, Geoffrey," she said in a very low tone. "You know I could not bear the life I was leading. I have been very happy here. Every one has been very good to me, and I have been very happy ; but—"

Geoffrey turned abruptly, and looked at her—looked at the graceful head, the blushing cheek, the faltering lips— and went straight up to her. She shrunk just a little at his approach ; but when he laid his hand upon her shoulder, and bent his head down towards hers, she raised her sweet candid face and looked at him.

"Annie," he said eagerly, with the quick earnestness of a man whose soul is in his words, "will you forgive all my mistakes,—I have found them out now,—and take the truest love that ever a man offered to the most perfect of women? Annie, can you love me?—will you stay with me? My darling, say yes!"

His strong arms were round her now, and her sleek brown head lay upon his breast. She raised it to look at him; then folded her hands and laid them upon his shoulder, and with her crystal-clear eyes uplifted, said, "I will stay with you, Geoffrey. I have always loved you."

The storm had blown itself out now—its last mutterings had died away; and through all its fury and despair, through all its rude buffets and threatening of doom, Geoffrey Ludlow had reached LAND AT LAST!

THE END.

Printed by W. H. Smith & Son, 186, Strand, London.

THE SELECT LIBRARY OF FICTION.

Works by the Author of "John Halifax, Gentleman."
2s. each.

Agatha's Husband.
The Ogilvies.
Olive.
Alice Learmont, *1s.*
The Head of the Family.

By ANTHONY TROLLOPE.
2s. each.

Doctor Thorne.
Castle Richmond.
Tales of all Countries.
The Bertrams.
Rachel Ray.
The Kellys & the O'Kellys
The Macdermots of Ballycloran.

By F. W ROBINSON.
2s. each.

Slaves of the Ring.
Wildflower.
One and Twenty.
Woodleigh.
Under the Spell.
Mr. Stewart's Intentions.
Woman's Ransom.
The House of Elmore.

By SAMUEL LOVER

He would be a Gentleman. | Irish Stories and Legends.

By W H. AINSWORTH.

Cardinal Pole.
John Law, the Projector.
Lord Mayor of London.
Constable of the Tower.

By THOMAS A. TROLLOPE.

Beppo the Conscript.
La Beata.
Marietta.
Lindisfarn Chase.
Giulio Malatesta.

By ANNA H. DRURY

Deep Waters. | Misrepresentation.

London : Chapman & Hall.

STANDARD AUTHORS.

ONE SHILLING.

Fcap. Svo, with Illustrated Cover, and well printed on good paper.

WHEN ORDERING, THE NUMBERS ONLY NEED BE GIVEN.

EXTREMES.

By Miss E. W. Atkinson.

" A nervous and vigorous style, an elaborate delineation of character under many varieties, spirited and well-sustained dialogue, and a carefully-constructed plot; if these have any charms for our readers, they will not forget the swiftly gliding hours passed in perusing 'Extremes.'"—*Morning Post.*

"'Extremes' is a novel written with a sober purpose, and wound up with a moral. The purpose is to exemplify some of the errors arising from mistaken zeal in religious matters, and the evil consequences that flow from those errors."—*Spectator.*

AN OLD DEBT.

By Florence Dawson.

" A powerfully written novel, one of the best which has recently proceeded from a female hand. The dialogue is vigorous and spirited."—*Morning Post.*

"There is an energy and vitality about this work which distinguishes it from the common head of novels. Its terse vigour sometimes recals Miss Brontë, but in some respects Miss Florence Dawson is decidedly superior to the author of 'Jane Eyre.'"—*Saturday Review.*

"A very good seasonable novel."—*Leader.*

COUNTERPARTS;

OR, THE CROSS OF LOVE.

By the Author of "Charles Auchester."

"'Two forms that differ, in order to correspond; this is the true sense of the word *Counterpart*.' This text of Coleridge introduces us to the work—foretelling its depth of purpose and grandeur of design. The feelings of the heart, the acknowledged subject of romance, are here analysed as well as chronicled."—*Sun.*

"There are, in this novel, animated and clever conversations, sparkling descriptions, and a general appreciation of the beautiful in nature and art—especially the sea and music."—*Globe.*

MY LADY.

A TALE OF MODERN LIFE.

"'My Lady' evinces charming feeling and delicacy of touch. It is a novel that will be read with interest."—*Athenæum.*

"The story is told throughout with great strength of feeling, is well written, and has a plot which is by no means commonplace."—*Examiner.*

"It is not in every novel we can light upon a style so vigorously graceful—upon an intelligence so refined without littleness, so tenderly truthful, which has sensibility rather than poetry; but which is also most subtly and searchingly powerful." — *Dublin University Magazine.*

TENDER AND TRUE.

By the Author of "Clara Morton."

" It is long since we have read a story that has pleased us better. Simple and unpretending, it charms by its gentle good sense. The strength of the book lies in its delineations of married life." — *Athenæum.*

"'Tender and True is in the best style of the *sensible* novel. The story is skilfully managed, the tone is very pure, and altogether the fiction is marked by sense and spirit."—*Press.*

"A novel far above the average. It is charmingly written, has sustained and continued interest, and there is a pure, healthy tone of morality."—*Globe.*

THE LIFE AND DEATH OF SILAS BARNSTARKE.

BY TALBOT GWYNNE.

" In many ways this book is remarkable. Silas and his relations stand forth so distinctly and forcibly, and with so much simplicity, that we are far more inclined to feel of them as if they really lived, than of the writers of pretended diaries and autobiographies. The manners and ways of speech of the time are portrayed admirably."—*Guardian.*

" A story possessing an interest so tenacious that no one who commences it, will easily leave the perusal unfinished."—*Standard.*

" A book of high aim and unquestionable power."-*Examiner.*

YOUNG SINGLETON

BY TALBOT GWYNNE.

Author of "The School for Fathers."

" Mr. Talbot Gwynne has made a considerable advance in ' Young Singleton ' over his previous fictions. In his present story he rises into the varied action, the more numerous persons, and the complicated interests of a novel. It has also a moral ; being designed to paint the wretched consequences that follow from envy and vanity."—*Spectator.*

" Power of description, dramatic force, and ready invention, give vitality to the story."—*Press.*

THE CRUELLEST WRONG OF ALL.

By the Author of " Margaret ; or, Prejudice at Home."

" The author has a pathetic vein, and there is a tender sweetness in the tone of her narration." —*Leader.*

" It has the first requisite of a work meant to amuse; it is amusing."—*Globe.*

FARINA:

A LEGEND OF COLOGNE.

BY GEORGE MEREDITH.

" A masque of ravishers in steel, of robber knights ; of waterwomen, more ravishing than lovely. It has also a brave and tender deliverer, and a heroine proper for a romance of Cologne. Those who love a real, lively, audacious piece of extravagance, by way of a change, will enjoy ' Farina.' "—*Athenæum.*

THE SCHOOL FOR FATHERS.

BY TALBOT GWYNNE.

"The pleasantest tale we have read for many a day. It is a story of the *Tatler* and *Spectator* days, and is very fitly associated with that time of good English literature, by its manly feeling, direct, unaffected manner of writing, and nicely managed, well-turned narrative. The descriptions are excellent; some of the country painting is as fresh as a landscape by Constable, or an idyl by Alfred Tennyson."—*Examiner.*

LEONORA.

BY THE HON. MRS. MABERLY.

"In the story of 'Leonora' Mrs. Maberly has described the career of an ambitious, beautiful, but unprincipled woman. Many of the scenes are drawn with great skill, and lively sketches of fashionable life are introduced." — *Literary Gazette.*

"Leonora is drawn with more than usual power. Her pride, her imperious will, her sins, her punishment, and her penitence, are skilfully wrought, and sustain the reader's attention to the last."—*Critic.*

ARROWS IN THE DARK.

By author of "Said and Done."

"The language is good, the narrative spirited, the characters are fairly delineated, and the dialogue has considerable dramatic force."

AMBERHILL.

BY A. J. BARROWCLIFFE.

"There is great power in 'Amberhill,' and its faults are forgotten in the sustained excitement of the narrative. There are in the book some of the shrewdest sketches of character we have ever met with."—*Press.*

"'Amberhill' is an exciting book, not belonging to any established school of novel, unless it be the defiant. There is a freshness and force, a petulant grace, and a warm-hearted satirical vein in 'Amberhill,' which will give it a charm to every *blasé* novel reader. The characters are vigorously drawn and have genuine life in them."—*Globe.*

OVER THE CLIFF.

BY MRS. CHANTER.

"One of the best, most interesting and enthralling novels we have seen this season. The style is very animated, and sparkles with wit and humour."

"One of the most successful novels of the day. No one will commence the book without finishing it to the last letter."

MISS GWYNNE, OF WOODFORD.

BY GARTH RIVERS.

"This entertaining and particularly clever novel, is not to be analysed, but to be praised, and that emphatically."

SOLD BY ALL BOOKSELLERS, AND AT RAILWAY BOOKSTALLS.

www.ingramcontent.com/pod-product-compliance
Lightning Source LLC
Chambersburg PA
CBHW021334110726
47900CB00005B/1466